Praise for Lenin's Harem

Born to an aristocratic life of wealth and privilege, but driven from the family home by resentful Latvian peasants, a young German struggles to survive and protect his love from the brutalities of a domineering brother, class struggle, war, and communist rule. The attention to historical detail and depth of introspection are worthy of Pasternak or Solzhenitsyn. Enthralling, reads as true as my grandfather's letters.
  Daniel Wagner, former Dean of the CIA's Sherman Kent School for Intelligence Analysis

William Burton McCormick vividly depicts the tragedies of the 20th century through eyes of a single Latvian Rifleman. With Wiktor Rooks, we witness the destruction of traditional society and its seemingly conservative values, to be replaced with new social, political and national ideas, innovations all ultimately perverted to hell by their adherents. The novel considers the eternal problems of humanity as cast through the dark prism of actual historical events.
  Professor Kaspars Klavins, Riga Technical University and Fellow, Royal Society of Arts (UK)

William Burton McCormick takes us right inside lives that would otherwise be not simply invisible to us but unimaginable.
  Suzannah Dunn, author of *The Confession of Katherine Howard*

An engrossing and well managed piece of writing, chronicling a fascinating and turbulent period of Russian and Latvian history while never once losing sight of the need to drive the narrative through the personal tale of its hero, Wiktor Rooks.
  Martyn Bedford, Costa shortlisted author of *Flip*

LENIN'S HAREM

A NOVEL

WILLIAM BURTON McCORMICK

KNOX ROBINSON
PUBLISHING

3rd Floor, 36 Langham Street
Westminster, London W1W 7AP
&
244 5th Avenue, Suite 1861
New York, New York 10001

Knox Robinson Publishing is a specialist, international publisher of historical fiction, historical romance and medieval fantasy.

First published in Great Britain in 2013 by Knox Robinson Publishing

First published in the United States in 2012 by Knox Robinson Publishing

Copyright © William Burton McCormick 2013

The right of William Burton McCormick to be identified as author of this work has been asserted by him in accordance with
the Copyright, Designs and Patents Act 1988.

All rights reserved. No part of this publication may be reproduced, stored in a retrieval system, or transmitted, in any form or by an means, without the prior permission in writing of Knox Robinson Publishing, or as expressly permitted by law, or under terms agreed with the appropriate reprographics rights organization. Enquiries concerning the reproduction outside the scope of the above should be sent to the Rights Department, Knox Robinson Publishing, at the London address above.

You must not circulate this book in any other binding or cover and you must impose the same condition on any acquirer.

A CIP catalogue record for this book is available from the British Library.

ISBN HC 978-1-908483-44-7

ISBN PB 978-1-908483-45-4

Map illustrations by Seth R. McCullough

Typeset in Adobe Caslon Pro by Susan Veach
info@susanveach.com

Printed in the United States of America and the United Kingdom.

Download the KRP App in iTunes and Google Play to receive free historical fiction, historical romance and fantasy eBooks
delivered directly to your mobile or tablet.

Watch our historical documentaries and book trailers on our channel on YouTube and subscribe to our podcasts in iTunes.

www.knoxrobinsonpublishing.com

*In memory of
Alice Davis*

Part One:

Pyrrhic Victories

Chapter One

December 1905, Courland

My brother always said they were watching us. From the fields, or the forest, or roadside, wherever they did their chores. I never gave it much thought. He was the heir and they were his concern. I, heir to nothing, could pardon watchfulness.

What happened afterwards, though, even Jesus would not forgive.

While our parents entertained the guests at the two-day Christmas ball inside, I sat on the manor's steps that evening distributing glasses of champagne to late arrivals, well-wishers and friends who'd enjoyed a walk in the crisp winter air of the Courland countryside. Unchaperoned for most the night, I'd frankly had more than a few glasses myself, too much for an eleven-year old boy.

It was in those later hours that I caught the voices on the wind. Far down the road, in the hollow, I could hear the singing of the working folk, those Latvians who spent their days farming the land for our family and the other Baltic Barons. Their Christmas songs drifting between frost-covered fir trees, harmonies moving slowly along as unseen carolers passed through the night. Voices, it seemed, from another world, one that touched ours daily but remained forever closed. How I wished to understand those Lettish songs.

With little to entertain me at the party, I got off the steps and found the old highway leading toward the peasant farms. Sipping champagne, by the time I reached the little thatch and log farmstead at which the carolers gathered, I was slightly cold, reasonably drunk, and completely surprised at the spectacle before me.

These Christmastime revelers were out in costume, Courland's native people *mumming* through the winter night. Letts of all ages wore animal masks, most in elaborate home-made disguises. Hairy stitched bears pranced on chains held by the mythic hero, helmeted Lāčplēsis. Ceramic goat horns rested on the heads of adolescent girls who danced with fake Jews in black hats and painted-on beards. I spied tiny old men whose trailing cotton beards sprang from their baby faces when they stepped upon them, while women dressed as spirits spun about me, the green stripes of their festive dresses showing beneath ghostly white sheets. All-in-all, a grand procession of adults and children, some dressed for the holiday season, others wrapped in their workers' clothes, marching together from the snow-covered fields toward the Latvian villages. All singing hymns of Christmas, a joyous chorus reverberating throughout the winter countryside.

My young eyes widened in wonder. Though I could not understand a word, these Lettish harmonies elated my spirit, brought me closer to the season than my family's stuffy, aristocratic ball ever had.

Why had my parents forbidden me to come here?

Fascinated, I could not resist following this procession as the mummers wound their way along the moonlit path. A Yule log dragged behind, they stopped at every home in forest or field, families dressed in red and green casting a year's worth of problems onto the timber as it passed.

For hours, through a string of villages, I trailed this parade. Fantastic figures and singing families joining at every stop until the alleys of the last town were swollen with costumed bodies. Funnelled into a narrow street, the crowd pressed so close my cap was jarred from my head, the champagne glass knocked to the muddy stones by a trio of deliriously dancing ghosts. With no pause to retrieve them, the tide swept me forward, breaking through on the far side of town where the land at last reopened into my father's fields. They came to rest in the yard of a most ancient farmhouse: stocky square timbers, a four-sided thatched roof and double smoking chimneys at the crown. A faded coat of arms hung from a wooden pole, reminding all that Letts were freemen, serfs no longer.

The march over, the singers gathered around the sacrificial Yule log, preparing for the celebratory burning. As the leaders toiled to light the icy log, the crowd at last seemed to consider my presence, masks turning my way, eyes lingering a bit too long. I suddenly felt outlandish in my fine jacket and shoes, far more foolish than the most absurd of these mummers. How I wished I were dressed as them, devoid of identity, free to mix undetected. How many recognized me as Rudolf Rooks's son, youngest child of the family that kept them for generations? So many faces, surely, would be familiar without their masks: Father's stablemen, farmworkers, woodcutters, perhaps even an elevated house servant down for the celebration. They all must be here. Yet there were no greetings, no holiday salutations, not even in the common Russian language. Their Lettish words buzzed mysteriously by my ears, the people passing close, but not once calling my name.

There was, however, an uncomfortable air of recognition in one silent watcher. Intense eyes beneath a swine mask, he clutched a drunken woman to his chest, her own camouflage slipping low, revealing her reddened face. I saw only a glimpse – Mrs. Bata, the wife of my father's foreman – then the Yule log caught fire and an eclipsing blaze rose up between us.

While last year's troubles burned into memory and the dancing mummers cast bizarre shadows over the snow, I tried to peer through the flames. There stood Mrs. Bata, now alone, her feline mask righted, but her man was gone. For a moment.

"Why are you here?" he shouted, appearing from the crowd, grabbing my shoulder and shaking me harshly. The voice was surprisingly familiar, the language not unknowable Lettish or even Russian but German, my native tongue!

This mummer squatted on his haunches, lowering down to my height. He shoved up his mask revealing the frowning face of my older brother.

"Otomars," I gasped.

"Wiktor, what are you doing here? At this hour?"

What was *he* doing here? Among the peasants. "I...I heard the songs."

He pulled me close, cold nose against my cheek, sniffing my breath. "You're drunk."

So was he, so what? "Mother let me have some champagne at the Christmas ball. Why are you dressed as a pig?"

Conscious that all the Letts were staring, Otomars lowered his voice, changed the tongue from German to a less conspicuous Russian; the adjustment difficult for my tipsy mind, I was not the language master he was.

"Wiktor, pay attention to me." He snapped his fingers in my face. "Does Father know you're down here?"

"No."

"Well, I'm taking you back."

So stern for a man in a pig mask. "Why?"

He didn't answer, simply dragging me from the crowd. He eighteen, I eleven, it was no contest. His face now visible, the Letts gave him a wary distance. Mummers silently watching as he stole me away into the night. Cowed and kidnapped by the first-born son.

"Why Otomars? Why can't I stay?"

We were a half kilometer from the village when my brother finally relented. The Latvians long out of sight, their beautiful songs only a memory, I didn't understand why we had to leave. "I want to hear them sing."

"Wiktor, listen to me," he said, voice firm as Father's. "There've been incidents all over Courland. In Livland too. I need you inside."

Incidents? What incidents? "I was only in the village, I go every day."

"Not alone, not past midnight, not when they've been drinking," with his free hand he cuffed my neck, "or you have."

"It wasn't much," I tugged at his grip. "You've had more than me."

He dragged me on. My resistance fading, we fell into silence, listening to the rhythmic crunching of our shoes in the snow. We were close to home now, the high windows of the manor house peeking over the bare trees.

I played my last card. "Then I'll just have to tell Father about Mrs. Bata and the housekeeper..."

He smiled, as if I weren't even in the game. "Do that and I'll mention where I found you tonight. Passed out drunk."

"I wasn't."

He shrugged. "Who's to say?" His grin had triumph. As always.

I was trying to conjure a worthy retort, some offsetting counterattack, as we arrived at home. Pale yellow and brown by day, the manor house was painted in midnight hues of silver and white, tree-limb shadows clawing across the front. The ground-floor windows darkened, the fires dead in the yard cauldrons, there were still a few trailing voices inside, the tinkling of piano keys from the parlor. Anne, at least, was still up.

In the worn slush before the steps, a crushed bouquet of roses. Flattened petals trampled under a man's boot print, an arc of purple and red leaves throughout the yard. Down the path toward the stables lay a dozen naked stems, most of them broken. Erich Kaltenbach had been here. Anne had rejected him again.

"Will he ever stop?" I said.

"Our sister's captured his heart, Wiktor," said Otomars, pulling a petal from the slush. "That's not an easy thing to forgo."

Yes, especially for a spoiled baron's son used to getting his way. "Maybe, Father should speak with Erich?"

"No, I will. Tomorrow." Otomars let out a sigh, warm breath rising in the winter air. "Let's get you inside."

I climbed the steps alone. "Aren't you coming?"

He remained at the bottom, brushing snow over the roses with the side of his boot. "No."

"Why can you stay out, but I have to turn in?"

He stretched out his hands. "Because I'm a man and you're still a boy."

"If you're a man, why are you dressed as a pig?"

He laughed, something in him warming at my remark. Otomars came up a few steps, pulled the mask from his head, slipped it gently over my face.

"I'll tell you what: Go inside, stay inside, and tomorrow night – after our parents are asleep – we'll trek down to the village together. Agreed?"

I couldn't see in this thing. "I…"

"One 'oink' for 'no.' Two for 'yes.'"

"Oink, oink."

"Good piggy."

He tapped my nose through the mask, playfully mussed my hair, all with a charm that made it almost alright, as only he could. "And nothing more about Mrs. Bata."

By the time I got the eye holes righted, he was gone, far down the path under the cover of trees. I was alone.

I considered going back, breaking my word, and following Otomars down to the Latvian villages again to make a point. But I was cold, a bit sleepy. Enough adventure for the night, tomorrow there'd be another volley.

With voices in the parlor, I could not risk detection. Probing questions at this hour, in this state, would be most unpleasant, especially from my parents. So, I went around the side of the house to rap on Erene's window and ask the faithful housemaid to let me inside in confidence.

As I passed round the corner, I gazed over the expansive lawn, divot-ed snow stretching down to grey stables. Still a few sleighs and carriages parked in the shadows, some guests yet to leave, or perhaps, staying the second night.

Beyond lay the little path that led to the main road to Mitau, a screen of fir trees running along one side. A man hanging by the neck from a branch.

I recoiled in horror, surprise, one thought in my mind: Erich.

The roses, the rejection…

I sprang from the porch, my mind not on the dead man, but on my sister. The guilt she'd feel.

But as I ran through the snow, I cast off the blinding mask, the corpse became clearer, a focusing silhouette against the moon behind. It wasn't Erich or even a man...

It was a burlap sack, stuffed and tied in the shape of a man. Dressed in an old coat, the collar buttoned to the chin, a painted waistcoat and knee-high boots to finish the illusion. The hallmark clothes of a Baltic-German gentleman, it could have been my father, or Erich, or Otomars; any of the landowners who ruled Courland.

I felt the deathly chill of the hour, took a few tentative steps forward, stood beneath the dangling thing, hoarse breath and drumming heartbeat the only sounds.

Rail spikes pierced the effigy at the head and chest, painted blood snaking down its icy form. And at the center, three words. Running from breast to belly:

Free

Latvia

Now!

Chapter Two

The old German gentleman burned in the sawdust sand, his burlap face shriveling to soot beneath the orange and blues of paraffin flames, silently wilting away as if he had never been.

I stood with Otomars in the loose dirt of the mulching pit, a shallow recess tucked far behind the grain sheds and well-hidden from the waking eyes of the manor house. The two of us worked alone in the late dawn of winter, the world still dark, the snow forever grey. Only our father and his Lettish foreman, Jāzeps Bats, were about for company, their distant silhouettes locked in conversation beneath the 'hanging' tree.

My brother prodded the effigy, turning it round with the heavy sod pike, feeding the fire every unexposed inch of fabric, his manner uncharacteristically quiet, his mind clearly elsewhere.

I fanned the smoke with the bare rose stems in my hand. "What do you think Jāzeps is telling Father? Down by that tree?"

Otomars grimaced, a growl in his voice, my brother taking last night's discovery much harder than I. "Bats will promise to speak with his workers, their families, stir up the dust a bit. That's all, Wiktor. He won't uncover the criminals. They never do."

Criminals? Such a harsh word over a stuffed bag, ugly writing or not. "You don't think they could still be about? The hangers of that… doll?"

"They're here. The villages probably." Otomars turned the pike thoughtfully in his hands, drilling it deeper into the sand. "If we're lucky."

"Lucky?"

"They could be among the house staff, the faces that smile at breakfast everyday."

"Never."

"Anything is possible, Wiktor." He nodded toward the tree. "That warning was hung over the road for our outbound guests to see. They want their threats to spread, to send word to the better classes. This isn't some drunken hooligan, there's intelligence at play, Brother."

"Father will find out who did this. He's…"

"I doubt that." Otomars stabbed the effigy, sending white sparks into the morning air. "You think our father is really suited to the task?"

"Don't you?"

My brother leaned forward, using the pole to balance himself. The fire's glow reflecting off his round face and wide forehead, flame light flickering with his thoughts. He gazed long upon Father, on Jāzeps, letting the stinging smoke tear his eyes.

"Father expects ghosts to protect us, Wiktor. Men long buried in their graves."

"Ghosts…"

"As real to him as any of us."

Father's voice interrupted, echoing toward us from the road. "Boys, how's it burning? Nearly finished?"

"Almost, Father." A final whisper to Otomars: "Ghosts?"

"Yes," he grunted, digging half-heartedly through the ash again, eyeing our approaching parent. "And they won't be enough, I promise you."

"Recognize this, Wiktor?"

Anne pounded away on the century-old Viennese piano; abusing the family heirloom no one else dared touch. "Well?"

"Edvard Grieg. *Piano concerto in A minor*, first movement."

"Excellent. How about this?" My sister's long fingers danced over the ancient keyboard, natural keys black, accidentals white, it didn't matter. Green, pink or purple, she'd know them by heart. "Not much of a challenge, I'd say."

Elbow on knee, chin perched on fist, I sat on the bench next to Anne. With my back to the piano, I took in every note, tried to discern every precious musical detail…

And strained to read the music sheets' titles warped and backwards in the polished skin of the vase nearby. "*Brahms' Concerto No. 2*, final movement in…in B-flat, major, I think."

"Very good, Wiktor. Let's try one more." Anne shuffled through the sheets looking for the perfect solo to stump me, any excuse to show off her latest mastery.

LENIN'S HAREM

A ballerina grown too tall, our seventeen year old sister had transferred her grandest artistic pretensions to this relic instrument fourteen months and sixteen centimeters ago. Forever perched on this padded bench, a siren in the family parlor, she now played daily throughout the year. Entertaining the passing world through summer's opened windows, notes descending with harvest leaves, serenading friends and suitors in the cozy privacy of winter. Always sitting, slightly slumped, remaining to all eyes 'the height a woman should be.'

A quick study, Anne. Impressive as she was deaf in one ear.

"Well?" she said, finishing the piece on a suspiciously chaotic flurry. "The verdict?"

I hadn't recognized a note, and Anne had shifted between sheet and vase... "Wagner?"

"Claude Debussy." Anne shuddered theatrically. "It's French. *Zut alors*, Wiktor, you need practice. We must buy you a music cylinder next market day." She raised an eyebrow. "And perhaps a pair of spectacles."

I smiled. Caught again. "No spectacles." I saddled closer to Anne on the bench. "And you can just lend me the cylinder Erich Kaltenbach bought you. Aren't there two in your room?"

Some shadow passed across my sister's face. Anne turned around on the piano bench, placed a gentle hand on my arm. "There'll be no more gifts from Erich Kaltenbach, Wiktor."

"Why?"

She looked over her shoulder as if to be certain no listener stood close by. Mother and Erene were off in the kitchen, Father and Otomars forever locked in the study with some guest. Anne's voice dropped to a whisper. "Albrecht Meer proposed last night. On our private walk." She put a finger to her lips. "That's a secret, Wiktor. Mama knows but not Papa. Not yet."

"Albrecht Meer?" *Again?* "Will you accept?"

"I did say, 'No more gifts from Erich,' didn't I?"

First, the Lett's hidden warning, now a hushed marriage proposal. So many secrets today...

We heard the creak of a door. Father emerged from the study, Otomars and their guest trailing behind. This man was a mystery. No one had told me we'd have a visitor on such a cold windswept Sunday. Yet there he was, a robust-looking man in his late thirties, nothing unusual in his dress, clothes perhaps a bit plainer than a gentleman's, but still proper enough, still something regal running through him.

There was a stern, self-importance to his manner that somehow reminded me of dusty paintings of old Prussian soldiers. Curious.

The stranger exchanged goodbyes with Father at the main door while Otomars took a seat near the piano looking rather sullen. Was this visitor's German language Baltic in style? Or did the kaiser's distant realm run in his accent? Difficult to tell.

"Who is he?" I whispered to Otomars, but he waved me off without a glance, his stare remaining on the conversation at the door.

Donning a felt jacket and feathered cap, the man gave a curt bow to all, then saw himself out. The room grew silent. Father walked over to the piano and asked Anne to recall something of Schubert's. She played beautifully, a hint of sadness in the music.

When the notes had at last faded, Otomars said, "Well?"

Father shook his head: "No."

"Otomars says we need guards."

"Nonsense." Father locked the rifle bolt, took aim at a crow settling on a stump in the snowy field. "For six hundred years our family has tended this land without incident, Wiktor. I'm not going to be the first master terrified of his workers." He let off his shot, a miss, the crow fluttering into the air unharmed. "Our servants are good people. It's an insult to us and to them."

Otomars should have known. Father had always been an independent spirit. He felt no allegiance to the kaiser, grumbled about paying taxes to the tsar. He had always said the Baltic landowners would be best served with self-rule, autonomous from any king or emperor, proudly on their own with aid from no one. To hire protection was disgraceful to him.

"If he's so worried, where is Otomars now?" said Father. "Your brother sits with the women instead of practicing marksmanship." He glanced down at me. "Sometimes I wonder if he really desires a country life."

Perhaps, my long silence softened him. As always, Father reined in his censure when it became too severe. "Of course, it is grimly cold, so who can blame Otomars, eh, Wiktor? One's fingers don't numb through two-layer gloves by the fireside."

Yes, certainly. The temperature out here was plunging. Air prickling and popping on my eyes, cheeks burning from briefest exposure. Wisely, Father had decided to forgo our usual Tuesday hunting session, instead settling for thirty minutes of target practice down near the Latvian villages.

LENIN'S HAREM

I thought we'd be alone given the weather, but the Letts were stirring, called by the sounds of gunfire on a slow winter day. Old farmers smoking their pipes in the cold winds, capped young men laboring to finish their workday chores, they all paused to watch, leaning on a far away fence as we shot ice balls off another. At least a half dozen of them, gabbing in their mysterious language. It made me think of secrets.

"I wish I understood them," I whispered to myself.

Father heard me. "The ruling classes choose the language, Wiktor. The Letts all speak Russian. And the best of their kind learn German. Doctor Gulbis for example. What good is it to learn Lettish?"

"But they can speak right in front of us. Without the slightest concern."

Father frowned, shoved a new shell into the rifle. "Wiktor, what's this all about?"

"Otomars says someone from the house staff hung that bag in the tree."

He laughed. "Who? Erene?"

"No. Dear Erene would never…"

"Matiss?"

"I couldn't imagine…"

"Exactly. Your brother finds conspiracies everywhere." He bolted the gun. "Our forefathers were crusaders, Wiktor. Fighters for the Cross. They conquered a wilderness, so we might live here in peace. And if they weren't afraid, why should we be?"

"They had soldiers."

"We are soldiers, Son." He passed me the rifle. "Now, take one more shot and let's go home."

I crouched down and found a secure position. As I tried to steady my shaking hands in the cold and find a worthy final target in the fields beyond, a sudden laughter interrupted my concentration.

It came from the Letts watching along the roadside fence. Unattended by those above, a little boy, perhaps three or four, imitated my marksman stance at their knees. An invisible rifle in his hands, he fired imaginary shots between the fence rails at Father and me. Laughing as he hit his targets, young lips mimicking explosion sounds as the bullets found their mark again and again. Ignored and un-hushed by his elders.

Chapter Three

The stone made a spider-web crack in the glass top of the table, then thudded across the floorboards until it found quieter grounds atop the rug near my desk. I stood back, away from the window. Somewhere a woman was screaming. Mother? Anne? No, it was the servant Erene in the entrance way, she had dropped the tray, a flat clang from the platter ringing through the room, the coffee cups in pieces, a puddle of steaming brown liquid seeping over the floor.

Staccato heart in my ears, I sprinted to the stairwell. At their base, near the door, I spied Anne, her arms locked around Mother whose face had turned grey as her hair.

"What has happened?" my own voice high and girlish with panic.

Our mother's words went unheard. Erene passed me on the stairs so quickly that she knocked me down. I fell to my knees, holding the banister to keep from falling farther.

Erene's words turned fear to stark terror: "We're on fire. They've set the house on fire!" She looked to Anne, then back to Mother. "Where's the Master? Mistresses where's the Master?" With each 'M' her voice grew shriller.

Anne shouted: "Out. We need to get out."

Erene's reply was incomprehensible, syllables merging, rising to a scream. My sister cut her off: "We must go."

"They'll kill us. They will." A quick and panicked utterance, it was not my mother's voice, foreign and cracking, though it came from her lips.

Somewhere off in the hall came the chiming of falling glass. "Who will kill us?" I gasped, hands shaking on the banister. What bandits, what army of invaders had found its way into our lands?

My head throbbed as I hurried down the stairs. At the bottom the heat was that of the kiln, my eyes quickly tearing, black clouds caressing the ceiling.

This could not be happening.

A group of servant girls, cries like seagulls on the Libau docks, ran past and huddled about Erene. She escaped them, pressed up against the door. "We must leave Mistresses, the smoke is growing worse."

Mother jerked her head around. "Where's Wiktor? Where's my baby?"

"Here Mama." I rushed to embrace her.

"We must go, Mother!" Anne pleaded.

"No, not until we find Rudolf. He was upstairs." Mother released me, tried to climb the steps, but Anne and Erene pulled her from the stairwell, their calls fading in the choking fumes, cries turning to gravely wheezes.

The thickening billows were overpowering. The insides of my throat cracking, I could no longer hold my breath and inhaled the searing clouds, my body rejecting each gasp in a spasm of painful coughs. Whoever was outside, whatever band of marauders ransacked our land was the lesser evil. They might kill us, staying inside certainly would.

Yet, even suffocating, near blinded, I hesitated. What might they do to Mother, to Anne, if we opened that door? It failed my young sense of justice. Our family had never hurt anyone, why should they want to harm us? This must be a mistake, some grievance against the wrong victims.

While I cowered at the door, the decision was made for me. The servant girls panicked, and despite Mother's command, they broke open the door and fled out into the night. If the smoke retreated momentarily from the blast of winter air, somewhere close within this new breath fed the flames. The vengeful gloom returned, stronger, doubly thick, carrying the scorching heat of its source. It burned, the hairs on my arms beginning to glow like embers.

Anne pulled our screaming mother out into the yard, arms still locked about each other they collapsed into the snow. Cries again and again for Father, nowhere to be seen. *Please, God, let him be outside the house.* Head dizzy, I stumbled to a knee in the ice, finally saw them, the enemy.

An army in rags. No successor to Napoleon, no endless hordes of Huns, it was nothing but a group of farmers. No uniforms, no flags, just a bunch of people in peasants' clothes. The men, hundreds of them, carried shovels, rifles, bricks and stones. Many shook torches in their hands. They had a greasy, dirty look to them, as if they were children of the hellish atmosphere that had just released us. There was no roar, no great swell of sound. Most stood there silently, letting a few do all the shouting. They screamed fierce words, most too distorted to understand. But I caught a few in Lettish: *Degt.* Burn. *Liesma.* Flame.

LENIN'S HAREM

To my horror I recognized faces in the crowd: Janis Stalts who fed the horses in the stables; old Matiss, who only yesterday returned from Rīga with Brother's newspapers; even faithful Rothberts who taught me Latvian sonnets during his breaks from fence building. They had treated us so kindly, so respectfully. Father had given them work, helped them feed their families. Why had they all betrayed us?

I could not run; they'd formed a wall around our home, watching as it was consumed behind. Sparks fell to earth around me, birthing little steam geysers in the snow. The great heat blistering my neck, I patted my head, prayed my hair was not aflame.

I glanced back, away from the vicious mob. The entire left side of the building, where Father's drawing room had been, was caught in climbing flames, the winds blowing the sparks across the roof. Dumbfounded, I slowly realized the constant screaming in my ear was Mother calling out for our father.

Where was he? I took a step nearer the house, but the blaze was only growing, the heat an impenetrable wall. Was it too late?

Averting my watering eyes from the pyre, I found Otomars standing a few yards away in front of the manor. He had his riding gear on, red coat, high black boots and leggings, helmet lying in the snow. He was talking to one of the mob, a thick man, with a deeply creased face sporting a blue work cap, their conversation drowned beneath the venomous crowd and Mother's hysterical screams. Otomars's stern expression showed not a trace of fear, as if he still controlled these rebellious workers. Heir to the estate, their master, even as it went down in flames behind him.

Another group of servants, coated in soot, burst through the house door. One stooped to tend a damaged limb, several others ran in mad circles trying to choke out the searing embers inside their lungs. A few sprang into the crowd, embracing... embracing who? Brothers? Sisters? Lovers? Husbands? Or traitors in our own household?

Fear began to ebb toward rage.

Otomars made his way across to the family, the man in the blue cap walking parallel, as if there was an unspoken battle line, some invisible moat separating them. My brother paused, put a hand on Mother's shoulder. She seemed not to notice, an uncomprehending look of terror on her face. Yes, I wanted to strike out at the traitors, to rip the torches from their hands, to shove their ungrateful faces into the ice, and show them that our family wouldn't cringe before their kind.

Half-bent, Father passed through the fire-ringed door. Either he'd doused himself to retard the flames, or he'd been taking a bath, because he wore nothing but his robe, not even shoes on his feet. Steam trailed from his uncovered head, in his hands his hunting rifle, on his face stark hatred.

Otomars shoved the gun from his hands, knocking it to the ground. Father dropped to retrieve it, Otomars swiftly kicking it to the feet of the man in the blue cap.

My jaw opened in horror. Our brother had betrayed Father, all of our family. Why? What cowardice was this? I sprang forward to help Father, but Anne gripped me solidly by the shoulder, shoved me to my knees.

"Wiktor," she whispered, trying to soothe my rage. "Pray with me."

They escorted our family down the hill toward the stables. I glared at each as we walked. So many familiar, so many faces from childhood, people I had long trusted. Even the house servants stood with them now, most averting their gaze as we passed. But those that didn't, they were the most horrible: the visions that would haunt my dreams years later. In their eyes I saw emotions undreamt until this night: hatred and mirth, pride and vindication. Some laughed in unrestrained glee. Others shouted out in Lettish, unknown words that I could not define yet felt their meaning. And their desirous looks toward Anne, so unconcerned by Otomars or Father, eclipsed only with a glance from the man in the blue cap.

My eyes found my brother ahead. He'd given up the family's possessions, home, everything without fight or protest. My fists balled in such rage that my nails cut deep into my palm.

At the stables, Jāzeps Bats and several others were standing about our wagon, taking out the cargo, removing the seat cushions, the leather lining, gutting the thing, leaving only the base wooden skeleton. They hitched an old plow horse to it and then motioned us in. I helped Mother step up into the wagon, then Anne, and finally climbed in myself. Otomars went forward and waited for Father to join him. He did not, remaining at the end, surrounded by his ex-servants. Some looked as though they might embrace him, others as if murder crossed their thoughts, most shuffled about uncomfortably.

Father finally climbed into the bed, the shake of the floorboards sobering my thoughts, reminding me this wasn't some horrible nightmare. Unable to stop her tears, Anne removed her knit stockings, tried to force them onto Father's bare feet while he sat unmoving.

Bats closed up the back of the wagon, the usual respect long vacant from his eyes.

The wagon steered out a wide path toward the main road. On the embankment above, the whole manor: roof, central tower, and surrounding rooms were now in flames. The arching windows glowed like the eyes of madmen. Echo after thunderous echo shook the countryside as the support beams cracked and fell to earth.

Anne leaned forward to Otomars: "Where can we go?"

"I'm thinking, Anne. We need to be away before they decide to put bricks against our heads."

Familiar-faced children ran after us, throwing stones at the wagon. One hit Mother in the throat and she crumpled over. Even that violence didn't rouse Father from wherever he was.

"It's not serious," said Anne, checking Mother's neck, "only a bruising, I'm certain."

"If we had had our gun…" I began to strike Otomars, landing heavy blows between his shoulder blades. "Traitor!"

"Stop it Wiktor!" Anne screamed.

Moving both reins into his left hand, Otomars reached around and grabbed my torso in a bear lock, pulling me over the gunwhale to his seat. My head locked between bicep and forearm, he whispered in a calm voice:

"Wiktor, what are you doing?"

Rage filled me, rage at my helplessness before the mob, at my helplessness before my brother. "You gave away our gun, our only chance."

He kept his eyes on the road, but pressed his lips against my ear.

"Giving away the rifle was our only chance, Wiktor."

Firmly he set me back into the body of the wagon, Anne tugging me down by the collar, forcing me to the floor-bed. "Sit still, Wiktor."

Otomars glanced back at her. "Anne, where should we go?"

"The Meer estate. Albrecht's family."

He nodded. "Yes, that's what I was thinking as well."

Otomars clicked the reins and the wagon jolted forward. When Anne at last released me, I drifted to the back, climbing past our parents. I sat there silently, trying to calm myself, to understand what was happening.

There were shapes in the darkness, figures on horseback trailing the wagon. An escort or did they mean to rob us? To murder us out of sight from the others?

"Otomars, there are men behind us."

"I know, Wiktor. I know. Help Anne tend to Mother."

We moved along for hours, silent except for hoof clatter and Mother's sorrowful cries. Up ahead, a slowly spinning axis of purple-grey smoke dominated the night time horizon. The great column, like the clouds above it, bathed in a jumping orange and yellow. In eleven years, I'd never seen anything so immense. Still kilometers away, I could smell the burnt timbers from here.

People were scattered along the roads moving in the opposite direction as us. Some carried baskets, others assorted household goods: silver teapots, lamp stands, bird cages. Two men passed by with a large rug rolled up between them, a woman's dress across one's shoulders, a riding helmet atop the other's head.

Anne twisted the hem of her dress in hand until it tore. "Albrecht."

We'd never make it. The roads were too congested.

Otomars stopped the wagon, turned around on his seat. "Father where should we go? It looks like something has happened up ahead."

He answered, saying something under his breath.

"Pardon me Father? I didn't hear."

"A man has a right to defend his home, Otomars. You had no authority to take that from me."

Otomars was silent for a long time. "I'm sorry, Father. It didn't seem you were thinking."

His voice was barely audible. "Well if you're doing the thinking, you decide. I don't care."

"Father?"

He said nothing.

"Papa?"

It seemed to me something died in our father that night.

Otomars caressed his brow, voice grave and breaking. "Anne? Where to now?"

"I don't know, Otomars." She too, sounded as if tears were going to claim her. 'Where are there soldiers? The Richter's manor?"

"Several hours at least. We shouldn't stay on these roads. We could go north?"

"Baron Kaltenbach, then?"

His reply was slow coming. "What do you think?"

"Kaltenbach then."

Otomars turned the carriage around and we headed for the north fork in the road.

As the night waned, there was no refuge from the choking haze. Everywhere there were orange bellied clouds and columns of smoke. It seemed people were always close by, yelling, shouting, screaming; all unseen in the thick gloom, the encroaching night alive with sounds. More than once we saw the dancing lights of torch bearers prowling through the nearby fields.

Soon we would know. This night was only the first.

Two hundred manors burned that winter.

Chapter Four

February, 1906

The fish swam round and round in the great wooden trough. Pike, carp, perch and catfish in a variety of sizes from tiny ones half the length of my little finger to monsters as long as my forearm. This was a pleasant place; tunneled into a hillside, cool in summer, warm in winter. The trickle of flowing water, running down wooden ramps from the ceiling into all the troughs gave a calming, tranquil relief to the mind. I had sat here for hours watching the fish in Baron Kaltenbach's hatchery. A smokeless fireplace in the corner gave just enough illumination. The flame light sparkled on the fish scales and off the water's surface, giving the whole room a magical, glowing faerie-like aura. A stranger would never have imagined how brutal the winter was outside.

I heard footfalls on stone steps. "Wiktor," cried out Anne.

She appeared in the entranceway, her head barely clearing the low arch. The light from the fire reflected off the water onto my sister's form, bestowing on her an enchanted glow, as if she were some elfin queen come to take me to wondrous realms.

"Wiktor," said this enchantress, "they're back. You need to come in now."

I followed her up the stairs, the cold gathering as we ascended, the biting Baltic winds sweeping over us as we stepped out of the cellar onto the surface.

Ahead, the baron's estate rolled away across open hills, crossing frozen streams and horse-huddled stables, before finally disappearing into acres of untouched forest. The snow trampled away by the boots of many men, the only virgin frost lay atop high tree limbs and across the expansive roof of the distant manor house. At our feet, the ground remained an ugly mix of brown and grey, the winter landscape scarred with creeping boot-prints.

The Kaltenbach holdings were numerous, many, many times those of our father. It took a full ten minutes to walk across to the residences. Everywhere there were clumps of men: *Selbst-schutz* mercenaries hired by the baron to keep his lands safe from revolution. As we passed their bonfires, each guard's hands and face turned toward the reviving flames, I could see the rifles across their backs and the 'skinner' knives hung at their belts. One painfully familiar fellow tipped his feathered cap as we passed.

Was he enough? Were these men enough? To protect us from all of Latvia?

A few minutes later I sat with Anne, wrapped together in an itchy wool blanket, warm within the blue and mahogany opulence of the Kaltenbach's baroque dining hall. The baron and his wife, Angelika, sat solemnly at opposite ends of the chamber, our parents on an ornate couch between. Their twenty-year old son, Erich, thin with a mane of curly black hair, leaned against the hearth, coffee in hand, repeating the news for Anne and me.

"I can only say that it was dramatic. The Russian forces were exceptional. They had no trouble overcoming any resistance the Letts put up. Really, it felt more like a hunting party. The danger was greatly exaggerated; we encountered nothing to give us pause."

Erich, Otomars and our father had ridden off with the Russian expeditionary forces to put down the Latvian revolt weeks ago. Two days after embarking, Father had returned, claiming he could no longer stomach the task. Since, he'd spent most of his time in his room. As far as I knew, he'd said nothing more on the matter.

Erich and Otomars had just returned. Our brother languishing in his quarters to change, Erich rushing in here to tell the tale still attired in muddy riding gear.

The ancient baron, too creaky and stiff for long conversation, croaked a rare question: "Are you quite convinced Erich that you broke their will to fight?"

"In Courland, I am certain. We took our leave when the troops turned north, Father."

"Then perhaps we can disband some of these *Selbst-schutz* men. These guards are costing a fortune." His smiled assumed agreement.

"Is that premature?" asked the baroness. "Erich says there are still brigands in Livland and..."

The baron raised a skeletal hand: "Silence!" And the room went so. When this brittle, reed of a man rasped this word all discussion was over. It was a strange, almost medieval mannerism from him but one that none dared challenge in his home. Our family's tenuous future hung upon obedience to his most eccentric fancies.

Everyone sat there uncomfortably, listening to the snapping and popping from the hearth, until the *Silence!* was broken by the creak of a door.

"Otomars!" exclaimed Anne, and she left the warmth of our blanket to embrace him. Everyone peeked from the corners of their eyes to see if the baron took offence, but he only smiled and said "Welcome." Discourse was once again permissible.

Realizing his ill manners, Otomars bowed before the baron, kissed him appropriately on the hand and elbow in submissive greeting. The recent ordeal had clearly worn on my brother, lines across his forehead, his eyes puffy and red. With his widow's peak and oval face, he looked far older than his eighteen years. Otomars asked a servant for a drink and refused all invitations to discuss his journey. It was only when he had received his cognac and was pressed by the baron himself that he agreed to answer questions.

"I am sure Erich has relayed most of the events, what can I possibly add?" His voice was worn thin, as if this were a retelling he'd sooner avoid.

"How did the Russian officers treat you? Were they hospitable?" queried our mother.

Otomars stood back from the baron, found a place to lean near the hearth, the firelight dancing off his face. "Fine, fine, Mother. They know how important our taxes are to Tsar Nicholas."

"Don't be cynical, Otomars."

The baron squinted in the chamber's light, his raspy voice carrying through the hall: "When you met the Lettish army in the field…"

To the family horror, Otomars dared to interrupt him. "Army?" He flashed a quizzical look at Erich. "There was no army, sir. A mob here or there. We had no one to defeat, they'd all gone home."

The old lord seemed confused. His son tried to answer: "Surely, Otomars that group at Kroṇauce?"

"Two dozen farmers? Hardly an army Erich."

Mother's voice was cracking: "But the land is secure, Otomars?"

"This was a punitive expedition, Mother. Punishment exclusively. We've done nothing these past few days to be proud of."

Anne wrung the blanket in her hands. "What did they do, Otomars?"

He turned away, looking back at our sister through a mirror on the wall. "We burned their schools, their churches, their granaries." He took another drink. "We...."

Erich burst out with praise: "Let me say, Otomars was magnificent. When they rounded up the Lettish prisoners, he picked their leaders out of the mob. Those that attacked your manor, organizers on the roads..." He turned to our parents. "Shaved whiskers, low hats, it didn't matter. They couldn't hide. What an eye for detail your boy has!"

Mother seemed proud, our father unmoved. Otomars only stared at the wall, his eyes avoiding the mirror.

Erich continued: "The army put them on trial immediately. Even two right in a wheat field for God's sake. They were hanged, when? I'd say not an hour later."

"Not an hour later," Otomars softly repeated, his reflection haunted by something far away. He took another drink.

My sister pulled the blanket close: "Are you sure they were the right men?"

"Of course he is!" proclaimed Erich.

"Who were they?" asked Anne. "Can you recall them Otomars?"

"Kēlers, Rihards Ābēlts, Andris Jansons. Bats was involved too."

All names I'd known, the faces of childhood. All traitors? All since executed? It seemed impossible. "Why did we kill them, if they didn't kill us?" I asked.

A hush fell over the hall. Everyone stared at me as if I had no right to speak. Finally Mother said, "Oh, Wiktor, don't be naïve. We could have died in the fire."

The others brushed aside my question, but my brother did not: "He's right... He's right. The next revolution will be bloodier. They won't spare us a second time." There was a terrifying finality in his voice.

Anne shivered against me inside the blanket. "Otomars, you don't think this can happen again?"

He said nothing. Erich answered for him: "I think they've learned their lesson."

"Otomars?"

"I don't know Anne. I hope not." He finished the drink, ordered another, turned back around. "We were lucky for the tsar's men", then realizing his omission, "and the baron's, of course."

I stood outside with my brother watching the people pass by in Rīga's Herder Square. It was one of those bright warm late winter days, the sun glaring off the snowed roofs of the city's center; the world seemed made of only three colors: blazing white, purest blue, and the soft red of brick.

There were Russian troops everywhere, searching pedestrians, breaking up discussions, watching from street corners. Even Otomars and I had been frisked – twice! – while waiting for our father's meeting to finish. Otomars said they were looking for revolvers and mistook us for Letts, rather than proper, landowning Baltic-Germans. It seemed to me the soldiers didn't care who we were as long as we obeyed.

Even with all the troops present, these Rīga Latvians still walked about as if nothing had happened. As if their crimes of the night were forgotten in the light of day. The very normalcy with which they acted enraged me. As though they thought justice had somehow actually been served and no atonement needed.

My anger increased when I saw men carrying signs. Signs written in all three languages with words like: "Higher Wages for Mill Workers;" "Support Land Reform" and "A Latvian Nation. Now!" Had they learned nothing? The soldiers frequently broke them up, but to my shock more often they let them continue. Silently, I wished punishment on the whole Lettish race.

Until I saw them. Father being so tardy, Otomars had taken us through a back street to purchase some luncheon fruit. On the way to this market, we passed a small plaza. Three men were being marched to the gallows right in front of us. A crowd stood about shouting obscenities in German and Russian. The condemned walked up the stairs, without swagger, without purpose. Not defiant as I envisioned rebels, empowered by martyrdom, but frightened, meek, contrite. These men did not want to die. One man was begging for mercy in Latvian, he kept falling into a fetal position, kicking with his feet until they carried him up the stairs. Another repeated "My God, my God," in Russian. One, he seemed the oldest with a long full-beard, began to shout out something, his voice muffled as the hood was pulled down over his head. I remember how the end of his beard stuck out from underneath, how it flew up as his body fell, and how it fluttered in the wind while he hung limp swinging like a clock pendulum. I was surprised I felt no relief with their passing; no vindication nor closure, only a sickly sort of waste in the pit of my stomach like the harbinger of a coming flu. It was not at all what I expected.

We met Father twenty minutes later, an equally sick expression on his face.

"What is it? What's wrong?" asked Otomars.

He took in a deep breath, held it, as if to pass one more moment when the secret was still his alone. Then he slowly released, and his soul seemed to come with it: "The insurance will not be paid. The company has folded." He half-heartedly reached out to put an arm on my shoulder, but mid-effort let it fall aside.

"There are too many claims."

Late at night, candle in hand, I tiptoed through the upper level of the baron's manor toward my brother's bedroom. The narrow hall was cold as outdoors, my toes icicles little warmed by the thin strip of carpet below my feet. Down this silent path I passed through history. A stern bust of the baron's great-grandfather on my left, another of some fellow called Cicero on the right, and ahead, the ancient Archbishop Albert of Rīga's antiquity, a must in the homes of the richer Baltic barons. These three ghosts my only companions at the midnight hour.

The walls about me were a mosaic of black rectangles framed in dusty bronze. Dark oil paintings faded over hundreds of years depicting wide landscapes and wider battle scenes, all populated by great men with the Teutonic Cross on their shields. Our ancestors, the Livonian Crusaders from the thirteenth century, conquering these lands, bringing religion to the Cours, Letts, Livs and other tribes of the region, saving their souls eternal.

They'd repaid us this winter.

As I neared Otomars's door, I found relatively recent subjects. The rich dukes of Courland from a few hundred years ago, standing on docks with sugar sacks and bananas, shrewdly appraising the goods from their colonies in the New World and Africa. Monies earned that went to the pope, and after him to foreign emperors, kings and princes in places I could never name. It didn't matter. The German landowners ruled the countryside – day to day at least. In the eighteenth century the Russians had come and our tributes shifted to St. Petersburg. Nothing else changed.

My brother's door was ajar. Softly as I could, I pushed it open, peeked inside.

He was still awake, sitting in a chair at the hearth, trying to read a letter by the fading fire.

"Otomars," I whispered.

He looked back at me, the lines of exhaustion on his face. "Yes, Wiktor?"

I stepped into the room, felt the welcome heat of the hearth and china boiler in the corner. "Anne is downstairs crying."

"I know."

"Why?"

"Tears of joy," he said without conviction. "She's agreed to marry Erich."

I felt something painful well up inside me, a tightening in my throat. "And Albrecht Meer?"

It took a moment for him to catch my meaning. Then he nodded. "As destitute as us."

Otomars motioned me over to his chair. "Wiktor, our lives are going to change, you know that, yes?" He folded up the letter. "Without insurance, there is no home, and there will be no harvest next autumn. Father's debts will mount."

"But the year after?"

"The banks won't wait." He put a hand on my shoulder. "And Anne's dowry? Much of the estate will go to the Kaltenbachs, more than a normal dowry."

I stared at him, not understanding.

"The baron does nothing for charity, Wiktor. He's wanted our land for years." Otomars squeezed my shoulder with his thick fingers. "I don't want you to become a Kaltenbach child. Work for them, run errands for their businesses until you begin officer training, but remember the Rooks name is yours, Rooks blood is in your veins." He looked me squarely in the face. "We have to start again. You and me, we're the hope."

My eyes drifted to the floor. "Of course."

"Good."

I let out a weary breath. *Officer training*, he'd said it. For the Baltic Barons, the first sons ran the estate, the seconds went into the military, or, if faint of heart, the clergy. But I had always wanted to go to university, to study the sciences. How could I ask Father for the tuition now?

And, my brother, so exhausted and sullen, without his birthright what would he do? "Where will you go?" I asked.

Otomars glanced down to the half-folded letter. He stripped off the address at the top. "St. Petersburg," was all I caught, before he tossed the rest into the fire.

"I have an offer of employment."

I leaned against the arm-thick mooring line, comfortable I would not slip and plunge off the wharf to the grayish Daugava River below. I had an invoice to deliver to the ship's captain, but he was taking his good time to appear on deck. Across the pier, I watched the newest refugees arrive and shove themselves in between those who had spent the night on the Rīga dockyards. Russians, Jews, gypsies, Estonians, Latvians all in the thousands. So many revolts had occurred in the previous year, so many people now were on the run from the tsar's justice. They clogged every inch of the harbor waiting for passage to Britain, the Americas, or anywhere outside of the Russian Empire.

I knew many among them were revolutionaries, murderers, or thieves. Like the ones our family had faced. Not that they wore signs that said: 'Traitor.' To the eye, they just looked like weary travelers; hungry, exhausted, seeking somewhere, anywhere to lie down on the planks of the teeming docks.

This was the hardest concept to grasp, how the mask of innocence played on our sympathies. Like that Estonian family across from me: a crying baby, the father missing a leg, the mother hobbled by some crippling disease. They didn't appear threatening. But I asked myself, how did he lose that leg? What crime might have he committed? Or this tall Jew near the seawall, shading his tiny pregnant wife and sunburnt son. Could they possibly be an enemy? Or those three Russian youths camped underneath the crane: too young to be dangerous now, but what will they be like in five years? Ten? If they're really loyal Russians why were they bound for other lands?

A middle-aged man, bald, clean-shaven wearing a thick weather-scarred overcoat walked down the gangplank from the cargo bay. He stopped and looked at me, balanced against his line.

"Are you from Kaltenbach Works?"

"Captain Skujenes?" I asked. "I've got a letter for you. The bill for the parts you ordered."

He took it, opening the envelope in front of me. He ran down the list checking against the charges he expected. As he did, we chatted about his journey from Oslo, how harsh the storms had been, and what he planned on doing ashore. He was a Lett, and I was thrilled that he hadn't mentioned my accent. Months of running errands for the Kaltenbach companies, foraying alone into the Lettish world with instructions from the bosses, had increased my Latvian speech remarkably. Maybe these damnable Letts could no longer detect a hint of German when I spoke their language.

At last I commented on the crowds marooned here waiting for passage, extending my vocabulary to the fullest.

"It's good they're leaving," the captain replied, folding up the invoice.

"I agree." I was glad someone else recognized the danger of these foreigners.

"Latvia is for the Latvians, Kraut."

Part Two:

Lāčplēsis's Men

Chapter Five

Summer, 1915

My mare whinnied as I turned toward the voices echoing up from the alleyway. These narrow Rīga streets were a poor place to ride a horse and now clogged with noxious fumes, both man and animal panted to take in enough air.

The sounds repeated. Soldiers definitely, soldiers close by, but this heavy smog smothered my world, clipped my vision to a few short meters. These men could be inside a nearby building, lost off a side street, or deeper in the alleyway. There was no way to tell.

A remorseful sigh, another burning breath, the greasy air slithering down my raw throat. There was *one* certainty, however: the German army was coming. Their artillery shells rained down on the city: collapsing abandoned wharfs, caving in walls, opening up craters in the muddy streets. Defeat after defeat this summer had made it inevitable. They'd be here by tomorrow. The Russians were doing what they had always done: backing up. Their one advantage, they could retreat for half the globe.

As an officer in the tsar's army my responsibility was to remove anyone of value from the area. Anyone who could operate machinery, sew a uniform, plow a field. Personal experience proved it was easier if we took the whole family and let them be sorted out farther from the front. It seemed half of the population of Latvia, having never left sight of their homes, was being moved thousands of kilometers into the heart of Russia.

Whether they liked it or not.

In theory my orders were simple, get the workers onto the carts to haul them away. If they would not be moved, shoot them so the Germans couldn't enlist them. In reality, this meant I rode about on a horse admonishing soldiers, stopping assaults, interrupting rapes. Looting, I slowly learned, was best ignored. The

Russian army was disintegrating, deserters in the thousands. Those who stayed expected additional compensation. It was understood, if unsaid.

On the city's main roads carts passed loaded with pale families, awakened and confused. An hour ago, asleep in their beds, now with one bag for all of them bound for places they couldn't even name. Most had never been farther east than Wenden.

These carts were often forced aside by speeding wagons full of machine parts, barrels of oil, wooden tubs of grease. The Russians were getting everything of value out.

And burning everything else. The fields outside the city last night were a turbulent sea of flame, crests of fire crashing together, breaking apart, only to be surmounted by the next, higher wave. Today the dockyards and factories were being torched. A coal black mountain had risen south of the city, dwarfing everything even the tower of St. Peter's church. The sun could not penetrate it and it was chilling in the heart to know that as I looked south onto this mountain shroud, our enemies must now be spying it across the river Daugava.

Mass burning had a different scent than the hearth, the variety of aromas was a terrible thing: scorched metal, vaporized refuse, old timbers, it was too much for the brain to process, and left me with a dull constant headache.

Two old Latvians, well past the age where they earned a cart space, shoved their way along the wall, fearful of being trampled by my horse, even more afraid that I would bark the command "Halt."

I tried not to have sympathy for them. These Letts had taken away everything our family possessed and had killed something inside my father. Yet, by circumstance I had spent many years on these docks running errands for the Kaltenbach family companies, working among the common Latvians. I had learned their language, understood a little more of Lettish thinking. There were a *few* good fellows in their numbers and, even if their brutish ways were unforgivable, I could privately admit that their open hatred for the Baltic Barons was not completely without warrant.

And, of course, they were the only men in the Russian army who really seemed to want to fight for Latvia. Admirable, given the way everyone else was falling back.

The throaty, rigid scream of an older man joined the chorus of younger voices. It echoed up from one of those small Rīga courtyards boxed in on three sides by apartment walls, the fourth entered by an archway low enough that it required me to duck on horseback. Inside, two soldiers stood, while a third harshly ejected a tenant from his doorway. Elderly, he collapsed onto the ground.

LENIN'S HAREM

I gained their attention with a guttural shout, quickly dismounted and approached the nearest. Closed in, the air could not escape and the oppressive summer heat thickened. A sauna full of singeing gas and smoke, clinging moisture collected beneath my uniform and sweat ran tickling across cheeks and nose.

"What is the situation, Corporal? Report."

He seemed flustered to see an officer, the others eyeing me timidly, waiting for his cue on how to react. They were all near my age, twenty, the corporal perhaps slightly older.

"Well, sir…" he paused to read my rank in the dense atmosphere. The smoke devoured illumination in these back-alley courtyards. "Lieutenant? This man is a machinist, sir. We were going to move him."

"He would move better if you hadn't thrown him to the ground." I gave the soldier a disapproving glance and approached the man who was picking himself up off the gravel. Then with a turn: "Where is your sergeant? Corporal…?"

"Korovnikov. Corporal Korovnikov. Our sergeant, he's gone off, sir. We've been on our own here for two days."

"There are many troops about, why haven't you found another commander?"

"See, sir… the thing is Lieutenant…he won't go."

Not an answer, he had avoided the question. Why?

A woman's scream from above, somewhere something glass shattered.

I started. "Who is up there?"

"One of our boys is getting out the last of the Latvians. They've been resisting."

I'd seen this too much in the past few days. "Get him down and the girl."

The corporal grimaced and gave a nod to one of the privates. He entered the building. A few moments later he exited with a sobbing adolescent girl and another Russian soldier. He couldn't have been seventeen. She was younger.

"What is your name, Private?" Somewhere an artillery shell exploded.

"Rezanov, Captain."

"Lieutenant," I pointed to my insignia. "Lieutenant Wiktor Rooks. And your other names, Private?"

"Dmitry Valentinovych , sir." He avoided my eyes. His face was flush with heat, his head unadorned, moisture dripping down his closely shorn scalp.

"Dmitry Valentinovych. Private Dmitry Valentinovych Rezanov." I said the name slowly, making it clear I was branding the name in memory.

"Yes, sir."

The corporal stepped forward, eclipsing my view of the boy. His tone sheepish: "Is there a problem Lieutenant?"

I kept my voice even, business like: "Private Rezanov is a rapist, Corporal. I want you to watch him." I looked at the others: "And you two escort this man to the main road so we can get him on a cart, I'll take the girl."

They didn't move. One of the privates yelled out, "You don't know...it's not true!"

I looked at the girl: Thirteen? Fourteen? Amber-haired, scratch marks on her cheek and neck, green dress torn across the shoulder. I knew. I watched the boy, accused of rape by an officer, his only response silence, trembling, looking at the ground. He knew too. If we were lucky, if *she* were lucky, he was the only participant.

She sobbed and tried to embrace the machinist. He avoided her eyes, kept her at arm's distance, stoically pushed her away. She collapsed to the cobblestones hysterical. Like the heat, these walls wouldn't let her cries escape. Again and again they echoed.

Corporal Korovnikov came forward. "You see Lieutenant, I know what he done was wrong, but... well, he didn't have to stay. None of us did. I mean you got to understand we could die when the Germans..."

"He ain't never experienced a lady," repeated the other private.

"Corporal, I want you to take Private Rezanov's gun and bayonet, and have your two privates escort this man to the main road, so we can put him..."

"I won't go." The machinist grew suddenly animated, yet his voice stayed firm, just able to penetrate the sounds of the crying girl. "This is our home. Jelena and I have got no reason to live in Russia. We live here, sir. Please."

These times were too dangerous for sympathies: "It's for your own protection."

"Sir, begging your pardon, but the Germans have never done nothing to me. Your men ransacked my home, attacked my daughter. I would be best unprotected by you."

The corporal broke in, "See! He won't go sir. Now orders are that we can shoot him, so the enemy don't get him. We've been trying to convince otherwise, but if they won't budge, well, what Dmitry did really won't matter."

"We're going to escort them to the road, not shoot them. Are my orders clear Corporal?"

He looked at his men. One put a comforting arm on Private Rezanov's shoulder. The corporal came back with the tone of a strained negotiator: "Clear, sir. It seems you'll bend the rules for these Latvians, while being awfully hard on your own men. Don't you think?"

Even in the sweltering heat and thick haze I could see the challenge.

"What is your full name, Corporal?"

He paused for a long time looking uncomfortably at the wall, then finally directly at me. His words started as a whisper, but gained volume with resolve: "I'd rather keep that to myself, sir."

Rezanov and the two others moved up behind him. Their rifles rising...

I shouted in his face: "I want your name, I want Private Rezanov's rifle, and I want that man escorted to the road." I willed him to respond. Without rank, without command, I was one against four strangers in a smoke-filled back alley.

A resolute frown from the corporal: "He won't leave. Orders are to shoot him. Seems that you are the one ignoring orders, Lieutenant. That kinda invalidates your command."

The guns went off, the machinist fell dead. Before I could move Corporal Korovnikov had bayoneted me in the lower intestines. He ripped it low, hooking my pelvis bone before pulling it out. There was no pain, only a hard, uncomfortable tugging inside. The last thing I remember was the girl's screams as my shoulder slumped against the wall and all went dark...

Chapter Six

Autumn, 1915, Livland

For three months I lay on a tiny cot in the army hospital with all my possessions packed in a trunk underneath me. The surgery had gone well, though I had lost a few centimeters of colon and taken some liver damage. The bayonet scar was hideous: like a huge fossilized centipede running from pelvis to stomach, but all in all the physical damage would soon subside.

It was my mind that worried. I replayed that morning over and over again, probing for alternative actions, imagining different endings. How had these men turned on me? How had my orders been refused? Why had I been stabbed?

As a child, I had always taken comfort in the natural order of things. A falsity. Our servants had turned on our family. These troops had turned on me. Was there anything I could trust? Anything, anyone who would do what was supposed to be done? Did I need to be kinder to earn respect? Or harsher? Was I too weak to lead?

It was a long three months. I tried not to think of the girl in the green dress or her father's execution. I rationalized that I hadn't failed them. These troops had betrayed them, as they had me. I said that every night before sleep. Told myself it wasn't a lie.

I'd given a report on the attack shortly after the surgery. A man in a tan uniform had filled out a form and promised investigation. I'd heard nothing more. I imagined the paper sitting in some mammoth inbox within an office abandoned from the war.

In the first month I had dreams that those men had found me here and snuck into the hospital to finish their work. I awoke in cold sweats. Apparently, I also spoke German in my sleep. A man with a head injury declared me an enemy spy, shouting out to the whole room his discovery. The nurse sedated him, and he was soon moved to a different ward. Nothing more came of it, but his accusations made me paranoid, fitful, afraid to embrace slumber. While my body healed, my mind became nervous, chronically exhausted.

Mostly, I sat. Sat and tried to make sense of everything. Sat and felt my belly tighten, and listened to the Russian nurse tell me this was a good thing. There was nothing to read, only an old copy of Chekhov's collected works and the Latvian poet Blaumanis's odes to country living. Both books soon disappeared. The room had a phonograph, but someone always needed rest. It was never turned on.

News of the war drizzled in. Miraculously, the German advance had been stopped somehow. Rīga had not capitulated. As autumn approached, there was even talk of an offensive. I perceived a pressure to deem everyone healthy. The doctors pried and pressed my tender stomach, weighed me twice a week. Intestinal wounds could take months to reveal that a body was poisoning itself. No matter how they wanted to be rid of me, nor strong my desire to be off this cot, everyone had to wait.

Time passed. I counted missing ceiling tiles, found patterns in the freckles on my arm and fantasized about passionate embraces with the nurse. My pillow leaked feathers and to distract my mind I invented games. After a sponge bath, I'd see how many I could balance on their side across my chest. A lieutenant from Wolmar and I challenged each other to see the number we could keep aloft with puffs of breath. He'd managed three, I five. Unfortunately, the effort agitated my wounded belly. He always won the stamina events.

Three days before my twenty-first birthday, when I had eleven feathers teetering on their side across my moist chest, I had a visitor.

A man in an officer's uniform, guided by the nurse, approached my bedside. He was so unassuming that I failed to acknowledge him until the nurse introduced us.

"Lieutenant Rooks, Captain Vereshchagin."

I brushed the feathers off with one hand. "Hello, Captain."

He had a piece of paper in one hand, a leather suitcase hung from the other. He was a trim, youngish sort. A man who wore a belt to keep his pants up, not his belly in.

He scanned the document. In a bubbly Russian accent: "If I were a doctor Lieutenant, I'd say you've got three days at most."

I started: "Excuse me, Captain?"

He answered with a preplanned cheeriness, pulling up a stool for a chat. "Of course, I'm not a doctor, so you've got nothing to worry about." He laughed. I didn't.

He was an odd, blubbery, smiling, young man: The type of officer who views war as a large, mostly pleasant, upper class game. He bantered about, asking how I was, what it was like in the field, all the while making a plethora of sporting analogies. I wondered if he'd ever been shot at.

Finally, when my morale seemed appropriately boosted, he got to the point:

"And there's more good news. The advance, as you know, has been stopped at the river Daugava. The Germans can't cross it."

"So I hear, Captain."

He pushed back his cap, revealing a freckled forehead and sandy brown hair. His voice went down to a whisper. "The Latvians, it seems will fight hard for this country. Truthfully, harder than our boys."

He said 'our boys' as if I were a Russian like him, yet there was a new gravity in his voice: "People will always resist fiercer in what they perceive as their homeland. High casualties, but they've stopped the kaiser fiends on the riverbanks. We should have seen this sooner."

Was he crediting the Letts for this defense? An astonishing admission from a Russian. I could only nod.

"We're organizing Latvian infantry battalions, *strēlnieki* in their language. Still part of the Russian army, but with their own officers." He picked a feather off my bare arm. "We want to attach you to one as a liaison."

I thought about what that really meant. Latvian battalions alone in the field. "So, I'm a spy?"

The metamorphosis was complete, he did not laugh. "You're a liaison. Lieutenant Rooks, you speak Russian, you speak Latvian. I am aware that you are fluent in German, which could have many benefits with prisoners of wars, or intercepting any sort of overtures from the enemy. We'll put you in with troops from Latgale and Vitbesk, they'll need help with the language."

"Respectfully Captain, you know I'm ethnically Baltic-German, the Letts despise us."

This time he smiled. "Well they hate us too, Lieutenant, but we can't leave them on their own. They might get the wrong idea."

I pawed for a way to decline. Alone with four Russians and they'd turned on me. What would happen adrift with hundreds of Latvians? Images of the mob outside our burning house. My wounded insides throbbed.

He snapped open his case and deposited an envelope on my blanketed lap.

"Letters from home. I'm sorry they've been opened Rooks, but they came across German lines."

His affability made me daring: "Afraid my loyalties might lie in Prussia, Captain?" Could I risk refusing this duty?

Again, he laughed. "No worries, Rooks. We have your oath to the tsar. And, we have people who will vouch for you."

I looked at the envelope. Slit open at the top, it had only 'Wiktor Rooks' written on it. No rank, no battalion. I surmised it must have been shipped inside a larger packet. Canned goods, blankets, boots, long taken by other hands.

"Two weeks Rooks," and the captain marched off to inform the nurse when I'd be healthy.

I opened the envelope. Inside was a letter in my mother's handwriting on white stationary. Unfolding it, a little pink sheet fluttered out. Putting aside Mother's letter, I read the tiny note:

"Dearest Wiktor:

I am sorry this is so short, I only learned your mother was preparing a parcel a moment ago. I will send you a proper letter soon. I miss you so much. Everyday I say my prayers for your safe return. I wear your locket always. There are so many troops about, that it is difficult to go outside without crying. Those uniforms make me think of you and how much I miss you.

The men here are such cads, they don't bow, they don't ask permission to speak to a lady. The things they say are beneath repeating. Not one is a gentleman like you. It reminds me why I love you so much.

I will write you a longer letter tomorrow Wiktor. Just know that I'm always thinking about you dearest.

Your amore,

Gitta"

My thoughts drifted briefly to the girl waiting for me at home. I tried to let them tarry, lingering on her fine features and loving smile, but my mother's letter begged to be read before the captain interrupted.

"Dear Wiktor:

I pray this letter reaches your hands, and finds you safe and far away from danger. We have not heard from you for the longest time. There have been many unfortunate changes in our lives. The Kaiser's Reich troops have entered our lands and have requisitioned the baron's estate. We are living with two dozen men on our lower levels. To make life more difficult, most of the servants have run off, though dear Erene joined us just before they arrived. It is a terrible amount of work; Anne, Genae, and all of us have had to supply them with food, night and day. They've eaten most of the stores, and I don't think there is a fry left in the fish ponds."

My mother was feeding the enemy, the people trying to kill me. I hurriedly continued:

"There is mud everywhere and the house reeks of cheap tobacco. Erich is at a loss (and terribly jealous about how some of them speak to Anne). Even though they are German, they are utterly common. They behave more like Letts! We can only hope for a quick end, so they can return to their homes. The baron and Erich are of the mindset that it would best if they actually took Rīga, that way the trade routes would be open again. Your father seems to just want them out, but what can he say? Such things are up to the baron and he seems to think we should help the cause. He even suggested that Erich enlist, and that sparked the most terrible row last night. Anne was so upset she could not even nurse poor Carsten. In the end, Erich is staying home with his wife and sons, as he should. I wish you were here too.

The only good news I can report is we finally heard from Otomars. His letter arrived two months ago. It seems he is still at the Ministry of Trade and Industry in St. Petersburg. He's been promoted to some sort of administrator role. It sounds like little more than a translator, but you know I never get all the details.

You are always on our minds. I say my prayers daily for your safe return when we can be a family again. Brigitta has asked to include a message which I've enclosed. She is a lovely girl and has been very helpful through all this. You should treat her better, Wiktor.

I hope this package gets to you before the roads to Rīga close. I wish I could send more. Our hearts and prayers are with you.

Your loving Mother and Family."

Supply them with food, night and day!
Best if they actually took Rīga!
We should help the cause!

Was she mad? Whether she knew it or not, her letter was treasonous. What was she thinking?

I tried to stay calm and focus my addled mind. The letter had been read by other eyes. Presumably the captain's at minimum. There must be others. Why was I being given an assignment? Why was I not in a room being interrogated? Harshly. With a letter like this, with a family like this, how could they not doubt my loyalty?

Vereshchagin was off doing his morale boosting routine to another bedridden officer. I interrupted.

"I'm sorry Captain, who was it you said had vouched for me?"

"If I were a doctor…. excuse me." He looked over. "What did you say Lieutenant?"

"Who was it, sir? Who vouched for me?"

He frowned: "Your brother, among others."

"Otomars?"

"Do you have another brother?" He found a seat at the other officer's bedside.

I sat up fully. "He's a civilian. Do you know him, Captain?"

"Not personally." He looked bemused. "People respect him, Lieutenant."

"He's just a clerk." How was this possible?

Vereshchagin sighed, stood up, then walked over and put a hand on my bare shoulder.

"If Otomars Rooks says you can be trusted, rest assured Lieutenant, you can be trusted."

Chapter Seven

"So why are you here Lieutenant Rooks?"

The major was a tall man, trim of build with a fleshy, full face, gigantic hands, and what I assumed were enormous feet inside the leviathan boots propped atop his desk. Red mud caked his soles and heels, a clue that he had returned to his office directly from the field.

"I was assigned here by the Twelfth Army Command, sir."

"Wrong answer."

I was unsurprised by his belligerence, he was of course a Latvian, but I still had not solved the puzzle of how to deal with him. Intellectually, I'd known that I'd be taking orders from Alfrēds Tentelis as soon as I was given the assignment, but now faced with his condescending hostility, I was finding the reality less than pleasant.

"What would be the correct response, Major?"

He slammed shut a drawer on his desk, withdrew his feet, and stood at full height with hands on hips.

"To throw the Germans out of Latvia, Lieutenant." He looked down at me, huge head eclipsing the paltry light from the window behind his desk. "How can you not know that?"

"That is apparent sir. I thought you meant my personal reason for …"

He shouted: "That is the only reason for being here!" He sat down again; the chair springs tortured by his velocity. "If I am going to have to feed you, if you are going to take space in our bunks, Lieutenant, you need to explain to me how you can contribute to driving them back into their lands."

There was a long pause. He must be bluffing. I had already been given my post. Would he defy the Russians and send me packing? He could only be testing me.

With an exasperated sigh, he finally said: "That was a question Lieutenant."

"Sir, I can contribute," I chose my words carefully here, "to the defeat of the German 8th Army, and the removal of all *Reich* Germans from Latvia, and the other territories of the Russian Empire, by performing all my duties as a liaison officer to the best of my abilities."

"What does that mean?"

"Sir?"

"You still haven't told me why I should feed you, instead of an additional infantry soldier?"

I was at loss for an answer. How I wished for an ounce of Otomars's savvy.

"My duties will include communication and co-ordination with other units, especially Russian brigades, aiding with contact with the High Command, translation of…"

He pulled out a ream of paper from his top drawer, tossed it in front of me. With disgust he said: "Write them down, exactly as they were given to you."

I started to unbuckle the large pack at my feet to dig out a pen. He impatiently handed me one from the inkwell on his desk.

I began to write in Russian. After a few Cyrillic letters, the major ripped off the page, crumpled it, and threw it across the room.

"In Latvian," he said.

It was slow going: I often spoke Latvian but seldom wrote it. My pen kept drying, requiring me to reach across the desk to Tentelis's inkwell. I copied all orders regarding communication, co-ordination, translation, and clerical work. I skipped Captain Vereshchagin's words about recording any signs of insurrection, nationalism, socialism or mob 'psychosis.' Those were best omitted.

Finished, I handed the paper to him. He read for a few moments and then tossed it aside. "Useless! Bureaucratic, paper pushing." He threw up his hands. "I already have too much communication with them!"

"Tell me," he scanned some document on his desk for my given name, "…Wiktor… can you fire a rifle?"

"Yes."

"Well good, at last a skill we can use. Can you shoot something other than pigeons, Lieutenant? Can you shoot a German?"

There was weight in his words and a hint of implication. I lightly thumped my palm on his desk. "Major, my family is in Courland. They are in the 8th Army's hands. I would like nothing more than to free them."

He leaned forward, his tone slightly softer: "I repeat: Can you shoot a German, Lieutenant? That's not an issue for you?"

LENIN'S HAREM

"I can shoot a German, Major. And I will not hesitate to order men to shoot them as well."

He only nodded. "Dismissed, Lieutenant."

The officers were billeted in a series of small wooden bunkhouses. Mine was on the end, the last stop before the road ascended a steep embankment covered with fir trees. Despite the dwindling autumn light, I could see the door, open to catch the breeze, a shiny tin '5' pinned to its center. Relaxed, light, conversational Latvian voices caught my ear.

Might as well get it over with…

I entered. The room was compact, smaller than I expected. An unadorned wooden interior, a single window, and against opposite walls sat a pair of bunks. In the middle, a little table with three officers about eating a thin, garlicky soup.

"Hello. Is there an open bed?"

One of them, a slight, wiry officer, with deep-set eyes, and a black pencil-thin moustache clinging to a pencil-thin lip, pointed to the far wall: "The top bunk's yours."

I threw my pack on the mattress and waited for them to rise in greeting. They did not, so I pulled up an empty chair and sat down.

"Mind if I join you?"

Nobody said anything. Was my accent that strong? Or had somebody prepared them?

"Rooks is the name. Lieutenant Wiktor Rooks." I extended a hand to the little officer. He didn't return it, only a slight nod as he spooned his soup.

Another officer asked: "Where are you from Lieutenant Rooks?"

I looked at him and fought not to show my horror. The speaker's face was erased; nearly featureless. No hair in the front, only light brown clumps sparsely along the back and side of the head. He had no lips and barely a nose: two uneven holes puncturing a smooth mound of flesh. There was a thick, leathery, red sheen to most his countenance, relieved only by promontories of pink skin coming down from the scalp or up from his neck. In all my months in the hospital, I had never seen such a bad burn victim. Not one that lived anyway. It was as if all his individual characteristics had been sanded away, leaving only pale blue eyes behind a tough, scarred, generic man.

I bought a little time to recompose myself. "I'm sorry. I didn't hear you. What was the question, Officer....Officer?"

"Lieutenant Gāters." I said, "Where are you from?" His words were raspy, his lipless sounds truncated, blending. A voice that would take some getting used to.

"Courland. The countryside, south of Mitau." My mind was not on my answer. Mitau was the German name.

The little moustached officer's voice was full of sarcasm: "Really? I'm from *Jelgava*." The same place. One city, two names, it all depended on your parent's tongue.

Gāters continued: "See, you and Seskis are like brothers. What do you do, Rooks? Trade? Industry?" He put his hands on the table. One scarred and puffed. The other no different than mine.

"I'm a liaison officer. Though I..."

"No, no, no. Your family what do they do?"

I stared at his face. Was it possible for him to even display an expression? Was there an agenda? Why was he asking these questions so quickly?

"We own some land. Just farmers really."

His blue eyes flared. He could have expressions after all: So, Rooks is that type of German. The *worst* type of German. His words were acidic: "Ever plow a field?"

My sympathy for his affliction was quickly waning: "Not personally. My father takes care of the crops."

"Has he ever plowed a field?" The eyes compensating for any expressiveness lost in the face.

"I don't know. Look, I just arrived..." I looked around for someone else to speak with. Moustached Seskis only grinned, clearly enjoying the spectacle. The third at the table, a bespectacled blond with thin, center-parted hair, kept his nose down in a book. I turned back to Gāters: "Have you?"

"Tell me Rooks, how did you get this land?"

"It's not mine. It'll go to my brother."

Seskis: "A little rich boy with nothing else to do joins the army..."

I ignored him. "It's been in the family for years, generations."

Gāters pressed: "Yes, but how did you get it? In the first place?"

What did he want from me? "That was hundreds of years ago."

"What exactly was hundreds of years ago?"

He wouldn't let this go, but I could not let them think I feared conflict: "It was a gift from Rīga's Archbishop."

LENIN'S HAREM

The blond got up, and plopped himself over in the bunk beneath my own, his eyes never leaving his book.

"Ah-ha!" Gāters put a good finger in the air, looked at Seskis, then back at me: "Why?"

I gave him what he was after, got it over with: "For spreading the word of Catholicism."

"So you force your religion on us pagans and take our land."

"I've never taken anyone's land nor told anyone which god to worship." I stood up to leave. Enough of this.

Seskis again: "What would you get if you made me Jewish?"

The bookworm on his bed added uncaringly: "Jews are The Chosen, not converted."

Seskis leaned back in his chair: "Well, maybe he does the choosing?"

Standing over Gāters, I could see a periodical he'd been reading spread out on the table. Cīņa: Rīga's illegal socialist newspaper. So that was Gāters's agenda.

"Quiet, Miķelis. We're having a real conversation here." Gāters motioned me over: "Okay, Rooks, sit down. So your family forces people at sword point to obey the pope and gets an aristocratic living for generations. Do you feel that's right?"

I didn't sit. "I'm not Catholic. My family's Lutheran. We're talking about ancient times. Are you Catholic?"

"No."

An atheist no doubt. Of course, if I had been burnt so, it might be hard to have faith. I continued: "How about you, Seskis? Catholic?"

"Maybe. Maybe not, though I can cut you a good deal for Judaism, Father."

Gāters: "Do you feel that's ethically right?"

"What's right?"

"Your family living off stolen land for hundreds of years?"

Stolen? This communist agitator turned my stomach. Now that I knew whom I was dealing with, I felt no need to pull the punches:

"Lieutenant Gāters, the only reason your own family exists today, is they pushed aside the previous tribe: The Livs, or the Letts or whatever. And perhaps some of my ancestors, long ago, moved a few of the tribes they found as well. It happens, it's natural. I'm not going to apologies for my family's prosperity!"

Somehow his scarred face hinted at satisfaction. He had goaded me into a class debate: "If that's true, why not just let the kaiser push us all aside, Rooks? If it's so natural?"

Seskis taunted: "Maybe, he'd rather share space with the Germans, than us Latvians. Is that true *Herr* Rooks?"

"No. No it is not." Though after this conversation who could say...

I went over, moved my bag off my bunk, and climbed in. I stared at the ceiling. They didn't realize the power I had. With one letter I could label them all communists and be done with them.

I could hear them chuckling: derisive, victorious laughs. One letter, that's all it would take.

Lieutenant Gāters would head that list. Seskis, too, though I couldn't recall if he had said anything blatantly communistic. Was he just belligerent? I'd need more time for observation. The blond had said little. What was his comment? I couldn't remember.

I started assembling the words of my report in my mind: "To the attention of Captain Vereshchagin…"

Leaves of all sizes and colors blew across the late autumn field: apple red, oaken brown, cheddar yellow, caramel and amber with twisting veins of purple, even stunning, ghostly off-white. They moved back and forth over the fading grass in little formations of their own. Stopping and mixing, before being taken on their way again; Like the soldiers marching on this field.

Yet, I thought, the leaves were better organized.

The troops did not look good. Latvians culled from all the Russian battalions, they had not worked together long. Throw in a very substantial number of new recruits, obviously attracted to the idea of a *Latvian* army, and we had what could only be called a mess.

Major Tentelis and his officers had quite the challenge ahead to turn these men into a battalion. Not my responsibility. I had quickly learned that a liaison officer has very little to do with troop development. I wasn't in command of anyone, and rarely, if ever, needed. So far, I spent my days simply walking behind Major Tentelis, observing what he observed.

The present drill required the men to march in waves toward targets at a short distance until their officer commanded them to stop. At that time the company would fall to the ground and await his orders to fire. Then they'd rise again, sprint ahead to burlap bags hanging on poles, and skewer them with bayonets. At command, they'd reform, turn around and begin an assault on the line of bags on the other side of the field. Again and again. All day long.

For occasional variety, they'd be given sudden turns, expected to spin in unison as if on a parade ground, or fire their rifles at an arbitrary set angle determined by their officer.

The company presently under scrutiny was commanded by our dear friend Lieutenant Seskis. His men were having more trouble than most. Whole groups of troops confused: turning opposite of their neighbors or firing at 45° when he called for 20°.

I enjoyed his failures, but was curious as to the cause. At one point I dared to ask the major about the miscommunication.

"Are these new commands sir?" They seemed basic enough.

He turned to me gruffly, looking as if my remark had been sarcastic.

"Did I give you permission to speak, Lieutenant Rooks?"

"No sir."

"Then don't speak." But I could tell his pride would not let an implied criticism remain unanswered. Without turning around he added: "There are many raw recruits and the experienced ones are not used to hearing orders in Latvian."

"Permission to speak, sir?"

He observed one charge until it was finished, barked out a critique to Seskis, and then turned toward me. "Permission granted, Rooks."

"Since time is of the essence, why not keep the orders in Russian, sir?"

He turned his back and said nothing more to me for a very long time.

As the day waned to dusk, the major and I made our way to the blond bookworm's field. He too marched his men until they skewered stuffed dummies, but after a couple of passes I noticed he never gave the orders to stop, drop and fire. They only sprinted from one end of the field to the other. I found this unusual. So apparently did the major.

"Lieutenant Juškevičs, get over here!" He screamed so loudly, I instinctively took a step back. There was something evil inside me that enjoyed the idea of my obnoxious bunkmates being given verbal thrashings.

"Juškevičs, what the hell are you doing? Your men haven't fired a round."

"Yes, sir. Major, we were practicing closing with the enemy, sir."

"Everyone is practicing closing with the enemy Lieutenant. Why aren't you giving the command to fire?"

I noticed Juškevičs didn't wear his glasses in the field. It made him appear even younger than me. He couldn't be a day over nineteen.

"We were practicing shock tactics, sir. The principal being that the quicker you reach an entrenched enemy, the faster you remove his advantage and even your odds."

"What?"

"If we lay down in the field of fire, many men may not get up. Recent tactical trysts…"

The major looked as if he'd explode. "Enough of this Lieutenant! I've told you before. If you don't have the courage to tell your men to fire, I will find someone who will."

He looked at Juškevičs with absolute disgust.

"Lieutenant Rooks, get out there and have these men fire at something."

"Me, sir?" I was a liaison officer, not an infantry commander!

The great man grabbed my arm in his bear paw, pulled me around, and shoved me forward. "You Rooks! And have them fire at something, or I'll line you and Juškevičs up and have them shoot at the two of you."

I walked slowly past the exhausted troops, still panting from their sprints across the grass. I could see the confused look in their eyes. Who was this? What had their Lieutenant done? They could all hear the major's tirade at Juškevičs. Wait until they found out I was German.

I'd be lucky if they didn't shoot me.

I aligned myself behind their first row. My heart was pounding, mind racing to remember my own training, desperate to recall what I'd casually observed this whole day. I had no sword, no rifle. Nothing to indicate a command was being given other than my voice. I took in a deep breath, until my lungs couldn't contain another atom and shouted "Forward!"

With all my might.

As loud as possible.

In Russian.

About two out of three stepped forward. Others slowly, independently, turned toward me their frowns deep and expressions confused. Seeing that their fellows had stopped, those marching came to a halt after a few steps, standing alone or walking back at leisurely, disorganized pace. The precise parade ground rows had merged into an amorphous clump of strolling, stationary, and befuddled soldiers with my one swift command. Everyone looked at me waiting for clarification. A buzz of questioning, Latvian voices rose off the field. Undeterred or unobservant, three or four solitary soldiers marched off into the sunset.

I sighed and waited for the major's comment. At least I hadn't said it in German.

"Rooks, get your ass over here!"

I lay on my high bunk, uninvited while my fellow officers played card games. I thought about today's humiliation. Embarrassed by Latvians in front of Latvians. Routinely denigrated by Latvians. And, for the most part, no one to blame but myself.

It could not have gone worse.

There was a rap on the post beam. Juškevičs appeared, standing on the floor, his bespectacled head even with mine.

"Lieutenant Rook?"

"It's Rooks…Yes?" What now? Had he come to thank me for destroying my chance to steal his command?

"Sorry. Rooks. I understand that you can read German?"

What trap was this? "Yes."

"A friend of mine, in the Rīga battalion, he sent me this book." He placed a thin, slightly faded pamphlet on the edge of my bunk. "Except, I can't read it. It's in German."

I rolled over, picking up the book with my right hand, and holding it out toward the light.

It was faded and worn on the cover, but the pages were crisp and clean, like it had been wedged on a crowded shelf for quite a while. The German on the front was clear enough: *The Field Service Regulations of 1908.*

"What is it?" I said.

"It's a tactical manual, Lieutenant. It's seven years old, but it's what the Germans had been studying."

"So?"

"Well, I was hoping you might help me step inside the mind of our enemy."

Chapter Eight

The tiny beads of perspiration reflected the moonlight off of Sergeant Līcis's skin, each a sparkling star in the constellation stretching across his darkened face. He remained crouching beneath the overhanging rock, a short distance from Juškevičs and me. The electric torch beam held strong from the nearby field; a shivering yellow spot, revealing black-green moss, tiny flittering insects, and grey veins on the slate stone above the sergeant's head.

The moment the light's oval disappeared he jumped up, his own torch flashing out into the valley. But it was too late, another beam, from another angle, shot down upon the rock close to where the last had vanished. With a brutal grunt, the sergeant recoiled again, taking cover from the light, waiting for it too to desist.

And so it continued, there was no escape: One beam shining down for a few moments, only to be replaced in an instant with another, forcing the sergeant back into his position. All the while, they were getting closer, and there was nothing our man could do to protect us.

Good.

Then he came. Leaping over the embankment, he landed nearly atop the crouching Līcis, shoving him back against the stone with one hand, flipping on his torch with the other. In the gleam, the sergeant's craggy face grimaced.

"That's checkmate," said Juškevičs.

The sergeant unearthed a profanity as Juškevičs and I stood up from our observation points in the cold trench. Juškevičs made several rapid handclaps, a fluttering sound like startled city pigeons: "Excellent, excellent. Perfect work Ojārs."

Sergeant Līcis came up, a slightly embarrassed look to his countenance, but also a hint of pride, like a father first beaten by his son at a foot race. These were his men, after all.

"I could never get a clear shot, Lieutenant. They had a beam on me the whole time."

Juškevičs could barely contain himself. He swayed in an antsy motion, his eyes twitching back and forth from the men in front of him to images conjuring in his mind.

He gave me a swift nudge to get my attention. "That's it Rooks. This is exactly what the boys in the 6th and the 5th have been saying. Well done. Well done, everyone."

To my surprise Juškevičs embraced me, hugged Līcis and then raced off into the night to congratulate his remaining man in the field.

Slowly, Sergeant Līcis and I walked back toward the barracks, a large, waxing moon transforming the depths of night to silver-tinged dusk. I could see swaying tree shadows ahead with empty, spindly branches, like long greedy hands clawing at the shrubs and digging among the flat stones sheltered in the open grass.

Yet, even with this visibility, Līcis had been unable to stop the assault on his position.

I watched Juškevičs approach the last soldier armed only with a heavy electric torch, and characteristically he hugged him too, strolling toward the barracks with a hand over his shoulder, already giving encouragement for tomorrow's drills. When required, he could be a far different man, little resembling the bookish, quiet resident of my lower bunk.

"He sure does seem happy, Lieutenant," said Līcis, a good-natured soldier that Juškevičs referred to as the 'best-sort' of NCO.

"He does indeed, Sergeant." Though honestly, I failed to quite see the significance of the achievement: Advancing two men in the dark against one was hardly safely moving an entire company under fire or breeching an entrenched enemy. Not even close.

But whatever the reason, it had made Juškevičs absolutely giddy.

Juškevičs and I entered the dark, silent Officer Quarters Number '5' shutting the door as quietly as possible behind so to not to wake our slumbering roommates.

"Please, Wiktor," his voice was barely hushed, "two minutes. I'll keep my hand over the shade..."

His enthusiasm was infectious. Using the moonlight seeping in through the lone window, I sorted through Juškevičs's stack of manuals finding the dog-eared *Field Service Regulations* near the bottom. Juškevičs lit a small lamp, cupping the glass with his hand, the shadows retreating to the corners of the room. "There's just one footnote I want you to read."

I swiftly thumbed through it, finding an illustration. "This one?"

"No."

Seskis, on top his bunk across the room, turned a sleepy, night-swollen face toward us, then collapsed into the pillow again: "Uhhh…What are you doing?"

"Me and Rooks are just checking some facts Miķelis, we won't be a moment."

"What time is it?"

"Nearly three o'clock."

Muttering profanities, Seskis turned his face to the wall. Gāters, his voice muffled by the rags wrapped about his head: "What cathouse have you two been at?"

"No cathouse, just trying some new tactics."

He moved the bandages aside, drops of moisture and salve slipping down his flattened face as he sat up. "In complete darkness?"

"It may be a little too unconventional for the major."

Gāters blue eyes glimmered, nearly green in this light: "What? What is it?"

Seskis screamed from his bunk: "Will you all go to bed? We have field exercises in two hours."

Gāters knocked on the bottom of Seskis's bunk: "Keep a lid on it, Miķelis."

He crumpled his rags, soaking up the mixture on his forehead. "What have you learned?"

Juškevičs was surprisingly cocky: "How to win, Guntis. Nothing more."

The spring rains fell hard in 1916. The mud made traction difficult, the German positions that much harder to assault. Gāters gave the order, and his men charged across the swampy field. The German rifles fired at will, smoke rising from each muzzle, linking with their neighbors to form a giant, grey caterpillar undulating above their entrenched lines. Men dove, men died, falling aside as Gāters, a vision of Satan in Hell with his tortured, reddened face, barked commands behind the drifting smoke, rising dust and writhing bodies, egging them on, driving them forward. At last, he ordered them to drop. Those still in line did so, and we could hear his struggling voice yell the command to fire.

A few Germans fell stricken by Latvian bullets, but most sat safe beneath the earthen walls. By the time our troops were up and charging again, the Germans had reloaded, sending more Latvians spinning to earth. It was a massacre. Gāters had no choice but to call them back.

This German infantry, entrenched on the embankment had kept Seskis's third company pinned down most of the day as well. A flanking maneuver along the ridge had only resulted in sixteen dead and a tongue lashing by Major Tentelis. I'd watched his charging soldiers, Latvians yes, but still living, breathing men, falling, slipping into that ravine as the German guns found them, their bodies clogging the rapids flowing through the valley bottom.

After these disastrous assaults, Gāters's men at long last took the misty hill across the field from the German trenches. It seemed that victory was at hand. The enemy was now cut off from their fellows, the gap growing ever distant as German 8th withdrew to defend their fortified lines against the massive 12th army assault kilometers away.

The Germans behind the embankment were left all alone, surrounded by our troops, with no hope of rejoining their army. Major Tentelis expected surrender. It did not come. Instead, within the hour, two more men were wounded having wandered within the surprising range of their rifles.

The major looked through his field glasses: "Seskis, reform, prepare for a second assault."

"Major?"

"Not now, Juškevičs."

"We can take the German position."

He pulled down the glasses. "I'm not going to let them chew up another company. One is enough."

"I don't need my whole company, Major. Just give me twelve men."

Juškevičs's soldiers moved in three groups of four; one squad laying down a continual suppressing fire: one riflemen firing, followed by the second, third and finally the last; while the other two groups huddled behind rocks, hills and ditches. When the Germans withdrew to safety behind their dirt walls, the other two groups crawled ahead, advancing a body length or two, and then crouching behind some new stone or shrub to hide. Then, the second began firing, providing 'cover' as the first and third picked their way toward the Germans. And so they advanced in rotation, one group firing, as two others crept ever closer.

At last, Sergeant Līcis was mere meters below the enemy fortifications. If the Germans could have raised a gun, they might have murdered him with a single shot. But the bullets from the other groups kept them locked inside. He unscrewed the top of the grenade, pulled it back and prepared to throw it over the embankment.

In the smog, a dirty, smoke-holed, once white, undershirt rose from the German trench.

They had surrendered.

Two days later I was summoned to the major's office. Upon being given permission to enter, I opened the door and found Tentelis sitting at his desk across from Juškevičs.

"Take a seat, Rooks" said the major succinctly, skipping preamble. "Well? What did they say?"

I sat down in a chair next to Juškevičs. He had an excited, expectant look, as if his next breath hung on my report. Frankly, I didn't want to disappoint him: "Well, Major, Lieutenant, the prisoners were unaware they had been cut off from the 8th army. I feel…"

"Really?" said Juškevičs, with more than a hint of glee. These last two days had been his after all. "They didn't know?"

"They were concerned. They knew a breech existed in the lines, but they were unaware of the retreat."

The major was more earthly: "Then why did they surrender Rooks? We hadn't killed a man."

"I think the best way to characterize it would be frustration, Major. Simple frustration. They repeated, again and again, they could never get a clear shot. We were advancing, they knew, but they never had a moment of unimpeded fire, or an upright target to kill. A couple of men simply quit, they had dissension down there in that mud hole, and it…"

"It… did what Lieutenant?"

"I would say it broke their will, sir."

My palm ached, the muscles on the back of my hand unable to keep a fist. I contemptuously threw the pen in the inkwell. My fingers were covered in ink, the last pink wrinkle falling before the conquering blue-black liquid.

I stood up, stretched my back, wiped clean my fingers, and tried to find some air in the stuffy silent barracks. Only eight more. Eight more translations of the wretched thing, and then I'd be finished. The major had better remember this.

Sergeant Līcis came to the door of the officers' quarters.

"Permission to enter Lieutenant Rooks?"

"Yeah, yeah." I waved him in and sat down for another pass at the task at hand. "I said you didn't have to ask, Herberts."

"Well, sir, Lieutenant Seskis gave me quite the going over for it last time." He picked up a stack of my translations. "Are these getting heavier, sir?"

"No, you're just getting older. " Another spasm in my hand. "Uggh…of course, not as old as me."

There was mutual humor in my remark, the sergeant was at least three or four years my senior. A good man for a Lett, from the eastern city of Dünaburg, he had too much to do to complain about the sins of the past.

"Trust me sir, those lines on your face ain't nothing but ink." He stacked one pile on top of the other.

"Don't mix up those pages. I alternated the sections."

"Not a problem, sir." He leaned back against the wall, papers resting against his chest. "You know, you're really helping him, Lieutenant."

"Helping who?"

"Lieutenant Juškevičs. This might not have happened if it weren't for you."

"He's read a lot of books Herberts; I'm just translating one. Not a lot of thinking involved on my part."

He carried the stack to the door. "All I'm saying is the major and those types are mighty impressed by him. Hope he's giving you a hand in return?"

"He's going to teach me to plow a field." I gave a quick, mirthful wink.

A stern, pensive reflection. "Goodbye, sir," and he silently exited through the open door.

Too far. Once again.

I cracked my fingers, and went back to writing.

LENIN'S HAREM

I lay alone beneath the massive yew tree, fully in bloom in the early days of summer, writing my letter to Captain Vereshchagin. It included a prompt analysis of all the battalion developments, a compliment directed at the 'initiative' of Lieutenant Juškevičs, and a recommendation for improvement of the courier system to other regiments.

As I wrote, distant names were being called out at random. A clerk distributed letters to the bunched officers waiting their turn near the barracks. Of course, there would be none for me. A year had passed with my family across German lines. What was happening? Were they still under the baron's protective wing? Had the Germans taken everything? I thought of my sister, and how I missed her. And our parents. And, yes, Gitta too. I tried to ignore the rumors of 8th army atrocities. They wouldn't touch the baron's class.

Would they?

I had nearly finished my report: "*Lastly, as to the matter of improper or counterproductive activities…*"

I scanned the mail group, finding Gāters's baldpate awaiting a letter. Or perhaps a periodical. Or anything. He had toned down the rhetoric since so many of his men were slaughtered. Still, there was no doubting his beliefs.

"Juškevičs!" the postal clerk yelled out. "Juškevičs?"

The lieutenant jumped out of the crowd, a large wrapped package in his hands. He simply radiated energy, bounding away from the others, halting only to recover his glasses thrown from his face in jubilation, before literally falling next to me under the tree.

"They're here Rooks. This is it!"

I didn't need to ask. I knew.

He ripped open the paper, the tomes fell out into his hands: *The Defensive Battle* and *Manual of Infantry Training for War* both in German, and a French work: *L'Etude sur l'attaque*.

"Which one's this, Wiktor?"

I looked at the spine. "*Manual of Infantry Training for War.*"

"And this?"

"Something in French, you know I can't read…"

"Then this must be *The Defensive Battle*."

I could see a lot of translation in my future. "Can't you get that in Latvian?"

"Are you joking?"

"Russian?"

"Maybe in St. Petersburg. Come On, Wiktor…Look, Infantry Training is thin. We can do that first."

"No, Juškevičs, not this time," but I knew he'd convince me.

Gāters walked up, tears pooling in his blue eyes, his lipless mouth somehow curled downward in a sob.

Juškevičs: "Guntis what happened?"

"My family…They've found them." He dropped to his knees near our tree; sobbing, it seemed, with joy.

Juškevičs crawled over, put an arm around Gāters shoulder "That's wonderful, Guntis." Juškevičs motioned for me to come over as well, but I decided to remain against the tree.

Gāters handed him the note. "They're in a work camp north of Moscow. It'd been so long, I thought…I dared not hope…"

I watched this scene unfold for a moment, and then returned to my writing:

as to the matter of improper or counter-productive activities…

I breathed in the sweet, aromatic summer air, and passed one more glimpse at Gāters's patchy head crying in Juškevičs's arms.

…there is nothing unusual to report.

Chapter Nine

Letts and Livs surrounded me, pressing against our carriage, their greedy hands reaching in, trying to grasp my uniform, to pull me into their smothering masses. The combined heat of their exhaled calls turned a cool morning into hottest noon. The crowd police could not keep them back, individuals breaking past, their swelling screams unearthing images, sounds, emotions buried since childhood.

Ahead, behind, trailing us, throngs of these peasants on either side of the road, fighting violently to get closer. So many faces, so many Latvians. The most I'd seen assembled, since, since…

Since they'd burned down my home.

Destroyed our family. Ended my childhood.

It was an unnerving experience. The troops marching down Rīga's cobblestone Kungu Iela, thousands lining the streets, a murmur of obligatory applause as the Russian Battalions passed at the head of the parade, only to be replaced by living thunder at the approach of the Latvian Battalions. I half-feared they'd break into our formations, overrunning the men long before reaching the river. Carried away by their own people, never even facing the enemy.

I searched the crowd. All were Latvians; so tied to nature, their physical appearance embodied the seasons themselves: hair woven in autumn's brown, red, and yellow; spring blossoming in eyes of blue, hazel, and green; shawls of winter white blanketing across every woman's shoulders, and summer's sun radiating in blinding smiles and warming cheers as the army passed.

Our kind, our class, was eclipsed today. I could not deny it. Even those not trapped in Courland would have stayed fearfully home. The barons remembered 1905 and had vehemently opposed this army's creation. Why celebrate another enemy entering the arena? Even the Russians shied away from this display, finding it too 'local' for their grand cosmopolitan tastes.

No there were only Latvians today.

I could feel it, radiating from every little boy, each old man, behind the rainbow of bouquets held by young women: A pride; a *national* pride; an explosion of Latvian identity. Everywhere there were flags, icons, symbols founded in folklore and history, hanging from every open window, posted on each free wall, pinned on the fabric of traditional dress. "We are not peasants!" they proclaimed. For them this was a first step, for the Russians a desperate last. What would happen when the Germans were defeated? Could things ever return to normal?

Even the normally fashionable Rīga dwellers were adorned in traditional garb this morning: beneath the women's shawls, long red, white and green striped dresses flowed from decorated bodices, their hair hidden under pointed white hats, or wreathed in a pinwheel of flowers; the men more modestly adorned in trim black and white tunics, vests and trousers; a wide hat of black shading grandfather's sun-spotted skin, while young men and boys welcomed the morning sun.

The car braked suddenly, pulling my attention forward. "Free Latvia!" yelled a young man, darting across the road, slipping between the marching troops and our carriage.

I followed his erratic run: jumping, waving to the mob, before finally disappearing into the opposite side. Free Latvia? From whom, my friend? The Reich-Germans? The Baltic-Germans? The tsar? Or all of them?

I tried not to dwell on his proclamation: A simple "Good Luck" sentiment certainly. It was the sort of thing young men do, to stand out, to impress girls, to pry another glass from their peers in the beer hall. But such words taken seriously, enthusiastically spoken inside this euphoria, could be dangerous. In 1905, they had.

Another rebellion was a real possibility, Captain Vereshchagin would agree, always reminded. And with the kaiser's forces lurking just across the river, a three-way war could finish the tsar and his army.

I could not repress a shudder. And without him, what would these cheering people do to our class or our family?

Or to me? Would these waving hands clench to raging fists? Rain down onto me, a thousand blows pounding my body into a bloody smear on the cobblestones? A stain to be washed away in the spring tempests? I would not forget, even though I walked among them, I was not of their ilk. This was their army. These people did not cheer for me.

A young Latvian woman, her sandy hair parted beneath the colorful band about her forehead, appeared from the side of the parade, a mosaic of flowers in her hands. As the car slowed to maintain proper distance behind the marching men, she was able to run aside, distributing stems to each in the open carriage: First Major Tentelis, his driver, the surgeon and finally me. Into my hands fell a yellowish carnation, the stem moist and pliable, the end crisp and freshly cut. I thanked her, as she began to lose pace, falling behind the automobile.

Suddenly it came to another shuddering stop, waiting for the soldiers to take the corner in proper procession. I could see Gāters ahead, coaxing the men to stay in formation as they pivoted. His hoarse commands were pebbles buried beneath an avalanche of cheers. The more it became obvious that the crowd disrupted his orders, the more their good-natured chorus grew. The men only stood stiffly, smiling, absorbing the adulation.

As we watched them the sprightly woman caught up with the car, pressing one foot on the running board, she elevated herself off the street to our level. To my surprise, she placed her arms around my shoulders, kissing me quickly on the cheek.

"Save us all, my Lāčplēsis" equating me with their greatest folk hero. I started to explain that I wasn't a Lett, when she kissed my lips warmly. While the onlookers howled in approval, this girl clasped my mouth firmly in hers. Then the car accelerated, she stepped off quickly, left behind waving.

I could not help but be touched. She was so…enthusiastic. A devilish thought: Latvian girls just might kiss better than our own. Otomars had always whispered this. A passion born in the fields, boiling since man's Vulcan origins, long ago refined out of the proper ladies in our circles. My brother had always spoken with carnal zest about trysts with the maid or a tenant's daughter, hidden kisses enlivened by their sheer secrecy. How dangerous to be caught with *her*.

I tapped my fingers on the black leather seat ahead of me. It was cool, slightly sticky in the morning air; my imprints dissolving slowly in the shiny interior skin.

No, I was not Otomars. It was improper to take advantage of one's position. House Master or military hero, I knew it unfair to raise her hopes, when a kiss was not a beginning but only an end.

I let out a surprisingly mournful sigh. So that was that. I licked my lips softly to wash her taste away, and fought to relax in the car. Trapped inside the swelling crowds, I shut my eyes, and tried to remember the last time I'd held Gitta.

Chapter Ten

October, 1916

The sound of thunder, an enveloping spray of mist punctured by wood and bone propelled fifty meters into the air, and the boat in front of me simply ceased to exist. The explosion shook our own tiny craft, throwing me down into the narrow wooden center, flung on top of a screaming soldier, another falling across my own back. Heavy red water, fragments of hull, lashed our shoulders, buffeted my helmeted head. In shock, I lay there while the boat rocked, rising so high on waves I feared it might overturn spilling us all into the boiling river; I could only cling face down, listening to the cries of the panicked man beneath me, feeling his quick breaths find rhythm with my own, slowly realizing we were both still alive.

An elbow in the back, the soldier on top righted himself, brought my mind back to our situation. I pulled myself up, our craft now passing downstream of the fizzling spring where the supply ferry had died. Green mists swirled about its bubbling cortex, like vultures hovering over the dead, hungry to settle again. There was no one to rescue, nothing to salvage. The currents carried away splinters of boxes, tattered pieces of cloth, fully uniformed limbs. A torso rolled like a lumber log against the upstream side of our boat. I used an oar to push it away, clinging tendrils of deadly vapor crawling up the blade from the water's surface, as if his spirit sought to drag the living down with him.

Far off another shell landed in the water, sending white foam and mist into the sickly clover autumn air. In this smog, we could not see the German artillery, their mortars seeking our little convoy as it crossed the Daugava stew. Ahead, both upriver and down, invisible cannons belched purple-red flares, a hundred caved dragons unleashing sulfur and smoke on our crusading knights. Their roars quickly followed by the screams of incoming shells. Months ago I'd learned to guess their accuracy, to find the distance by the pitch, reading the anguish in the air splitting around me. Every volley, each lapse between brilliant ignition and falling whistle played a variant of the same tune. Which pitch, which key would serve as life's valedictory?

I sailed toward Saulkalne, where we'd spent the last three months in gallant misery. An hour south-east of Rīga, Saulkalne was a large bridgehead on the opposite side of the Daugava, one of the few places on the South Bank still in Latvian and Russian control. In many ways it felt like an island, the German front lines cutting off the mainland, the river a barrier behind entered or exited only by a water crossing. For seven months Russian and Latvian battalions, two each in rotation, had held these two square kilometers of shelled earth, despite ferocious German assaults. Supplies ferried across the river often failed to arrive, many boats ending in a geyser of foam, shattered hulls and bodies carried downstream, flowing out to the Baltic itself. Men killed kilometers upriver, mourned from Rīga's widowing bridges, but buried at sea.

As a liaison officer, I'd taken far too many trips on these exposed boats, often summoned at the whim of some Russian officer who wanted to hear in person: "What was going on across the Daugava?" After one near miss had spilled the entire crew into the muddy river, I began to keep track. Twenty-two crossings before this trip, the same count as my age. Would I make twenty-three?

I feared these passages more than anything in war: isolated, clinging to a pitching wooden target, unable to move, counting the seconds until we reached the other side. Once across, we were comparatively safe, the stalemate between the kaiser's 8th Army and our battalions, offering a more predictable, knowable risk.

Until today. The Germans had changed everything.

Hours before I had been standing with Gāters on the North Bank, watching an intense German artillery barrage on the Russian troops across the Daugava: Lightning flashed up and down the line, echoing explosions chasing herons from the river's surface, pillars of flame offering glimpses beneath the horizon's smoky clouds. We knew the 8th Army was trying to break the Russians. For over an hour it had continued. Within the sparse pauses we'd heard puzzling sounds drifting across the waters: the anguished cries of men. Not the sharp, common screams of the freshly wounded soldier, but a fog of hovering, agonized moans. Like the calls of a thousand spirits unleashed from Hell.

Twenty minutes later, the yellow-green mist rose above the dusty smog of combat, slowly windblown toward the river. Beneath, a dozen men fled down to the banks, dropping their weapons, discarding packs, helmets and jackets, so they might run faster from the advancing shroud.

At my shoulder, the atheist Gāters whispered: "My god."

I folded my arms to pin my trembling hands, the shudder carrying to my weakening legs. God had little to do with this, Lieutenant. We had heard the stories from France.

The first group reached a small ferry, desperately unmooring it from the black wooden dock. At the top of the embankment, the greenish smog was cresting, like a breaking wave on the ocean shore. Nearly enveloped, a mounted soldier whipped his horse, taking the riverbank's slope at a full gallop.

Heavier than air, the clover mist seemed to accelerate, seeking the river itself. The rider's beast lost its footing, falling toward the muddy bank, a brown dusty trail as it slid to a stop, head hidden by the river reeds. The man abandoned his steed, running along the water edge toward the dock, screaming out to the drifting ferry, the cloud now a hundred meter-high wall toppling over him.

The ferry too far, he dove into the expansive river, desperately swimming. The soldiers on the boat reached out helping hands, even as those at the helm gunned the engine, daring not to tarry.

The gas eclipsed the shuddering horse, the haze spreading across the water, rolling over the swimming man, the first wisps caressing the stern of the fleeing boat.

Farther inland were more explosions. Fresh, dark green clouds were thrown higher into the air, like ominous forested mountains towering behind the thickening hills spreading toward us.

"How much, Guntis? How much are they using?"

There was a horrible cracking of heavy wood, like a mammoth oak felled in the forest. The ferry had run aground full-speed, farther down on our side of the river, sharp brown stones puncturing its eggshell hull. One man was thrown out, landing in the greening waters, carried down stream. None of his comrades moved to aid him. Instead, each lay doll-like loose, coughing, choking, pleading for help.

Gāters and I sprinted for the distant boat, picking our way over sharp rocks, and around muddy inlets. As I cautiously slowed to navigate a flow-slickened stone at the water's edge, a sparrow passed my shoulder swooping low for insects on the river's surface. Suddenly the arc of its flight ended, falling leaden into the flowing grey-brown water, the swish of the bird's tiny body as loud as the bells of St. Peter's tower.

"Run Gāters! Run!" And the two of us fled uphill, trailing a Russian artillery crew just now abandoning their gun.

I closed my ears to the screaming men below. "God forgive us."

As I climbed up Saulkalne's dock ladder, a shell found the river edge upstream, showering my back with clumps of steaming mud, fist-sized drops of water, burning reeds and smoking black leaves. I protectively clutched the package to my chest. No rusty nails, old glass, barbed wire in that explosion, thank God. None of those. And nothing worse.

I shook my head, the mud chunks sliding off my helmet to the wet, aged planks beneath my running feet. At the end of the pier stood Major Tentelis, tall and impatient, as if my errand had only been a quick jaunt down the office hall.

His look was expectant, controlled, but I knew him well enough now, nearly a year in his service. There was a hint of fear in the wavering of his hand as he returned my salute. He prayed for good news, but dared not expect it. My next words might bring orders of his court marshal, the imminent destruction of his men, or both.

"Well Rooks?"

"The entire Second Battalion is coming, sir." I pulled the package from beneath my jacket. "With the masks."

His long face breathed a sigh of relief, tipping his hat back as if to let his anguished mind have some air. When the Germans had launched their chlorine attacks, the Russian Battalions were alone here. The 12th Army brain trust had ordered the Latvian troops to cross the river to reinforce immediately.

Without waiting for gas masks to arrive.

The Latvian company commanders, following the lead of Captain Kļaviņš, had refused the order, holding out for the equipment. To the Russians it was treason. To the Latvians, it was simply survival. Everyone could feel the porcelain 12th Army cracking.

While others haggled, Major Tentelis had crossed the Daugava to assess the scene himself. So he was the last to know.

I smiled. "They caved sir. The generals "discovered" 40,000 masks they had forgotten about. Expect them on a railroad car in the next two hours, our men shortly thereafter."

Relief mixed with regret in his voice. "They think of us as cannon fodder." Tentelis wearily looked at me: "Do we have to fight them as well?"

I dreaded that possibility, literally meant or not. Yet, right now I could hardly blame him. "I doubt that, sir. The masks are coming."

I unwrapped the soaked package, inside were two masks, two pair of goggles. The former resembling a bloated surgeon's mask, the cloth covering stuffed with treated cotton. The latter, the thick leather bound spectacles chemists and pilots sported. I handed one of each to the major. He stuffed them in his greatcoat pocket.

As we turned away from the docks, I let my eyes wander to take in our surroundings. The world on this side of the river, wore a hazy, shifting green sheen. Vapors still carried on the wind, and toxic mists lingered on the road, scampering away from the breezy motion of our steps. Overhead, the sky's palette was over-mixed; the jaundiced clouds turning the afternoon sun a thick sludgy grey.

I trudged inland, spying nearby the horse abandoned by the fleeing soldier. Its body lay on the riverbank, head fallen into the brown waters, a black little rapid flowing over its submerged snout. About the body lay the rigid forms of several black ravens. Having descended too early for feasting, they had soon joined the meal.

As I walked behind Tentelis, I noticed the gas pooled thicker in still places; a dark clover lurking in the hollow of an oak tree; seeping into old footprints; laying still on a mud puddle; or sleeping in the shadows of marker stones. It hurt my eyes, refusing to be in focus, always remaining indistinct, fuzzy. Greedily, it sought man's possessions, a tint inside empty bottles along the path, a fully brewed soup in abandoned helmets on the riverbank. Wherever there was shelter from a breeze the gas congealed. Like the spirits of those killed seeking to hide from Gabriel's gathering chariot.

Dead birds littered the landscape. An entire flock of geese, having fallen to earth roughly in unison, their distorted formation running across the roof of an empty barracks, disappearing into the shriveled field behind. Watch dogs lay chained, tethered forever to their posts.

Following the major, we took the long desolate hike past the stacked wood of the bunk houses, through a maze of sandbag and mud walls, down, down and down again toward the trenches. A world haunted by phosphorescent ghosts, but vacant of men, there was barely a soldier in residence. Even the artillery guns lay empty, abandoned. The corpses of animals were everywhere, the grass shriveled and brown, but so few soldiers, living or dead.

"Major Tentelis, where is everyone sir?"

"Along the first line. Every remaining man is dug into the fortifications. We can't let them know how badly they've hurt us."

And exactly how badly was that? "What is the present situation here, Major?"

He did not turn around. "Distressing. I've been a soldier twenty years, and never seen anything like this. I'm told at least two thousand dead."

"Two thousand? In a single hour's bombardment?"

"It could have been worse. One battalion was on leave. Unfortunately," he stopped, pointing back toward the river, "they took the masks with them Lieutenant. The men here had no protection."

"None?" There had been whispers at headquarters, but nothing like this...

"The usual 12th Army mismanagement, yes? Too bad the Germans chose to douse us with chlorine in our very moment of vulnerability." There was grey despair in his eyes. "Such the coincidence."

A horrible coincidence. "What else could it be, sir?"

The question transformed him, sparking a cruel sneer: "Tsar Nicholas's court is full of bootlickers Rooks, some of whom have loyalties resting in the opposite trenches. Nothing is secret for long."

Another barbed reference to the Baltic-German aristocracy? My family certainly had no access to the tsar. I was sick of Tentelis's rhetoric. Such a typical Latvian: finding conspiracy, blaming my people for Russian incompetence. Certainly a topic for Captain Vereshchagin's report.

I responded without thinking: "We're not always the villains, Major." Fortunately, my muttered remark went unnoticed by my commander. Or appeared so.

Privately smoldering, we passed into a flooded tunnel, green-stained water rising past our heels, the bodies of mice riding the waves our steps created. The major took off his cap, tucking it somewhere inside his long coat. He pulled his mask over his head, and secured his goggles.

"I'd put yours on for safe measure. The chlorine is mainly at rest now, but there are still pockets lingering in these passages."

I took off my helmet, started to drop it at my feet, only to remember the chlorine vapors licking our muddy boots. Instead, I pinned it between my knees, and pulled the mask over my head, letting it hang about my neck. I tightened the goggles, replaced my helmet, and pulled the cloth up over my mouth. It was odd how donning this mask made me feel so alone. My breathing was constricted; the warm exhales reflecting back into my nostrils. Despite the mammoth size of the eyepieces my vision seemed clipped, the margins now black and ominous as if I peered out of a deep cave. A strand of green mist had infected one goggle, forcing me to remove it all and start again. I felt tired, short of breath, the mask blocking the intake of oxygen.

I could not imagine fighting in these things. The Germans had upped the stakes again, turning the air itself into a weapon.

Damn them.

My own breathing filled my ears. If the major was speaking it was nearly impossible to hear him. He motioned for me to follow, moving farther into the blackness of the tunnel. For a few moments, I felt as if we were in Verne's *20,000 Leagues Under the Sea*, armored in our own contained environment, helmeted explorers walking along the inky ocean's floor.

Till my eyes adjusted, and I beheld our surroundings. No, we were in a far different tome, pinned in the burning pages of Dante's *Inferno*. We'd tunneled into Hell itself.

The underpass was clogged with the dead. We could not move forward without climbing over one, often several. Seeking shelter from the chlorine, they must have fled down into the passageway, trapping themselves in a low confined space where the toxins built fastest. A sad and lethal mistake. Most were curled up, bodies in fetal positions, heads buried beneath sandbags, wrapped inside jackets, all in an attempt to protect their faces, to find one last gasp of passable air. One at my feet, his blue eyes fixed on the ceiling, had torn a handkerchief and stuffed it inside his mouth to filter his lungs. The cloth's tail fluttered as I passed, stepping over the man's waist to follow the major.

Tentelis had stopped, waiting for me in front of a mound of dead Russians piled nearly to the roof. How many? Ten? A dozen? It was hard to say. The survivors beyond must have just tossed them down into this hole.

A whisper came from his mask. I motioned that I could not hear. He moved closer, his covered mouth pressing against my ear. I knew he was shouting at the top of his lungs, the words were drawn out, elongated, but still I could barely understand him. It was more than the mask. There was an odd, voluminous noise coming from beyond the bodies.

"Be careful here, when you climb over Lieutenant. Don't stand up, you'll be above the trench wall!"

With that, he began to surmount the corpses, gingerly placing a boot in the gap between one soldier's chest and another's leg, like a mountain climber finding footholds in the sheer face of a granite cliff. Slowly, he progressed, liquids and film affixing to his uniform as he crawled over.

The major disappeared into the graying light of the opening near the ceiling. If there was a ladder it must be buried behind the bodies. There was little choice. I tried to find a step, a footrest that did not unnerve me walking on the dead. I put my boot on someone's upper arm, pressing up, finding my next step on an exposed shoulder. My grip slipped slightly, my hand falling from a thick thigh to the next soldier's open mouth. I shuddered, and apologized to the deceased. Discovering a wide neck to grasp, I pulled myself higher.

I slid through the gap, mindful of the major's warning, and threw myself straight down, rolling into the grey paste of the trench. An acidic, burning stench caught my nose, making my eyes water even through mask and goggles. I struggled to my feet, keeping my shoulders bent in fear of sniper bullets. Hunched, I followed the major through these channels.

Always horrific, the filthy dugouts had descended into something worse than I had imagined possible. A wretched noise shivered my soul: the din of 10,000 men, coughing and hacking in an anti-chorus, the retching ignorant of rhythm, every gasp moving to its own time, finding its own awful key.

Trailing behind the major, I stared at the poor souls who manned the walls. A hierarchy of men lay soaked in these muddy ravines: the living, the dead, and those somewhere in between.

The relatively healthy pressed forward in the fortifications, one foot on the firestep, holding rifle at ready, or loading the machine gun of his partner. Their faces were blackened, exhausted, ankles deep in mud, or yellowish water. Denying to their officers and themselves any tickle that might catch in their throats. Few had any obvious surface wounds, but by countenance and body language, most looked physically broken, gas hollowed into brittle shells. Even so these Russians kept their positions.

The dead mirrored the living: forming a parallel line along the rear of the trench, the corpses often strung two and three together. Mostly uncovered, their mouths opened in a last gasp, stains of foam on some lips and jackets, the arrogant gas pooling in the throats of others. Stones in a human wall, like the dugouts themselves, continuing as far as I could see in the dimming light.

These were hard enough to accept, my mind desperate to deny such horrors, to cast them out as nightmare. But those in flux were by far the worst. Men writhing in the mire or propped fitfully against a bag wall; trapped in fits of retching, never-ending spasms of hoarse coughs. Their respiratory systems destroyed, it was physically impossible for them to stop. A soldier held by his comforting fellows continued to gag until the yellow-white foam turned red, until it was too painful to breathe in again and finally, often after tens of hours, he succumbed. Then his comrades pinned a few words to his departing soul and stacked him with the others.

I passed a man at his post. He had wrapped himself in his coat so completely, hiking it up to his shoulders so that I could see nothing of him. Only the muzzle of his rifle protruded between the buttons.

The major stood ahead, his mask down, goggles back; he leaned forward freely speaking with a soldier. The Russian's jacket was tied loosely about his waist, though he still sported his helmet. His uniform sleeves were rolled up, and his long undershirt seemed to have been shredded to the elbow, as if he had been attacked by a pack of wild dogs. His accent possessed a hint of something else. Finnish? Polish? Or the unrecognizable cadence of another isolated village in this endless Russian Empire?

"Three gases, sir. At least as much as we can count from the shell bursts. The second was the worst, it caught the lip of the trench behind you and the explosion pushed the stuff right up the channel at us. Like a bullet down a barrel.'

Tentelis looked him over: "You seem in good health son, was your coat the only protection?" If the Russian was offended by being called the diminutive 'son' by a Latvian he did not show it. He seemed pleased to be receiving an officer's attention.

"On the first gassing, yes, Major. After that, we got some piss rags, and did the best we could."

I interrupted: "Piss rags, Private?"

"A filter in a pinch, sir. I'd call it a 'field' adoption of something Captain Kļaviņš suggested."

Tentelis broke in: "Can I see one son?"

"Begging the major's pardon sir, but I distributed them all. And I'm kind of out of cloth." Somehow he grinned. "Kinda out of piss too."

This man had been gassed three times today and could still smile. Amazing.

Twenty minutes later, I sat waiting on a sandbag, shaking a strand of fading green fog marooned in the bottom of a tin can. It slithered to the lowest point, trying to keep up as I rolled the cylinder in my palms, like a rodent trapped in a perpetual running wheel.

I sat while others prepared for battle, aided the wounded, fought for one more breath. Of what value was I? To others? To myself?

I thought of those soldiers lying in the boat earlier today. Could I have held my breath, carried at least one up the embankment? With Gāters help, possibly. But we had only fled. Both of us.

I rejected these thoughts, searched for optimism. Perhaps, the mass retching had subsided slightly? A comforting idea until I realized the reduction only could mean more men had perished. So tragic. There were rules even in war. Things so terrible, so against natural law, that they should never even be conceived, much less implemented. Had the scientists, the politicians, the kaiser seen what their weapons do? Could they possibly walk down this trench and say to themselves: "This is good."?

Tentelis stood across the dugout, still talking in the dusk with the same Russian sentry. They seemed to be getting along swimmingly. I admitted myself a tad jealous. A Russian and a Latvian; A soldier and an officer chatting for so long, did the major forget all his claims of Russian betrayal?

War seemed a strange place to forgive hatreds. They were birthed here, not buried. Why was this soldier pardoned, but not my people? Why not the landowners, Major?

Perhaps I was concentrating too much on these musings, or maybe I had grown too accustomed to battle, but I did not hear the whistle of the shell. It exploded close behind, sending brick, mud and shrapnel ricocheting against the outer walls. Another and another, lighting up the dusk, following in rhythm down the lines. Somewhere a man screamed. And then I saw them. The dirty green gases rising from blackened craters, blowing through the trench like sea fog beneath a pier.

When would they stop? With trembling hands I donned my gear. My breathing so fast, the mask pulled concave across dry lips.

I turned to the major for guidance. To my surprise, he had removed his own mask, placing it on the face of this soldier. In the horror of the moment, I could barely think. Why? Why? An officer, a battalion commander, giving protection to a common foot soldier. A Latvian helping a Russian. Those he said plotted against him.

LENIN'S HAREM

Major Tentelis gave a quick pat to his shoulder. "Your post." The man stood shocked for a moment, and then climbed up toward a machine gun nest. Ignoring me, Tentelis ran off in the opposite direction. Seconds later, the cloud rolled in, quickly fading light and color to memory.

I ran in the major's direction, imagining his thoughts. *I won't take shelter, while the soldiers suffer.* Perhaps, perhaps. Or maybe something more basic, more human. A simple sacrifice, made to secure a fellow man's life. *A soldier, who'd survived three attacks should not have to endure a fourth unaided.* I could hear him saying those words.

But now Tentelis was exposed himself. Who would aid him?

Shame covered me as thoroughly as the gas. We were about to die. It felt nearly a certainty, and there was something in the nature of the major's sacrifice, which made me want to pass on the same. To give Tentelis my mask, to let him know I understood.

Later, I would spend many hours pondering these brittle seconds. Blessed by a richer life, why was I suddenly willing to gamble my future for an ugly, common Latvian? One of those who had already taken so much from me. An unbalanced equation certainly. What had overcome me?

But at that moment, it was all I wanted. To force my mask on him, to give my pampered, meaningless life for someone who would sacrifice his own for another. To prove I would do so.

I chased the major, as the green mist penetrated everything: the other men, the weapons, the trench walls themselves. I could feel it soak through my clothes, sneaking underneath my sleeves, crawling down my neck. A drying wetness, it dampened the surface while sucking moisture from deeper within my skin. I felt dehydrated, as if my flesh was growing dusty, flaking away.

The mask too was smothering. My limbs grew weak, my lungs straining to pull thick oxygen through dense cotton. It came too slowly. I could only stumble forward in the glued mire, each step shorter, weaker than the last.

The major fell ahead of me, pulling in his knees, wrapping his coat over his head. I kneeled at him trying to pry his hand free, to make him grip my mask. I paused a moment before removing the precious device, cloistering my clothes about me as tightly as possible. I took one last gasp and pulled it off. I grabbed the major's wrist, pressing the cloth into his palm.

Take the mask. Take it.

He pushed me away harshly, rocking me back on my heels. I propped my free hand into the mud to prevent rolling onto my ass. The mask fell free between us.

I scooped it up. He must understand. I can aid him, as he had the soldier. In all this death, he needed to let me help him.

He wasn't looking at me, head down inside his coat. Did he know what I was offering in this lethal gangrene gas? Could he sense who I was? I reached out for his shoulder. Here! This is life!

My heart a machine-gun, my own body crying out for breath, terrified, drowning, I lost control of my bladder, the warmth of urine running down my pant leg.

I remembered the soldier's words. Perhaps, we both could live! Hold on a moment more, Major.

I began tearing at my shirt, my jacket. The material was thick and hard to split, the effort eating up the oxygen in my lungs. Just a small part, please. Any piece that would come loose.

Something within him decided to move. His face eclipsed, he struggled to his feet, his back to me. I could hear his choking already. No, this way! No. No. No. I held out the mask. Take it!

The major gained his balance, and still hunched over, ran down the chaotic trench. Disappearing quickly into the astral fog.

It was my last sight of him alive.

By the time I rose, my head was dizzy, my steps unbalanced. Desperate for air, I pressed the filter to my lips. The gasping breath brought a measure of slithering toxicity with it. It seared my mouth's interior, a burning coal slipping toward my throat. I gagged, biting into fabric as I donned the mask fully. My senses were spinning, drunk. Which way had he fled?

Somewhere guns were firing. I sought higher ground, seeking a moment's rest to regain my wits. Dropping to my knees in a puddle, I leaned back against a wall of sandbags. I considered ripping off the cloth, better poison than asphyxiation. But those eternal coughs hounded me, dissuaded, reminding me of the queue between Hell and Purgatory.

I was lost in a blank green world. The major was gone, disappearing with all the land's features, bettering me in his death.

Damn him.

I sat trapped on an island, a grim shroud descending from the green skies. Useless, I curled up in the lonely mud, pulled my coat over my head, and for the second time that day begged for God's forgiveness.

Chapter Eleven

Great beasts gathered around the watering hole.

Or so it seemed to me as the morning window light reflected off the cold polished meeting table, gently mixing white, blue and brown over its surface like the pooling colors of some secluded, sylvan pond. Lounging along its edge was the Russian 12th Army staff: old men hidden behind wiry white whiskers, their full bellies jingling the bottom of dull medals when they coughed, shifted in their chairs or belched some half-hearted complaint. Sleepy, aging lions more tired than threatening.

Of course it was easy to be brave when you weren't standing in front of them as bespectacled Captain Juškevičs now was. Promoted to replace Major Tentelis, his bouncy energies were the springs of an annoying gazelle in this pride's lethargic midst. Occasionally, they'd take a lazy swat at him, but no one really had the energy to finish the Lett. He bounded about, safe while the old beasts slept, satiated from their extensive breakfast.

Nothing he said was reaching them. His terms were dryly technical. His ideas, so bold to the men, were ridiculous to this audience. They asked few questions, gave fewer suggestions. These men had made their careers with the old strategies, crafted methods that had allowed them to surpass their fellows, to rise to the status where Grand Duke Nicholas, indeed the tsar himself, entrusted them with the Empire's very survival. No denizen of a tiny province was going to tell them how to win the war. Not one barely out of his teens, certainly.

Juškevičs's nasal voice seemed shriller in the echoing, musty chamber. "Despite a four to one enemy superiority, Lieutenant Briedis was able to…."

"It's Colonel Briedis, Captain," sparked the plump Bulgarian General Dimitrev, awakening from his sleep to swipe at the gazelle. "Don't you know your own leaders?"

A purple-faced officer laughed at this remark. Or was it a snore? Either way, his eyes remained shut.

Juškevičs adjusted his glasses, pressing them higher along the bridge of his nose.

"Yes, but it was 'Lieutenant' then, wasn't it? Or was he a captain at Misa? Can someone check that?"

Desperate to move him on, I nodded as if taking the note, only scribbling the word 'idiot' on my paper. *Stay on the subject Heinrichs, and for God's sake don't correct them. What is the benefit of embarrassing a general, please?*

He continued. "Nevertheless, this decentralization will often bring the men out of the range of a company commander's voice. What to do? What to do?"

Even I couldn't listen anymore. I found myself seeking the shelter of the window's view. Outside, past the empty November trees, I could see the grey flowing Daugava, across the Saulkalne bridgehead half-hidden in mist. Last night's rains had washed away all the smoke from the daily battle. They called it 'Nāves sala' now, the 'Isle of Death.' An appropriate christening. A month ago I had nearly died there. Three thousand had been less lucky.

October had passed. A month where I'd tried to change everything, tried to matter.

I had initiated this meeting, planned it, written up the schedules, and pried compliance from the Latvian company commanders, citing benefit after benefit. Essentially extorted the Russians officers, implying to each, that everyone else who mattered would be present. *I understand the importance of recuperation General. Not to worry, I am sure your fellows will be fair when they dole out the roles in the coming offensive, sir.*

I certainly hadn't conceived the brewing Winter Offensive, but I could do my best to glue Russians and Latvians together before it began. The 12th Army, and for the first time, all nine Latvian Battalions striking at once.

The goal? One dear to my heart: The liberation of Courland itself.

To throw the Germans out of Latvia.

I took one last glance across the river. With morning rays breaking through the storm clouds, Nāves sala looked rather peaceful, slandered by its young name. Hard to believe two battalions lay waiting in the cold mud for the next German attack.

The seasons move on, no matter what men do, a poet once said.

A heavy sigh. Perhaps this meeting should move on as well. No one was even watching Juškevičs anymore. Despite his grand gestures and oft-quoted statistics, the decision was made long before this conference started two hours ago.

Only our surprise guest seemed even to be conscious, and he was certainly more focused on the mannerisms and reactions about the table, than anything said across it. I'd invited Vereshchagin as a matter of courtesy. He'd said "No."

So why was he here anyway?

One of the staff assistants entered through the rear door, uncomfortably willing his footsteps to mute. He crept along the circumference of the table, each general, every colonel looking up, hopeful of being pulled from the dreary meeting. At last he bowed, whispering something to Vereshchagin, before passing him a folded note.

Vereshchagin took a quick scan of the message, politely excused himself, and walked toward the door. As he did so, he brushed along my shoulder, the words "Please join me," whispered into my ear.

I was uncomfortable leaving a meeting I had arranged, especially one that was failing so spectacularly, abandoning Juškevičs on the sinking ship. Still, Captain Vereshchagin was not to be ignored.

Juškevičs, his cadence now pleading, asked for questions. There were none.

I stood up, watching our young commander's eyes turn my way. I put up one finger. "One moment" I mouthed, using the cover of silence to slip away.

Outside, Captain Vereshchagin was watching a Latvian regiment practice marksmanship, his face and stance, registering his disgust.

"These Livs know nothing about war, Rooks. Look at them, firing on their own. Where is the discipline?"

"With present reload rates, it makes more sense to have them fire at will rather than sit inactive."

He lit a cigarette. "You sound like that wet-nursed captain in there. Who does he think he is? Telling the generals what strategy to use."

Was that rhetorical? When I didn't answer, he did: "Rooks…this desire for the Latvians to break down their forces, to give their men responsibility." He paused, waving his cigaretted hand in tumbling passes as if trying to find the words. "Is it an attempt to shift the blame, to scapegoat the soldiers for their officers' on the field failures? … Tobacco?"

His words out, the hand gestures stopped, a thumb hooking onto his broad brown belt. His index finger tapped the buckle, as if timing the seconds to my response.

"No thank you sir. We are only doing what we think is tactfully advantageous, sir."

"We?" The tapping stopped cold.

"Well you assigned me to this battalion, Captain. So, yes, 'We'"

I did not like his facial reaction to this. I continued: "*They*, Captain, are merely doing what the Germans have been doing. The kaiser's troops have delegated authority, broken into smaller tactical units and backed us up from Prussia all the way to the banks of the Dauga…"

"Lieutenant, I'm hearing the same thing in every Latvian battalion. Untrained troops making battlefield decisions…"

I pooled my courage. "No, sir. They're training them sir. That's the point, to deepen the knowledge down the ranks."

He nodded, as if finally comprehending. "A Lett's a Lett, a Cour's a Cour, regardless of rank?"

"That's not what we're saying at all…"

He seemed irritated at the correction. "Are you their propaganda officer, or my liaison man, Rooks?"

Suddenly the deadened conference seemed less uncomfortable. "I am your liaison, sir."

"Good." He took a few more puffs on his cigarette, watching the men run about the field.

Finally, he turned back to me. "Do you think this some type of Marxist subversion, Rooks? A give the power to the common man, common soldier philosophy?"

I found myself disagreeing with him again. "No, I don't think so, Captain."

His hand flew up in disgust. "Stop arguing with me Lieutenant! In every Latvian battalion I go, I see it. Every report I receive says these units are infected with communism and nationalism. Like gangrene, we must cut it off."

An exaggeration, surely. "I wouldn't say so, sir."

His eyes rolled. "Except yours, Rooks. Except yours. Not a word." He angrily poked my breast, the ash from his cigarette tumbling down the front of my uniform. "Are you trying to tell me that in all these battalions, by chance, yours is the one without the slightest sign of Marxism? Or that not a single one of your men hopes he is fighting for a Latvian nation?"

"Sir, there are sympathies here and there, but nobody's planning to overthrow the government."

"I want these sympathies in your report, Rooks!" He poked me harder, pressing fabric into muscle. "That's an order, not a request!"

He stepped back, took in some air. After several moments, his face softened, his words almost apologetic in tone: "Really, Wiktor, you've been here a year. You haven't given me one lead, one hint of anything worth addressing. Is my man blind?"

"No, sir."

He moved over, put an arm over my shoulder. "Rooks, you've got a good name. I don't want to put you in the battlefield. I don't. But if you can't get it done back here, what can I do?"

I didn't want to be in combat, no sane man did, but I was repelled by this idea I had to be sheltered. "I am not afraid to fight, Captain."

He smiled, looked into my eyes. "I know that Rooks, but are you afraid to talk?"

"No."

"Then six names. In the next report, at minimum." He patted my shoulder supportively, all problems apparently solved. "Find me the worst and give them to me. Whoever they are."

I nodded, wanting to end the conversation without a verbal commitment, but his eyes wouldn't release mine. "We have an understanding then, Wiktor. No excuses."

We re-entered the meeting hall. Juškevičs was still droning on. "We've adapted their use and have had extended success in the field. There is no doubt that the enemy has had an enormous advantage employing their own variations of Boers tactics against…against more conventional opposition."

That did it. Juškevičs's enthusiasm had taken him too far. By 'conventional opposition' he meant them: the generals, their men, their old ideas and everyone here still awake knew it.

A few stood up. Several rapped on the table.

Meeting adjourned.

We just might be home for Christmas. Or a few days afterward, at any rate.

The men took a moment to pose for photographs with the captured German cannons, straddling the giant barrels, leaning against the bases, trying to look their best for fathers, mothers and girlfriends; for lovers not yet met, for sons and daughters unborn.

No matter how slow the camera's shutter, or painful the touch of arctic winds, they remained unmoving. Proud smiles; cockily raised chins; a swagger in the way each leaned on his comrade or puffed out his breast.

This is how it was. This is what we did.

Nearer to me, hundreds of German prisoners sat on their knees, loosely herded into an oval collection. Their hands long since dropped from behind their heads, they attempted to clear out dry spots in the snow beneath, begged for cigarettes, or used a palm to dam an icy bullet wound. The surgeon still busy with Latvian troops, they knew it would be a long while before aid came to the enemy.

The Offensive had begun in the predawn morning two days before Christmas, an unusual time to attack certainly. It would have been even a greater surprise if it had been Yuletide for the Germans as well, their calendar nearly two weeks ahead of ours. Well, if not a Christmas gift, our troops had certainly given them a bad New Year's hangover.

Briedis's forces had moved quickly under cover of a blizzard, refusing artillery protection for fear of alerting their enemy. Snipers eliminated German sentries; snow-white soldiers silently threw snow-white mats over barbed wire fences dropping into the trenches before most of the enemy could fire. They drove them out of their fortifications, forcing them past their rear defenses. All the small unit tactics, all that marksmanship, finally thrown back against their creators.

Over two days with heavy losses, we'd pushed them south, Briedis's men taking the impossibly fortified 'Machine Gun Hill' on Christmas Day, our forces, under Juškevičs's command, supporting their flank. German prisoners came streaming down the hill, so many in fact that it was becoming difficult to keep them all penned in.

That would not be a problem. The 6th Siberian Rifle Corps would soon be here to aid and relieve us, the usual Russian tardiness not withstanding.

Though I wish my runners had returned …

In the meanwhile I interviewed prisoners, my German fluency for once an asset rather than a stigma. I reclined on a wooden chair obtained from some abandoned farmhouse, its back supported by a thin birch tree, my feet propped on an old stump. A little fire burned, close enough to keep me warm, a coffee pot within a slightly straining reach.

Two at a time, the prisoners were taken out of the group. Those who seemed agreeable were given a tin of warm water. Those less so, were harshly returned to their fellows.

LENIN'S HAREM

Close-up, the German troopers were thicker, redder of cheek, better fed than our own. An oddity, they were fighting a two-front war, you'd think it'd have been they who were starving. Yet somehow, it was our portions that arrived late, rotten, or never at all.

The latest were typical enough: a tall, pox-faced blond who seemed very eager to converse. Name the topic, anything not to get shot. Probably a clerk or bookkeeper's son, his quiet life interrupted by the Calls of State. His partner, a private raised in the beer halls and rowdy docks of Hamburg was a different sort entirely. I imagined him joining the army early, drunken on hops, pride and glory. Slapping buddies on the back in the queue, bragging he'd be the first to trim the tsar's moustache. To him this war was a great brawl to win, a sort of extended barroom tussle. Capture only meant he was now swinging with one arm pinned behind his back. His face was beet red, his black bangs surprisingly long, and every time I asked him a question I got the same response.

"Go to Hell! Traitor bastard."

I only folded my hands and smiled. "Your opinion was noted the first time Private."

I turned from him, concentrating on the one willing to talk. With so many prisoners, I had that luxury. I'd let Gāters stick a couple of men on the 'misguided son of Industry' as he'd call him. I nodded, and two soldiers escorted our belligerent friend off.

"You call yourself a German. Traitor bastard. Go to Hell!"

Some side would always label me a turncoat. "Quite the poet, your friend."

The blond broke a nervous smile. Yes, he was the type. He'd probably expected to spend his life snugly pressed into a dark wooden chair, penned in a dusky office, sheltered behind stacks of ledgers, wielding nothing more fearsome than a fountain pen. To find himself a prisoner in frozen Russia with thousands of men wanting to kill him, well… that was certainly a grievous error. And he'd like to balance the books as quickly as possible, I was quite sure.

"Okay, Bernhard can you identify which city your last supply train came…"

I noticed Captain Juškevičs had wandered over to the far field to conference with Seskis while the two guards were still away trying to weed out another interview prospect. A moment of privacy! An opportunity to vary the topic a little.

I waved off his coming answer. "Private…Bernhard…were you ever sequestered on a land called 'Rooks Muiža?' The manor is in ruins, but some of the stables and the surrounding houses still stand."

His face seemed to widen, flattening as he strained in thought, his pox scars pulled oval with the effort. "No, sir... never even heard of it."

"Near Jelgava. Mitau, you might know it as?" I refilled his tin with hot water from the fire. "Take your time...the names can be confusing."

He only shook his head "No."

I could see the soldiers returning with another prisoner. "The Kaltenbach estates then? He is a noble of some reputation, a baron, you must have heard of him? A huge farm off the old Rīga road?"

Bernhard just shook his head, "No, no. I am sorry. I am not withholding..."

I waved him off again. "No, no. I know that. Tell me, what has been happening in Courland? How are the people being treated?"

"I can't say really, I've only been here two weeks."

Two weeks? "Where did they have you stationed before?"

"Near Neuve Chapelle."

"In France? On the Western Front?"

"Yes."

So far away. "Why did they move you over here?"

"There was word of a large assault coming. I'm just a soldier, I go where I'm told."

"A few weeks ago?"

"Yes, of course."

How? How did they know of the Offensive? Our Captain would have to be told. *Both Captains.* I cursed. Somehow, the kaiser's generals always anticipated. Maybe, the stories about the tsaritsa were right, she was German after all.

An internal irony. Major Tentelis would have approved of that thought.

As I pieced together my next question, Bernhard, grew surprisingly bold, seizing the privacy for his own use: "Sir, you seem like a good sort...the tea and all. Why are you with these..." He looked about, lowering his voice further. "With these Slavs? Why aren't you helping your own kind?"

Latvians were Balts, not Slavs, but still there was something sincere, even innocent in his tone. Could I talk to anyone from any army without being accused of betrayal? "Because you're in our lands, Private."

His green eyes widened. "So, are they sir. The Russians, I mean."

Yes, Private, so they are. But that was another topic...

I pulled my pocket watch. Nearly three p.m. Yes, these lands were full of Russians. Though I was beginning to have doubts about the Siberian Corps.

Safe from the nearly rioting troops, I slammed shut the door, at last giving privacy to some of the officers. Seskis in his anger picked up a kerosene lamp, and tossed it against the quarters' wall. The glass shattered, and burning flame ran up the wall, pooling red and yellow at the corner of the ceiling.

"Jesus Miķelis! You'll kill us all," yelled Juškevičs, pulling a sheet off the bunk, and pressing it to the wall to smother the blaze. I grabbed a pillow and rushed to assist him.

"Let it burn!" Seskis was in a horrible rage, shattering a wooden chair against the wall, a leg rattling across the card table. "Let's burn the whole god damn place down."

Juškevičs and I had nearly absorbed the flames, only a trailing bit of liquid light crawling along the ceiling. Gāters grabbed Seskis behind, his permanently swollen hand pressing hard across the little man's chest to restrain him. "Calm down, Miķelis. Calm down, let's not make it any worse than it is."

"Any worse? How could it be any worse, Guntis? They left us out there to die! Every one of us! Every single goddamn one of us."

Gāters's hold softened, turning from a restraining grip to a sympathetic hug: "I know, Miķelis, I know, we were all there."

The screech of a pulled chair. Juškevičs, finished with the fire, sat himself down at the table, his face buried in his hands, his leadership falling away. "They just don't care. I tried to tell them what the Germans would do. I tried… No one would listen."

They were right. Right, and they didn't even know as much as I. To them, the incompetent tsarist army had been unable to penetrate, unable to advance, moored in their nineteenth century tactics. As liaison officer, I now knew the truth: The 12th Army hadn't *tried* to engage the enemy.

The Siberian troops had never shown, claiming they had gotten lost on the way to the front. Lost? *Go south, go west, the front stretches to the Crimea!* If true, the incompetence was unfathomable, without precedent. And if not true, what then? *What did that mean?*

No, no, our masters had stayed safely back, unleashed their Lettish watchdog on the trespassers. A pity the dog was injured.

Even where the Russians had actually relieved our exhausted forces, they gave the land away. They would not fight to keep Courland, not die for this country. All the gains squandered as the 12th Army performed its only capable maneuver: retreat.

For two weeks everything the Latvians won, the Russians lost. Twice, thrice, our battalions had to recapture land they had died for only the day before. Over and over again, as the Germans moved in more and more troops. The whole Winter Offensive ground to a halt.

It was so obvious now. To the generals this was still foreign soil, with Russia proper not starting for hundreds of kilometers. Let the locals absorb the casualties, let them all die first.

And now there were rumors that Colonel Briedis hovered near death, wounded capturing 'Machine Gun Hill' unsupported for the umpteenth time. Just another Latvian sacrificed by the tsar.

If these men knew the truth, they'd rebel. Attack the Russian troops, burn the houses, perhaps ally with the Germans. It would be 1905 all over again. Worse, the Letts had an army now. They were better than the tsar's men and they knew it.

But this time, this time, maybe they had a just reason. Such thoughts seemed obscene, but maybe they, maybe I…this was the land of my birth after all, maybe…

Maybe I should rebel too, rebel against those pigs in St. Petersburg.

I looked at Juškevičs, wanting desperately to be the leader, but only crumpling over nearly in tears. All his plans, his tactics misused. I watched the deformed Gāters bear hug little Seskis, attempting to soothe his righteous anger. Outside the cries of the wounded, waiting for attention, for medicine or for last rights. Early counts had eight thousand dead. How many more to come?

I kneeled at my bunk, opening the rolled bag with all my possessions. I pulled out a black bottle of balsam.

I slammed it on the table in front of Juškevičs, and reaching into my bag, birthed four shot glasses. For one night, Vereshchagin could go to Hell; everything said was off the record. "Alright, men let's have a drink to the tsar's health."

I sat alone in the frigid back office, scribbling away in the poor light provided by the underfed kerosene lamp. Someone had tried to enrich the fuel with grease. The resulting smoke irritated my nose, made me sniffle, adding only to my poor mood. What I would give for a warming fire?

I flipped through the casualty lists, pages and pages, pausing for a moment to write down a name:

Corporal Imants Ronis. *Number Three.*

LENIN'S HAREM

I scanned further down the paper, found a soldier from Ogre killed on January 3rd. Private C.Y. Arons. *Number Four.*

Four dead? Was that too much? I was going to have to add someone alive eventually.

My stomach rumbled. When was the last time I'd eaten? Two days? Yes, yesterday morning. One piece of stale bread. No butter to be had.

I paused, bought time looking at the newspaper clippings pinned to the wall. *The London Times.* Paris's *L'Aurore.* Incomprehensible languages, peppered with little words, bits of meaning ducking between verb and noun, yet altering the entire sentence. An absolute mystery.

The translators told me the articles were full of praise for the Latvian Riflemen and damnation for the Russian leadership. That a month later the world knew, knew how we'd been robbed. I suspected they embellished their readings to raise morale. Certainly, the world wasn't sending any food.

I pulled my coat tighter desperate to warm myself, returned to the problem at hand. Maybe if they were all in the same unit. I could claim I was investigating, watching, when the Offensive began. One of those tragedies of war, a whole group trapped in the wrong location, wiped out.

No, it was too much the coincidence.

I put my face in my hands. This was not going to work. He'd never believe.

A knock at the door.

"Enter."

Sergeant Līcis poked his head through.

"Hello Herberts."

"Good evening, Lieutenant." He took off his hat, revealing a slightly balding head, the respectful tone reminding me of Father's old driver. There were still some Letts who remembered the politeness, the old ways. "I am sorry to interrupt."

"What can I do for you?"

"Captain Juškevičs's going to address the men in a few minutes. He'd like to talk to you first."

Couldn't he see that I was busy trying not to betray them? I shuffled my papers, annoyed. "Did he say what he needed?"

"I think he wanted to get the official position, you being the Russian representative and all, sir."

"What position, Herberts?"

There was a dawning of realization on his face. Slightly uncomfortable, he stepped forward entering the room fully, closing the door softly behind

I could see the brim of his cap twist in the sergeant's hands. "I assumed the news came from you, sir. Then, you don't know? You haven't heard?"

There was something frightful in his tone. "Heard what?"

"The tsar, sir. He's gone."

Chapter Twelve

September 1917, Rīga

The dark silhouettes of zeppelins and observation balloons glided along the morning horizon. Brooding manmade storm clouds eclipsed only when they silently passed behind St. Peters bulbous multi-platform spire or the bubbled steeple of Rīga's Dome Cathedral. Too remote for our artillery, the enemy safely watched from the heavens. Preparing. Coordinating

For whatever was coming.

The German cannons had spent the dawn firing up and down our river defenses, a long curtain of smoke, an extended symphony of explosions, but little real damage. It was all a feint, a screen, to hide where they were going to ferry the Daugava, to disguise their strike at Rīga herself.

I scribbled these thoughts on the paper. A new government, the same field reports to the same generals. Not much had changed since Prince Lvov, and then Kerensky, had replaced the tsar. Perhaps the nationalists and radicals in our midst had become bolder, more open. An observation, I would have been forced to disclose to Captain Vereshchagin.

If I could find him. He had simply disappeared. Lost in the administrative changeover? Missing in action? Laying anonymous in a field hospital? No one seemed to know. My backlogged letters remained unsent.

I sealed the envelope, turned to my runner. "If there is a written reply, Private, I'll be in the East trenches conferencing with Lieutenant Gāters by noon."

I handed the little Russian the parcel. I was a bit skeptical he could actually complete the route anymore, a victim of the horrible new gas used to finally drive 12th Army forces from Nāves sala: An odorless monstrosity that blistered the skin even when the lungs were shielded, his flesh was a patchwork of black scabs and pink swells, slowly healing along forehead and cheeks, still heavily crusted on the back of his hand as he folded my envelope into his leather bag. His agony as he shuffled away told me countless lesions lay hidden beneath his uniform, ulcers rubbing painfully against cloth, always infected, never fully healing months after exposure. Perhaps nineteen, my messenger moved like an eighty-year old man. Was he still in the field from duty or from desperation?

Either way, God help him.

I looked at the grey smoke drifting in from the tortured river, an unnatural fog flowing over the pier, between the city blocks into the populous Rīga streets.

And God help us all if they used the weapon here.

***

The explosion threw me back against the rear trench wall, dirt and rock ricocheting off my chest, my face. I lay there unable to breathe, small avalanches of soil draining onto my back from the smoking earthworks above. When at last the shock wore thin, enough senses returning that I could intake one struggling gasp, a smoldering mouthful of dust and fumes came with it. It was then I heard the sound. Growing shouts even more fearsome than the whistle of an incoming shell.

German voices nearby.

The cadence of childhood, the sheltering language of my parents, forever bound to memories of bedtime fairytales and Christmas Eve celebrations, now turned to the cold calls of doom.

They'd crossed the river.

Gāters crawled over to me, his mannequin face shadowed by an earth-caked helmet.

"Rooks are you alright?"

I tried to take stock of my body. Everything hurt, but seemed intact. Attached at least. "I don't know…I think so. Gas?"

He shook his head, brushing dirt off my shoulders. "No. Not if they're sending their own men."

I heard a Latvian scream "Breech! Breech! B…" His words cut off by machine-gun fire.

A nearer man yelled: "They've broken through!"

"Come on Rooks. We need to get you up." His great puffed hand took hold of my jacket, the other beneath my arm; he pulled me upright into a sitting position. My body felt shifted, twisted, as if organs and flesh had been suddenly rotated around bone's axis.

LENIN'S HAREM

I bent myself awkwardly up to a knee, just in time for Gāters to shove the cold steel pistol into my hand.

"They'll be coming, Rooks. It's the best I can offer."

I was so scared; I don't remember if I thanked him.

The machine-gun fire grew louder, several mortar explosions farther down the trench blowing smoke and screams our way. I could see our gunners, forced behind the protective walls, ducking under piles of sandbags. The German suppression fire had trapped us all. Bullets knocking bottles, cans, everything unsecured to the trench floor.

And yet, the German voices seemed to be receding. I found one Latvian machine-gunner, foolishly up and firing in the hailstorm of incoming bullets. His angle continued to slowly rotate, having started in the front of the trenches, he now seemed to be aiming along them. And then behind them.

"Guntis, where is that soldier firing?"

He did not hear me, enveloped as he was in his command. I dared a look, peaking through the gap of the crater that had nearly been my grave marker.

Through the dust and smoke, I could see German soldiers running, attacking our second line of defenders. The enemy armed with rifles, mortars, machine-guns, every type of light weaponry one could imagine. It was difficult to tell from the distance, but their uniforms looked different, thicker, padded.

"Gāters!" I howled.

There was no answer. I found the decrepit Russian runner, and sent him to fetch the lieutenant. By the time he arrived, the first wave of Germans was disappearing in the smoke, another moving up to follow in their wake.

"Guntis, where are they going?"

He didn't answer, only watching with his field glasses. "Past us..." his tone more a question than an answer.

This was so unusual. When you broke into a fortification, you fanned out along the enemy line, destroyed their ability to fire on your fellows, consolidated your gains for the next assault. But to just keep moving deeper? Why? They'd be cut off. Surrounded. The Germans were better soldiers than this.

A bullet's near miss forced me to recoil. Today's second reprieve. Somehow curiosity momentarily conquered fear and I risked another glance.

Yes, I could see them running by us. Leaving our fortifications, machine guns and cannons all heavily suppressed by fire, but unassaulted. They simply ignored our defenses, lines of men penetrating deeper and deeper.

So, so quickly.

Like lightning.

My mind returned to my duties. The generals had to know. I slipped away, down into the darkened bunker, found Gāters already there, screaming orders at a wounded sergeant. I picked up the phone to advise the Russian command of the situation.

It was dead.

"Gāters they've cut the lines."

He turned from his tirade. "Already? Madness."

I cupped my ear to block out external noise. Nothing. "It's out."

"To leave our cannons and go after telephone wire. What priorities are these?"

"I don't know." There was something unnatural in the air. They made me nervous these Germans. Always raising the bar. With their toxic gasses, their zeppelins and airplanes. Their lightning warfare.

I slammed the receiver into its catch. "Gāters these are your men, what should we do?"

He sent the sergeant scurrying off to some duty. "Maintain our ground."

"Even with them behind us?" Maybe it was our men who might be cut off.

"Yes. We still hold the defenses." He picked up his pistol, stepped up toward the trenches. "What else can we do Rooks? Without 12th Army approval?"

Something in my expression must have registered with him. He hesitated at the door. "See if you can get a runner to headquarters."

I told the Russian to go. He looked horrified.

"Sirs? They're behind us. It's suicide."

A good point. Gāters sent him anyway.

I tried the phone again. Still dead.

Dead, I feared, as this city.

Chaos. Chaos, apathy and starvation. How appropriate to be sitting in a schoolroom.

A little less than sober, I sat on a child's desk looking out a frosty window. On the corner across the street, I could see the wooden exterior of the spa our family had visited when vacationing here as a boy. I remembered the plump half-Russian woman who ran it, how she always called the patrons 'lover.' Such a little word, yet it had annoyed my mother no end. One June, Mother's irritation even cut the holiday short, forcing us all on the next train down to Mitau. Oh, how angry Father had been.

So many years ago. The place hadn't changed. Not since then, not since medieval times they said. Not until now.

Yes, poor little cobblestoned Wenden. This quiet resort town had found itself swamped with a retreating army. Beaten and bruised men, desperately needing a drink but with nothing left to buy one. Everywhere there was despair: in the slumped bodies behind frigid alleyways, in the cracking voices echoing from forced-open taverns, and hidden in the evasive eyes of the locals. Churches and schools, restaurants and homes all billeting bitter, wounded alcoholics. Without Rīga, our army had little claim to being the country's defenders. Instead, they'd descended into rude thieves and unpaying thugs ripping the community apart. A victorious army was a load to bear, a defeated one a devouring curse.

Disaster had followed disaster, unseen but rhythmically predictable, like waves lapping on a midnight beach. Rīga had been lost, and now famine was crossing all of the Russian Empire. Starving, the people had consumed the infantile Kerensky government, another set of pretenders pushing themselves into power. With luck, the Bolsheviks just might last until the next catastrophe.

And being new rulers, they'd sent someone to explain the new rules. The speaker checking his notes in this crowded lecture hall was the third in a month. He was immaculately dressed in light brown and red, his slightly graying hair greased back in thick wavy strands, like the graceful chrome lines adorning the hood of some elegant automobile. His spectacles rested firmly on plateau cheekbones. His features were handsome, slightly exaggerated, deeply recessed, as if his face belonged carved on the side of a building or atop a monument, instead of fashioned on a flesh and blood man. Rumors were he was a different sort; that he was not an administrator, but from the War Ministry itself. A humorous distinction in a government so young, did that mean his office was across the hall or around the corner from the others?

I looked around the Liv schoolroom. On the walls the simple geometry of children's drawings; the weathered faces of fading maps; posters adorned with the enforced Cyrillic alphabet. The last a bit ironic since there was hardly a Russian in the room. They'd all gone home, broken by defeat and so many upheavals in Petrograd, as St. Petersburg was so unseemly labeled. The new Bolshi War Minister had even tried to spin this to the world, calling the mass desertions a 'demobilization.' As if that changed anything. The 12th Army didn't exist anymore. All that remained was a gang of defeated men with nowhere else to go. The Latvians simply had no homes left to hide in.

The speaker clapped his hands quickly. "Greetings, my comrades. I have much to say, so let us begin." I was surprised by his voice: A Latvian. A Latvian speaking to them in Latvian.

"First, I have just come from a meeting in Petrograd with Commissar Trotsky. We want you to know how the People appreciate the sacrifices you have made. I must make special note of the Zemgale regiment, heroes and examples to us all." His voice dropped off here, as if to sanctify his words: "We should all honor their memory. Many, many good men died so that the 12th Army might safely withdraw from Rīga."

Yeah, pretty much all of them. A clever opening, Kerensky's government had never bothered to acknowledge this selfless defense. Many in this room had a friend among the fallen. Indeed, I thought the Bolsheviks were smart to send a Latvian. Sons of farmers, dockyard workers, most in this room were naturally receptive to communism. To see one of their own in authority…well that *was different*. The tsar had never done that.

"I have spent many weeks meeting with the People's War Council. We have recognized the innovations in battle of our Latvian comrades." He paced from one side of the room to the other, keeping all involved. "Seen how your bravery has kept the German invaders at bay for two years. We ache for your losses, losses unnecessarily magnified by the cruel interference of the tsar's incompetent officers, and the misguided rule of the illegal Provisional Government that followed them in tyranny. I tell you my comrades, before we leave this hall today, we shall reverse those wrongs!"

He was playing to their prejudices. I could feel the room spark; eyes awakening, minds sobering. Reverse? This wasn't the usual propaganda speech. Maybe he really had something to say.

He spoke faster, gathering momentum. "We shall build a new army. A People's Army." He raised his hand in a fist. "A Red Army!" He let the statement hang in the air for a moment, catching their eyes, returning confident smiles. "And we want you! Each of you, all of you to train it! To forge it!" He spread his hands out wide like a preacher on a pulpit. "To lead them, my Latvian comrades! No more tethered to the past, we ask you to show us the way! To cast free the yoke from the good people of the world."

An electric murmur ran through the room. *Promotion. Advancement. Authority.* And unsaid, but in all their minds: To leapfrog the Russians. Giving orders, not taking them. After so many generations, could it be true? History balancing itself before them.

He could see their excitement and fed off it. His breathing seemed rushed, as if preparing for some tremendous effort. He jumped up on a desk, seizing the moment for a mighty proclamation.

"In return, the People's Government promises…" he paused, the great salesman about to close the bargain, letting them breathlessly beg for his final words. *Promises? Promises what?*

"Tell us!" yelled gleefully desperate Gāters.

Our guest's words were understated, as if to let the content carry the volume for him:

"Self determination for Latvia."

Their own country. At last.

The room exploded in a roar. Men stood up clapping, whistling. With a few words he had resurrected them all, brought them back from extinction.

But not me.

Juškevičs caught me at the door. "What is wrong with communism? With equality for everyone?"

I just wanted out, so uncomfortable in this room. "It's not for me Captain." I moved to get by him. "I'm the rich oppressor remember? Enemy of the People."

He blocked my exit, my reflection leering back in his glasses. "Nonsense. I've vouched for you, so has Gāters. You'll have to pass an interview, but we can prepare you."

He had actually attached his name to mine? An aristocrat? A German? Such a risk Juškevičs, so unwise. And Gāters too, of all people? Amazing.

"I'm a landowner, Heinrichs. It's not possible."

He pulled his hand from the doorframe, placed it on my shoulder, his face growing remorseful. "Wiktor…Poor deluded Wiktor. You aren't any longer. It's time you accepted that my friend."

"…No."

I shoved my things into my bag, my leather civilian shoes refusing to find a compact angle. I pulled them out again. Perhaps rolled in my summer jacket.

I wasn't sure where I was going to go exactly. My home, my family lay in guarded Courland. Even the most distant relative, the most estranged acquaintance was locked in occupied Rīga.

And Otomars? He had never returned my letters. Had he fled the Revolution? Certainly, he was not among its victims. Not my brother, they'd never get him. Never.

I saw my future: No shelter. No work. No family. Maybe that was what appealed to the Latvians in communism. How nice to share, when you have nothing.

There was some truth in that.

Across the room Seskis had nearly finished his own packing, only sorting through accumulated odds and ends on the shelf above his bed.

I compressed my toilet kit, slid it down the inside curve of the sack. "Aren't you going with them?"

He kept his back to me. "Nope, I'm heading out of here before someone puts a gun to my head."

"What do you mean?"

"Colonel Briedis. Trotsky shot him, seems he was saying the wrong things. I'll bet their recruiter forgot to mention that?" He took his insignia off his collar and deposited it on the shelf.

Seskis was always so belligerent, harder to understand even than Gāters. "Well then, where are you headed?"

He held up a shot glass, two nipples painted on one side, a pair of dice on the other. "Is this yours?"

"No."

He shrugged, cramming it into his sack. "Don't worry, Rooks, I'm going to fight for my country. There are men arming themselves…" He looked at me as if he'd said enough. "Plenty of them."

I thumbed through a copy of the *Communist Manifesto* given to me by Gāters, then tossed it into the bin. "So are the Bolsheviks, it seems…"

He smirked. "I'd hold on tight to everything you own, Rooks. Every empire in the world is going to want their piece of "All the Russias." The Germans are here already. The British, the French, they'll be coming soon enough. It wouldn't surprise me if the Japanes…"

"Do the odds scare you?"

Seskis smiled. "Course they do. What frightens me more is the winning."

"How so?"

He leaned comfortably on his bag, looking a little like a man saddling up to a tavern bar. "If somehow we succeed, if we beat back all their enemies for them, we have to pray the Bolsheviks keep their word." He returned to his packing. "Throwing down our lives for strangers. Again. Maybe we are stupid peasants."

"And how are your vigilante mobs different?"

"If we win, we've won. Don't need to go begging for a promise."

I retrieved the *Manifesto* from the bin. It was *something* to read after all, better than counting cannon fire all night long. 'How many men do you think you can raise? Really Miķelis?"

"Don't know. But they got one more with me than without." He pulled his bag's drawstrings tight, snapped the buckle. "Things are about to get really complicated, Rooks. Life's been simple up to now."

He threw his bag over his shoulder and headed for the door.

"See ya, around Rooks. Try not to get killed."

I wandered down Wenden's twisty stone paths; the little town uncomfortably clogged with solders and ex-soldiers neither knowing quite where to go. Friends becoming enemies. Enemies becoming friends.

I passed under the high steeple of Saint John's ancient church. I knew this town well, all those relaxing summers. Off a side street, I found a little inn we'd stayed at fifteen years before. The woman there even spoke German, claiming she remembered our family. I somewhat doubted her, but appreciated the friendly sentiment. She gave me a small room atop the stairs, overlooking the busy Rīgas Iela, a little pot of flowers on the window desk. I stayed there a week before the remnants of my wages were spent. She let me remain another two nights, never replacing the flowers, before asking me to leave.

That night, I camped in an alcove between a restaurant and a little porcelain shop looking out over the crumbling, half buried remains of a Livonian castle. Built by the heroic Knights of the Sword, its snow-covered stones broke the surface here and there, a half-collapsed keep the last sign of glory long passed. The ugly newer tower of Count Sievers eclipsed much of my view, surpassing it in all ways but majesty.

I sat on that bag, propped against the restaurant wall, facing the old castle, a silent refugee trying to stay alive through the night. Frost covered my shoulders, glued my unshaven whiskers together. Passers-by stared, laughed, shuffled their feet a little faster away.

I lay there the following day.

And the next.

I passed a little tavern on Palasta Iela. A sign claimed they sought a shopkeeper. Inside, I was told the job was given to the owner's nephew. A good boy by all accounts, he needed the work.

I returned to my bag in the alleyway, ice water seeping into the indention where I sat. Soaked, I pulled my limbs close, fought the coming fever.

Stared at the castle.

I found myself knocking on a grey, weatherworn door. A tired, squint-eyed Juškevičs answered, his spectacles hanging from his shirt pocket.

"Wiktor?…Do you know the hour?"

"Why me, Heinrichs? I'm an aristocrat, rulers from birth."

There was a softness in his weary eyes. "Does it matter?"

"It does."

He released a slow breath, the warm air fogging his hanging lenses. "I read the letters, the ones to Vereshchagin"

That was not possible. "All of them?"

He nodded. "The major assigned me the task when you arrived." He shrugged innocently. "When I took command, I continued."

I stood there stunned.

He opened the door further. "Come in Wiktor, let's get you some soup."

Chapter Thirteen

The train tracks stretched to the horizon. Parallel rails drawing ever narrower, diminishing, vanishing where snow met darkening sky. Cold irons marching to infinity in the immeasurable Russian wilderness.

I thought we could fit all of Latvia between here and the skyline; so incomprehensibly vast was this land. All of Courland certainly. My whole homeland, all I'd fought for, was only another meaningless wedge in a far greater nation.

And yet I missed it so.

I straddled the rails, one foot on either side, the ash of my cigarette falling in the frozen mud between. A newly acquired habit: tobacco. One to calm the hunger pains, to warm fingers and lips, to keep the mind occupied during the long inactivity of military life.

To my left, my men filled every doorway, leaned against every column of the little wooden railway station. Some sat on its flat roof huddled by the fires glowing in the metal cylinders provided, those perched in the vacant trees across the tracks, forced to make due without such luxury.

Farther down the track, a group of our men lay in the snow firing at cans, bottles, and branches, all propped up on a skeletal wooden fence. I could hear the cheers of victory, the bitter moans of defeat. These were my troops now and they were going to practice marksmanship whether it made them 'undisciplined' or not. Among the lesser sins Vereshchagin would have noted.

They were lousy shots really but slowly improving. I'd bested most of them, finishing fifth in the last unit contest. I was secretly a little pleased with myself, even as their captain I had to be publicly disappointed with them. Not bad carrying two years rust from liaison duty.

And it had earned me some much-needed respect, imperative in my current situation. Especially, since I had such a hard time connecting with these Latvians.

But these soldiers should have been better shots. They needed to be if they were going to survive, if I was going to survive.

"Captain Rooks!" yelled the young Lett on the roof's edge. "The train is coming. I can see the smoke."

I peered north in the dimming light. I certainly couldn't see anything. Either he was mad, or his sight was far sharper than mine. If correct, he certainly should have done better in the marksmanship contest.

Yet slowly I saw the white-grey billows, only little candle wisps now, but thickening to a string of kettle puffs. They were coming, indeed. I could not help but feel the excitement.

"Alright men, let's get ready." They scrambled to their positions in front of the station. Several marksmen scampering up the coal chute ladders to take their sentry posts.

The train from Petrograd, I'd never get used to that name, bound for Moscow. The Bolshevik government was getting out, the Germans, the White Armies, the British all getting too close. Rīga was lost, and now St. Petersburg was at risk. Communists or not, they were retreating to the traditional tsarist capitol, the heart of the Russias. Symbolism be damned, they needed safety.

And it was up to the Latvian Riflemen to get them there.

I'd been given the responsibility to keep this station secure. Not much of a task, really. There were no crowds in the late winter weather to cheer or threaten them, and only a few nearby villages lay in the unfathomable immensity of Russia. Nothing around but isolated farmers who wanted to keep their eyes shut, to ignore every change in government. Just go about their simple lives.

I must admit I enjoyed the assignment. With all their pestering questions about my beliefs, nobody in the Bolshi staff had even inquired about my experience. It was my first military command for this army, any army. I had Juškevičs to thank for that I was sure, but I didn't really think this new government had any choice. Things were stretched too thin to have 'liaison' officers, administrative officers, anyone really who wasn't in the combat chain. Except propaganda officers, of course, those were mandatory. And I wasn't quite ready to join their ranks.

The train was visible, a shiny black cylinder, growing larger and larger, an expanding shadow on a snow-white canvas. I could discern the separate cars, found myself wondering which one the party leaders were in. That being information privileged only to those Latvian units actually onboard.

Well, I had a bet with Juškevičs and I planned to win it. All this socialist sharing be damned …

As the train rolled up, I could see how heavily protected it was. Men atop the engine, leering out of doors at the end of every car, hanging tightly to steps and ladders as they approached the station, rifles at the ready. The entire government of the largest nation on Earth aboard, if something should happen …

Well, Russia couldn't be thrown into more chaos.

I stepped off the tracks, climbing up to the station. As the engine passed, I could see Lieutenant Līcis sitting on the lip of the coal car behind the conductor's booth. When he saw me, he grinned, pulling phantom strings as if to sound the horn.

I could hear his 'Toot…Toot' as the engine slowed, releasing its steamy sighs, finally coming to a halt beneath the coal funnel.

I motioned to my men, the lever pulled, the black shale falling into the payload chute, a grey haze thrown up into the twilight sky.

At regular intervals, riflemen approached the train, halting before every door, at every step mindful of any person that wanted to get on…or off.

I walked over to the engine. Līcis's face was slightly blackened from sitting near mounds of coal during the long journey. He was wrapped in several layers of clothes, the outermost being a thick yellow-brown fur coat. It made him look rather like a great stuffed bear hung high in some Wenden banquet hall. As with most things, he didn't seem to mind.

"Hello, Herberts. Any trouble?"

He tipped his cap back, a band of pink skin visible along his scalp. "No, Captain, everything's been top efficiency. Major Juškevičs even had a few loaves of bread delivered at the last station."

I grinned. Always so positive Līcis, even when fleeing the capitol.

"Good…. good." I took a quick look about. "And in which car might I find the richest butter?" his reflecting smile showing he caught my intent, "For all this bread, Lieutenant?"

He laughed his polite laugh. "Fraid you've been outbid, Captain."

"What? You're joking?" Oh, no…

"Sorry, sir. Butter's hard to come by this winter. It's a seller's market." He patted his breast. "Vodka warms the heart, delivered at the last fuel stop as well."

Damn Juškevičs. "And you call yourself a communist, Herberts?"

"More of a 'Socialized opportunist,' sir."

There was a slight disturbance a few cars down. I could see a thin man in a small cap standing in one of the train's open doorways, shaking hands with a growing crowd of my soldiers.

"Excuse me," I shouted up to Līcis, quickly parting his company.

I marched over to the car; the young man perhaps a few years older than me, was precariously balanced on the exit step, grabbing hand after hand of excited soldiers.

This was all I needed, my men distracted, grouped in one spot, while some assassin armed with pistol or dynamite crawled into the caboose.

"Alright, alright, break it up." A few moved off, but most kept reaching for the man. I forced myself into the crowd, shoving by them, standing between them and this celebrity, an epidemic of disappointment sweeping their faces.

"To your positions. Now!" They moved away begrudgingly, slowly backing to their assigned duties. This wouldn't help my popularity.

I turned to the man in the train. "I'm afraid I need you to return to the car, this a security risk."

The man sneered, said something under his breath, but moved back inside.

A moment later, the signal went off, the train having finished refueling. Our men at each end of the station gave me 'all secure' signs. I waved back, and the engine began to churn, slowly pulling car after car away, resuming the long trip to Moscow.

My eyes followed making sure our guards kept watch for any late assailants that might lie in the snow beyond the station. When it had finally disappeared into the distance, I let the men slowly relax, gave them an hour to prepare for their own trip. Free, they clumped into groups, gabbing, buzzing about their encounter. Annoyed, I grabbed the arm of one who had mobbed the car. "Who was that anyway, on the step, Corporal?"

He actually rolled his eyes, answered as if I should have known; as if my very authority was called into questioned by my not knowing.

"Only, the greatest Latvian Bolshevik, sir. The man who stood up to the British Empire…"

Chapter Fourteen

Summer 1918, Moscow

High in the heavens a silver cross burned red in the setting sunlight, as His must have at the moment of Ascendancy, while far below, the terrestrial crowd of Letts stared intensely at me excitement and anticipation in their eyes. As I spoke, the man recoiled, horrified at the truth of my words, my opponent quickly pulled something from his belt, violently rushing toward me.

And thrust his knife into my chest.

I staggered back, ripping the blade from the assassin's grip, trying desperately to pull it from my wounded breast. I lost my footing, fell hard to the wooden floor. I could hear the roar of Latvians cheering, clapping.

Betrayed.

I let out a few gurgling moans, a desperate cry.

And I died.

A nudge. A nudge in lieu of Resurrection.

"Get up, Wiktor. We have to change the scene."

The voice of God?

No, of Juškevičs. Somewhat the letdown.

He kicked me again. "C'mon, get your ass off the stage."

I sat up slowly: "A little respect for the dead, Heinrichs."

"If I didn't respect you alive, why would I respect you dead?"

I got to my feet, stumbled away, the little wooden stage trembling under my weight. I thought it might be a tad insufficient for the locale, this collection of planks hastily assembled in the middle of the Kremlin's Cathedral Square. A crude, temporary construction, a brown smudge in the expansive courtyard surrounded by great golden domes, towering swallowtail fortifications, and the five spires of the eternal Cathedral of the Assumption; all looming down in the summer twilight. A plaza where Imperial coronation festivals had been held, across whose stones the leaders of the Orthodox Church had led a thousand grand processions to its Four Holy Cathedrals; and the spot where nervous virgins shuffled their feet as Ivan the Terrible selected his brides. Used by the tsars for centuries to greet foreign dignitaries or for the Imperial family to enjoy the greatest musical and theatre performers of their times, it was now the sole dominion of a bored regiment of Latvians.

The surrounding marvels fading dull after months of duty, the soldiers had grown to staging plays to entertain themselves. And so awful were these, such an insult to the art of theater that the officers had decided to show them how it was really done.

I wasn't sure ours were any better.

Of course, there weren't that many actors to choose from. The Latvians had been separated into nine Red regiments, eight sent off to the far corners of the globe to fight the tsarist loyalists, the separatists, and all those empires trying to grab a piece of Russia from the new government. The 9th was garrisoned alone to guard the Kremlin, which in effect, had made us Moscow's police force, or the Bolshevik watchdogs as we called ourselves.

For now, at least. Things were changing.

My acquaintances had managed to stay together, Juškevičs and Līcis both commanding companies in the 9th. Only Gāters had been sent away with the 4th to fight the turncoat Czech People's Army. A move that had made the ardent Bolshevik very excited, desperate as he was to fight for the cause, while the ambitious Juškevičs had sulked, being stuck 'sitting around.'

Me? I was happy to be far away from the front lines, death of boredom being preferable to death by cannon fire.

Not that our off duty time was dreary. I had never seen a city so large, seemingly without end. We spent hours wandering the town trying to take it all in. Moscow had not the architectural beauty of Rīga or St. Petersburg; instead it was a never-ending series of drab grey and brown buildings stretching out from the Kremlin epicenter, a numbing uniformity broken only by the occasional reflective dome or jutting spire of an Orthodox church.

I never dared explore alone, often forcing Līcis or Juškevičs to accompany me. While the revolution had been relatively bloodless in Petrograd, it had been plenty violent here with fatal clashes still a daily event. Indeed, well into this summer, gangs of armed protestors still prowled the streets ready to confront any adherents to opposite ideologies. And with so many dead, mourners took daily acts of vengeance, escalating the blood cycle in beatings, shooting, and arson. Others used this shrouding chaos to commit theft, burglary and their own innumerable heinous crimes. To say the Moscow streets were safe would be the boldest of lies.

And yet, there was also something grand afoot, a potential for greatness, a real sense of hope in the air. Writers and philosophers, students and laborers, all mixed in the cafes, taverns and restaurants, walked in animated discussions along the Moskva River, and debated issues on the artisan walkways of elegant Arbat Street. Late evening gatherings were filled with people from throughout the world, pilgrims here to partake in the rebirth of society itself. Everywhere there were Latvians and Poles, Jews and Byelorussians, Lithuanians and Romanians, Czechs and Serbs. A sprinkling of Westerners bringing support from the great cities of the world: Paris, London, Madrid, New York, Mexico City, and Rio. Even a few words of German might be caught on the wind, sprouting from some thought provoking discussion in the late hours of the evening. All mixing in such numbers, that nationalism, religion, ethnicity and class seemed distinctions of sullen, stale minds. There was a sense of history, that this enlightened generation would finally address society's age-old ills.

And then there were the women. As a young man, I could not help but notice: tall and blonde, painted in make-up, and sporting jewelry as if the revolution had never happened. Never in Rīga had there been such beauties. So great were their numbers that a soldier might spend every ruble of his wages in just one sunny afternoon distributing flowers to the smallest fraction of girls he fancied. Many a night my twenty-four year old heart was crushed by the rejection of my just-met true love, only to see a far lovelier vision crossing my way at the corner.

And there was something electric about a city, where in equal measure the very next street might bring Venus incarnate, the bold trial of a grand new philosophy, or the deadly menace of armed thugs bent on destruction. By comparison, the gentle hills and forests of Courland suddenly seemed tame.

No, Moscow was not a boring town.

The library was quieter in latest evening, when I found it easier to concentrate. No distracting rallies or speeches in the courtyards outside. No drumbeats from military marches on Red Square or cries of crushed protests passing over the Kremlin walls.

I pulled my pen from the forms, placed it pensively on the desk. In the autumn Moscow's universities offered courses in two areas of interest: anatomy and physics. My garrison responsibilities would not allow time for both.

Anatomy would inevitably lead toward medicine and a doctor's life was tempting. Certainly it would keep me in good stead socially, to again don a little of the airs, the trappings of my aristocratic past, and beyond this tenuous communist state the profession would return a handsome, livable wage. And to rescue a few lives, when I'd seen so many lost…yes, this would help my soul tremendously. There were no drawbacks to such a noble pursuit.

But in physics I could lay a foundation stone for astronomy, and in this I could claim the heavens, near eternal, untouchable by man. With Earth a smoking cataclysm, it seemed attractive, comforting to study His more celestial creations, to know there was something ordered somewhere in the universe.

I laughed internally. And, if the Bolsheviks really planned on turning all the churches to planetariums, as was now being debated, well then there might be plenty of opportunity to report my findings. I imagined myself, standing at the pulpit, a hushed congregation stretching out before me inside the glistening halls of the Church of Christ the Savior. Their approving roars as I proclaimed: "Comrades, we have just found another moon around Jupiter!"

I laughed again, pausing in my thoughts to assess the musty wooden shelves on either side of me. A sparse collection of books in the Rifleman's Library, certainly, but it was growing. A few Latvian tomes snuck in between the Russian masterpieces, the distinct letters on the spine upsetting the rhythmic ranks of their Cyrillic neighbors. I hoped they wouldn't be removed as improper or nationalistic. Why was Russian the accepted language of all the Workers, but Latvian the diction of a nation? When Latvia had never been a nation? Was this ironic or hypocritical? I couldn't decide.

I pulled out a collection of Alunāns's poems. All dedicated to cultural identity, all screaming for a Latvian state. But would Latvia ever be a nation? It seemed less likely now. In desperation, Lenin had given it away with countless other territories when he signed the Brest-Litovsk Peace Treaty in March. The only way to stop the advancing Germans: Here, just have the land. Leave us alone.

It had cost him support among the Soviets, even his own Bolsheviks. And it had the Riflemen screaming betrayal.

Justifiably so. If I went home now, by the agreement I'd be a Prisoner of War. No parents, no Anne, nothing. A locked compound wasn't much of a homecoming.

So instead, we were marooned in Russia, forced to live in a palace. How strange the twists in life's path.

I picked up the pen again. What other such turns might lay ahead? Maybe I shouldn't count too much on those courses in the autumn.

Captain Jēkabsons appeared from behind a Spartan bookcase. My assassin in yesterday's play. Short, muscular, compact, the type of man who looked impossible to tip over, but really hoped somebody would try. He donned an offended air at my every appearance. Though he barely knew me, he seemed to thoroughly despise me. I hadn't bothered to inquire why.

He carried books in his hands, a scowl on his face. No greeting as he passed me, he found an open shelf, and started to shelve the volumes.

I tried to bridge the gap. "Hello Captain."

He said nothing.

I threw out another olive branch. "Is that Krišjānis Barons in your hands? I rather liked his *daina* collections." *If not his politics, but then manners are all about the unsaid, aren't they Jēkabsons?*

He let out a small sigh, as if acknowledging me was a defeat. "So do I."

Ah, victory! "Where did you get these?"

"In Jelgava." He briskly shelved the last one. "About time I got rid of them. I've been lugging these books around for years."

He squatted on his haunches, looking through a lower shelf for some book.

"Jelgava? Are you from Courland?"

"Whole family is."

"So am I."

His answer was slow in coming, suspicious. "You know Rooks, they told me you were from Rīga."

I frowned. "No, from Courland as well."

"Which town?"

Shit. "A farm…near Jelgava."

"I see." He pulled out some book, turned it upright, and reshelved it. "Why the interrogation, Rooks?"

"Only being friendly." I pressed my pen to the paper. "Would I be too much the inquisitor to ask which town you hail from?"

"No town. A hovel, twenty people, off the Kaltenbach Estate road."

"Kaltenbach? My sister married..." perhaps it would be better not to complete that sentence.

He folded his arms, looked at me oddly.

"I should say, my sister was married near there."

"How did you slip through the cracks, Rooks, and end up guarding the Kremlin? Bribery?" Not waiting for an answer, he turned and started to walk away. "Do the political commissars know we've got a landed German sitting inside our ranks?"

I shouted after him. "They do! And they know I've been fighting for the cause, Captain! Can you say the same?"

His squatty body passed behind the bookcases, but his voice carried over them. "Of course, I can. I believe in it."

I went back to my writing, trying to concentrate on my academic decisions. I had no time for unfounded accusations. Ungrateful Letts.

A moment later, Jēkabsons came back with another load of books, and slammed them down on the desk before me, eclipsing the top of my sheet.

"Tell me Rooks," his face in mine. "Who did your sister marry, again?"

I met Juškevičs in the shadow of Saint Basil's Cathedral, shading the end of Red Square, its great tear-drop domes like the swirling, multicolored turbans of eight Eastern wise men sitting in judgment of all these changes before them. Stoically, they watched the silly marching men, the reactive speeches, and the changing tenants of the Kremlin. Knowing they'd outlive them as they had all the others.

Juškevičs was squinting, his eyes shrunken to unknowable brown slits, the spot of sun on his face revealing tiny blue veins flowing across his forehead. "So, how's your day been?"

I frisked my pocketed shirt for a cigarette. "Exhausting. Vandals, protestors, anarchists, you name them, I probably arrested them today."

He said nothing, only silently handed me a cigarette.

"Thank you. Just another day, really. And you?"

"Fine."

I searched my pocket for a match. Juškevičs's sunspot had dissolved leaving him in the cooling shade. Yet he still squinted.

"Going out to Khodynka for the holiday, Heinrichs?"

"Yes. And you?"

"I'm having drinks with Alisa."

More silence. He didn't seem very verbose this afternoon. I gazed up at the sky, purple-black along the horizon. "Looks like we have some thunder coming in." I found a match, gave a quick glance to Juškevičs. "I heard half of the Congress walked out over Brest."

"Yep." Another solemn, one word answer.

"The Left Socialists in particular."

He only nodded.

We stood there awhile smoking, watching crowds mull about on mammoth Red Square, a few worriers beginning to scatter before the storms grew near. Farther back, beyond the Kremlin walls, I saw two men secured by a rigging of wire and rope climbing the spire of Savior Tower. When they reached the top, they worked for the longest time, discarding the tsar's double-eagle emblem and adding a hokey looking red star. A neon beacon in the blackening sky.

I used this to breech Juškevičs's self-induced silence.

"Look at that! Those are horrible. A cheap wooden star on top of a tower like…"

"They're rubies."

"Rubies?"

He shoved his hands in his pockets, rocked back and forth on his heels. "Hundreds of them, worth a fortune."

I nudged him with my forearm. "I guess they really are communists then."

"Why?"

"If they can make something so valuable, look so bad." I laughed.

He didn't. "I'd watch your language, Rooks."

"What do you mean?" Why was he acting this way?

"I mean be careful what you say. People are beginning to notice."

I shrugged, took a puff. "It was just a joke Heinrichs."

"We're still on duty Captain. You'd better call me Major."

With the summer rains, they'd move the play's second performance inside to an ornately pained pink and white tsarist banquet hall: Cherubs and angels, damsels and wild beasts peering from the baroque ceiling. A far more appropriate venue to kill a king, I thought.

Jēkabsons stood in his worker's attire, shouting out into the sticky evening air.

"You, sir, are the enemy. Tyrants such as yourself cannot be allowed to shame our people in oppression any longer."

"Quit your prattling lackey, go and fetch your master some soup." Boos and hisses sprang from the crowd as I spat these words. At some level, I wished I'd read the king's part before accepting Juškevičs's offer to play it. It seemed the audience felt me a little too appropriate in the role.

"Enough, my lord, I will deliver a far hotter meal to you than porridge!" And again he pulled the knife from his belt. A touch of genuine fear, as I saw the velocity of his attack, the way the painted blade reflected some wayward lamp beam. There was something too real in the motion.

He shoved the knife in again, finding the spot beneath my blanket-cape. I felt the impact, minimally absorbed by the pillow beneath my tunic. Only a fake wooden blade but thrust with real power. Harder, I thought, than it need be.

I pinned the weapon to my chest, stumbled back, fell leaden to the hall floor. Moaned my death cries once again.

As the hero made his triumphant last speech, immortalizing man's struggle with tyranny, I chanced to spy up at him from those moist floor boards. He walked in a circle, trumpeting his soliloquy to the cheering soldiers. As he stepped over my corpse, his eyes caught mine. There seemed true hatred in his glance.

Such fine acting, Comrade Jēkabsons.

The lightning flashes no longer illuminated the speckled window shade, at last leaving the room dark and still. Pounding thunder had ceased to shake the little apartment from outside, a warm silence settling in after the passing summer storms.

I stroked her blonde hair, gently arranging it in a fan across her bare shoulders. She always slept in this same angle. Legs and hips intertwined with mine, but her naked back at a distance, our bodies forming a 'Y' on the mattress.

Such a nice way to spend a holiday, even if it wasn't really my own. When the Latvian regiment celebrated, I celebrated.

And I couldn't think of a better way to do so.

I ran a finger down the slope of her back, lying to myself that I hoped not to disturb her. Let it circle round where her flesh melted into mine, and softly drew up again, meandering toward her shoulder. I found her body enveloping, consuming, with a thick frame that might someday don considerable weight, but now, in her youth, only pulled her flesh tighter, sheathing her in alluring canvases of smooth, taut skin. All strung between womanly curves. How I adored it.

I smiled. Strange then, how she laughed at my own. Made little off jokes in the calm between lovemaking. Perhaps, that was the time to make them? When a lover is full of pride, least threatened by a minor puncture to self-esteem. I wondered if a German girl would do so? Or a Latvian?

I thought not.

I had been coming to Alisa's for weeks. It hadn't taken long to get her to give up this body. A little vodka, a lot of dancing. And once she succumbed, how she seemed to enjoy each indulgence, the movements growing faster, more risqué with every meeting.

And yet, there was a distance. She would still not kiss me, not fully. A peck on the cheek, a quick clasp of the lips, but not a kiss of real passion. Nothing even as heartfelt as that Latvian girl's during the parade years ago. Were all Russians like this?

I tried to pierce the veil of her sleeping mind. *"I will give into carnal desires, it is what we both want, yes? But my soul? Not yet. You have not nearly won that."*

The opposite of Courland's high society, where a maiden might kiss you early in the courtship and talk so romantically of a future, of true love, houses and children, but for the sensualities you must wait and wait. And wait, again. A heart given first, more freely than a body. The less valuable commodity? A bit naïve the Russians would say.

So different. I wondered which was right?

The thunder returned. A knock at the door.

Should I get it? That might be the gentlemanly thing to do. But perhaps Alisa didn't want it advertised that I was here?

Another knock. A continuous pounding. With an anguished moan, Alisa drew herself up, pulling the sheet off the bed to wrap about her, leaving me bare on the sweaty mattress.

She went into the next room. I could hear her talking to someone at the outside door. Her mother? Friends? Another lover? Who?

And what was the hour?

The words grew quicker, harsher, too faint, too fast, for my comprehension. Soon,

I heard the door shut, her footsteps on the floorboards.

She returned, the damp sheet clinging in the humid night to every nuance of her form. The trace of a nipple, the slight indention of her navel ...

I felt warm desires rising again. I reposed on the bed, let her have a good look at my body, naked on her mattress. I patted the bed, coyly smiled. "Is he gone?"

In a tired, slightly exasperated Russian, she said: "It is for you."

At the door was Līcis, his face a mask of worry. Behind him the world had disappeared, a thick grey fog dissolving everything but a running automobile. Between the mists and the glare of the car's invasive headlights, I could barely tell it was he.

I quickly buttoned my shirt. "Herberts, what are you doing here?"

"We gotta go, Captain. There's been another revolution."

"What?"

"Yeah, all hell's breaking loose."

Chapter Fifteen

"Things are going mad Wiktor. The German Ambassador's dead. It looks like we're at war again. People are being arrested, and nobody knows who's in charge."

I slammed the rear car door, took one last look at Alisa, a slight wave as she shut her apartment door, but her expression unreadable in the thickening fog.

Līcis was in the front passenger seat, some young soldier his driver. I leaned forward from the back. "Tell me everything, Herberts, from the beginning."

He half turned to speak to me as the car reversed into the street. "Alright, we got this call that there's been trouble at the German embassy and the Kremlin's sending a bunch of a diplomats over to deal with it. Nothing new there, right? Watch the pole Kaspars!"

The car lurched in a sudden turn, accelerated forward. Līcis shook his head. "But I kinda knew there must be a big problem because our own officials wouldn't go without protection. So, who do they send? My guys. A whole squad."

I leaned closer, finding it difficult to hear over the revving engine. "Which officials?"

He held up three fingers. "Chicherin, Karakhan, and…"

"Really?"

"And get this: Dzerzhinskii!" Even in the darkened car, I could see his eyes light up.

"Dzerzhinskii? The Cheka's Dzerzhinskii?"

"The same. I was guarding the goddamn head of the secret police!"

"Incredible."

A deep pothole tossed me against the leather interior, demanding a glance out the window. We were barreling down some unidentifiable street, the great black hulks of buildings rolling by on either side like mammoth steam ships cruising on a foggy sea.

Līcis continued. "That's nothing. When we get to the German embassy, there's another Bolshevik big fish waiting for us: Radek. And he's carrying his own gun

Wiktor. I mean even with all us around to protect him, he's sporting this huge cannon. It looked like a siege weapon. I swear to you it was as long as my thigh." He held his hands wide, his shadowed face framed by the smoky grey of the windshield behind. "I mean, these are our dignitaries headed into the embassy for Christ's sake. Just like a little army."

The car lurched again, taking some corner at full gear. "So, we get inside and the place is just shattered. Turns out a bomb went off right at the bottom of the stairs. They got Ambassador Mirbach's body lying under a sheet. The assistant German ambassador Riezler, or the ambassador-in-training, or whatever the hell he is, is acting insane. Shouting, screaming about how the assassins fired at his head and this is grounds for restarting the war."

"What assassins? Who were they?"

"Two guys from the Left Socialist Revolutionaries. Came in sometime after two o'clock demanding to see the ambassador about an urgent matter. Riezler claims they had documents from Dzerzhinskii himself authorizing the meeting. You should have seen his eyes when he heard that!"

"Could they have been real?"

Līcis sat forward in his seat, trying to see anything in the mists. "Only if Dzerzhinskii's one hell of an actor! Who knows, they could've forged anything. Anyway, Riezler told us when Ambassador Mirbach came down, the killers pulled out guns and started shooting. Take a left here, Kaspars."

The car shuddered into its turn. "I saw the place, Wiktor, there were bullet holes everywhere. They had chased the ambassador through the living room, and next thing you knew one of 'em threw a bomb and Mirbach is dead."

The car revved into full throttle, I clung to the vibrating seat in front of me.

Līcis turned back to me. "Then these murderers scaled a three meter fence, hopped into a waiting sedan, and disappeared into the city."

"My God, Herberts."

There was a horrible thud, something large bounced over the hood, ricocheting off into the swallowing fog.

"Tell me that wasn't a person Kaspars!" demanded Līcis.

"A dog, sir."

"There's more, Wiktor. So this under-ambassador was saying that our officials weren't appeasement enough. That if they didn't get Comrade Lenin over to the Embassy right now, he was going to telegraph Berlin and tell 'em to declare war. I mean this little German ass was demanding our Head of State, show up, and show up now.

"So at five o'clock Lenin showed up! And Riezler was calling him on the carpet. Really, no respect at all. Demanding an apology, saying if the assassins aren't caught and punished immediately, he's assuming Lenin's government authorized this and Brest is dissolved. I would have punched the son of a bitch."

My body felt the forward pull of deceleration. "And Comrade Lenin?"

"He just asked technical questions. Where were the shots fired? Describe the assailants? What time did they arrive? No emotion at all. Completely cold, as if somebody had merely dropped a few eggs on the market floor. Too bad, but it happens everyday."

The car was slowing to a stop, stuck behind others confused by the weather.

Līcis tapped my arm to draw my attention back to him. "Meanwhile, Dzerzhinskii's livid about the bombing, finds out that the killers are being sheltered by Popov's sailors in the Pokrovskii Barracks. So he goes down there, without us, and demands that they give up the assassins or he'll have the whole Central Committee of the Left S.R.'s shot."

Kaspars interrupted. "It's really congested up ahead, sir."

Līcis ignored him. "So what do they do? The sailors arrest Dzerzhinskii instead. Suddenly, the Head of the Cheka's a hostage!"

"My God!"

"These sailors are out in force. There's a state of emergency. Colonel Vācietis's meeting with Lenin right now. Nobody's around, they're all at the front, so they're trying to get all our guys back from holiday before these Left's sailors decide to storm the Kremlin. Try finding a few thousand Latvians in this fog quickly." He smiled with his usual optimism. "Luckily I knew where you'd be these days, Wiktor. See what you miss, when you spend the night in bed lover boy."

I only sneered.

Līcis turned to Kaspars. "Why aren't we moving, Private?"

"I don't know sir." I opened the rear door, stuck my head out. Up ahead, the fog shrouded silhouette of another vehicle. I could tell by the phantoms hovering ahead of it, that men were stopping cars.

I sat back down.

"What is it Wiktor?"

"I don't know."

Kaspars honked the horn.

Līcis got out, and as the ranking officer, I felt obligated to join him.

As we wandered toward the next car, Līcis asked. "Are you armed?"

"No."

"All I've got is a pistol. The private has a rifle in the automobile."

I could see a man on the side of the road open the passenger door of the car ahead of me, reach in and try to pull someone out. Yells and screams burst through the night.

I started to rush to their aid, but Līcis grabbed my arm.

"Damn." Līcis cursed. "It's Popov's sailors, they're taking hostages."

"What?"

"Bolsheviks, they've been seizing them all night."

Two more phantoms approached. One screamed: "Get in your car. Now!" The two of us backed away, Līcis motioned for Kaspars to unwind his window.

The men in the fog were still advancing, while a sailor beyond seemed to be beating a screaming victim into submission.

"Kaspars," whispered, Līcis. "Can you pull this thing around?"

I looked back. There were several cars behind penning us in. I went to the next, motioning for the driver to roll down his window. The young man looked frightened and refused. I tapped on the glass, but he only shook his head, no.

Two of the sailors had reached Līcis, screaming questions, orders. I knew they could see his Rifleman uniform.

Kaspars stepped out of the car. One of the shadows yelled: "Get back in there!"

Our private ignored the order and pointed his rifle at the sailor. I could hear Līcis calmly say: "We're on government business, I need you to let us through."

I came up behind. "And that man on the ground, release him."

With Kaspars pointing the gun, they silently backed away. To follow Līcis's instructions? I had doubts.

I could see more men coming through the mist. A dozen? Two dozen?

Līcis said: "Leave the car, we need to get out of here."

The three of us moved on foot down the line of vehicles. Found a man in a horse-drawn cart. I thought briefly of taking it, but there was no time. More and more shadows were appearing on either side of stopped automobiles.

Quickly I crossed the street, the poor lamplight preventing me from being exactly sure where we were. Perhaps, Strastnoi Bulvar …

There were more figures coming the opposite way. Allies? Enemies? Or innocents? Anyone unidentified was too risky.

I heard yells behind. A couple of the figures had started to jog our way, a few now fully running.

Kaspars brought his gun to bear, but I quickly whispered: "No." Instead, the three of us ran toward a side alley. There was an entrance to a Georgian restaurant, long since closed for the night. I could hear more shouts coming in the blackening fog, forcing us deeper into the alley.

Our pace built until we were sprinting. With no lamps in this back street, our vision was nearly useless. Only the faint glow of the city lights on the clouds above gave us any ambient illumination.

There were more trailing shouts, though we should have been invisible to them at this distance.

I heard Līcis scream. A step later, something hard and metallic smashed against my forearm. I let out a loud forbidden curse, a calling siren for any that followed. A large iron fence closed off the end of the alley. Invisible under these conditions, I had run into a post full force. At my feet was Līcis, a brutal scrape across his nose. Kaspars rushed up behind, halting before he fell over his officers.

"Are you alright? Did you break your nose?"

Līcis grimaced. "Not my face, I think I tore-up my ankle on the crossbar."

Kaspars and I pulled him to his feet, allowed him to put weight on the injured leg. He winced a little, but said "Not a problem, I'm fine." Līcis was always fine.

We listened a moment, the alley quiet.

"Do you think they've gone?" asked Līcis, massaging the wound on his face.

"I don't know."

"Well Captain? What should we do?" The older of us, Līcis almost seemed to enjoy his junior status, throwing these decisions over to me.

"Over the fence." I found a foothold on a crossbar and climbed over, avoiding the spikes atop its posts. Kaspars handed me the rifle through the grill and then helped Līcis surmount it. He grimaced noticeably on landing.

The private followed. I handed the gun back to him.

"How far are we from headquarters, Kaspars?"

"Six, maybe seven city blocks, Captain."

Līcis scowled. "Four at most."

Either way, new voices behind propelled us farther along into the night.

We walked for a few minutes, taking the alley turn, desperate for any light in the sullen blackness. There was little talk. We simply wanted out. At last I could see the white orbs of street lamps, feel a comparative breeze, even hear the unmuffled pops and stutters of a passing automobile. An exit.

And then the light suddenly cut off again.

For a moment I thought a thick patch of haze had simply blown by eclipsing the lamps. Until there were voices, then shadows passing through night's misty curtains, heading briskly toward us.

"Shit." whispered Līcis.

We could see their silhouettes: five men standing shoulder to shoulder, fencing in the alley's exit. In the thickened night, I found no facial features, no dress, nothing but four large, husky shapes, the fifth shorter but bulldog broad. These men whispered to themselves; the words just below audible, the language indiscernible at this distance.

The phantoms marched nearer, a compressing wall shortening the space in the alley with every second.

"Lieutenant, they've got rifles" noted young Kaspars in his lowest voice.

Indeed they did, long thin rectangles swung from shoulder to hands as they advanced. I could hear the bolts lock from here.

Līcis gritted his teeth. "What do you recommend, Wiktor?"

I was afraid to speak. Utter Latvian and they'd know me a Bolshevik. My Russian would never pass for native, nor our uniforms at close distance.

"I'm not sure."

Kaspars started to raise his weapon, but Līcis pulled it down. Outnumbered, any threat would only get us massacred.

Silently, they marched closer, too compact, too numerous to shove through. I wanted to flee, my body tugging at my unresolved mind, but I'd never pass the alley turn behind before they fired. Yet, each step nearer only increased their accuracy, made more lethal the moment of truth.

Somehow, we needed their identity while still masking our own. Before one demanded my name with a gun barrel pressed into my chest.

A few had their rifles raised. There was no time.

"Parlez vous français?" I yelled.

"What?" spat Līcis.

I could see one lower his gun, two others turning to their neighbors muttering confused whispers in the night fog.

"Je ne parle pas russe!"

The short one called out: "Who are you?" The accent familiar. "Identify yourself."

Līcis let out a long breath. "Thank God, Wiktor. Latvians."

I nearly fainted with relief. "Yes, thank God, Herberts. I was out of French."

I threw open the barracks door, helping to support Līcis, who had developed a painful limp. Inside the musty, smoked filled room a thin assortment of officers looked up nearly in unison. Then as quickly returned to their musings.

Juškevičs ran over, aided me with Līcis. Helped to sit him in a chair.

"He scraped his ankle. We had some trouble."

"It's nothing" said Līcis. "Just need a sip of alcohol."

"Popov's sailors?" Juškevičs asked.

"Yeah."

He relayed a vodka bottle to Līcis. "Did they know you were Latvian? They might have ignored you."

They had seen Līcis and Kaspars's uniforms at the car; there was little doubt…

"Why do you think so, Heinrichs?"

"They want to keep our men out of it. A couple thousand sailors can't stop us, not all of us, at least."

Līcis took a sip of vodka. "Anything new happening, Major?"

"The Left S.R.'s have seized the telegraph office, Herberts. They're sending messages to all of Russia, all the world, saying that they're in charge." Juškevičs couldn't hide the fear on his face. "Renewing the war with Germany, calling the Bolsheviks agents of Berlin."

I started. And the regiment was just waiting in their bunks? "Then why are you all sitting here? Why aren't we out fighting this?"

Juškevičs's face grew anguished. "Men are still trickling in, Colonel Vācietis is meeting with Comrade Lenin as we speak…and there is some debate on …on the merits of what the Left Socialists have to say…"

The way his voice trailed off, left little doubt what he meant.

It was nearly 1:00 a.m. and the arguments raged over and over. They might ebb for a while in morning exhaustion, but every time a new group of officers returned from holiday, the same issues would cycle again. Little pockets of debate round every electric light in the barracks, like blinded moths colliding above the campfires.

Captain Jēkabsons pounded his fist on the table. "Too much time in Germany. Lenin's their patsy. They financed the Revolution, put him in charge to give everything away." He shouted to the men. "What a sound investment! He promised us our homeland and handed it to the kaiser months later." A few nervous cheers followed his remarks.

It was late, my head hurt, my arm throbbed, and I'd listened to this idealistic runt for hours. Enough. I got off my bunk, entered the fray.

"What choice did he have? Really Captain?"

Jēkabsons glared when he saw that the dissenting voice was mine.

I took off my hat, spread out my hands, beseeching them all. "Be realistic my friends. We can't fight the world all at once. There are a thousand tsarist loyalists coming in from Europe every day." I turned to Juškevičs sitting at the table. "The British, French and Americans are plotting our destruction." I sought undecided eyes in the gloom. "The Czechs have turned on us. The Japanese are prancing around Siberia. Of course, Lenin made peace; it was the only hope of stopping the Germans from rolling into Petrograd."

I threw my cap on the table. "Let us kill the wolves, before fighting the bear." Somewhere, somebody clapped. Juškevičs quietly added: "Well said, Wiktor."

Jēkabsons gave no pause, pointing directly at me. "Lenin gave away our country, don't you remember that Rooks? Betrayed his promise." He turned to his fellows. "New philosophies, but the same old Russians! Any lie to keep us fighting for them." There was a swell of agreement outside the lamplight.

"How can he keep his promise if the Revolution doesn't survive?"

He moved into the crowd, taking the argument to them. "How many Latvians are out there dying? On the Volga? In the Crimea? In the Urals? All who think their sacrifice is for their homeland. A wage the Bolsheviks can't pay."

I slapped a palm on the table. "The Germans already had all of Latvia, Jēkabsons. Be truthful. What Comrade Lenin bought us was time."

He stayed with them, back to me. "Of course, Captain Rooks would agree to the occupation…he's a German."

I could feel their eyes turn on me. So many officers I didn't know, judging me, labeling me.

My words could not be colder. "I'm from Courland. As you are…"

Līcis interrupted sitting on the floor, his back propped against a table leg. "I was in the embassy. I saw the way Lenin reacted to the German officials. Hard. Cold. He's no stooge of theirs."

"But he still came when they called. At their disposal…" Jēkabsons made a mocking, submissive bow.

I took command again: "Given the situation, how could he not? What kind of…"

There was a knock at the door. A staff sergeant popped his head in.

"Colonel Vācietis is back. He wants you all on the plaza in five minutes."

Juškevičs asked: "What's the early word?"

"Preparation for assault on the telegraph office, Major."

Juškevičs looked around at the assembly, his voice steady, strong. How he had grown into leadership these past years. "There it is. Our Commander is going… Do we follow?"

There was only silence.

"We've got a meeting in five minutes."

They uttered no sound. Each man fearful to be the first. Even Jēkabsons. Even I.

Juškevičs pushed back his glasses. "Well boys? Are we at war with Germany… or not?"

The smoke from the mortar shells billowed from the walls of the Central Post and Telegraph Office, mixing with the remainder of the night's fog to block out most of the early morning sunlight. The humidity coated my face, demanding I constantly wipe away tickling beads of sweat and moisture. My listless men supported the artillery brigade, keeping away the protestors, the curious, and those with 'disruptive' potential. I patrolled our ranks trying to stop any brutality toward the captured as they were lead away. There would be plenty of official brutality awaiting the Left Socialist Revolutionaries soon enough, they didn't need an improvisational harassment right now.

I felt a bit of morning drizzle. More rain? Or had the thick air finally condensed to liquid around us? I didn't care. As soon as this was over I was going to spend the day in bed. Let my sergeant mind the men and fight the weather.

Juškevičs came trotting over to me. "Let's go Rooks."

I didn't even try to hide my disappointment. "What? Where Major?"

"They need more support at the Pokrovskii Barracks, the sailors are putting up quite a fight."

I shouldered my rifle, wiped clean my face once again, and motioned to my sergeants. Sleep would have to wait.

Seven hours. Seven hours it had taken to finish off their resistance, to rescue Dzerzhinskii and the rest, but at last we were home. I stumbled toward my bunk, several of the other officers trailing in after me. When was the last time I slept? Forty hours? Fifty hours? My stomach was rumbling, but it would have to wait. All I wanted was sleep.

I collapsed onto my bed, tried to muster the energy to pull off my boots. I could see the other officers flowing through the doors: Juškevičs, Jēkabsons, and countless comrades I didn't know. I wasn't sure where Līcis was, attending to his ankle perhaps.

Within this crowd of men, I spied an obvious stranger. Heavy, middle-aged, decked in a fine grey suit, he was distributing little blank envelopes to the officers. I saw them rip the letters open, varied looks of satisfaction, pleasure or confusion on their faces.

The man spoke perfect Russian, better, clearer than mine, but even he had a hint of an accent. Very slight, but unmistakable.

German.

He passed my bed, handed one to me. "As promised," he said, the inflection Reich not Baltic. How had he gotten into our barracks?

Even so, the envelope attracted my curiosity more than the man. I cracked mine open, heard the late-arriving Līcis ask: "What are these?"

"Rubles," answered Juškevičs in a distracted, counting voice.

I fanned out the bills in my hand. Heard the coins rattle around in the envelope's bottom. Yes, rubles, but not rubles alone.

"Marks as well, Herberts." I held one up in my fingers. "Don't overlook these."

Chapter Sixteen

I watched them cheer, the Latvian soldiers, like excited children freed from the schoolhouse an hour early. They all saluted Jukums Vācietis as he approached his black staff car, some even shredding discipline and breaking into waves. For all of them, it was a momentous, previously unimaginable day.

And, I must admit, it was a great day for me as well.

Vācietis had been made Commander and Chief of the Red Army, and now was setting off to defend the entire Western Front. A reward, I suspected, for squelching the Left S.R. uprising only three days before. The hushed cynics might even have called it a mandatory repayment. The same cynics who now dubbed us "Lenin's Harem."

No matter. The Latvians cheered because one of their blood was at the head of a Russian army. Yes, I could certainly accept and understand that.

But Vācietis was also from Courland specifically, born under the same skies as me. There was pride in that knowledge, transcendent of class. A man from our country had ascended so high. He'd walked the same lands, perhaps explored the very woods I had in childhood. A relative of Vācietis might even have tended our family farm.

Such a thought. Even if true, I shouldn't be thinking it. Not here, not in Red Square.

I mused at myself: Oh, shut up Wiktor. Shut up and clap.

I joined the cheers as he got in the car. Found myself waving even, waving to a Lett.

Juškevičs was as euphoric as me, insisting on getting a drink, a rare demand from my bookish friend. Arms thrown over each other's shoulders, the two of us turned around to find Līcis standing behind, his expression the complete opposite of ours. I'd never seen him this upset.

"What's the matter Herberts?"

"Gāters was wounded at Sizranj." He squinted beneath the hot July sun. "They don't expect him to live."

"Rooks!"

"Just a minute, Major!"

I looked down at the little girl. She was dead.

I laid her head on the wooden walkway outside her Moscow apartment, closed her eyes, tried to find something to cover the blood.

The soldier beside me was trembling as the sergeant pulled his rifle away. I felt for him but there was nothing I could do to change this. Only God could.

"It was so dark, Captain. I couldn't see."

"I know Private." I stood up looked at a boy in a helmet. A Lett from Goldingen. Claimed he was eighteen, probably sixteen and so far from home.

"I heard a sound. I thought it was the terrorists."

What were the words? What should I tell him? How could I say anything, when there was nothing to be said?

"This can happen in war, Zvirbulis." How trite, how insufficient, why could I never rise to the occasion in these matters? A wall between me and the rest of the world.

"Captain Rooks!" repeated Juškevičs's distant voice.

"A moment, Major!"

"She was hiding. I saw movement behind the door…"

I put my hand on his shoulder. Is this what an officer is supposed to do? Are these the words I was supposed to say? "Let's get you some water, you're not a bad person, Private, it's just a mistake…"

"Just a mistake?" He was crying, actually crying. The wrong words. Again.

"No…I don't mean…."

"Captain Rooks! Come here! And that's an order!"

"Sergeant, help the private here. See if anyone knows where the girl's mother is."

I handed off the weeping boy to the other soldier, and walked down the smoky city street toward Major Juškevičs's position.

One life ended. Another irreparably harmed. Why can soldiers massacre the enemy, or fire into a crowd of armed protesters and then drink and carouse that very night? Sheltered by anonymity and self-preservation, perhaps?

But when it was an innocent and the soldier is alone. Well, then nothing disguises the murder in it, especially to the murderer.

I found Juškevičs standing impatiently in front of the steps to an underground apartment, his stance resembling more and more Major Tentelis's.

"I'm sorry Major. One of my men killed a bystander, a young girl. Got confused in the gloom."

"I'm sorry, too Wiktor." There was a long pause. The closed off end of the street was hazy with gun smoke, the shootout having lasted far longer here. The informer had said the tsarist loyalists were in one of two apartments. Juškevičs's men had found a hornet's nest. Ours was empty, except for the girl.

He led me down the steps. "They weren't just tsarist supporters, Wiktor. Turns out they were Okhrana fugitives. Damn tough to flush out, too."

The Okhrana, the tsar's secret police. A brutal bunch. Many had opportunistically turned 'Red' after the revolution and joined the Bolshevik's Cheka. The rest hid in back rooms, aided enemy armies, continued to plot counterrevolution in the nastiest of ways.

"How do you know they were Okhrana, Major?"

"My 'Party Chaperone' tells me two of them were known operatives. More reliably, we found explosives, multistage fuses. They were definitely preparing something vicious. Lob a bomb in the Bolshoi Theatre, perhaps? Blow up a few Committee members?"

I passed into a smoky cellar, acidic smells burning thick in the air. There was a splintered table along one wall and an unhinged door that had been used as a shield: It's bullet-riddled exterior almost cut in half, but not nearly enough protection to save the three bodies piled behind, their corpses in various states of destruction. Soldiers stood around in the shadows, the danger over, using the quiet to calm down.

Juškevičs stepped over a broken chair, ducked under a shattered swinging light bulb. "This was a real bloodbath Rooks. We killed all five of them, no surrender."

Terrible, I was sick of death. How many more dead bodies would I have to see in this life? What was the human limit?

He took me into the next room, a little back pantry with broken cups and plates littering the floor. Bloodstains ran from a smear on the wall, another corpse laying at the bottom.

"This one's machine pistol took a nice gouge out of Saulītis's arm before we got him." Juškevičs looked sharply at me, a bloody fingerprint smudge decorating one lens on his glasses. "I thought you'd want to know Wiktor."

Once again I found few words. "Captain Vereshchagin."

I sat on the shuddering train across from Līcis, nothing but silence between us. He might have been on the other side of the world, lost as I was in my own thoughts:

If Vereshchagin really was Okhrana had I unwittingly worked for them too?

"It's better that Guntis's family already knows. At least we don't have to relay the news, Wiktor. The conversation will be easier."

"True, true, Herberts."

In the eyes of the communists would that make me Okhrana as well?

Līcis opened Gāters's little box on his lap, the warm midday sun passing through the car's window, illuminating the interior. Inside tin pins, folded notes, a badge, his insignia. And something rectangular, glass and reflective. "Do you think it's right, giving them back all his stuff?"

If they found out…Juškevičs, he knows already. Certainly he will keep this quiet.

"Do you think so Wiktor?"

"I'm sorry Herberts, what did you say? The way this train rattles…"

He pulled out a framed picture, handed it across to me. "His family will probably want this? Right?"

It was a photograph of a group of Rifleman officers in front of the walls of the Kremlin. Dashing, handsome young men, Līcis and I among them. And there, near the center, was Gāters. The contrast was obvious.

Līcis voice cracked a little. "I mean do they want to remember him this way?"

Disfigured? They must have seen him so, surely a photograph these last few years. But who could know for certain?

I handed the picture back to Līcis. "It shows him as a Rifleman. His parents will be proud."

Līcis slipped it back into the box, closed the lid. "He has only a mother. Their father caught ill in the refugee settlement. I don't remember what Guntis said it was."

"How long ago?"

"Last year, I think. At least that's when he told me."

A son and a father. A family robbed of its men.

LENIN'S HAREM

After getting off the train in Cudovo we hired a husky old Russian driver to take us by cart toward the nearby village of Sipoli. A pleasant enough trip, the September sun was still warm, the air not yet carrying winter's chill. Indeed, a balmy current rose off the vast flat Volchov swamps behind as the cart meandered up a slight incline toward the village. The surrounding trees decked in the rich colors of autumn, no longer any nagging insects to bite the ear, yet no early snows to slow our journey. A perfect time to be outdoors, in the wilderness. How I would have loved to have taken a forest detour for some pheasant hunting.

If my body could manage it. I tried to crack my back. The six-hour rail journey north from Moscow, all on that horrible wooden bench, had given me a painful ache in the rump. By contrast, the thin pillow in this little buggy felt like the down of my parents' old bed. In the afternoon sun, I thought I just might nod off.

I closed my eyes and let my thoughts drift with my consciousness. I had not been close to Gāters, but Līcis hadn't wanted to come alone. Said he felt uncomfortable meeting with the family of a deceased friend by himself. I understood that. And if Gāters had really vouched for me, really helped convince the Bolsheviks to ignore my family's past, then I owed him that much certainly.

I must have drifted off, so startled was I when Līcis exclaimed: "We're here."

I opened my eyes.

I was in Latvia.

A narrow dirt path wound between Lettish houses, so familiar in design: the single story, the double chimneys and the same wood-plank exteriors, in every window box, a host of autumnal flowers. Outside the nearest home, children jumped rope, singing Lettish songs. A town, like any small town in Latvia, like the ones dotting the land near our old homestead.

Magically I'd been whisked from the heart of Russia to Courland.

I was home.

Līcis seemed as astounded as me. "My God, Wiktor. It is just like Latgale."

The cart gone, we stood at a distance watching the three young girls skipping rope along the dirt road. A fourth sat off to the side, counting their time. It had been so long since I'd seen this sight. Since I'd felt the joy in a child's game. Years?

Yes, years.

Līcis waved briskly at one, then continued down the path looking for the Gāters family home. Yet, I remained rooted just watching. Just listening to their giggling voices, to the rhythm as the rope struck the ground.

"Hold up Herberts" I implored, gently motioning for him to come back. "I want to stay awhile."

Ieva Gātera was a thin woman, with deep-set eyes, and eyebrows of such faint amber that from a distance she appeared to have none. She might have been forty, still pretty, but time was beginning to find its foothold. There was an extra line beneath the eye, a deep crease separating mouth and cheek, a coming grayness at her temples.

And yet she was tidy, together in her light blue dress and wool shawl, remarkably composed for a woman who had lost a son while still mourning a husband.

Her house was equally well kept. Poor certainly, but there was no squalor. Every item had a place: blankets were folded square to the plank wall, pots and bowls rested symmetrically on a rack near the old, but undeniably clean, iron stove, a surprising number of books were arranged alphabetically on a shelf above my head and three twig brooms lay smallest to largest in the corner nearest the door.

So fastidious a woman, had she always been so?

"You will stay for dinner? After such a long journey? We can afford to be hospitable to Guntis's friends."

Līcis answered for the both of us. "Of course we will."

I nodded in agreement, sipped my onion soup, and stared at the picture in my hand: a younger Ieva with her bearded husband, her two daughters, one just a toddler and perched on her lap; and standing proudly behind his mother, her son: Gāters.

It had never occurred to me that Guntis might once have been handsome, that he hadn't always been a disfigured monster. Of course, at some level I had known that must have been the case. But I, as everyone, had struggled to ignore his affliction, to assess him on deeper values. Never really considered what he might once have been.

Yet, there he was. Alive, happy, staring back at me; ignorant of his coming fate. Smooth of face with a curl in his hair. His robust locks might have been brown or amber as his mother's, so hard to tell in the chrome tint of the photograph. He'd once had full lips and freckles. Dear God, he'd had freckles. And those too had been erased as he had been.

Līcis, sitting on the stool next to me, had regained a little of his good cheer: "It looks just like a house in Latgale. Don't you think so Wiktor?"

I put down the picture, ran a finger along the green and white patterns in the weave of the rug at our feet, the fibers tickling the skin. "Most definitely. Did you bring these things from Latvia, Ieva?"

Her face conjured images of the forced evacuation, a foolish, unthinking question on my part. "No, we had little room. There are so many Latvians in Sipoli. We help each other."

Līcis piped up again. "How many live here Mrs. Gātera?"

She sipped her own soup. "We're practically the whole town. When released from the camp…there was nowhere to go. People cling together in these sort of times."

"Is there any work?"

"Some of the men work the trains. There are a few farms. Not much." Something in the way she answered made me a little uncomfortable as if Ieva were feeling pressed by these enquires. I glanced at Līcis to suggest he desist, but he didn't look my way.

Herberts continued: "And you?"

She nodded, white hands straightening a folded blanket on the chair next to her. "Men pay me to have conversations with them, Lieutenant."

Līcis frowned. "How does…"

Her voice was breaking: "Twice a week, I take the train from Cudovo to Petrograd." She picked up her soup bowl, placed a fresh cloth beneath. "I am employed this way, so my daughters needn't be."

The house creaked in the autumnal winds. Ieva broke a sad smile. "Just talk, I mean. You'll find I'm full of topics." Her eyes moved from Līcis to me. "Men need to be listened to sometimes. Wives, lovers, they can have agendas." She looked more than a bit forlorn, a little desperate for agreement. "Don't you find it so Captain?"

I put down the cup "Of course, Ieva."

Līcis spooned his soup, an uncomfortable, perplexed look on his face.

"Mother!" came a little voice from outside.

She smiled, glad for the interruption. "Ah, the girls have returned from their chores."

A young woman entered through the open door. She was about twenty, dressed in a white bodice, a light green dress beneath. A full-jawed face framed wide near-turquoise eyes. Her hair was black, tied in a long braid down the back, the end thrown over her right shoulder so that it fell across her expansive breast. She was simply the most beautiful woman I had ever seen.

She was Gāters's sister?

"Lieutenant, Captain, this is my daughter Agnese. Agnese these are friends of Guntis's." Ieva's voice gave way at the mention of her son.

"Hello Lieutenant." Agnese curtseyed. The fullness of her breast, the angle at which it hung away from her ribs as she bent toward Līcis sent shocks of aching arousal through me. And when she turned her blue eyes my way, I actually felt fear, inadequacy.

"Hello Captain."

"Pleased to make your acquaintance." *Oh, for one moment's embrace...*

I could see those eyes flare, a questioning expression on her face. My accent. So had her mother. "It's alright Agnese. Captain Rooks is "Red.""

"Yes, "Red.""

"Please call me Herberts." Līcis smiled at her, smothering her palm in his hand. "None of this "Lieutenant" gibberish."

"And me too." I added wisely.

She seemed slightly puzzled by my remark. Clearly, Līcis had the advantage, the same ethnicity as her, knowing the customs, the little references and intricacies of their culture. I couldn't believe a short, balding, Lettish lieutenant was going to out maneuver me for a girl. *This girl.*

The voice again: "Mother!" It came from the rear door.

Ieva motioned to her daughter. "Agnese, go help your sister at the water pump."

Desperate to make amends for my "race" I suggested: "Please, let me."

She might have been ten years old and recently sprouted from cherubic childhood, or a waif of fourteen all too hesitant to bloom. Either way, the two full water buckets hanging from the pole across her shoulders were too much burden for the girl.

I stepped down into the yard. "Let me help you with those."

She broke the quickest smile, returned to the strain. "I have them. Thank you."

I put a palm beneath the pole, trying to ease some pressure off her back. If she noticed my aid, the girl didn't say a word.

I could hear Agnese chuckling from inside. Līcis was making the most of his time.

"May I ask you a question?" I looked stealthily back at the house. "About your sister?"

She made no verbal response, her face both perturbed and expectant. I suspected questions about Agnese were not infrequent.

I knew she must find it odd, harassed by a complete stranger, but there was really no time to lose. "Which flowers does Agnese prefer? Is there a fragrance that she often wears?"

One bony knee briefly buckled, struggling with the encumbrance. I offered again. "Really, let me take one of those."

Whether it was pride, the attention lavished on her sister, or some perpetual anger of adolescence, the girl shouted her answer. "No! I said I can do it!"

Immediately, her mother's voice broke the air. "I don't like your manners, my dear." Ieva came to the doorway, arms folded across her breast. "Be nice to our guest Kaiva."

Chapter Seventeen

January 1919, Rīga

The Latvian Riflemen had retaken Rīga.

Marching triumphantly down Kungu Iela, all that we had struggled for had finally come true. Only a year after its creation, the Latvians were leading the Russians to reclaim the great city on the Daugava. At last.

But everything else was so wrong.

The crowds welcoming us were smaller, more subdued than I thought imaginable, a fraction of those who had cheered us here all those years ago as we marched out to meet the enemy. Instead, most of the citizens hid inside their homes, doors bolted and curtains drawn. It was more than the frosty winter weather. A palpable dread hung in the smoky air. Some Latvians bystanders even wore contorted, hateful expressions as their own troops passed. They seemed to fear us more than the retreating Germans, a travesty that tore at my very soul.

I knew the reason. The British, so afraid their empire would be infected as the tsar's had been, had spread their arsenic to every strata of Rīga's population. Repeating countless lies of the coming Red Terror and the atrocities the Riflemen would commit on their very own people. Months spent dreaming of liberating this city, of becoming heroes, of thankful handshakes and emotional embraces, all vanished. Now their own citizens looked upon them as the latest invader, just another terrible occupier. The newest plague sent to wipe them from the Earth.

It was heartbreaking to see the men spurned so, unembraced by those they loved. In a war full of betrayals, this was by far the worst. My fellows robbed of their very reason for fighting, of their families, of their friends, of their purpose.

And our opponent was little better off, falling back again and again as our steel columns forced them across the bridges, out of the city proper. Defeated in the West, by treaty the German troops had fought for their new British masters here, a human wall meant to pen the communist swell in the East. But they were not the same warriors we'd faced. Gone was the tenacity and innovation that had made the kaiser's soldiers such irresistible opponents. Now, they reminded me of the tsar's old men: alcoholic, unmotivated, unwilling to die to preserve the patch of foreign land they defended. Their Prisoners of War spoke repeatedly of their own betrayal in Germany. Undefeated in the field, they'd been 'stabbed in the back' by the despicable politicians in Berlin. All they wanted to do was go home.

On both sides of the contorted lines, the city's smoking ruins marked a land of disillusionment, where dreams died as well as men.

But there was another foe, a new enemy waiting somewhere outside Rīga's limits, one whose dreams were still very much intact. The vigilante mobs like the one Seskis had joined had grown into an army. More accessible to the common Latvian than the wide journeying Riflemen, those that sought a Latvian state had swelled their ranks while we had been in Russia saving the Bolsheviks. Supplied by the British and the Americans, and trained ironically by German officers, they were a growing threat. Very soon there would come a horrible day when Latvian would face Latvian to determine the country's future. A day everyone knew was fast approaching, but it seemed nothing could prevent.

I walked slowly along the great river, found Juškevičs standing on the bank, his field glasses scanning something in the distance. Far downstream my bare eyes could see the glint of ships at the mouth of the Gulf of Rīga, nothing but sparkling shards beneath a backdrop of mountainous grey clouds.

The frigid draft coming off the river waters forced me to pull my coat tighter. I'd lost a glove in the fighting, my bare hand tortured by the arctic sea air as I fashioned the buttons. "What are they Heinrichs?"

"British frigates. Freighter escorts."

Supplying the Germans, now properly back on the other side of the river, no doubt. "Which one's got the Ulmanis government on board?"

"None. That ship's long gone. Far, far, out of range of our guns, probably safe in Courland by now." He pulled the glasses down, briefly. "Sorry."

How come everything I'd ever sought was is in Courland? "It's alright. I guess that makes us the proper government."

He returned to his scope, his voice colder than the winds. "When the Germans owned Rīga these past fifteen months were they the rightful government?"

"No."

"Then we aren't until the people accept us. And trust me, Pēteris Stučka isn't going to win us any new followers." Such a nasty tone. In the history or warfare had any victors ever been in a sourer mood? All that sacrifice …

The two of us stood in silence, the day's reception floating in our minds.

I'd been sober too long, far too long. "I need a drink"

Juškevičs surprised me. "Yeah, me too."

Perhaps I'd lost my mind for a moment? Or an hour? Or two? After all, it had been a wild evening. Juškevičs had misplaced his glasses. I had lost my grandfather's pocket watch and my sole remaining glove. There were other foolish things perhaps, but I couldn't quite remember them at the moment. I had never been this drunk and it felt good. To embrace the release, to lose all responsibility, to become a passenger in my own body and just see what happened.

I stumbled along, through the dark, medieval streets of oldest Rīga; a stocky red-headed Latvian girl named Zane supporting my weight while Juškevičs leaned on a roundish little black haired beauty of his own. Was she called Laura? Or Lara? No matter. They were as wine soaked as us, and since it was well past five o'clock in January's freezing morning, our foursome was desperately searching for a new place to drink.

I shouted because I could. "No, darling. We were *both* part of Lenin's Harem. But ole Juškevičs here's been spoiling for a fight, and I've got the wrong blood in me, so we had to transfer." Zane shrugged indifferently. I hadn't slipped into speaking German, had I? Perhaps, if I talked a little louder. I found her ear, yelling: "It seems some people didn't like me guarding the Kremlin."

Zane recoiled. She'd heard that alright. I sought out Juškevičs in the dark street. "Heinrichs, who was it that didn't like me? Can you tell me that finally, please? Please?" I shouted a third "Please!" just to sway him.

He was practically ignoring me, his hand half down Laura's blouse. "Sorry, can't do that Wiktor. Where is this tavern Laura?"

"Off the next alley." She said nearly slipping on the icy cobblestones. Juškevičs held her closely, his lips pressed against her cheek. "Careful, Laura, if you fall we might not get up again."

"I might like that."

"Did you hear that Wiktor?" He tossed his head around, "Laura might like a fall with me!"

"It was Jēkabsons wasn't it? He always hated me, Heinrichs. I know it was him, the little bastard."

He said nothing, deep in a sloppy, over-passionate kiss with Laura.

"I tell you, Zane, it was Jēkabsons. Little short guy, jealous of me in every way. Napoleon in worse clothes." She seemed surprisingly uninterested in Kremlin intrigues, trying to pull herself from my grip. What was the matter with her?

I held fast. "Zane, you don't understand. Heinrichs got us transferred, transferred just so we could come and rescue you ladies. Aren't you grateful?"

Apparently Laura was, because Juškevičs had maneuvered her into a dark recesses in the near alley. I couldn't see much in the gloom, but the few soft moans emanating from restless shadows indicated something was afoot.

Zane seemed less appreciative, she wouldn't even kiss me. "Just one," I begged, tugging at the tails of her coat.

"No," she yelled, pulling her jacket free. "Leave me alone."

I was wobbly without her support. "Did you hear that Heinrichs, the lady isn't grateful?" I looked to Juškevičs, but he was busy with his shadowy undertakings.

I returned for Zane, but she had disappeared. Now, that was unfriendly. I stumbled a little farther into the alley past Juškevičs. "Zane?" I whispered. "Zane?"

I careened from wall to wall, moving deeper into the off street. She was nowhere to be seen. How rude not even to say goodbye. After I had given her my grandfather's watch.

Of course she could be standing right in front of me with the alcohol fog I was in. I took another step, crashing over a pile of open trash. The smell of rotting meat and onions filling the narrow passage. I gagged out a final: "Zane!"

Nothing.

Well, who needed her? Just another girl. There were thousands in this city more appreciative than her. Or should have been. Damned British.

I dug my fingernails into the dusty, ancient bricks, pulled myself up again, stood precariously, while brushing onionskins, orange peels and assorted slimes off my pants, leaned on the wall as I continued. Was this the way I'd come?

No. No. A different route. Here, the alley opened into a little courtyard, a four-way intersection, with the exit across from me twice as wide as any other. There was a beam of moonlight breaking the cloudy sky and a solitary lamp fitfully glowing above a door on the opposite side. Off in one corner, a thin, rickety old-style wagon, a lumpy tarp thrown across its bed. Somewhere, a door was creaking in the breeze. I leaned back against a near wall to rest a moment, found gravity dizzily increasing.

I must have passed out, for I was soon lying prone in the cold dirt, one elbow propped on a slight outcropping of brick. Had I dreamt them or were there voices only a moment before?

The courtyard smelled of urine. I tried to relax, let the acidic odor clear my head. Where was Heinrichs? He had taken my grandfather's watch. I must ask for it next time I saw him.

Voices again. Heinrichs? Zane? Zane, that was her name, yes?

No, no, the words weren't Latvian. They were…they were German?

"Heinrichs…. Heinrichs. The funniest thing happened to me."

"Wiktor? What is it that you need?" He seemed agitated, standing at the tavern door, Laura on his arm holding a single burning candle in her hands. He made no motion to let me in. "Well?"

I put a finger to my lips. "Sshhh…. You'll wake the owner." I sidestepped past them. In the dark interior I could see several thick, long banquet tables crossing an unadorned wooden floor. A second lit candle rested on the polished surface of a wide bar, its glow casting a shimmering white halo over the assorted bottles on the shelves behind. Along the rear wall, a skeletal stairway climbed up through the ceiling. Under lit, the whole room appeared cavernous, gloomy, mysterious.

Heinrichs shut the door behind me to cut off the draft. "Laura's father is the owner, Wiktor, and he's not in. There's no one to wake."

I could barely contain my excitement. "I found a wagon full of Germans."

"What?"

I started laughing hysterically. "They were all hiding under this tarp. It was so funny. I could see them move every once in awhile. A little ripple here, a face peeking out there, they looked like puppies in the wash basket."

He let go of Laura's waist. "Are you serious?"

"Oh yes." I kept nodding until he understood.

"We need to call the watch. To apprehend them."

I put a hand on his chest to stop him. "No, no, no. You don't understand."

"What do you mean?"

I just shook my head. "They weren't the enemy. They were like me. Local Germans, nothing unusual."

"Baltic-Germans?"

A few more nods, then I pointed to my chest with both hands. "Like me."

He looked at me incredulously, seeming to sober by the moment. "The aristocrats are raising their own army too, Wiktor."

"They are?"

"Yes, they are. And you know this, Wiktor." He moved away from Laura, closer to me. "We talked about it at length this evening."

I needed a chair. "I don't know. I'm too drunk."

His face was shadowy, but his voice too clear. "Not that drunk, Wiktor. You told me you feared your father, your brother might join them."

Clearly he didn't understand me. "No, no, no. Heinrichs, they're just like me. Nothing to fear …"

"Men need a reason to hide in a wagon, Wiktor. We can't let this pass."

I stumbled away into the echoing gloom. "They're gone, anyway. A driver came out and took them down the road." Where was his sense of humor?

He followed. "Can you still identify the wagon? It cannot have gone far."

I crawled up on a table, curling to sleep. "No… I am too drunk."

He took the candle off the bar, set it next to my face, the heat, the light disturbing my attempt at rest. "You're not too drunk. Wiktor, let's go. Which road did they take?"

I shoved the candleholder away, hot wax spilling to the floor. Juškevičs quickly righted the base before the whole thing fell. "I said I'm too drunk, Heinrichs."

I closed my eyes, but his voice was still there, echoing in my head. "Wiktor I am ordering you to go. Captain Rooks, now!"

"It's no use Heinrichs, I am too drunk. I'm going to sleep." I was so disappointed, why hadn't he thought it funny? Just like puppies…

"Disobeying orders Wiktor. Do you know the penalty?"

He was so serious. I rubbed my face with my hands. "You won't do anything to me, I'm your friend." I rolled over, more comfortable on my side. The table was so thick, it didn't even shudder. A good bed.

He gripped my jacket, pulling me upright. Eye to eye.

"Now, Captain Rooks."

I pushed him away, a rough forearm detaching his grip on me. "I won't." Why wouldn't he let me sleep? I'd had enough of him and his arrogant Lettish 'orders.'

I sneered directly at my assailant: "You owe me Heinrichs. I could have turned you into Vereshchagin many, many times." I rocked back onto an elbow. "Gāters wasn't the only Lett with communist propaganda under his pillow."

These words caused a transformation in Heinrichs, his own drunken, dull eyes slowly clearing. And the dumbfounded expression on his face hardened to seething rage. Handing his candle to Laura, he stepped back, undoing his shirt, button by button, a look of fiery menace in his sobering eyes that I had never seen before. Not even on the field of battle.

By the third button his undershirt was visible. Laura put a hand on his shoulder, but he only shrugged her off, keeping his eyes locked on me.

Finally he took the shirt and hung it across the back of a chair, slowly, efficiently, using the posts of the frame to support the shoulders, so it hovered there as if still filled by the spirit of a man, insignia shining a Vulcan red in the candlelight.

He took two steps toward me: "Okay Wiktor, okay. I am just a man now. There is no uniform. I am no longer your superior officer. Only a man, and I talk to you as one."

I had said too much. I slid off the table, trying to settle myself on the floor. "Heinrichs let me…"

He waved off my overture, pointed to the ceiling. "I am going up to Laura's room for one hour. One hour to sleep off these spirits. When I come back, I'm going to put that uniform on. Be an officer again. And then Wiktor, I'm going to do one of three things."

I nodded even though I didn't understand.

"A squad of our soldiers is billeted not two blocks from here. Either, I am going to commend you highly for having contacted them and initiated the arrest of those men in the wagon as an appropriate action for an officer of the Red Army."

He leaned closer. "Or, I am going to punish you harshly for having failed to apprehend this enemy when given the opportunity. And ignoring my orders to do so."

He stood there a moment, his angry panting the only sound. "Or possibly, I will not be able to find you. Then I will only assume you have deserted… to whatever army now calls your allegiance."

I took a wobbly step closer: "Heinrichs listen to me."

His fist struck me hard below the left eye, staggering me back so far that I needed a hold on the heavy table to keep myself upright, the contents of tonight's wine churning in my stomach.

"That is for jeopardizing our men." His shaking fist casting rhythmic shadows across his face, Laura white as a ghost behind. His hand slowly unwound, steadied, a single finger remaining leveled at me. "And for daring to abuse our friendship."

I found a bare wooden chair, lowered myself onto it, massaged the burning in my cheek, felt the skin already expanding.

He turned away, took a staggering step sideways, shaking his hand in pain as he made toward the stairs. Laura approached him, but no longer amorous, he pushed her away with a concussive violence I thought Juškevičs could never possess. He soon disappeared up the stairwell. Laura following tentatively, unsure of her steps in her own home.

Slowly, over an hour's time, the remaining candle diminished until the starved flame became a single fading ember and finally evaporated in a wisp of spinning white smoke.

I sat alone in the night listening to my own breathing.

When Juškevičs came down again six hours later, I was still sitting alone, the vision in my left eye long choked away by unattended swelling.

Silently, without salutation, without preamble, Juškevičs went to his shirt. Removing it from the back of the chair, he slipped it over his shoulders, pushed his arms through the cuffs, never taking his eyes from me. Slowly he buttoned it again, from the bottom up, last night's dark glare on his face, far more horrible now under dawn's ashen hue.

When the collar button was securely fastened, he stuffed the tails into his trousers, and approached. Standing silently before me.

I felt the need to speak: "Heinrichs, I am sorry… I was drunk." I still was, really. But sober enough for regrets.

He spat on my boot. White and thick, the mucus hung on my toe for a few seconds, before seeping toward the floor.

Wordlessly, Juškevičs marched toward the door, steps echoing long and hollow on the tavern's wooden floor. When he reached the exit, he threw it open, letting in the painful, burning morning rays. There he hesitated, keeping his back to me, his voice was calm but acidic.

"My report will say that Captain Wiktor Rooks failed to pursue an opportunity to capture probable enemy soldiers and was grossly negligent in his duties to follow up on suspicious activity"

I only nodded, sat hunched on my hard wooden chair.

"And that I strongly recommend no advancement on your next grade review."

I watched the saliva puddle beneath my toe, used the boot to rub it into the wood grain, flattening it to a damp smear on the floor.

He stepped outside the tavern onto the doorstep. Cast one last comment to me, before slamming the door thunderously.

"And only that, Captain."

August, 1920 Moscow

"To Līcis!"

Everybody raised their glasses for my toast. "May he and Karina never part!"

Līcis laughed his hearty laugh. He, Juškevičs and I each downed our full glasses of champagne in one swallow. Was that the sixth or the seventh tonight?

The three of us sat at a lonely table underneath the sole undimmed lamp. If there was anyone else in the restaurant we had not seen them for hours.

Līcis bobbled his head. "Oh, how the room spins, so early. That is not a good sign." But he laughed like it was. "A fine toast, Wiktor. A fine toast. I would like to return the gesture to you and Alisa."

I only shook my head. "Don't bother. She's not speaking to me once again. These Russian women, they are very headstrong. You'll find out soon enough."

"No, not my Karina. She is sweet, only a little kitten."

Juškevičs muttered, "You think so, but she'll be the tiger after your wedding day. This one will watch you like a hawk, I can tell."

Līcis shrugged. "Tiger, hawk, kitten, am I marrying a woman or the zoo-keeper?"

I laughed. "You are inebriated."

He poured more Champagne into my glass. "And you should be too. This may be our last night together since Juškevičs is leaving us."

"Yes, off to fight General Wrangel. I can't say I envy you." Two whole regiments had just been eaten up in that Crimean meat-grinder. The nastiest of the White Armies, the Volunteer Army of Southern Russia had been a constant threat for years. Countless Latvians had lost their lives fighting down there, Gāters not least among them. And now our friend might join them, it made me want to make amends.

"Soon, you'll be saying you can't envy *them*, Wiktor. Just watch what we can do." Juškevičs pointed to his head. "I have some ideas."

Līcis laughed over-hysterically. "Heinrichs with his more ideas…To Heinrich's ideas."

We all toasted again, each downing another glass. The room was indeed spinning.

I snapped my fingers in remembrance. "I have news. I received a letter from my mother today. Came through the Latvian Consulate. After five years, finally in touch."

"That's fantastic." Līcis quickly threw an arm around me, Juškevičs only nodded approvingly. Some scars still hadn't quite healed.

"It seems they have stayed in Courland all this time."

"We must all visit them." cheered Līcis.

"That's not so easy my friend." I started filling their glasses for the next toast. "But listen to this: My brother was a translator for the English and the Americans in Archangel." I pounded lightly on the table, spilling a little Champagne on the cloth. "Can you believe it? We were fighting on the opposite sides."

Juškevičs propped his fist beneath his chin. "Why didn't he join Bermont-Avalov? From what I know of your family that army seems the sort of thing he'd support." There was a chilling seriousness in Juškevičs tone that reminded me of that horrible night in the tavern. It might be better to distance myself from any more disloyalties.

"We're talking about my brother, not me, Heinrichs." I shook my head, hoping it was enough of an explanation. "He'd never ride a losing horse. And the aristocrats indeed lost, yes? Much safer to play with the British and Americans, as he did. And he's already set himself up in the cushy new Rīga government."

"Doing what?"

"Who knows? The letter didn't exactly say. If I know him, he'll be king by the time I get home." I needed a cigarette.

"Are you going back?" Juškevičs sounded disapproving.

"When I finish my second degree." I suspected I was the only one returning to Latvia. Līcis was marrying a Russian woman and Juškevičs was wed to the Soviet army without a doubt. "As long as I can stay stationed in Moscow, I figure three years at most to get them."

"You'll end up married to Alisa." Līcis's tone was certain. "Her charms will take you."

"Perhaps they will." They were nice charms.

I tried to think of another toast. The big news of the week, of course, was the Soviet government's announcement that it had 'now and forever' renounced any claim to Latvia.

"To Comrade Lenin. In the end, he kept his promise."

Their replies were long in coming; Līcis only slowly raised his glass, an ambivalent look on his face. Juškevičs not at all. I had quickly killed the festive mood.

For a few moments I was left waiting, the glass growing heavy and sticky in my hand. Finally, Juškevičs brought up his own. "I will toast the man, but I don't like him leaving my homeland a puppet of the British." He drank. "We will go back there some day."

Like the true military strategist he was, Juškevičs still relived daily the loss to the Latvian National Army; mistakes made, alternate actions that should have been taken, new strategies needed.

While I was secretly happy to have Latvia a free market, I felt for him, thrown out by his own people. Forced to divert men to defend against other Soviet enemies like Wrangel, they'd fought their countrymen severely undermanned; given Rīga away, were pushed slowly out of their homeland. A very bitter pill, most of the Riflemen desperately wanted a second chance.

"Invasion is not revolution, Heinrichs. The movement must come from within." I enjoyed preaching communist theory to him, whether I really agreed or not. Hopefully it alleviated his doubts about my intentions. He'd never treated me the same after that night in Rīga.

He turned to Līcis his tone consciously trying to lighten the mood. "Wiktor doesn't think like a military man, Herberts." He made a deliberately audible whisper. "Too much time spent with women."

Līcis grinned. "I will certainly toast that Heinrichs."

And we all toasted women, the only thing truly worth fighting for anyway.

Part Three:

Homeland

Map by Seth R. McCullough

Latvia Between the World Wars

Chapter Eighteen

April 1924, Riga

I had come home with no home to return to.

I lugged the heavy trunk up the gangplank until the steward stopped me. "Only passengers from this point forward."

My mother's waxen face wore a perpetual, painted-on despondence. She had reached that age where her make-up no longer highlighted her beauty, but covered creeping blemishes. Even so, the anguish beneath all the powders was too real, too natural. She pestered everyone continuously. "You're sure you told Erich the hour the ship arrives, Otomars?"

My brother put a comforting hand on the shoulders of both our parents, a bridge linking them as they climbed the boarding walk. "I told you, I gave all the information to Anne. You'll be fine Mother."

She was trying to hold back tears, as much for leaving her sons, as for departing her homeland. Otomars embraced her, drowning even his body in her great brown fur coat.

I offered Father my hand. For the first time in a long while, he took it. His eyes met mine, a face mirroring my own thirty-five years down life's road. Would I look as sullen? Glare as stoically at the world's crimes?

"I'll see you in August, Son." He slightly smiled, even patted me on the shoulder with his free hand. Perhaps the reality of the separation had thawed him.

When he turned to say goodbye to Otomars, Mother hugged me tightly, the heat of her coat, too much in the blossoming warmth of April. But there was not another item that could be stuffed into these trunks. More elegant worn than carried, she had insisted, a little pride in the leaving.

"We'll come early Wiktor. Your Father and I will spend some time with you before the wedding." Her eyes were swollen, her cheeks puffy from days of crying. A whisper in my ear: "I'll talk to him."

"That would be nice Mother"

Otomars and I stood along the pier, waving as the towering bow of the cruise ship pulled away. Father gave only one slight acknowledgement, and then stood still, holding our weeping mother as they both took a last look at Rīga's skyline.

It would be a new life for them, one they hadn't wanted but were forced to accept. I hoped it wouldn't slowly kill them.

The Bolsheviks had been defeated in Latvia, but the end result had been similar. The new Latvian government had seized all Baltic-German farms, every single estate, distributing all the land to the homeless, to war veterans, to refugees; giving it all to their own kind.

Without compensation. And with the Germans defeated and the communists in power in Russia, the gentry no longer had anyone to protect them, no one to call in to vanquish the peasants one more time.

The aristocracy was finally gone. A bloodless 1905, the old world vanished forever.

A hand on my shoulder: "They'll be all right, Wiktor. The Kaltenbachs will take good care of them. They'll love Lübeck. I've heard it's like Rīga."

Like Rīga, but not Rīga. And certainly that German city was far from the rural majesty of Courland, or Kurzeme, as the Latvians were now insisting it be called.

The boat's stern was pulling away, headed down river, out to sea. The people on the deck had all melded into one. No more individual than the anonymous pigeons fluttering about the dock.

My brother let out one last long breath. It was all too real now. "Do you want to get some lunch Wiktor?"

"Sure."

I sat across from Otomars in the little café along Rīga's Stabu Iela. He looked so old. He was not the same man who'd trekked off to St. Petersburg years ago and time had not been kind to him. He had put on considerable weight, shaven his whiskers, seen his hairline retreat high atop his head. At 37, he hardly resembled the dapper young man I remembered.

LENIN'S HAREM

But his eyes, his eyes were the same. Fiery, mischievous, always one step ahead of mine. If his appearance had metamorphosed, well underneath he was still my brother. More serious, colder perhaps, but that could be expected given the change in times.

I wondered if he saw any of the boy left in me.

"When some of their things arrive, I'll go down and help them sort through it. You might come along if you can, Wiktor."

I blew on the surface of the steaming coffee, still too hot to taste. "I'd like to. Do you know the cost? By ship to Germany?"

"Would you like me to help with the fare?"

"No, Otomars, that's not what I meant." Always the older brother. "If they need me, I'll come."

He was silent a long moment, swirling the bread in his gravy. "Have you thought any more about Erich's offer to run the saw mills?"

What a drab life that would be: Fighting over labor issues, negotiating prices on buzz saw parts, and if the government seized Baltic-German industry as well… "I'm going to turn it down, Otomars. I really think the University will offer me tenure next term."

He forced down another bite of his biscuit. His fifth. It looked almost painful. No wonder, he had gained such weight.

"Have you told Gitta?"

I cautiously tasted the coffee. Just cool enough, but desperately in need of sugar. "Yes…She's less than pleased."

He folded his thick hands above his plate. "Can I tell you something? As your brother?"

I could sense another lecture coming. Yes, there was no doubt. This was the same Otomars.

I spooned in some sugar, took another sip of coffee. "Be my guest."

"Break it off with the woman. You don't love her." The lightness of his expression, failed to diffuse the magnitude of his words.

"Of course I do."

He grinned. "No, you don't."

Were we children, arguing in such a "yes-no" fashion? I tapped my spoon on the counter. "Yes, I do. I wouldn't be marrying her if I didn't."

"You can't stand her. I've got eyes Wiktor, there's no affection between the two of you. I hate to see you so miserable."

He put his hand up for another cup of coffee. "And if you are going to marry a girl you don't love, at least find one with something to offer."

"She's got plenty to offer."

He leaned back, completely comfortable in this sort of debate: "Like what? Conversations about wall hangings? Drab observations on shrubbery arrangements?"

I should have been angry, defending my fiancée, but instead I found myself subtly laughing. A little truth in his observations, how she did ramble about decorations.

He read my mind, gained a stronger smile, quickened his words. "And come on Wiktor. Those bulbous eyes? She's not a beauty. Our groundskeeper was more attractive."

"Stop it, Otomars." And stop smirking Wiktor.

He leaned forward. "Do you want to see that face passed on to your children? Gangs of little bugged eye creatures saying "Hello Father," when you return home. Really?"

No, don't laugh. Throw your coffee in his face.

His tone turned darker. "You really don't think she waited for you all this time? Nine years? No one waits a decade. When you had only courted her for a few months before the war? Madness. Nothing but a series of lies meant to guilt you into marrying her." Out of coffee, he drank from the water glass. "It's simply that nobody else would have her."

"That's absurd. She told me she had throngs of suitors." I stopped my laughing, ashamed for having started it

He raised his eyebrows. "Nine years but nothing permanent. While all her friends got married off? I guarantee a few of those Prussian officers had a taste of her."

I returned a cold stare. Otomars didn't flinch. "A pity when you haven't."

This was no longer funny. "A lady doesn't…"

"A lady does, she just doesn't mention it. A hypocrite says she hasn't, when she has."

"Otomars…this is my fiancée you're…"

"All he had to do was go on about some fictional manor house in Munich, and she'd swoon. God, mention a fern and she'd rip his clothes off." He paused while the waitress poured him a fresh cup of coffee, then motioned for her to leave the pot. "It's not like Gitta brings any wealth to this marriage. Her family's been robbed of their lands just like the rest of us. You're going to be stuck in a very narrow townhouse for a long, long time with her. Are you sure you can stand it?"

"Of course I can. I love her."

LENIN'S HAREM

"If you did, you'd have struck me by now, dear Brother." He stuffed in another section of sausage. "And you know it."

I sat in the box seat next to Gitta. She in a shoulder-bare fashionable white dress, I decked in hat and tails, both lightly clapping as the curtain came down to end the opera's first act. The balcony allowed a wonderful view of the stage in Rīga's fine National Opera House, all sheathed in emerald and gold with several marvelous sparkling chandeliers hanging from the ceiling. Yes, I thought, it rivaled, perhaps even surpassed, the Bolshoi in Moscow. Smaller, less ornate, but the contrasts between the elegant bronze adornments and the beautiful green walls were far more striking than its Russian counterpart. No, it was simply the most elegant theatre I had ever attended.

And it had better be at these prices.

Gitta turned to me, her blonde hair combed over, pinned back behind one ear. Otomars was mad, her eyes were not bulbous. She was even pretty in this lighting.

She put a hand on my knee. Affection. She must want something.

"Wiktor, can you get me a cigarette?"

"Of course, darling." I got off my seat, started back toward the door to the hall.

"Wiktor?"

"Yes?"

"Please make sure they're Ruhtenberg. The last brand was…" she flicked her hand, as if shooing the words away, "they were musty."

Yes, yes, of course. The most expensive. I mouthed silently to no one: "We must keep Gitta in the life she is accustomed to, mustn't we."

I waited in the queue as the opera patrons selected packs from the cigarette girl's tray. I could see Gitta through the open door, sitting in the little box, happily gazing out into the free space of the theatre. As if clairvoyant, she turned to look back, caught me staring.

I gave a faint smile, a little wave. Only thirty or forty more years of this…

She only struck out her hand, pointing a gloved finger past me.

I mouthed again: "What?"

She pointed again, frowning.

I looked back. The last customer had bought his goods and exited, leaving the cigarette girl waiting. I quickly apologized, looking into the tray to make my selection.

"Let's see, she wants Ruhtenberg's finest…"

"Is that what you smoke Wiktor? Such expensive tastes."

I looked up surprised. I wasn't such a frequent opera patron that the staff knew my name.

I stared at the girl. Nineteen, twenty? There was something oddly familiar about her.

She returned a wide, polished smile. "Kaiva. Guntis's sister. Remember?"

"Yes…yes, from Sipoli." What a small world. I hadn't recognized her in adulthood. She was thinner, smaller, more finely featured than Agnese with her mother's light amber hair parted down the middle. Not the head-swiveling lightning bolt that her sister was, but attractive certainly. Very much so.

I took a quick look over my shoulder. There were no other customers, though I could see Gitta beckoning for me to come back.

She could wait. "When did you get to Rīga?"

"Almost two years now. Agnese's husband is quite the nationalist, desperate to live in the new state. They dragged me with them."

Agnese married? Too bad.

The bell went off. The call to return to the seats for the next act.

"I better hurry." I found the cigarettes, reaching into my pockets for the correct change. "How is your mother? Still in Russia?"

"Yes, she met a man in Cordova. Nice enough, I suppose."

I reached out to hand her the money.

"Don't worry, it's my pleasure."

"Oh, I couldn't. Please…"

"Nope. I insist. A little sharing, my Comrade." There was a permanent effervescence in her voice, a cheerful perfection in her smile.

"Why, thank you."

The lights dimmed.

"I really must go."

"Is that woman waving in the seat with you?"

I turned to find Gitta motioning for me to hurry up. Even in the low light, I could see her perturbed expression.

"Yes, my fiancée."

She considered this a moment, then leaned into my ear, the cigarette tray pressing firmly against my stomach. "When you make love to her tonight, I want you to think of me."

"What's the matter Wiktor?" Gitta whispered. "You look like you've seen a ghost."

I sat down, passed her the cigarettes. The orchestra had just started playing the opening movement. "That cigarette girl was the sister of an old army acquaintance."

Gitta glanced back toward the closed door. "I don't like the way she looked at you."

"Shhh…Nonsense." *It was more in what she said, anyway.*

Despite the rising music, Gitta seemed bent on having a conversation. "You might remember, I had three proposals while you were conscripted on the wrong side. Two of them from rather handsome German officers."

I motioned for her to keep it down. "Yes, well I am very happy you waited for me." Such the old spinster, unmarried at 26. How many more times would she mention her devotion? Her chastity? I sometimes wondered if I were engaged from love or martyrdom. *Maybe, Otomars's theory was…*

"I am happy I waited too dear."

I hoped she was finished, but in the comparative lull of the second orchestra movement, Gitta felt compelled to embellish: "I am just sad you missed the parties. Oh, how we danced on the baron's manor. In the summer, he put out the most fantastic assortment of lamps. Blue, yellow, pink. A last hurrah for all us, and you were off in some ditch."

Yes, *in a ditch*, as if I were off building sandcastles. "I'm sorry I missed that too." *Now, shut up.*

"We lost nine years, Wiktor. We could have been married by now."

A sigh from my soul itself. Yes. We could be.

Other patrons were staring. She lightly touched my hand. "If you work for the Kaltenbachs perhaps we can still afford a large family. A house in Majori?"

"Enough Gitta."

I could see them turn, looking for the usher, but still she persisted: "Why not? You need to think of…."

I took her by the arm, escorted her out of the balcony, into the hall. She looked shocked. "Forget this Kaltenbach nonsense. I like astronomy. I like teaching. I've worked very hard to have the opportunity to pursue them."

She turned her back to me, threw her hands up. "Well, I guess we'll have to give up the opera tickets. It'd be nice to have *something* left from the old days."

Far off in the darkened hall, I could see the silhouette of the cigarette girl silently watching our exchange. An usher approached, but she stopped him, let the two of us continue.

Gitta paced in small circles, finally turning around to me. "You know Wiktor," she pointed a gloved finger into my face. "I'm not always sure you're willing to do the things necessary to keep me happy."

I let out a long breath, surprisingly more sympathetic than angry. "I think you may be right, Brigitta."

"She threw the cat at me."

"No?" Kaiva put her hand to her mouth in disbelief.

I sat next to her on the granite steps of the great baroque National Art Gallery, its towering columns and high arching windows all gleaming perfection in the morning sun, a brilliant backdrop for my sudden revelation of emancipation. "It"s true. Right there in the apartment. She was stroking the poor thing in her lap, and the moment I told her it was over, the little beast was flying through the air."

Her eyes grew wide, pupils large and black in the morning light. "Was it injured?"

"No. And neither was I, thank you for asking." I rocked closer in exaggerated laughter. She didn't move away.

Her hair pulled back in a bun, she had an academic and serious appearance as the two of us sat quietly looking out over the busy street. We watched the light crowds marching up and down the many steps at the entrance of the spacious gallery. A slight breeze ran up the incline, carrying snippets of discussion, bubbles of conversation, all mixing into a soft mosaic of human voices. I let myself just float away with them, after all those years of war to simply relax.

Kaiva attracted my attention by touching my hand. "So, what did you think?"

"It's not what it used to be. Before they had all the Dutch masters, the Italians, the German painters. I don't mean to offend you Kaiva, but now it's Latvian, Latvian, Latvian. There is no selection."

She nodded, considering carefully my words. "You must understand Wiktor, when a people have been forced into the shadows for so long, they have a need to show what they can do. It's their turn in the spotlight." She gave me a half smile.

LENIN'S HAREM

"Not such a bad thing for a little while, is it?"

"Perhaps not."

I sat quiet a moment, remembering her words at the opera. Two weeks later, and I could still not escape them. "Do you want a sugar ice?"

She licked her lips. "Hmmm…Absolutely."

I put my hand up. "No, no stay there. My turn this time, Comrade." Such a political word, and yet it had almost become a pet name between us, a coy reference to the past.

I trotted off, slipping behind the massive stone structure of the gallery into beautiful Esplanāde Park. Fully in bloom in May, a long stretch of grass and trees running through Rīga's center, its green slopes decorated by lounging couples of every age and class. There were well-prepared diners having fully catered meals on colorful blankets in the shade of the great Russian Orthodox Cathedral, gaggles of racing school children tended by shepherding school mistresses, and slumbering wanderers who on their purposeful journey to some important destination, had foolishly attempted to cross, succumbing to the park's beauty and the comforting warmth of a Rīga spring morning.

I dared not tarry long, fearing I too might fall prey to these Elysian charms. I quickly found the sugar ice vendor, his odd little ice box hanging by thick straps from his shoulders while his little striped hat precariously fluttered in the breeze. As he dug out the treats, I spied an old woman carrying a basket of roses along the park's path.

An idea crossed my mind.

I hurried back toward the gallery before the ice melted, and another petal fell from the dozen pink roses pinned against my chest. I dodged interlocked couples and young boys on high-wheeled bicycles, lost a few petals to two exuberant young girls gliding past with squeaky wheels on the bottom of their shoes, disappointed friendly dogs begging for a pleasant scratching behind the ear.

Such an excursion just to impress one young Lett, could I even tell my family that I was seeing her? A Latvian? They would be livid.

Perhaps, I'd let Otomars in on the secret. He'd enjoy that. This was all familiar territory for him. I could imagine a ribald nudge from him at the table, a little male to male understanding.

Surely, there would be no need to inform anyone else. This couldn't lead anywhere, could it? Only a distraction until I met another German girl, a more agreeable version of Gitta, yes? A lark, a fling, a spring tryst, as much a product of the warming weathers as any emotion of the heart. Yes, that was all.

There was no earthly reason I should be this excited to give her these flowers. None.

I climbed the steps at the gallery, clumsily trying to keep the roses behind me. Found Kaiva basking in the sun near the top, eyes half-closed, simply enjoying the late morning warmth. She had unpinned her hair, letting it fall freely over her shoulders, passing from academic to angelic in this heavenly light.

I must have been out of shape for my heart was racing.

"Here you are," I handed her the cone of ice, "and it seems I found you something else." I pulled the flowers around.

A slight, if confused smile crept onto her face. A pleasant look certainly, but not the overjoyed expression I'd hoped for. Had I erred?

She took them, her finger running through the blooms. "Thank you, Wiktor. So thoughtful." Her voice was low, muted.

What had I done? Too many? Too materialistic? Too presumptuous?

She plucked one out of the bunch, held it aside. "You've never courted a Latvian before have you?" Her dawning grin almost teasing, was she mocking me in some secret way?

"No. Were these too soon?"

She was squinting in the light. "Not if they reflect real feelings."

"Too," I hated to broach it. "Too capitalistic?"

She laughed. "Only if you swindled them from the local gardener." She passed the one rose to a little boy, his other hand clasped behind his mother as they climbed down the steps from the gallery. He giggled a smile. A flower from the pretty lady.

She watched the child a moment, the rose bobbling slowly away. Head thrown back taking in a little more sun as I waited confused. Finally, Kaiva stood up, pressed the roses between us, and gave me a gentle kiss. "An odd number of flowers is for romance, Wiktor."

I kissed her again both relieved and thrilled, enjoying the seeping taste of her lips. A light pressure in the locking that somehow bound something far stronger. It was a long while before I forced myself to separate and ask: "And an even number?"

She winced good-naturedly. "For the gravesite."

Kaiva and I lay in her bed, locked together once again, intertwined well past dawn for the third night running. My chin softly atop her head, her head firmly resting on my chest, bodies recovering for the next intimacy, minds effortlessly spinning to unexplored topics. For nine hours we'd lain here this night, the subjects turning, branching down surprising, invisible paths; looping, doubling back, splitting and mending again. We'd talked of childhoods, of wars, of cigarettes and astronomy, of burning manors and refugee camps; debated Rīga and Moscow, Courland and Sipoli, the merits of Alisa's body, and the type of paint needed to repair a red star; spoken wistfully of that first night at the opera, of Guntis as a boy, and her first lover named Mātis; marveled mutually at the weight of a full water bucket and the size of Gitta's shoe collection; mourned in turn the pain of third degree burns, the straw padding in Agnese's brazier, and the nature of Ieva's solitary work; and listened with equal patience to tales of Guntis as a soldier, her third lover also called Mātis, Anne's ballet that one snowy Christmas, and Guntis as a communist. Finally we came to Otomars and his many affairs. Somehow, it had to end with him.

"I guess he's got the money to take care of them. I don't know how he does it." I reached out for the bottle on the table. Empty. "I'm not sure he'll marry a single one."

Her reply surprised me. "Ritualized monogamy is ridiculous, anyway." She said it so matter-of-factly as if to be beyond debate. "The only rational for its societal dominance is the need for accountability in the children produced."

Only rational for its societal dominance? Such text book commentary. Was I sleeping with a political commissar? A social theorist? What kind of pillow talk was this?

She continued, her free hand fluttering about, talking as relaxed as if she were muttering about the evening dinner. "If we ever truly achieve a socialized state, there would be no need for monogamy." She leaned farther over me, turning her face up to see mine. "In a capitalist world somebody has to pay for a child's upbringing, yes? That's what a dowry is. To cover the costs of the bride and offspring. Ideally, the State should support all children equally. Then what does it matter who the father is? Or even the mother?"

Ah, yes, I reminded myself. She was Gāters's sister. Was the whole family this way? Something devoured with Ieva's stew? Or was this some way of keeping her brother alive? A form of hero worship? She couldn't really believe these things?

"But that would be anarchy. You could end up raising someone else's children. Someone else could raise yours."

I felt the tremor of her shrug along my body. "So? How is that different than adoption? Or marrying a woman who already has a child? Would you care for them less?" She put her head down again, the heat of her breath warming my chest. "It's what your brother is doing. What was his name again?"

"Otomars."

"Otomars's mistresses will find other men eventually, men who'll raise his kids. I would hope for their sake, those children are loved by these foster fathers."

"Well, I would hope so too." Such strange thoughts. And yet it was electric to be with a woman that had more to talk about than the color of the drapes.

I looked down, her trim little body pressed firmly against mine. So unconventional. And only twenty.

"Then we're agreed."

I wasn't sure about that. "And love?"

"Love too. Why can't you love more than one person? Why must one individual have every attribute you admire? Or desire? It's not realistic. A myth forced on young girls to keep them happy as the property of a sole man."

"What about diseases? Syphilis and such?"

She glanced up again, looking surprisingly young. A little girl concerned by her breach of manners. "I'm not saying you don't need to be careful, Wiktor." She put a hand lightly on my cheek. "It's more theory than practice."

Thank God. "So, you'd never actually follow them."

She gave me an evil glance, fully the woman again. "Well, maybe for you, if Gitta gets you back." She snuggled aggressively against me, pubic hair tickling my hip. "We'd still have to meet in secret." Kaiva pulled herself up, smooth skin rising against mine, gave me a light kiss on the mouth. Then another.

These playful flirtations turned passionate. She pushed me back against the mattress; sprinkled light kisses slowly down my chest, my stomach. Her flickering tongue circling my navel. I could feel the silken skin of her breasts against my legs, rough nipple tickling across my thigh as she descended, every kiss only slightly lower than the one before.

Until she stopped.

"Where did you get this scar?" She ran her finger along the wide, hairless mark running up from my pelvis. "The war?"

I felt the flush of embarrassment. The scar, they always asked about the scar eventually. "A deserter bayoneted me when I tried to stop him from killing two Latvians."

She rubbed my stomach tenderly, soft circular motions matching the turning thoughts in her mind. "Were you able to save them?"

"No." I ached inside. Sad for disappointing her. "I'm sorry."

I could see her eyes shining up at me in the darkness. "You tried Wiktor. Most your…most wouldn't." Kaiva kissed me again, ran a hand along my thigh.

"I knew you were different."

Chapter Nineteen

Otomars was in the driver's seat once again.

"Ready?" He said, looking back at me with a mischievous grin on his face.

"Ready."

His foot hit the accelerator and the sedan lurched forward, wheels spinning slightly before they found solid earth on the snow blanketed road. I held tightly to the rope handle, as we were suddenly jolted into motion. Fighting to keep my skis pointed straight, I maintained my tenuous balance, desperate to stay upright, to avoid the groove from the tire.

The car began to go faster, the rural landscape whizzing by in a featureless blur: the white cones of snow-covered trees, the extended brown rectangles of icy roadside fences and beyond them, the slowly passing dollhouse of a distant farm.

Kaiva hollered in ecstasy; straddling the other tire groove to my right, her hair pulled out from beneath her knit cap, it fluttered free behind. She even boldly put up one hand, taking a glimpse at me, daring me. *Come on Wiktor. Show me.*

I mimicked her. It was little problem for me, a boyhood spent in the countryside. Snow skiing from behind an automobile was not so different than being tethered to the rear of Father's wagon. A bit faster yes, but that simply made it all the more exciting.

As Kaiva let out another joyful yell, the tip of her ski caught the snow's groove and she began to wobble. Not an experienced skier, I could see her overcorrect, only worsening the problem. She was going over.

I let go, the car disappearing, a flash of clear November sky, and then the cool shower of powdered ice as I reached the ground. I lay back laughing, heard the "wumph" in the snow as Kaiva hit a few meters further on.

I sat up. Found her farther down the road wiping a glaze of fresh frost from her face. Watched with great amusement, as slightly dumfounded, she searched for her cap lost somewhere in her latest snowy tumble.

My laughs echoed in the open countryside. "You beat me, my Comrade. I had no chance." She only scowled in response.

"I think your hat is over there."

She scooped up her icy cap, tried to beat it clean across her trousered thigh. 'Wiktor Rooks, I will not let you, let me, win.' She marched over toward me taking a sudden lurch as she stepped into deeper snow.

I burst into laughter as she fought to extract herself, to somehow maintain her dignity. 'In two years have I ever let you win, Miss Gātera?'

Kaiva donned a half smile when she reached me. "Get your brother back over here." She slapped me playfully over the head with her snowy hat, a haze of biting ice settling into my hair, sliding cool across the top of my ears. "Just 'cause Otomars can't drive straight doesn't mean I need a sympathy fall."

The sedan pulled up, its exhaust an unwelcome industrial intrusion in the fresh country air. Otomars stepped out, a grin on his face. His latest – was it Rasa? – joined him from the passenger side. "You two are such the graceful pair. Considered figure skating?"

" 'Fraid you'll have to get back in the car, Brother." I looked at Kaiva's eyes, exuberant even in mock outrage. "The lady demands another rematch."

I walked with Kaiva through the little streets of Jēkabpils. With a few minor exceptions, it was a uniformly horizontal town. Nothing but single story houses made of long wooden planks, bunched along straight roads. A simple little hamlet on a bend in the Daugava as it stretched toward the Baltic Sea. Hours upstream from Rīga, the mighty river was not yet so wide, and a local fisherman standing on the bank could shout greetings to his counterpart casting for trout from Krustpils, Jēkabpils's mirroring town on the other side.

Kaiva liked to take me on these side trips. I suspected she hoped to open my mind further to her ideas. With time and the mutual discovery that follows in the wake of initial lust, she had correctly surmised that her great Red Rifleman was not really much of a communist. Not one at all actually. If this was the single flaw in our relationship, it seemed to do no damage, even opening things up for a lively, debate now and again. But since she'd started working for the underground communist newspaper, Kaiva had doubled her unspoken conversion efforts, suggesting lectures, books, or even a tired rally here and again. As if I hadn't had enough exposure to these after five years in Moscow.

When I declined, she would go anyway. After I discovered she regularly attended with one of the more handsome writers from her paper, well then, I decided perhaps the communists just might have more to say after all.

So, here I was, far from Rīga in this flat little town in snowy late November, wondering what it was exactly she planned on showing me. She'd been atypically quiet about the subject. Was this meeting more than a speech? Something greater than the usual canned and repetitive 'fiery' oratory? Who could say? I was happy just to spend time with her.

She led, her arms full of goods she had bought at the market square. Loaves of rye bread, pīrāgi buns filled with bacon and ham, potatoes, cucumbers, a head of lettuce, tomatoes, chicken breasts, and a glass jar of some local salad cream, all loosely wrapped in a quilt she'd brought from home. Much, much more than we would need for our return trip to Rīga. Were these for the guests? The lecturers? To free the minds of Marxist philosophers? To satisfy the bellies of young revolutionaries? I'd learn soon enough.

I had a free *pīrāgis* bun in my hand. Boyishly, I lightly bounced it off the back of her head, catching the pastry on the ricochet. She stopped to give me a quizzical look, but as soon as she turned back, I threw it once more.

"Stop it Wiktor." Her voice was ambiguous, difficult to tell how much farce there was in her agitation.

So I did it again. Arms full she was at my mercy.

"Stop it, I mean it." But there was a slight laugh in her exasperation.

One more time then for good measure.

"If any pieces get stuck in my hair, Wiktor." She turned and threw one at me. A quick duck and the bun sailed harmlessly over my shoulder dropping into a patch of melting slush.

"That was your lunch," she pointed, shaking her head at my immaturity. "We need to save the rest."

Feeling the mood had been appropriately lightened, we found ourselves approaching the end of the lane, the last few houses giving way to a series of half-collapsed sheds; off kilter, slanting, all in danger of being swallowed by the tall grass sticking out of the snow about them. Our dirt road a quagmire of melting ice and mud, it could only be that Kaiva had taken us down a wrong turn.

"Is this the right place?"

"Yes." She handed me the bundle in her arms. I juggled them, fearful of losing a potato, dropping a tomato or another precious bun.

She trudged out into the snow, through the patchy grass, until she found the half-hidden marks of a low, worn path. She followed it a few steps and then knocked lightly on the door of one of the sheds, the apex of the roof barely taller than she.

The door slowly opened and inside I could see a man sitting in an old, rust-marked wheelchair. He was somewhere close to thirty, unshaven with longish brown hair, and a deep brow that kept his eyes hidden in shadow. Within his shack I could see a worn space where the chair must rest, and a low, tiny blanketed bed along one side. Apart from a few odd items hanging from nails on the walls that was all it contained. The whole compartment was not four meters square.

Could a person really live there? Would he not freeze?

Kaiva gave the man a quick greeting, hugging him as he wheeled out into the snow, and then she motioned for me to join them. "Wiktor, this is Gotfrids. Gotfrids my friend Wiktor."

I wasn't sure who this fellow was, but I didn't like being introduced as a 'friend.' Not after this much time in courtship. What did that tell me about our relationship? Or this man?

With the ground turned to slush and little room in Gotfrids's tiny hut, there was no obvious place to have the picnic that Kaiva had now evidentially been planning. She soon discovered an abandoned shed that had collapsed completely to earth. Prying away some of the higher, dryer planks, Kaiva and I quickly assembled a little wooden raft in the snow to set ourselves and the meal upon. Gotfrids ate from the confines of his chair, the wheels rolled right up to the edge of the rough platform.

He was a quiet man saying less than little. It seemed Kaiva had to pry even simple answers out of him. He eyed me suspiciously as she assembled the sandwiches, mixed the salad. Only nodding or grunting in response to my passing small talk.

Despite his introversion, she was openly friendly to him. They clearly had known each other a long while. Slowly, much more from her statements than his, I found that Gotfrids too had been in the refugee settlements in Russia, and Kaiva had met him there as a girl. They spoke frankly of the state of his degenerative disease, one that sapped the strength from his limbs, had forced him into this wheelchair, and left him unable to work. Marooned Gotfrids in a wood shed at the end of a muddy street.

She seemed so comfortable with him and Gotfrids equally uneasy with me. What was the cause of his mistrust? Had they once been lovers, my presence a painful reminder of his loss? Or as a Latvian, did he despise my German roots? I shook my head at my own suspicions. Perhaps he just feared strangers. An understandable enough mentality in his current health.

I spent another hour or two, learning very little more about Gotfrids, mainly listening to Kaiva update him on her life. She leaned an arm across his knee as they talked, head almost in his lap, but she spoke so glowingly of me, of my kindness, of my struggle for The People in the Russian Civil War, that any jealous impulses arising from their intimacy were held strongly in check.

When we left Gotfrids, he thanked her, only making a small acknowledging nod toward me before wheeling himself back into his miniature home, the door to the outside world closing behind.

I had not gone far down the street before I asked: "Who is he?"

"A friend. Someone without another soul in the world." She took a sad look back at the crooked little shed. "He sometimes sleeps in that chair. It's becoming difficult for him to pull his body up into bed."

"I'm sorry to hear that." Trite again, Wiktor.

"That's what I'm talking about. Not bloody revolutions." She gripped my hand tightly, eyes carefully alert to my reaction. "Not burning manors, Wiktor. It's not about wars, it is about accountability. The State should take care of him, Gotfrids has no one."

"That's what the Church is for."

She looked around, mockingly. "Where is the church now?"

"I don't know." She could be so overly literal.

She gripped my hand harder. "I'm going to spend New Year's Eve with him. Give Gotfrids some company to start off the next year."

I was more than a little offended, such an important holiday, and she'd be spending it with another man. Even an invalid, it was a little…

Kaiva seemed to read my thoughts. "If he sleeps in the wheelchair, I'll sleep in the bed. If Gotfrids has the strength to reach the bed, I'll rest in the chair."

"That's not my concern. What about your absence? The faculty party?"

She gripped my hand. "You'll have me every other day of the year, darling. He needs a friend."

I remembered her introduction. "A 'friend' like me?"

"No, you're a lover." She reached up and kissed me on the cheek. "A wonderful,

wonderful love. But for that lunch at least, he had to be the most important one, for his well-being. Don't you understand?"

I nodded, if only to give me silence to consider my thoughts.

Together, we both passed back toward the market square taking a different route than we had come, walking hand in hand along a little ridge that set the bank of the river apart from the town. Below, in a little fenced-in yard was an apple tree, its stretching branches wearing a sprinkling of frost. In this waning autumn, it was completely devoid of fruit, except upon the very end of one long, spindly branch, where there hung a single golden apple.

"Isn't that pretty? So late in the year."

She nodded. "Yes, I love the contrast of gold against the tree's brown and the snow's white."

So striking was it in this landscape that I thought to reach off the heights of the ridge and pluck it for my lady. Unable to grasp it, I descended the slope, and started to straddle the yard's fence when Kaiva interrupted.

"Leave it, Wiktor," I looked back at her, a lovely shaped shadow still atop the ridge, "for someone else to enjoy."

Under looming grey skies, Rīga's central open-air market was filled with desperate shoppers shoving, pushing and jamming themselves into each stall; bodies thickened by layers of winter clothing, they packed around every display table, haggling, bargaining, all hoping to get enough goods to weather the coming winter storm: an icy tempest brewing menacingly out in the cold Baltic Sea. Kaiva had disappeared somewhere in this chaotic mass of people, searching for some sort of garnish which poor Agnese could never do without. Now alone, I fought for the seller's attention, trying to force the dwarfish owner to take my money for the potatoes in my hands. Unfortunately, he was locked in negotiations with an anxious and toothless old lady over the turbulent price of cucumbers. I had to wait my turn.

I could feel the temperature dropping through my jacket, beneath my cap. Landfall tonight they said. This was going to be a very uncomfortable few days.

It was surreal, fighting for food with the common Latvians. I really had joined the working masses hadn't I?

The sound of a solid thump, and my black leather cap flew from my head, momentarily resting on the shoulder of a man facing the other way, before sliding between the bodies to the market floor. That had been no breeze, someone had knocked it off!

I started to bend down, squeezing myself between the people, while at the same time trying to look through the crowd to find my assailant.

A short man, in a long black coat pointed at me, even as he was disappearing into the crowd. "We beat you Rooks. I told you we would, you son-of-a-bitch."

Seskis! After all this time!

I thought for a moment his insult might only be a little ribbing, a machismo gesture at a former comrade. But no, Seskis hadn't returned to me, hadn't even stopped. No care to converse, no desire for even the shortest reunion. Strictly a taunt. Nothing else.

I reached the gravely floor, lost in a forest of legs, thick coat-tails drifting across my vision like fog on the pier. I found my cap pinned under the heel of some unobservant buyer, still perusing the produce above. It took several accelerating taps on his leg before he finally moved off.

I forced myself to my feet, nearly being crushed by those seeking a better position at the table. The cap was mud caked underneath, smashed, with a shoe's sole imprint across the brim. What had possessed Seskis to do this? A man I hadn't seen in years. Not even a salutation. No question about my well-being or the affairs of our mutual comrades?

Very strange.

That night, as the howling December winds rattled the shutters, and frozen gusts sputtered beneath a jittery door, I lay huddled with Kaiva. Both fully dressed, buried underneath several blankets, body heat for once a higher priority than romance.

I mimicked Seskis's expression. "The anger in his face as he shouted; I'd never wronged him." I brushed her hair for a few moments with a free hand, before returning quickly to the safe warmth of the coverings. "It seems he hated me so. They *all* hate us so." I grimaced. Unthinkingly I'd opened up a far wider, sorer, subject.

She thought for a moment, tucking her head beneath my chin. "Wiktor, darling, I don't mean to offend, but did you…did you ever ask yourself why?" She pulled back to look into my eyes. "Consider the cause of this malice?"

"Of course, every time I remember my boyhood going up in flames." There was an anger in my voice, one usually kept in check when discussing the issues between our peoples. Seskis had tapped into something within me.

Her cadence was calm, even sweet. "And what did you conclude?"

I knew what she wanted to hear. An answer that would match her beliefs, reaffirm her faith in her lover. Some logical, Marxist rationale that would throw the blame squarely back on my kind, but I felt too passionate at this moment, too confessional to be tactful: "Because they wanted what we owned. It's simple really. Our nice life, our things, they were there for the taking. So they took them."

I felt the friction of her nodding. "I'm sure your family had many nice possessions." Her tone remained calm. "Your people, the German aristocrats always donned the trappings of rulers, but let us be honest…they never took the responsibility."

"What do you mean?"

Her words were measured, unrelenting, "I mean, they collected the taxes, managed the serfs well enough. But when some new enemy appeared on the horizon, the Poles, the Swedes, or finally the Russians, your ancestors were all too happy to negotiate, to preserve your own way of life at the expense of your workers."

Another communist myth. "We fought too, there were many great generals…"

"A few, Wiktor. A few. But when Peter of Russia brought his army, three-quarters of my people perished in defense of their homes. Three out of every four, darling. The countryside was littered with our corpses." Underneath the covers, her hand found mine, always her way of communicating unity when her words grew too rough. Yet, she still said them, still thought them: "But the aristocrats, Wiktor, they fashioned a deal, merely changed the delivery address of their tributes. How had their lives changed? A new language to learn, a new court to charm, is this fighting for us? Leading?"

"Ancient history."

My response agitated her. "You think so? It's happened in your very family." She peered up at me, breath warming my face. "When the Germans took Courland in the Great War, Baron Kaltenbach, your own sister's father-in-law, had an audience with Kaiser Wilhelm during his visit to Jelgava. You told me so yourself."

"I had nothing to do with that."

She ignored my response. "What sort of things do you think they talked about? The weather? The price of shoes in Berlin? Or do you somehow believe Kaltenbach demanded the kaiser take his army and leave our people in peace? Did he spit words of rage and defiance while at the emperor's feet? I have my doubts, Wiktor."

She turned her back to me, cocooning her body against mine. "Have there ever been more Judas rulers? To bargain with the enemy against their own subjects? Of course the Latvians want you…I'm sorry…them…out."

"That's just one opinion."

There was a long silence. To let the discussion end thus, might have implied meanings. I returned to my original point: "But why Seskis specifically, Kaiva? I had fought against the Germans alongside him. No deals then."

Her voice was leveler again, almost sad. "Some people can't differentiate the group from the individual. They need to keep us all in separate hat boxes." She turned head up from the mattress, almost able to see my face. "There are those at my newspaper, who ask again and again why I am seeing you?"

Was that to imply she sometimes wondered the same? "And what do you say?"

"Only that you're different." She put her head back to the pillow.

"And that I love you very much."

New Year's Eve, 1926 Rīga

Otomars and I sat smoking in the back room of Fisher's Auxiliary Club in Rīga. A posh dining and drinking establishment in the cellar level of an extensive Jugendstil building running along Pils Iela. Owned and frequented by British dignitaries, businessmen, and high-ranking military officers, it had become Otomars's new favorite watering hole. Many nights he could be found sitting in a thick leather chair, lost in the sauna-like haze of its dark wooded and emerald green carpeted cigar room. A secluded rear chamber very similar, I imagined, to those that must exist in cosmopolitan London.

His answer was typically calm: "Some colleagues at the Ministry simply asked me for a recommendation, I had never heard of this Vereshchagin fellow."

I nodded, greatly relieved at having finally found the courage to raise the subject after all this time. "He wanted me to be more than a liaison, I was effectively…" I whispered this, though I was unsure why, "a spy."

He smiled, keeping the cigar locked between his teeth. "And were you a good one?"

I thought about that for a moment, took a long puff of my own. Such a different taste than a cigarette: fuller, more overpowering, the dry flavor lingering in the mouth so much longer. "I'd say I might have been too sympathetic to my targets."

"A danger, I suppose for everyone involved in such an undertaking. Yes?"

"I mean their ideas were reactive, excessive even," I lightly tapped my cigar in the ashtray, "but understandable seeing how they were being treated."

He switched vices, removing his cheroot for a sip of beer. "Well, it served you well these sympathies. You could not have survived the Bolsheviks without playing their game."

Finished with my cigar, I folded my hands, sinking deep into the chair's comfortable padding. A man could fall asleep here and die slowly, happily, of smoke asphyxiation. "It wasn't so much a game, Otomars, as opportunity. And they were offering freedom, choice. Or so they claimed."

Even in the dark, underneath the haze, his eyes disagreed. "Well let's just say you picked the winner. And philosophies aside, that's never a dumb move."

"They certainly didn't win here, as Kaiva never tires of reminding me."

"Not yet at least." He took another puff. "Don't think the game is over, Wiktor. Isn't that what your young belle is working for?"

I closed my eyes. Yes, I could just drift away in this chair. "They have no support. The economy is too prosperous. Everybody's happy in the present boom."

"You're thinking too local, Brother. There are 100 million very committed communists just over our eastern border. Thanks in no small part to your little adventure in Russia."

I opened an eye, frowned at him. "I was already in the Russian army when the government changed over, what choice did I have?"

His silence was response enough. I changed the subject.

"This is pretty exclusive. How did you find this place?"

Cigar in hand, he pointed to the ceiling. "I know the landlord of the building. When the tenant changed from brothel owner to three Scottish gentlemen last year, I asked if he might find a way for me to gain membership. Three days later, I was drinking whisky and eating fish and chips."

His satisfied tone told me he preferred this topic. I resumed my comfortable rest, knowing full well Otomars would love to expand his answer to include some personal philosophy, if I'd let him. Another lesson for his little brother.

I was right. "Politicians come and go, Wiktor. Governments rise and fall. We've had four in the last twenty years. At least. The key to this life, Brother, is in knowing the people who will always be in position to help you." He paused for an inhalation, while I subtly smiled at his predictability. "If you want a train ticket, don't bother the Minister of Transportation, he'll be out with the next coal shortage. Befriend the guy who switches the rails, greasy or not, he'll work there forever." I gave him a gentle nod, trying to embrace sleep. Keep rambling, Brother.

"The men who really run things, Wiktor, are not in the newspapers. And they don't want to be."

Yes, so much to learn. Thirty-two years old and still needing constant instruction.

I heard the clinking of glasses. Opening my eyes, I saw a young woman set down a tray with two steaming mugs of coffee, the aroma of caffeine pulling me unpleasantly back from my attempt at slumber.

Otomars said something coyly to her in English. Her response seemed affable enough, and they bantered back and forth for a few minutes in that mysterious language. Though I caught very few words, her tone, her body language, seemed agreeable. By the end of the discussion, the young Brit even trailed a light caress along his shoulder as she went off to fetch the next order. How did he do it? Twice her age and nearly triple her weight, what could she see in him? My brother's charm with the fairer sex had always amazed me. Just another unknowable aspect of such a multifaceted man.

A satisfied grin on his face, an eyebrow triumphantly waving, he returned his attention to me. "What do you think of English women, Wiktor?"

"I don't know if I've really been exposed."

"I think they're charming." He pinched the air between forefinger and thumb. "A tad heavy, perhaps. All that greasy food. But still such cherubic, nice round faces."

I shrugged. "I believe I'll stick with Kaiva."

He looked incredulous. "Yes, but for how long? You shouldn't get her expectations raised. It's not fair."

"Her expectations? I hope to marry her." Maybe my brother wasn't such an astute observer after all. It had been two years, what did he think I was doing with her?

"Wiktor, no…she's not what you need." He crushed his cigar in the tray. "Right now, you're still swept away in lust. You're not thinking about the difficulties it would bring."

"I know…our parents."

He sat forward in the chair, elbows on knees. "The whole clan, Wiktor. The Letts took everything from them. Now one will be part of the family? And a communist too! Father's health is a little dubious as it is."

"I mean she's so different. A woman who is not just window dressing." Could he not feel the excitement woven into my very voice?

Otomars frowned, a wisp of smoky haze crawling along his high forehead. "Anne's not window dressing."

"Yes, but Erich treats her like she is."

He didn't say anything.

"I love Kaiva, Otomars, isn't that enough?"

"No, it won't be." He smiled reluctantly. "But when you're in love you think that it will."

"And can you see that I am?"

He stared at me for a long moment, before finally nodding. "Yes, I can see that."

Was I actually about to win a discussion with my brother? Was this possible? "So do I have your blessings? I may need an ally with the family."

His eyes were somewhere off in the gloom. "I can't always protect you Wiktor."

I answered with disappointed silence, so he continued, eyes meeting mine. "But of course you do."

I sat with Kaiva in the sands of a midnight beach, the eternal July sun briefly testing the ocean's waters, leaving only its halo to turn the underside of offshore clouds a painterly pink.

I thought I could still detect the stray notes of the American Jazz musician playing his saxophone in the outdoor amphitheatre in nearby Majori. Or was it only the rhythmic waves lapping on the Jurmala sands? Or the voices of boisterous campers round a fire far off in the direction of Rīga?

No matter. I breathed in the warm, salty air. The great city was only a half hour by motorcar away, but its high spires and ornate facades were nearly unimaginable in the relaxed serenity and natural majesty surrounding us, the beautiful Baltic Sea stretching out in front, purple and blue waters churning beneath eternally lit skies. Sheathing trees behind, a great sylvan veil eclipsed all signs of man's encroachment. Yes, it was only thirty minutes to a different world entirely.

The faculty dinner had gone well at the resort restaurant nearby. Tenure at last. It was all perfect. This had to be the place and the moment.

"Kaiva, will you marry me?"

Her face remained surprisingly unsurprised, and a little sorrowful. She put a hand to my cheek, the grains of sand in her palm less rough than her words. "Wiktor, you know how I love you, and how deeply that love runs. Must I become your possession too?"

I felt a constriction in my chest, a painful contortion in my stomach. Not an unexpected answer, not completely. I just…somehow I thought the moment would carry her along as well.

She could see that she had hurt me,. "Wiktor, you make me happier than any man I've ever known. I can't imagine my life without you. It would be such a darker world."

I nodded.

Her eyes were swelling. Why was my wonderful offering turning her so sad? "I've spent three years with you, Wiktor. I want to stay with you."

I picked a grain of sand from her lips. "Forever?"

"Very much so."

I felt slightly better, sniffed away any coming tears. She wanted to be with me after all. For now that would need to be enough.

I gripped her hand tightly. Kaiva smiled, a tear running down her own face. Yes, she would stay with me.

I'd convince her of the rest.

Chapter Twenty

May 1928, Lübeck, Germany

It had taken me six more months to get Kaiva to finally agree, and another four to convince my parents to meet my betrothed, but at last we were all at dinner.

Fiancée and family nearly through the meal and no fatalities: A miracle.

But there was still time.

Despite these less-than-latent tensions, I had tried to enjoy the evening.

Theirs the larger apartment, the dinner was held at Anne and Erich's rather than our parents', a beautiful modern dwelling with a magnificent view of the river Trave and all seven of the town's great naves from their high balcony. And if the furniture was more decorative than comfortable, and the staff recently reduced to one biweekly Danish maid, well they still seemed to live an elegant enough life, far better than mine, certainly. Only the masterly oil painting depicting the baron's old tree-shrouded manor, hanging prominently above the empty hearth, gave any hint of the magnificence of glories lost.

To my relief, our parents seemed surprisingly robust in their new environment. Yes, Father had complained repeatedly of weakness in his legs, and Mother warbled on about the disaster of her new hairstyle, the one that looked exactly the same as everyone she'd ever had, but, all in all, they'd surprised me with how well they were adjusting. Or as much as I could discern in the first night of a busy five day visit.

Erich looked nearly identical to his wedding day, barely a crease in his forehead, his dark locks even longer, bushier, and rather askew. A little, I mused, like the unkempt coif of a recent Nobel Prize winner, the German physicist Albert Einstein. I almost made the reference, but doubted anyone at the table would catch it. Or care to. My well-read brother, maybe, Kaiva, perhaps...

Anne was, if anything, thinner than she had been as a young woman. Four children hadn't expanded her waist or rounded her cheek at all. Her boys, Carsten and Elias, were absent on some school expedition, but both of my young nieces,

Jana, five, and Bettina, three, continued to terrorize my sister by escaping to their spacious balcony. She would watch them from the dining table, through the sliding glass doors, and though the terrace railing was high enough to keep her daughters safely penned inside, they'd still given her an unrestful, fitful dinner. Through four courses, I hadn't seen her relax and finish one.

Erich, my father, and his elderly bachelor friend Rothbart, a fellow Courland exile who had taken up residence near Berlin, spent most of the dinner engaged in their own dull little conversations, preoccupied with hunting, fine tobacco, and upcoming motor car races. It was only during this last dinner course, when they'd turned to politics, that Kaiva began to drift away from Otomars's less-than-engaging account of his recent trip to Helsinki.

I saw her eyes wander, passing between the speakers, following their conversation. Up until that moment, Kaiva had made me undeniably proud, the perfect lady all evening long. Complimenting Erich and Anne on the food, the décor and their generous hospitality, she'd then spent an ingratiating twenty minutes playing with my nieces in the drawing room before the meal. A wise tactic: win over the children first, recruit these boisterous allies to help charm the more aged later.

Even in the most trying moments Kaiva had astounded me with her self-discipline: Feigning interest when Mother went on extensively about the Christmas bouquet she received from Gitta, who apparently was still unwed, poor girl; barely rolling her eyes when Erich called the local help 'lazy and slow-witted.' And she bit her lip triumphantly as Father explained to Rothbart that I had been a 'prisoner' of the Bolsheviks during the war.

But it didn't last.

Erich shook his head sadly, the way he always did when expecting empathy. "I can't just keep paying these attorney fees. If the League of Nations won't act on this next petition, I think we should find another avenue to protect our interests."

Rothbart put down his fork, and clapped his hands excitedly. "I know just the group."

This was just too much temptation for Kaiva. "Why do you feel the League should take action?" They turned to her, surprised by the sudden breach of their privacy. She slowly sipped her soup from the spoon, curious eyes watching Erich patiently for a reply.

His response was less than bemused. "The Latvian government illegally seized our estates. We are appealing for international pressure to return them."

Kaiva looked about the table. "I'm sorry. I don't understand. You're living in a fine apartment, we're drinking…"she crouched slightly, reading the bottle's label, "sixteen year old wine." She peered up again, a strange innocence in her tone: "Your life seems more than comfortable. Why do you need more?"

My mother failed to muffle her words in the palm of her hand. "A lady doesn't talk politics at the dinner table." A remark clearly directed at my fiancée though her eyes never left me.

"Now, Mother…"

Erich seemed to find it undignified to even have to defend his position. "I'll say it again, my dear. Because your government stole…"

Kaiva corrected him, pointing lightly with her spoon: "They're not *my* government, Mr. Kaltenbach. I'm a communist."

Mother's fork rattling in her plate, she suddenly found something to attend to in the next room. Kaiva's eyes followed her into the hall before returning to Erich. "And I have plenty of issues with the present Saeima but land reform is one of the few things they've done right."

Father broke in, wielding the butter knife like a lance. "I was born on such a seized estate, my dear. As was Otomars and Anne and your future husband, if it should come to that." Anne put a tender hand on his shoulder, whispering in his ear. He lowered the knife. A little.

A good idea. I put my hand on Kaiva's knee, but nothing slowed her. Quite the opposite, she seemed invigorated by the debate. "Yes, but you were only a single family of five. Can't you see?" She actually smiled at Father. Could she not understand the effect of her words? "Your farm probably now supports two or three full Latvian families."

She returned to Erich. "And the baron's? I don't know how large it was… perhaps a half-dozen? A dozen? A small community?" She looked about as if somebody would supply the missing estimate to bolster her argument. No one did.

The smile again: "It's simply a better use of the land."

Erich's face was turning red. "That was my father's land they stole, Kaiva." His use of the past tense was painfully telling with the baron too unwell to attend tonight.

I squeezed Kaiva's thigh like a market melon, but she only took my hand, holding it softly beneath the table: "I understand that it has sentimental value Erich, but that can hardly surmount the need to feed more people. The fact that your father possessed it…" she looked briefly to the ceiling thinking of the best comparison, "makes the estate a trophy of sorts."

Yes, she liked this word. "Its value was in what it represented to you personally, not in the soil's most efficient use." She scanned their faces as if she'd find agreement. "And frankly, I am not surprised the League of Nations hasn't responded. There are greater problems on this Earth than worrying about returning people's trophies. No one at this table is starving."

Erich was taking the breath needed to shout something terrible when Otomars wisely decided to speak up. "Miss Gātera, Wiktor tells me you want to be an editor. Is that correct?"

Kaiva seemed cheery, as if this was a healthy discussion rather than the terrible, divisive affront it had been. "That's my dream, yes." She took another sip of soup, turned to me: "This is really good, try some Wiktor." She offered a taste from her spoon, pushing it toward my mouth.

"A little later, thank you."

As all proficient public speakers can, Otomars expanded his voice without raising it: "But in a communist entity, the government assigns your vocation, placing the individual at the labor needs of the State. Yes, Kaiva?"

"Correct."

"So, if they need sheep shavers and you want to be a newspaper editor that's just too bad. The government hands you a pair of shears. True?" My brother repeatedly clicked the nails of his thumb and pinkie as he timed her responses. Did anyone else notice this habit?

Kaiva was up for the challenge. "Well presumably they would qualify me, so your example is ludicrously extreme. But if that's what the people needed, it's no different than if a corporation rejects…"

"If a corporation rejects you in your chosen field, you go to the next company on the street." He rolled his hand in the air. "And the next and the next. But if a communist government rejects you, where do you go? You have no other options, Kaiva."

"Then I'd shear some sheep."

He leaned forward, heavy forearms resting leaden on the table. "Does that sound like freedom to you? Would that make you happy? Being told this is what you had to do and it was illegal to do otherwise?"

She let go of my hand, so she too could prop an elbow on the table. "Of course not, no one likes to be forced…"

Otomars rocked back, the table lurching free of his weight. He snapped his fingers in the air. "'Forced!' a good word. We'll keep that one. And when you were 'forced' to leave for that refugee camp, did you feel your family's reaction to the loss of their home was overly 'sentimental?' A mere 'trophy' lost in the war?"

Her eyes recognized his tactic, a little less zest in her voice. "No, it was extremely traumatic…"

"Exactly, 'traumatic.' A traumatic experience the loss of one's home, no matter the rational behind it." He spread out his palms. "Perhaps then you can relate to others at this table?"

She nodded. "Yes, perhaps so."

"There is theory and there is experience Kaiva. Can you reconcile them?"

"I can…I can. And I apologize if I offended anyone." She seemed genuinely contrite, smiling to our disapproving relatives each in turn.

Still, either her principles or her pride wouldn't let the fires fully extinguish. "But it doesn't dispute the benefits of land reform."

Otomars nodded as if conceding the point. "It doesn't. I am simply illustrating that our life experiences are not so dissimilar. No one around this table should be so quick to judge."

He stood up. "Not poor hosts." Though he only looked at me before turning his eyes squarely on Kaiva. "And certainly not guests."

There was a hovering, uncomfortable silence. I once again lovingly gripped Kaiva's knee.

"Now, if you'll excuse me." Otomars bowed slightly. "I think our mother may need assistance."

I leaned over the railing wondering if it would just be easier to jump over it. A three story fall? Surely it would be a quicker, less painful demise. This evening couldn't get much worse.

How wrong I was.

Kaiva had only been in the water closet a minute or so when Otomars found me, had my arm firmly in his grip. His voice was slow but seethed with rage. "Let me ask you something Wiktor: Would you let someone talk to your family like that if they didn't have a vagina?"

"Otomars!" I pulled my elbow away from him violently. It took all my will not to strike him. No, no. I backed a step. All I needed to cap this night was a physical altercation with my brother.

He used his bulk to block our conversation from the other guests. "You tell me she parrots her brother. Yes? Would you have kept quiet as long if he had been saying those very same words? Let him justify the loss of your home so flippantly? Let him chase your own mother out of the room?"

"He's dead Otomars." I tried to look past his shoulders. "I think you all are being a little excessive…"

His face eclipsed mine. I feared I might tumble backwards over the rail. "Did you raise objections to this sort of talk back in your army days? No? No wonder Vereshchagin thought you were such a disappointment."

"She has her own views."

"I don't give a damn what her beliefs are, ostracizing Erich is never a smart thing, Wiktor." He shoved a finger into my chest so hard, his drink spilled out of the other hand. "He keeps our parents fed. And he has to because of people like your little girl there."

I tried to speak, but Otomars wouldn't let me get a word in. "I'm going to have to spend the rest of the night repairing the damage she's done."

I held a hand up, pushed myself away along the rail. "I'll talk to Erich."

"No. I'll talk to him. You just keep Kaiva clear of him." He turned and walked toward the dining room. "It's time you grew up and pulled your weight in this family, Wiktor. I'm tired of solving all the problems."

I sat there a few moments, trying to calm down. Just let the warm spring breeze flowing over the balcony carry my stress away. As justifiably sensitive as everyone was to leaving Courland, I was fairly certain that Erich was over-reacting. Sent scurrying to the back rooms by the words of a twenty-four year old girl, a fine baron he would have made.

I noticed his wife was still in the common rooms, Anne standing comfortably with her two daughters at the dessert table. She didn't seem flustered. Why was the new family master under siege?

I let out a long sigh. Otomars censure annoyed me. I'd done everything the family had ever asked. Now I was begging for just one thing in return: To accept this woman, for the night at least. Was that too much?

Kaiva joined me. Of course, she was no saint either. "A trophy," what was she thinking? She hadn't even asked if my mother was upset. Was she so oblivious?

LENIN'S HAREM

She leaned on the rail next to me, looping her arm under mine. "Did you notice Erich and Anne at dinner?"

You mean before the train wreck? "No…In what way?"

"They don't talk. They don't touch. She never says a word to him, really to anyone."

Welcome to German aristocratic society, Kaiva. "I think the girls are a distraction. Anne's best one on one. And her hearings not…"

"She doesn't love him."

My agitation showed through: "Keep that thought to yourself, okay? For once." If that opinion got out…

She looked offended. I rubbed her hand slowly in apology. "All I'm saying, Kaiva, is they've been married a long while now, the fires can cool a little."

She watched Anne spooning pudding into a bowl for little Bettina. "I wonder if she ever loved him?"

"What do you mean?"

She put her free hand to her lip. "I'll bet there was someone else before, a ballet partner, a stable boy, some perfect memory which still holds her heart." She paused, leaned her head on my shoulder. "Doesn't your sister remind you of my mother a little?"

I thought about this observation. Anne was towering, terribly gaunt, blonde and elegant. Ieva smallish, compact, amber-haired, tidy.

"No. Not really." Not in the slightest actually.

"I think she does." She gave me a kiss on the cheek. "I'm going to talk to her."

I gently clasped her hand. "Kaiva, don't you think you've…"

She gently swatted my arm away. "I'll be good, Comrade" a fading whisper, silently mouthing that last dreaded word. She gave me a flash of mischievous grin as she trotted away. I watched her step right into conversation with Anne, putting a bare arm around the taller woman's waist. To my surprise, Anne let her keep it, making small talk with my fiancée.

I sat there a moment, leaning against the railing. They would never accept her, even as Anne laughed at something Kaiva said, even as both women knelt to engage my nieces in play. Even then I knew. I could not keep both these worlds. One had to go.

Yes, she was an outcast here, but strangely, it was I who was standing all alone.

I had stood there a long time, when Otomars approached with two drinks in his hands. His face contrite, he handed one gin to me, an obvious peace offering.

I took the initiative: "So, how's Erich then?"

He laughed, a completely different man than the maniac of an hour before. "He's better. He thinks you're insane but nothing worse than that."

Erich was certainly not my largest concern. "Our parents, they hate her, don't they?"

He nodded, a light smirk on his face. "Yes, they do. But really Wiktor what did you expect?" His hand, the one that had gripped my arm so harshly now comforted my shoulder. "Always thinking with your heart."

I stood silently, so he continued, his voice more comforting than his words. "You must remember Wiktor, her people, yes not Kaiva personally I know, but her people torched our house, stole our land, have effectively forced our parents out of their homeland. They are older than us; it is not as easy for them in this new world."

"And did you bring a nice, humble girl, happy to be moving up into a finer class? No, you brought a fiery argumentative communist. She's not very tactful. Couldn't she just nod and eat the ham?"

"You mean like Anne does? She wasn't always so mute."

"That's a cruel thing to say about your sister, Wiktor."

"I know, I know, I'm sorry." I put my fingers to my temple, to dam the breaking headache. "I'm going to be alone at the wedding, aren't I? No one from the family will come?"

Otomars's face shown in the late city lights. "Are you still going through with it, Wiktor? After the reality of tonight?"

I nodded. "Yes… There is no comparison. These family dinners occur once every few years now, Otomars. But in every hour of every day, she makes me happy."

"Even these last hours?"

I looked at her over with Anne and my nieces. Both women were still sitting on the floor playing some sort of word game with energetic Bettina, Kaiva's arm snuggling a sleepy Jana against her shoulder.

She had been so concerned for my sister's happiness, misguided fears, yes, but still genuine in their intentions.

"Yes, even now, Otomars." I downed some gin, let out an endless sigh. This would be the last I'd see of my parents.

Otomars just shook his head, but there was something surrendering in his voice, a tint of the long absent mirth. "God you are a fool, Wiktor, a complete and utter fool."

I smiled remorsefully. "Well, if you're going to be a fool…"

He bear hugged me across the shoulder, shaking me supportively. "But you won't be alone at that wedding."

Chapter Twenty-one

November 1938, Moscow

I stepped off the bus, squeezing between two sullen servicemen into a bitter cold and grey world. Beneath dull skies, I shoved through the oncoming passengers, an assortment of shadows and shapes adorned in the plainest of clothes, all pressing together too tightly to breathe, and finally found a little room on the uneven concrete slabs that served as a sidewalk. I gathered my bearings, checked my belongings, and quickly made my way down the street. I was late.

The landscape was not the one I remembered. The outskirts of Moscow had seen the most construction in the past decade, the city having swollen with forced industrialization and countless refugees of collectivization. Huge monolithic tenements dominoed toward the skyline. In every direction, rose a dozen of these faceless grey boxes, devoid of decoration and expression; vertical grid works of concrete, their architects confusing uniformity for equality. A nightmare of regularity. Never pretty, Moscow had not aged well.

Continuing, I stepped into the road's gutter to avoid a thick mob of old ladies grouping for another truant bus. Heads wrapped in drab scarves of faded green or washed-out blue; their haggish features mutely watched every step as I passed. I nodded, but not one matron acknowledged my gesture. Was this the fate of all those magnificent Russian beauties? To turn small, square and silent? A travesty of nature. Had it always been so? Something ingrained in their genes? Or was this some engineered by-product of imprisoning rural people in this cold, faceless city? To squeeze them into something smaller? Better to stack them in those countless concrete towers?

A phantom conjured from my past: Could statuesque Alisa have withered so? Turned to a cubic spinster?

No, no, forever twenty-three and perfect. I cast such aging images from my mind. As all icons, she was best left undisturbed.

I rounded a corner, beneath darkening clouds. It was already cold this autumn, a long harsh winter beckoning. I tightened my jacket; found the little side path: a white dirt gap between posts in the low skeletal fence. Just beyond lay a compact treeless park. It might have been a field used for sport or the joyless playground of a nearby tenement, but its true nature lay in the lines of low unadorned headstones. The newer ones typically Soviet: flat squares unembellished. Even in death, it was dangerous to display pride in anything other than the State itself.

A chilling breeze crept up my ankles, fluttering the letter as I unfolded it:

Fifth row in, eighth plot to the right off the path.

I stepped off the dirt onto the flaxen grass, heels sinking deep into the soft mud below, quickly made my way along, somberly counting. Some tombstones had flowers, others a painting propped against them. I felt impossibly old. Alone.

It was the seventh plot, one earlier than I'd been told. But there was no doubting I'd found the correct grave. The emotions took me. I dropped to my knees, felt the earthen moisture seep into the shins of my trousers.

Heinrichs Juškevičs
Born: August 1896 Died: May 1938

Treason, Heinrichs, they'd said treason. Oh, what had been done? What act was possible?

My mind drifted back to his rare letters: tame, complacent, understated all. So typically Juškevičs. That one phone call last March, his voice filled with pride, full of successes, no hint of doubt.

I plucked some grass from the earth, snapped a few grey-brown blades in my hand, letting them flutter away on the breeze. What had he failed to mention? Kept hidden from me? Some ill path taken? An unwise decision that had pulled him into something brewing and sinister? Cautious Juškevičs, it was so unlikely. Or was this all a horrible mistake? The Soviets seemed to be finding so many sinners now; could a few innocents be taken in the harvest?

I looked at the little granite marker, feeling the two meters of earth between me and my friend. So close was Juškevičs, only a man's height away. What had once been an ambitious learned being was right here, and yet irretrievable, his remains no more alive than the stone bearing his name. I pounded the earth in front of me, cold mud sticking to my hand. Damn. Damn. What had happened?

I looked at the plain headstone. Assembly line cut, marginally polished, made without thought, without care, by people who never knew Juškevičs. There was no mention of his rank, stripped in the denouncement, taken days before his life.

I fumbled inside my coat pocket, withdrew a grainy remnant of chalk from my lectures, scratched 'Colonel' in front of his given name. Vandalism? Sacrilege?

Vindication. Juškevičs's sin could not have been so great, that it erased twenty years in their service. I would never believe that.

I stared at the name, watching the looser bits of chalk flow away on the breeze. Buried here so far from his native lands, would anyone come to mourn him in Moscow? In this locking land? Would they dare cry for an Enemy of the State?

The periphery of my vision found movement. Turning, I spied a little white dust cloud spinning between the rigid steps of a thin man in a long black coat, walking along the cemetery path. He discarded his furred hat as he approached, exposing a hairless fish-pale skull; flat and wide like a seashell, deep ravines stepping down the forehead. My soul crept along my spine, the stiffness of his gate and lifelessness of his countenance a bit too reminiscent of the corpse, as if some nosferatu had silently risen up from the very stones around me. And as he grew closer, I could see the deep gullies cut around his eyes, leaving two pale green islands adrift in molted, receding skin. He appeared ancient, far, far too old for a man not yet fifty.

But then there was that smile, immortal, it would outlast Heaven itself.

"Līcis."

"Five children, Herberts? How do you feed them all?"

He sipped the cognac, rolling it in his glass as he listened. The dim little bar was packed with husky factory workers, the smell of alcohol running a distant third to the acidic scents of machine oil and cheap tobacco. Līcis seemed to know the bartender, for the two of us were served noticeably quicker than most of the other agitated customers. So much for the brotherhood of communism, not when spirits were at premium.

"It isn't always easy, so many mouths. We buy all the goods from the state stores." He laughed. "Karina is as forbidden to approach the farmer's market as I am…" Līcis stopped to think about this for a moment, rapping his knuckles lightly on the barroom table. "As I am the whorehouse, Wiktor. One step inside is grounds for annulment!" He slapped the wood, chuckling again, enjoying his earthy analogy.

"Annulment? After seventeen years?"

He shook my comment away. "And you Wiktor? Still no children? Trust me; they keep you young my friend."

Despite his appearance, in so many ways he seemed the eternal child: boisterous, fidgeting with his drink as I spoke, all too antsy to spill out the next mirthful critique on what I was saying, very little seemed to have changed on the inside of Līcis. If anything, he had grown more confident with his eccentricities, unhindered by what others might think, freed by the melting of class distinctions.

I wondered why time had ravaged his body so. Military life? Alcoholism? An unmentionable illness? Would I dare broach it?

I returned to his question. "I know they do, Herberts. It's Kaiva, for a long time she didn't have time for a baby."

"A woman without a child is like…" He struggled for some appropriate metaphor, contorting his face for several seconds before admitting defeat. "Why not then, Wiktor?"

"She works so hard at the newspaper in Rīga. It's her life really. She absolutely believes in this communism. It was a bit of an obsession with her. I have several long-winded theories on why."

"'Was an obsession?' Have her opinions changed?"

I finished my flimsy ale. "No…no, not at all Herberts, if anything when the Ulmanis government drove the party underground, she only doubled her efforts. I never saw her."

"And thus no children?"

"Well something happens to a woman when she gets into her thirties, Herberts. Even to Kaiva. I won't lie; a child is all she wants now. And she's a fearsome woman when focused."

"I'm surprised your back has held up." He gave me a ribald smirk. "So, you'll be buying drinks soon, my friend, I'll have mine in advance." That nearly toothless grin again, he raised his hand for the barkeep.

I shrugged. "It's been nearly two years…perhaps you should wait on that order."

The ravines on his baldhead deepened, his green eyes turned curious: "Two? Is everything…"

"Fine, fine…She's been having tests. My brother knows the best doctors in Rīga."

He looked into his empty glass. "And you as well?"

"Please, Herberts." And we both laughed heartily, perhaps a little too much so, as it was followed by a lengthy silence. The glasses clinked lonesomely when the barkeep gave us another set of drinks.

Līcis renewed the conversation. "How's the family?"

"Never hear from them. My brother keeps in touch, but I'm the one who married the communist."

He toasted me supportively. "And a Latvian. Moving up my friend."

"Well in Kaiva's case, yes…other Latvians I am less sure of."

He ignored my jibe. "Ah, well if she blossomed into anything like her sister…"

"You should see Agnese, Herberts. As round as a teapot."

"No, no, no. Don't say such things." He rocked back in his chair, a palm thrown melodramatically over his face. "A man must have his dreams, Wiktor."

"Not a man with five children."

More brief laughter. More heavy silence. Thoughts hung like ghosts over both of us.

I dared exorcise them. "Herberts?" I girded myself for the weight of the question. "What happened with Juškevičs?"

His answer was surprisingly fast coming. "Treason. Simple as that." He settled the point by striking the bottom of his glass emphatically on the table.

Such a harsh condemnation for our old comrade shocked me. From the usually jovial Līcis, so canine loyal to his friends, it seemed impossible that he could agree with the verdict.

"C'mon Herberts, you can't believe that Heinr…"

"Yes, same as all the others, as Eidemanis, Alksnis, and Jukums Vācietis." His voice boomed toward me. Other heads turned.

I stared in disbelief. "But it was Heinrichs!"

He shook his head, emphatically. "No, he was like them. Laicēns, Peters, Knoriņš, Daniševskis, Bērziņš and those many others too. All the same. Traitors."

I actually thought about standing up and leaving Līcis. How dare he? "And do you believe all these crimes? These are your people, Herberts. Our comrades?"

"Of course I do." But in his lonely eyes a desperate caress, a pleading. "You understand me now, Wiktor; they were all as guilty as Heinrichs Juškevičs. The *exact* same level of guilt as him. Every one of them."

I started to reply, but he grabbed my wrist harshly. "I have five children, Wiktor."

His voice found an even higher pitch. "We are very thankful that the State protects our sons and daughters from its enemies."

"But…"

I could feel the sweat from his palms smother my skin. "Five." His tearful eyes held mine. "You'll know what I mean, Wiktor, when you have that son of your own." He smiled, not three bottom teeth remaining, but still he held my wrist firmly: "A blessing coming very soon, I'm sure, my dear friend."

It was well past three o'clock in the morning, when I arrived back at my home in the Mežaparks district of Rīga. A series of small houses on a slight hill, populated by young professionals, university staff, career bureaucrats, people that had found a minor, if stable, respectability; a pleasant cove to comfortably pass their lives.

Along the road a few parked cars were covered in early winter frost, beyond the tiled paths into small fenced front yards were all blanketed in an ethereal layer of white.

But not mine. Typically efficient, Kaiva had already swept our walkway, our steps clean before any of the neighbors. A welcome homecoming. I unlocked the door, made my way into the house.

The bedroom was completely dark. I tried not to disturb her as I deposited my coat on the dresser. I was unsuccessful.

Her voice was raspy, throaty from sleep: "How was it?"

"Sorry to wake you." I pulled my shirt off, threw my pants over the chair. They could be hung tomorrow. "It was horrible. Seeing the grave… and Līcis, he looks ill." I fought back emotions. "He sends his love though."

"I'm so sorry, darling." She fluffed an unseen pillow. "Perhaps he'd like to meet us, if we visit Mother in Sipoli?"

"That's an idea." I slipped into the bed next to Kaiva, a hand on her thigh, a welcoming kiss over her shoulder.

And a taste on her lips. "Yum…brandy?"

A slight smile in the dark, a slighter caress across my chest. "Yes. It's a cold night."

"Freezing." I pulled up the blankets, snuggled against her. "Moscow's sure not the same."

She sighed. "I know Wiktor. It's the Russian mentality, not communism. You need to differentiate…"

LENIN'S HAREM

"You should see the place. I can't imagine living like that."

"Give it time, my love." She pulled my hand around her waist, intertwining her fingers with mine. I kissed her lightly on the shoulder.

I was thoroughly exhausted by the trip from Moscow and more than a little relieved that Kaiva wasn't pushing for an attempt at conception. She only lay silent, fading into sleep with her hips snug against mine, torso turned away.

As Alisa had slept all those years ago.

So many shadows from those years in Moscow coming back these last two days, dormant for nearly two decades, they seemed to inhabit the very air, hover around my mind, pass silently into my bedroom.

Of those memories, Alisa had been by far the most pleasant. I slipped my hand away from Kaiva's grip, snuck it underneath the ties in the back of her nightgown, ran my fingers lovingly down from her shoulders as I had Alisa's in her youth. A sin to touch my wife and think of another woman? So much slighter, my love. A smaller, thinner woman, the journey shorter, with quicker turns, and shallower slopes, but no less pleasant. More so, actually. Her textures so familiar, the knowledge of her body only reminding me how long we'd been together, and how much I loved her.

My finger found a thin imperfection: low along a rib, a groove in the skin, some long deep scratch. New or unremembered? Impossible to know.

"Poor girl." I kissed the back of her neck, stroked her hair for a few minutes, and quickly found sleep to the rhythm of her breathing.

And tried not to dream of friends long gone.

It was three weeks later that I got the telephone call.

"Hello."

The man's voice on the line spoke in husky Russian, flat and truncated. "Wiktor Rooks?"

"Yes."

There was a burst of electric crackling on the other end. "Captain Wiktor Rooks?"

"Formerly. May I help you?"

"I am preparing a hearing on a Major Herberts Līcis. I understand you served with him at length in the past?"

A hearing? "Yes, many, many, years ago. To whom am I speaking?"

Despite the interference, I could hear him wet his lips. "Titov."

"What sort of hearing, Mr. Titov?"

"Preliminary investigations of illegal activities. We would like to interview you regarding the character of Major Līcis."

"Illegal activities?" My stomach knotted. It was not possible. Not him too. "No, never, not Herb…not Major Līcis, I can tell you he is an upstand…"

"We need to conduct the interview in person, Captain. For identity verification and any secondary questioning that might be required."

"In person? In Moscow?"

"Yes. Can you come immediately?"

I leaned against the wall, tried to clear my mind. Overcome horror, surprise. "I have a lecture tomorrow. Can we not do this over the telephone? I could send a statement by telegram."

The voice was utterly calm: "You will need to cancel your engagement. The hearing is tomorrow evening. We need to have your deposition well before that time. Can you take the overnight train? One leaves Rīga at 19:10."

"I don't know…I don't know." Anything to help my friend, to save him from the fate of Juškevičs. "I haven't the papers ready…for the crossing…"

"We can telephone the customs office ahead of your arrival to overcome any issues. If you truly feel Major Līcis is a likely innocent, then it is most important we hear your views."

"Of course." I heard the door slam. Kaiva was home from the newspaper. I blocked the mouthpiece, shouting into the other room. "I'm on the telephone."

There would be hell to pay for canceling my lecture, but images of Juškevičs's gravestone, of the fear in Līcis's eyes pervaded my vision. I could not abandon him. Not Herberts. "Alright…What do I need to bring? How should I prepare?"

"Just yourself. Are you in contact with anyone else who might be familiar with Comrade Līcis?"

"No."

Kaiva entered the room, a sheet of yellow paper pressed to her breast. She was white as a ghost, her expression terrifying. I cupped the receiver again. "Are you alright?"

Wordlessly, she handed me a telegraph sent to her newspaper. More Soviet executions yesterday, she had circled a name in the third column.

Herberts Līcis

"Please Captain Rooks, if you can make the evening train we'll have a car waiting to assist you at the border."

I stepped away from the wall, holding Kaiva breathlessly. Slowly lowered the shaking receiver toward the latch:

"Captain Rooks?"

"Hello?"

"Hello? The connection is poor Captain. Please speak up."

"Captain Rooks, can you hear…"

Click.

Chapter Twenty-two

August 1939, Rīga

"Wiktor it's been nearly a year. You need to calm down."

Otomars leaned forward in the little outdoor café, his face furrowed in concentration as his huge fingers crushed a tiny lemon section sending a spray of cloudy juice squirting into his herbal tea. "You'll develop an ulcer."

He was right, he was always right. "I know, I know. I should just let it go. But it's not so easy, Otomars, when your life is threatened. The dreams…"

"Why are you so certain that your life was endangered? Nothing's happened since. It could have been a mistake. A macabre clerical error." He found a spoon to mix in the juice. "I still maintain the caller didn't realize your friend had already been hung. The truth is a possibility in any conversation."

"He was shot, not hung."

The waiter came by, depositing the sugar jar in the center of the table. He tarried a moment too long for Otomars already had another task for him.

"Can you lower the awning a little? The sun is right in our faces." The adolescent server muttered something less-than-serviceable as he slinked away, but my brother was indeed correct. The noon sun was intrusive, sweltering in late August. There was hardly a square meter of shade on the entire open expanse of the great Cathedral Square before us. The sun at its apex in the cloudless sky, even the huge Dome Cathedral, dominating the far side of the plaza, cast no merciful shadow for sinner or saint alike. Once the tallest tower in Europe, it had long since been surpassed by Saint Peter's only a few blocks away, but its mammoth square-domed roof remained magnificent scenery for a cordial luncheon with Otomars. It was almost worth enduring the temperature.

Now spooning in the sugar cubes, Otomars returned the topic to my troubling telephone call. "As I have said before, at worst it can only have been the Soviet military or some toothless faction of their government. As long as you stay on this side of the border you've little to fear."

"How can you be so certain?"

He raised an eyebrow. "Because if their secret police or some intelligence organization were truly after you, you'd have disappeared right here in Rīga." His spoon quickly stirred the tea, clinking like wind chimes in the breeze. "There are too many extra shadows on the wall these days as it is."

Now that was comforting. "There have been other things as well. You know, twice in this last month I've answered a ringing phone only to have them hang up at the sound of my voice."

Otomars shrugged: "People dial wrong numbers, Wiktor. Operators connect bad circuits." He tasted his drink, pausing slightly before nodding to himself in approval. The right mixture. "You can't live a life of paranoia."

The awning lowered slightly over its wooden frame suspended above us, another half meter of cloth between us and the searing sun.

"Ah, that's better." Otomars soaked up the change in atmosphere, peacefully closing his eyes but still speaking. "Perhaps this will comfort you: I am considering seeking the magistrate position for a district in Latgale, based in a little town 30-40 kilometers outside of Rositten."

That was a surprise. "Do you think you can get it?"

The tiniest of smiles graced his restful face: "If I seek the position, Wiktor, I'll obtain it."

Always so confident, my brother. "You'd better remember to call it Rēzekne then or they'll lynch you the first morning."

He opened his eyes slightly, expanded the smile. "Old habits die hard."

I chased a fly off my sleeve. "A bit remote isn't it?"

"I don't like the way the political weathercock is turning, Wiktor. If there were any truth to your experiences, they would be a prime example. It might be good to have a refuge that is a little…off the map, should we say?"

"And give up the spectacular apartment, this fashionable city life you've built for yourself?" Had the eternal playboy turned recluse?

He gained a playful animation at my question. "No, no. I can do most the reviews right here in the city, only a few days a month out there, maybe a little more at first." He sipped his tea, took in a breath of the cooling air. "Let's not panic, Wiktor. We'll just lay some roots, an option if ever needed."

The bells of the Dome Cathedral rang long and heavy in the burning air, each weighty vibration carrying a wave of scorching heat along with the deep, ominous sounding.

I watched a well-dressed young couple near the Cathedral's entrance turn to each other, a bit of laughter, a raised eyebrow or two between them, before they continued arm-in-arm across the white stones of the square.

Otomars had spied them as well. "Oh, caught again!"

"What do you mean?"

He pointed loosely in the direction of the Cathedral. "The Letts say that if the bells sound as a woman passes beneath she is unfaithful."

A strange myth. "Why only the women?"

"Well, if it rang for the men it just might not stop," Otomars laughed, looking to me for agreement. "Rīga would never sleep. Clang, clang, clang all night long."

"Yes…true enough." I looked at my pocket watch. "I must leave."

"So soon?" Otomars seemed deeply disappointed. "We just found the shade."

"Sorry." I got up from the table, deposited a few bills for my half of the meal, pinned them to the tablecloth with the sugar jar.

"I have an appointment."

"You can pull up your trousers, Mr. Rooks." The doctor wheeled away from me on his low little rolling chair. "Everything looks normal."

Somewhat the relief. I hopped off the examining table, fumbled with the buttons.

Pen in rubber-gloved hand, he continued to scribble on the paper in the folder atop his low little desk, asking questions without glancing up at me: "This scar across your pelvis, what did the army doctors say about internal damage from the laceration?"

I fastened the top button, sat back on the padded table. "I'd lost a few centimeters of colon and took some liver damage. They thought it was minor." If there was more, either I'd forgotten or they hadn't told me. It had been over twenty years…

Doctor Roberts looked about my age, early 40's or so. Plump, balding, legs spread wide out, he scooted himself about the room atop his low, three-wheeled wooden stool. Powered only by his churning feet, he kept his arms folded, the whole torso compact and together as if to reduce air resistance. In his white coat, with shiny scalp reflecting the brilliant ceiling light, he rather reminded me of a newly hatched chick: Legs broken through the shell but body still encased, running around the nest bumping into things.

His whole examination room was built in miniature. The shelves were low, his desk lower, it seemed everything was designed so he needn't get off that damn stool.

"Any injury to the testicles during the original assault? Severe bruising?"

"Not that I can remember." He dashed off my answers in quick, hard pen strokes, recording my words in some sort of brutal, truncated shorthand.

"Any before or since?"

"No."

He paused the interrogation to scribble some more extensive notes. The examination room was smallish and amply lit by multiple rows of bulbs along the high ceiling. From sky blue walls hung detailed anatomical illustrations of both genders' genitalia seen from every imaginable angle, in every conceivable state of health, illness, or pubic development. Pictures cluttered with labels, dotted lines and strange, unnatural words like 'urethra' and 'fimbraie.' It all had a way of taking the sexuality out of sex, turning it into a squishy amalgamation of sacks and tubes, secretions and glands. No romance, no eroticism, all biology. No more, or less, interesting than a dissected frog.

"Any reason to believe you've recently ingested any toxins? Been exposed to pesticides?"

"None that I know of." Dr. Roberts had a strange way of peppering me with questions, while remaining locked to his little desk, staring down at his forms. It felt more like an interview with an accountant or an auditor. I could be talking about stockroom inventory as easily as my own body. The inflection and interest were always the same. He was supposed to be the best in Rīga, but I found his bedside manner sorely lacking.

"Anything unusual in the consistency or colour of your semen? Is the discharge black or especially milky?"

God such questions. "No. I don't think so. I must say, I don't really examine such materials."

He looked at the clock, wrote something down. "No worries. We'll get a sample." He gave no pause. "Ever had any kidney damage? Or disease?"

"No. None." I'd been in here thirty minutes. Could this go on much longer?

"Any other injures? In your combat days or since?"

"A concussion once. Nothing else really."

He rolled his stool over to a shelf crowded with thick leather-bound books, and a few wooden visual aids. He pulled a few more blank pages from a stack of unused paper, then wheeled back to his desk. As he did so, his tone broke a little from his usual clinical voice, slightly warmer, more human. "Where did you serve, Wiktor?"

My mind was on other things. "I'm sorry?"

"Where were you stationed? I was in the Daugavpils battalion."

"The Daugava front. The city defense mainly and the Nāves sala bridgehead." I thought it best to omit my years in the Red Army. Otomars's friends tended to be rather anti-communistic.

"Nāves sala?"

I didn't like the way his face lit up at the mention of that horrible defense. "Yes, Saulkalne."

He tapped his pen repeatedly on the back of his neck, gently rocking back and forth on his little wheels, as some new thought ran through his mind. "Tell me Wiktor," he made a quick note, and turned toward me for once looking directly into my eyes:

"Were you ever the victim of a gas attack?"

I was a shocked man in a city of shocked people.

I stood on the packed trolley bus, as despondent as my fellow passengers, but for a far different reason. Their faces were a blank from the horrors occurring just beyond Latvia's borders. From the war in Poland, our south-eastern neighbor being hungrily devoured by both Germany and the Soviet Union; from the surprise declarations of war by Britain and France on one aggressor, but not the other. I guessed one monster was enough. I could hardly blame them.

The passengers discussed events even now, some whispering in the seats, others yelling across a dozen people to an opinionated fellow at the bus's far end. All the while I stood silently hanging onto the horizontal stabilizing bar. My life was a perverse shadow of my fellow riders', my fellow citizens. At night, they anxiously sat by their radios, counting the minutes until the news broadcast of the day's tumultuous events, while at home, I guarded the sole telephone awaiting the next call from Doctor Roberts's office. As Rīga's city dwellers stared in horror and disbelief at the headlines off the freshest newspaper, so did I recoil at the paltry numbers on the latest test results. An odd parallel of suffering and shock, that somehow made me feel even more isolated. Theirs was a comradeship in fear: they gabbed and debated in plazas, churches, taverns, and up and down the halls of my university. Mine was a world of false smiles, tears behind locked toilet room doors, desperation denied, submerged and dormant. Hundreds rallied for one side or another, or marched in hope of peace, while fully alone I made clandestine clinic visits at lunch or slipped off to the doctor's office between lectures. I stood apart, separated from the whole globe it seemed. Even my friends. Even my own brother. And especially, necessarily, impossibly Kaiva.

The bus lurched to a halt; I shoved my way through this mob, the sole exiting passenger at this stop. Only a few suburban blocks to home.

Lost in thought, I headed along the sidewalk. One last test, the results due in a few days. The medicines would make no difference. I could sense what the outcome would be. My training in physics had given me an inherent inkling for probability. After all these trials, it was a statistical certainty. There could be no happy ending.

But it bought me a little more time, another reason not to tell her. A few more days to figure out the proper words. And what those words might mean to my marriage.

For two months, I'd stayed silent, but tomorrow or the next day, I would have to finally confront my wife. I knew a little part of her would die, which meant nearly all of me would.

I passed through my leafy yard, climbed up the front steps, fumbled for the key. But Kaiva already had the screen open, greeting me in the doorway.

There were tears in her eyes. She must suspect. I'd waited too long.

This was going to be impossible.

She embraced me. A passionate kiss, her lips moist from crying. As she pulled her head away, I had a better read of her face. Happiness? They seemed tears of joy.

"Wiktor," she cried. "I'm pregnant."

Chapter Twenty-three

December 1939, Rīga

Otomars's toast brought tears and a little laughter to the assembly in his Rīga townhouse. The gentry dressed in an array of colors and the latest Prussian fashions showed their approval by raising their glasses in tribute, as much I thought to the eloquence and wit of my brother, as to my sister Anne and her husband Erich Kaltenbach returning for the first time in sixteen years.

Across the densely packed room, I smoked my cigarette and looked out my brother's balcony. It was a snowless day, the late afternoon sun hiding between gaps in the narrow streets. Pastel colored city blocks, three to four stories tall, adorned with rows of green and white shuttered windows, stretched off into the sleepy haze. Orange tiled roofs gave a comforting uniformity to every street. At ground level, many displayed the decorative windows of shopkeepers. Christmas was coming soon, and Parisian and American goods gently nudged aside Latvian for passer-by attention.

The building directly across was taller than most, five stories with a vaulted roof extending past the requisite orange tiles to surpass its neighbors. A bright yellow in the Swedish style, its face sported grey trim and decorative oval placards. Opposite my level were three storm windows. Inside, I could see Yule tide decorations complete with Christmas tree, Nativity figurines, and hanging cut-outs of Father Frost. On the carpet an idle child must lay, for every few moments a balloon of pinkish hue would rise from the floor, floating past an open window, only to drift slowly down again. I tried to remember those long ago days when I could simply sit and bounce a balloon above me.

On the ground floor, the yellow walls gave way to several large pane windows through which I could see patrons enjoying their afternoon tea. Outside, wire frame chairs sat tucked beneath little tables adorned with tiny candles. At one, three Russian servicemen dressed in their army greens, talked exuberantly in their off hours. They, like all of us, wondering about the meaning of recent events.

In front of them, the bustling Alberta Iela dimmed in growing twilight. Suit and hat men scampered home late for Friday dinner, in their haste separating fragile interlocked couples out for an early evening stroll. At the corner, an old woman and young girl, separated merely by sixty years, paused as if to survey this very building.

Otomars's residence was in one of those magnificent apartment buildings constructed during the Jugendstil boom of the early 1900's: the outside façade a vibrant sky blue decorated with luminous white masonry and a robust assortment of animal and human figures. Paramount among these was the bare face and nude torso of a distinct young damsel. No nymph of the architect's imagination, the great Eisenstein had immortalized his own lovers in stone, each residing eternally youthful above while passing pedestrians aged with every sortie below. Like a painter, or a poet, every unique work dedicated to the current enamor of his heart.

A whim entered my mind. Could this old woman have been the maiden who adorned these walls? Her skin, creased and spotted, once been the twin of these smooth figures who had defied forty years exposure to ice, sun and rain? Perhaps, she had come to show her granddaughter how she looked all those years ago? Remarking with a mix of melancholy and pride: *Wasn't I beautiful? Wasn't I something, little one?*

But like her, the city was always changing. If you listened carefully, you could hear the sounds of heavy machinery: the cranes moving mammoth girders, the mixers pouring foundation concrete, 10,000 rivets bolting steel to steel, all in haste to finish before the last ray of winter light was gone. The new Russian Naval Base down in Rīga's harbor was well underway. As was the air force base at Kuldiga; the artillery guns placed at Mazirbe; and the Red tank battalions at Priekule and Vaiņode. Indeed, there were now more Russian troops in Latvia than our own.

Having the protection of the Soviet army, forces I'd served in, and helped to build, should have been a good thing. Kaiva tentatively supported their presence. "All brothers and sisters, workers united against capitalism and fascism," she'd said. But even her voice had doubt. So many of those brothers who'd fashioned it, who'd risked all in its creation, were now gone. Some like Juškevičs and Līcis cannibalized by their very own. And a few nights recently I'd laid awake, listening to phantom knocks by Mr. Titov at our front door. Would they dare in Latvia? In a sovereign nation?

Yes, this…this unsolicited occupation by Russian forces made me truly uncomfortable. There was no other way to say it, it felt 'tsarist.'

I was soon joined on the balcony by a tiny, tiny man: Thinning white hair, a symmetric bow tie capping a perfectly pressed blue suit.

"So, Wiktor.… You're saying to yourself, how can I give my ole friend Peisach the proper respect? Well, no need to get up my boy, that cigarette will do."

He said so with such a disarming laugh, as if we were oldest, closest of friends. Of course, I'd only met him once: at Anne's wedding, when I was just a boy. He had that charm about him. I immediately handed him a cigarette.

With a wink, he took a puff, and mocked a cough. "God, Wiktor you always did have terrible taste in tobacco." He tossed it over the railing, and shuffled around in his coat pocket. "Here, let me show you what men of style smoke."

Peisach Ulmann had been the business front for Erich's father for years, managing the tobacco company, the metal ware factory, and all those saw mills. He had finally bought Erich out, a milestone everyone knew was coming since the day Baron Kaltenbach had died. Most assumed Erich had no interest in industrial pursuits. Now that it had finally happened, the room was filled with gossip as to why.

They had been together so long, the baron and Peisach. As shrewd as the baron was tough, their success had few rivals. This little Jew, shielded from the persecutions of the tsar by the barons, had made them a lot of money. Now he'd be doing it on his own.

He handed me a cigarette from his own company. I lit it, and took a drag. There was no difference. I smiled to myself and said: "If this is your best Peisach, I know that suit is Russian made."

"Italian." His few free hairs waved back and forth in the terrace breeze. "All you're doing is proving my point son. Your sister got the brains as well as the looks." He put a hand on my shoulder.

I took another puff, and couldn't help but laugh. "Now, how did you know me? It's been thirty years."

"You're sitting by yourself. Can I have light?" I lit his cigarette. "People don't change from childhood, they just get more wrinkles."

"I'm just taking in some air."

"Course you are." He took another puff. "In the merchant world 'just' is a synonym for 'not.' You know the word synonym, don't you Wiktor? If your employee says he's just about done, it means he's not done. If a customer is just thinking about buying, it means he's not buying."

Outsiders looking in, the Latvians used to have an expression: "You can't separate the German and the Jew." Maybe that was still true…

"Now, if I were you…."

Otomars interrupted Peisach with a clap on the back. He congratulated him on his acquisitions, and then faded into some alien tongue. Yiddish? Was there a language my brother hadn't mastered?

They conversed for a few moments in this dialect. Ulmann offered Otomars a cigarette, but he declined, answering in German: "Soon Peisach, thank you. Wiktor, may I speak with you please?"

"Sure."

"Excuse us for a second Peisach. We'll be back." The elderly guest only silently nodded.

Escorted by my brother, we crossed the crowded room. I wondered what he wanted to talk about that required privacy in the middle of a busy party. My stomach sank, and this irked me. How could he still have this effect, even after all these years?

Otomars was intercepted by elderly Diāna Strausa, who without hesitation began to regale him on his choice of cuisine. I used this moment to slink off to the serving table to get myself another brandy.

At the table I found another man pouring just such a drink. He filled his glass one-third, and then seeing me waiting, asked if I'd like one as well.

"Please." He was dressed in a grey pinstriped suit, angular faced, 40ish. His brown hair waxed straight back, right in line with the pinstripes.

"Are you Wiktor?" His German was very thick. Not a Baltic, maybe Bavarian.

"Most days. I'm afraid you have me at a disadvantage, sir." I wished he'd hurry up and pour before Otomars escaped.

"I am Lukas. He filled my glass two-thirds, placed the bottle on the table and offered his hand. 'From Regensburg. Your brother has quite the place."

I shook with my right, scooped up the brandy with the left. "It's nice. He's renovated it recently." Where was Kaiva?

He turned salutation to conversation: "I think it was Erich who mentioned to me you were an officer. Did you serve under Bermont-Avalov? I have friends you may know."

I sensed an awkward discussion ahead. "No, no.... I was a Rifleman. Spent most of the Independence Wars in Moscow." Except, of course, the retaking of Rīga.

His eyes widened. "The brother of Anne Kaltenbach is Red?"

"Was...recruited by their military. I can't say I fully endorsed them."

"But you still fought for them, nonetheless." This seemed to upset him. "And do you agree with all these Soviet troops in your streets? The bases being built near here, the air strip they've constructed at Libau? In Lithuania, in Latvia, all over the Baltic?"

"A mutual agreement, an offer by the Soviets of assistance." An internal sigh. I'd answered this question many times in recent weeks. From everyone that knew my past, or remembered Kaiva's involvement with the newspaper.

"And what of the Finns?"

"Well," I wondered how I had maneuvered myself into defending Russian foreign policy, "they declined the offer, and..."

"And were invaded by the Red Army." He moved closer, I could smell the alcohol.

"Tell me, honestly, Wiktor, as a Rīga resident, as Volksdeutsche, do you think it would have been any different if Latvia had said 'No!' ? Would they have been spared invasion?"

"I ...I don't know..." I sipped my drink to buy time.

He would have none of it. "Do you trust Berlin?"

An odd question, had we shifted topics?

A martini in his left hand, Otomars motioned me over to the swinging doors. Suddenly, his conversation seemed more attractive. I put out the cigarette in my half empty glass, said goodbye to Lukas, and made my way through the guests toward the kitchen. As I went, I caught a glimpse of my wife. All of eloquence in a steel blue evening dress, her milky bare shoulders and flashing perfect smiles caused pangs of arousal even as my brother's hand upon my shoulder commanded attention.

Otomars, straight-armed the door, and took me inside his bustling kitchen. I smothered in the buttered aftertaste of tonight's duck. The smells of alcohol, burning chocolate, and the wispy, sobering aroma of soap garnished the air.

At the sink, the pots and dishes were dutifully scrubbed by ageless Erene. She was being handed pans at a frustrating rate by an adolescent girl, bowed up in a white maid's uniform.

"Ladies," said Otomars, "you can take your cigarette break now."

"Just did, Mr. Rooks," said Erene. "Thank you."

"Do you still have cigarettes, Erene?"

"Yes sir."

"Then be a dear, and run along and smoke them. Take Viola."

With a domestic understanding Erene guided Viola through the rear door.

I slid my finger along the crusty edge of the mixing bowl. The frosting's surface was hard and stiff, but beneath pockets of moisture made it pleasurable. I licked my fingers: "I was having quite the chat with a Regensburg guest out there. Who is he?"

"Some friend of Erich's." He dismissed the subject with a wave of his hand.

"What's this all about Otomars?"

"Sit down Wiktor."

I did so, moving a chair away from the cluttered kitchen table. "So?"

For a moment there was nothing but the sounds of the party through the door. Otomars took another chair, set himself across from me, looking for once uncomfortable despite his immaculate coat and tails.

I anticipated: "This is about Kaiva again?"

My brother put his hand on my forearm: "Wiktor everyone knows, she is so obvious, the smiles, the glances..."

"I don't want to hear it Otomars. This is between Kaiva and me."

"And everyone else, Wiktor. You know, I know, she knows, they *ALL* know what is afoot."

I cautioned my brother. "I don't want to know his name Otomars."

This was all I needed. Every so often Otomars had made references to Kaiva's supposed paramour, but he had seldom been this direct, certainly not with a gaggle of guests outside.

Otomars seemed sullen. "Where's your pride? Are you going to let her humiliate you in front of all our friends?"

"They are not my friends Otomars." How could I make him understand? Could I have stomached to tell my brother the truth? "This is a personal matter. I am not eight years old any longer..."

"She is no good, Wiktor. She's unfaithful, she will not listen. I know you don't like to hear this, but Kaiva is too liberal. She doesn't subscribe to the older morals."

"I know her views. I knew them when I married her." I stopped to hush my own voice. "That does not mean she's being untrue."

Otomars remained level: "I hear you Wiktor, and I respect what you say, but she...

she is hurting you. And I don't want to see that happen, this is not the first time."

"She is not hurting me." How he loved to play the patriarch.

"Don't be defensive Wiktor. I'm trying to help you. Let her go. If she wants to run off wi…"

"I don't want to know his name!" I stood up and walked away. People in the other room must be able to hear.

Otomars too gained his footing. "You need to face this."

"No, please. I'll deal with it. Just don't tell me." I could not know the name, not dare see my suspicions confirmed. Then it would be *his child*. *Their child*. Not ours. How could my brother, with his pride, understand that?

"Just don't say anything Otomars. I'll handle it, alright?"

"Let her go, Wiktor." He came up behind me, for the first time in a whisper: "There is a girl in my office, very pretty, Latvian. I know you like the type. Demure. Submissive. I'll introduce you."

Better my brother thought me not much of a man…"Let's just hold off on that awhile, alright, Otomars?" I walked out the kitchen door before he could reply.

The hours passed. Many top hats were donned by exiting crowds, others caps found themselves resting on shelves, atop the dining room table, wedged between pillows in the couch, even a few stacked like waste baskets in the corners of the rooms.

I found myself trying to make small talk, all the while observing both Otomars and Kaiva. I read intent with every smile from her, avoided every gaze from him.

Otomars had me spying on my wife. Such paranoia, it would drive me to an early grave. The best thing to do would be to join into a conversation: The room was abuzz about the news of the day: The German battleship, *Graf Spee*, which had disabled three British cruisers off of Montevideo a few days ago, had been scuttled. Berlin's trumpeted victory against the Royal Navy had actually been a draw. The disappointment in the room was palpable.

Our brother-in-law had no hesitancy sharing his views with the crowd about him. The years had been kinder than expected to Erich. He had maintained his thick shock of hair, now a solid, sugarcane white. He still carried the sneer-smile, though it had a more agreeable nature than I remembered it. Indeed, there was something regal about Erich now, a power, a confidence that attracted throngs of slightly subservient admirers.

Time had been less kind to Anne: wire thin as a youth, now past middle-age this trait had turned to a skeletal, cadaverous quality. Her eyes were hollow and distant, and each salutation, every query, required pulling her back from somewhere else. Her hearing was failing in the good ear, and with it she seemed to be fading from existence, becoming a fixture, a decoration at her husband's side. When pressed, she insisted that nothing was wrong, though she seemed to find nothing unusual in the asking.

Otomars said he had taken Erich aside to discuss Anne's health, but for once our brother had met his match. His only report: "Frequent headaches."

Finding this scene depressing, I turned to a group on the balcony. Here, this strange Lukas was lecturing: "They have the men who bombed the Chancellor in custody, another example of British terrorism…"

I had enough of war talk and decided to find Kaiva. Lukas noticed my sudden departure, and broke off his rant to follow me.

"Wiktor!"

There was no avenue of escape. "Yes Lukas. Don't let me interrupt…"

He sprinted up to me. "I am sorry Wiktor, I ambushed you before. We got off on the wrong foot…"

"Really, it was not such a problem. I need to speak to…"

"Do you think me so bad? Advocating Berlin? All we are trying to do, Wiktor, is reclaim what was stolen at Versailles, nothing more, nothing less."

I started to respond, but he continued:

"And all the Russians are trying to do, my friend, is retake what they lost in their own civil war." He straightened my lapel, patted my shoulder. "Your country, Wiktor, and Estonia, Finland… You know this, I can see it in your eyes."

He moved even closer. His face filled my vision. "The people of Germany see this. Your people, Wiktor. We are moved. We'll help, you've but to ask."

There was such earnestness in him. I nodded, if only to end this.

"Just ask Wiktor. Everyone in this room wants to know the same thing. We won't abandon you." It felt like he was courting me.

"There are thousands of *Volksdeutsche* leaving Latvia. Tens of thousands. Our government is letting them settle in Germany, in New Prussia, in Poland. With your own kind, with your sister and Erich. Half the people in this room are going. Consider, life outside of the Russian shadow."

"In Poland?"

"Yes, it is safe there. The fighting is over." He calmed down, stepped back to a reasonable distance. "No one wants any more bloodshed. The French, they don't want to die. Neither do we. Sooner, or later the British will accept this, and we all can get on with our lives…"

His arguments for a peace were logical, progressive, even impassioned. The German overtures appealed to reason, even a paradoxical pacifism. All you had to do was overlook the fresh corpses of Poland and Czechoslovakia.

Still, there were aspects that made sense. No one but the British wanted this violence to continue. The French had declared war three months ago and done nothing. There was little doubt they would fold, if the English only would listen.

And maybe if the British settled down, the Russians would stop building defenses in our city. Maybe they'd pull up their troops and go home. Maybe.

I did not have long to consider. Through an open door I could see Otomars and Kaiva in a heated exchange. Why hadn't he left well enough alone? I hurriedly dodged guests and reached the library entrance in time to see my wife throw her drink in Otomars's face.

"How dare you!" she yelled, as he took a handkerchief from his breast pocket, and began to wipe the alcohol from his countenance.

"Deny it." Otomars said, soaking up the liquid pocketed about his eyes.

"You hypocrite! Do you even know the name of that girl out there?"

"I'm not married, am I Mrs. Rooka?" He hung emphasis on those last syllables.

I arrived behind them: "What is the problem here?"

Otomars stuffed the handkerchief in his suit pocket: "Close the door please, Wiktor."

Kaiva plucked the martini from my hand and re-doused my brother's face.

"Kaiva…"

She ignored me. "How dare you! Who do you think you are?" I could not remember her this angry. I grabbed her by the arm, and started to drag her away.

"Let me go. God damn it, Wiktor."

Otomars had the rag to his face again: "Please, Wiktor, close the library door."

I ignored them both, dragging my wife from the library into the stunned crowd.

"I said let me go, Wiktor." She tugged at my arm like a bull terrier. "How many bastards have you fathered Otomars? Hypocrite!"

At last she relinquished physical resistance, as I forced her ahead of me, step by step down the stairs. The worried staff placed the coats in my free hand.

"And the lady's bag?"

"I'll fetch it in the morning, Erene. Thank you." I pushed Kaiva out the front door.

"You don't have to shove, Wiktor." The storm had ebbed, a frank embarrassment seeping in.

"Sorry, but we need to leave."

Her voice was low: "You could have said something."

It was cold outside, more illumination coming from the Christmas decorations and display windows than the slow lighting street lamps. A crisp frost hung in the air.

I reached the car, parked at the curb, a white Mercedes Benz borrowed for the occasion. In the back, two stuffed suitcases for a romantic weekend in Sigulda. A wine bottle sat free on the backseat floor.

Whether she felt ignored, or had regained her strength, Kaiva directed the next attack at me. "You're spineless when it comes to him."

"Just get in the car." I opened the passenger door and pressed her shoulder to bend her down. She refused, taunting me: "Spineless!"

I pressed harder, and pushed her into the passenger seat. On principle, she resisted, releasing a scream of pent up rage.

She sat. I threw the coats in her lap, and slammed the door.

"Is everything alright here?" One of the Russians from the café had crossed the street to investigate.

"Yes, everything's fine, Corporal. We can handle our own affairs."

He leaned down to the window. Through the glass he repeated:

"Is everything alright here, Madam?"

Kaiva, head down against the dashboard, only nodded an affirmative.

The soldier returned his cold gaze to me. I gave him a solemn, silent look, and stepped around to the driver's side. As I slid in, I noticed two of his comrades standing in front of the car. They remained in place, even when I started the engine.

Frustrated, I gave two swift honks of the horn. Slowly they parted, a meandering, defiant walk. A walk that told the driver they moved only because they had to.

For now.

Chapter Twenty-four

April 1940, Rīga

The tiny metal case was smothered even in a ten year old boy's hand. "It looks just like a spy camera."

Otomars gave me a mirthful wink: "Well, you would know Wiktor."

I returned a smoldering stare from the far railing.

He laughed. "You are much too sensitive. Really you are." Otomars put a hand on his son's shoulder even as the boy found his next photographic target. "Commercially available, built right here in Rīga by VEF. Just a better fit for Grants's pocket, isn't it?"

A fit? The camera was not ten centimeters wide, not three centimeters tall. It could blow away in the breeze, certainly up here. How could the pictures come out at all? Not at this height off the street.

Otomars looked back at me again, raising an eyebrow. "Nothing covert about it."

Grants shifted back and forth against the railing, trying to find the right angles as he took picture after picture of the Rīga skyline from the little observation platform half way up Saint Peter's enormous steeple. Iron railings and crossbars offering perilously little protection from a seventy meter plummet to the cobblestone plaza below.

The whole city stretching out before us, the streets nothing but little inlets connecting numerous odd shaped plazas, all penned in beneath the old town's beautiful stone masonry and the prickly spires of a dozen other churches. But even this steeple's greatest rival, the arching roof of the nearby Dome Cathedral, bowed beneath the towering majesty of Saint Peter's. The highest point in Rīga, the view was breathtaking and in the warming air, all our problems felt as tiny as the people flowing in and out of the distant green patches that marked the numerous city parks. High perches had a way of doing that, making everything individual seem insignificant. Mine was only one life after all, a shame to waste it fretting.

The boy turned to his father: "Otomars let me get a picture of you two from the plaza."

"Excellent idea Grants." He smiled at me, amused by his son's enthusiasm.

Grants descended the stairway to the lower platform, taking the long, twisting route to the bottom, his unruly brown hair blowing freely in the open platform as he disappeared to the levels beneath. The boy seemed anxious to please, friendly enough certainly. A bit runtish, wide-eyed and hollowed cheeked, I'd found very little of Otomars in his young features. Not so unusual, I supposed, some children displayed predominantly their mother's traits.

I wondered if my own son or daughter would wear Kaiva's amber locks, see the world through her piercing eyes, smile above my wife's preciously slight chin?

I took in a breath of morning air. Or would the child have another, unforeseen combination? A few months would tell.

I crossed the platform toward my brother. "He looks just like Rasa, especially around the eyes."

He stared out into the spring sky. "I'm glad you didn't say that while he was up here."

"Why?"

"He's Jūlija's child."

"Oh."

During the ensuing silence, I watched ant-like pedestrians marching near the grey-flowing Daugava, where the city turned from stone to wood in the Maskavas District; so named because the old road to Moscow ran through its long dusty streets.

Even at this distance I could recognize the Soviet uniforms. There were so many these days. Perhaps I was wrong. Maybe a few problems were more noticeable from high above.

I pointed it out to Otomars. "Look at the Russian troops all over the town, after we helped build their…"

Opening up this frequent topic seemed to annoy him. "Wiktor, you know things happen in this world for reasons other than to simply ruin your day. You do realize that, don't you?"

"Of course I do, but there are so many troops. Are they protecting us or laying in wait…"

He sighed. "Think. Seventy-five percent of this country's exports go where, Wiktor?"

"I don't know…" My vocation kept my attention focused light-years from Earth, certainly not on local economics. "I'd guess Germany?"

"Germany."

"How is that relevant to what I'm saying?"

Otomars directed me to the other side of the platform, pointed downstream to a large steamship headed to the port. "And you see that? A Swedish cargo freighter." He turned slightly down river toward the Gulf of Rīga, found an approaching convoy to his liking. "And there:" His arm dotted about. "Swedish ship. Swedish ship. Swedish ship. Swedish ship. All filled to the gills with iron ore." He turned his face to me. "Entering the continent through Rīga, bound by rail for whose furnaces? To build whose Panzer tanks? Whose airplanes? I'll give you one guess."

His palm clapped against the railing. "Of course the Russians are going to shut that down. *Betrayal*? Why do you take everything so personally, Wiktor? I doubt very many members of the Politburo curse your name at night."

"But they're not at war."

"They will be if the German army keeps growing. No, the Russians would be fools not to close this valve."

He leaned forward on the railing, his quiet voice seemed to be speaking more to himself than me. "And then the Germans will open it up again."

How many invasions was he promising? "I've been through battle, Otomars. There were times I feared no one would be left."

"Only the dead have seen the end of war, Wiktor." He stood up, as if girding himself to the reality of his words. "The worst of man's assorted evils, but it is survivable. You've a front line," he stuck out one arm, the other hand hop scotching back and forth over it, "and on either side you've got administrations. A man can find shelter there." He dropped his arms. "If things stay relatively stable, one could even prosper."

Otomars kept his disturbingly pensive voice even as he turned to me. "No, it's the beginnings and endings that are most dangerous. When the sides are changing," his eyes were somewhere over my shoulder, finger pressed against his lip, "then it can be tricky."

"That's pretty mercenary…"

His eyes returned to mine. "Not such a bad label really, Wiktor. Mercenaries are at least honest, upfront. Some people lie to themselves, some lie to others, but in the end everybody in war, as in life, does what's in their own best interest. If you'd accept this truth, maybe you'd relax, stop being so hurt, so disappointed in everyone all the time."

"Disappointed?"

"In our parents," he nodded in the direction of the Russian soldiers, "in the Soviet Union…" He leaned hard on the railing, a sad gaze holding my eyes: "in Kaiva."

My voice was only a whisper. "She hasn't disappointed me."

Otomars left the balcony's edge. "You're an honest man Wiktor." He clasped a hand on my shoulder. "And honest people don't like the truth. Isn't that the greatest of ironies?"

I didn't dignify that with a response. "So, you really think there's going to be war?"

He waved. Grants had made it out to the plaza, now a tiny figure pointing his invisible camera up at us in the steeple.

"Definitely."

Oh God.

"Ready Wiktor?" Otomars put one arm around me, waving for the picture with the other. "Smile."

June 16th 1940, Daugavpils

I helped Kaiva rise from her seat in the massive Daugavpils stadium. Nine months pregnant and overdue, she surely should not have come to the great songfest. But it had become a tradition between the two of us, a ritual of summer, and Kaiva was not one to be told she shouldn't do something. Her belly massive, the weight pressing on her spine, bladder and kidneys, she stood tilted, her grip heavy on my arm. She lasted only a song or two before I had to help her back to the concrete seat, a cycle that had gone on repeatedly for the past two hours.

Formerly Dünaburg, Līcis's hometown in the extreme south-east of the country was the largest settlement in Latgale and the gateway to the East, where the Russian river Dvina was rechristened Daugava as it flowed into Latvia. Every year, celebrating the rituals of summer, thousands upon thousands met in this stadium to embrace and renew their Latvian heritage, to sing songs of joy and truth, to stand as citizens along the waters of the river that defined both their oldest traditions and youthful nation. Such a cultural Rosetta stone was this event that an ethnic German and a communist had attended for the last six years, leaving a little less the outsiders, more in love with each other and the land they inhabited each time, a transformation neither expected, denied nor regretted.

And in this turbulent year, I felt an even stronger need to embrace this renewal, to cleanse the past and start afresh. Kaiva instinctively must have known this. I suspected it was the reason she'd insisted on attending despite her doctor's advice.

At first glance, the thousands of singing girls were as beautiful as ever, hair wreathed in flowers of yellow and purple, and the greater assembly decked in traditional clothes of every tribe of Latvia. Latgalians, Semigallians, Selonians, Cours, Ests, and Livs had truly succeeded in celebrating both unity and diversity simultaneously.

But the harmonies floating on warm summer air felt slightly off this year, the choruses an octave shriller as a few of the young maidens fell aside, eyes downcast, voices breaking mid-song. And the music seemed a bit more subdued, the musicians at the pipes failing to summon the usual air from their lungs. This was the year, the moisture in the eyes of old women sprung from sources other than elation and pride, and the elder men, their faces grown longer than their beards, complained repeatedly of the humid vapors rising off the nearby river. Indeed, this year's celebration had more than a hint of bitter sweetness woven into the traditionally exuberant proceedings.

When not distracted with aiding Kaiva, I found my eyes repeatedly returning to the empty official boxes on the opposite side of the stadium. The seats unoccupied, only the Mayor of Daugavpils remained. Arms crossed, his face an expressionless mask, so many eyes questioning his loneliness, more and more crying for his solitude as the night wore on.

The radio broadcast before the celebration had told the story. The absent officials were in Rīga, called back to an emergency meeting. Moscow had given Latvia six days to create a new government, one that would be 'more friendly to the Soviet Union,' or it would be forced 'in its own defense' to install one. The same ultimatum given to Lithuania only yesterday and communist forces had occupied Vilnius by this morning. I'd be surprised if Estonia would last the night. With Soviet bases and tanks already covering our homeland and thousands of troops massed on the borders could there be any other outcome for Latvia?

A despairing atmosphere rose from the crowd, tens of thousands of people together, yet all feeling a collective isolation. Otomars had said the Soviets would wait until the West was distracted. And indeed, no one was watching, the world's eyes fixed on the German tanks rolling down the Champs Elysées in Paris. The

Baltics stood alone, fell alone, not even the lead story of the day.

I felt for them all. Planning to attend a christening, they had instead held their own wake. It was a show of faith in their culture's durability that they chose to sing at all, to display one last moment of solidarity in these closing hours. The tears were flowing, because there was absolutely no doubt: We'd lost the country.

And a week later we lost the baby as well.

Part Four:

Cornerhouse Latgale

Chapter Twenty-five

June 14th 1941, Riga

The first knock came at a little past three in the morning: A hard, a-rhythmic banging on the front door. In this hour, with such ferocity to the pounding, it was simply impossible to ignore. And even while shaken harshly from slumber, I knew the meaning. This would be the night.

In the bedroom, Kaiva turned her face to mine, a wordless stare from the pillow, the fear in her eyes matching the dread in my stomach. I pulled on my robe, walked down the hall as the pounding resumed, louder every step nearer the source, and finally switched on the lamp in the foyer. The familiar metallic click as I pulled the bolt, cracking open the wooden door to let in the humid summer night.

In the porch light, behind confused fluttering insects, stood three Russian soldiers, rifles across their chests.

"Let us in," said the nearest curtly, his arm forcing my door open farther. They shoved into the entrance way, backing me up by their very collective weight.

Behind them a civilian, a small middle-aged man in a brown suit and a crisp, pointed little felt hat. I had seen him before…somewhere.

"Wiktor Rooks," said the man. "You need to come with us. You have thirty minutes to pack your things."

"What…what do you mean?" Under the foyer light, his feature's clearer, I made the connection. He was a neighbor who lived a few blocks over; I'd often seen him out walking his grey poodle in the morning as I went to the university. He frequently let his pet run loose, I remember him calling it. The dog's name was 'Elena' I thought.

I had never gotten his. "Where am I going?"

"You will be together."

My stomach dropped even further. "Together?"

"Your wife" he checked a piece of paper tucked in his palm, "Kaiva, she will need to come as well."

I stood there a moment, as the soldiers shoved past me, penetrated deeper into the house. "We're not going anywhere with you. What is the cause? Have you a court order?"

The words passed effortlessly through his thin lips. "We mean to annihilate your class, Mr. Rooks."

"What? What do you mean?" I was dizzy; I could hear Kaiva shouting at the soldiers behind me as they entered the bedroom.

He checked a wristwatch. "You've twenty-nine minutes, Mr. Rooks."

After we both dressed, while Kaiva pulled garments from the dresser drawers, I passed into the little pink-walled side room: a study-turned-nursery-turned-abandoned storage area. Boxes cluttered the floor, the shelves filled with Kaiva's literature, my journals and papers strewn across the dusty desk. I moved aside a small box of charts and star maps, still not re-hung, to find the small leather suitcase. Quickly, before any soldiers followed me in, I dumped out Kaiva's pamphlets, found an old window curtain to cover them and returned to the bedroom case in tow.

Despite the summer season, she shoved sweaters and her winter coat into the bag, its body bowing round as if about to burst, even as I threw on my weight to close it.

A call from the other room: "Eight minutes, Mr. Rooks."

Hurriedly, we packed the larger suitcase unable to exchange much more than worried horrifying glances. The soldiers were never beyond hearing distance, the man lurking in the hall, pestering us both continuously about the location of any valuables we might possess.

I looked into the doorway, a young soldier staring vacantly back, not even malice in his eyes. This was nothing to him, another job, an irritation that kept him up late tonight. Surely, we had been different? My men not so ambivalent when we'd arrested tsarist conspirators all those years ago in Moscow. It had been important then, they were dangerous to the State. Terrorists, counter-revolutionaries, yes?

Some part of me wondered if this was how it had been for Juškevičs and Līcis. Did their soldiers arrive at the same late hour? Did their enemies take wives and lovers with them too? That had been in Russia, I told myself, not Latvia. Was there still a difference?

LENIN'S HAREM

With no time remaining, we found ourselves in the hall, two lives stuffed into two suitcases. His hat tipped low, keeping his eyes in shadow, the little man seized the smaller bag, rummaging through the hastily packed contents. "Is there any jewelry in here, Mrs. Rooka?"

She didn't answer. Kaiva wasn't much for ornamentation, not by nature a sentimental woman, but in the side pockets he found a pair of earrings I'd given her on a distant anniversary. In a shirt pocket, he twisted his fingers around the tarnished silver necklace that had been Ieva's. Quickly, he stuffed them into his suit pockets. "We confiscate these bourgeoisie trinkets."

His hypocrisy threw me into a rage. Full of malice, I stepped forward. "That's just a fancy name for robb…"

One of the soldiers shoved the muzzle of his rifle under my jaw, thrusting upwards so hard that I had to retreat to my tip-toes to avoid being impaled on its cold steel. He stood against me, giving a few extra pushes to make his point, keeping me off balance, pressed back against the wall, Kaiva's shrill voice screaming for him to release me.

Unbeckoned, the civilian grabbed my hand, tugging at my wedding band.

"Don't…"

He ignored my plea, forcing the ring off. This too he shoved into a coat pocket. The man turned to Kaiva deeper in the interior. "And yours…"

She shook her head, backing toward the bedroom. "No."

In an instant, another soldier struck her hard against the jaw with the butt of his rifle. She ricocheted against the door frame, collapsed to the ground. A long, hollow moan, as she lay on the wooden floorboards.

"Kaiva!" I shouted with steel against my Adam's apple.

"Your ring," the civilian demanded of her, his voice calm and level.

She only lay there, half-stunned. When the assaulting soldier stood over her, bending to grab her hand, she kicked at him from the ground, heels digging into his groin, bruising at his legs. Enraged by resistance more than injury, his rifle slammed her face again and again, the thumps thick and hard, horrifyingly on the target.

I forced my jaw past the rifle, but my own guard sent a hard blow into my stomach, dropping me breathless to the floor. "Leave her alone." It barely came out, the air gone from my belly. I felt the gun's muzzle on the crown of my head. "Please, just leave her alone."

Her assailant paused before his last battery. The blow, slow and aimed, it struck solid. There was a moist cracking sound, her arms dropping limp, as her legs ceased flailing. I could see her hips turn as she curled up in a fetal position, her face obscured by the boots of the soldier hovering above me.

"Leave her alone."

There were wet, repetitive sobs as the civilian stooped to finally pull off her ring.

A few minutes later we were out in the street, carrying our suitcases quickly through the warm morning's semi-darkness. Parked along the curb was an old, rusty-green flatbed truck, several sullen, stunned families waiting in the rear. Leaning against the cab, a solitary soldier, his light machine-gun ensuring there was no thought of escape.

As I helped Kaiva into the bed, I recognized one of the women inside, a receptionist in the administration at my university. A man who could only have been her husband and three boys huddled with her along the opposite side. The others were unknown to me: a mousy-looking man curled in the corner nearest the cab, an elderly couple, belongings all tied in one great bed-sheet bundle, sitting silently against the wheel hub.

It was only when I had found a space, as the vehicle began to pull away from the curb, and my home fading into memory, that I found a moment to truly examine my sobbing wife.

Kaiva's face was covered in blood, pooling thickest around her nostrils and mouth. A hemorrhage was growing along her right cheek, so expansive I feared it might take her vision. The bottom of her jaw was curved, swollen half the size of a melon. Her upper lip split, the depths of her mouth erupting a fresh, oozing blood. I moved toward her, tail of my shirt in hand to clog the wound. When I tried to press it to her face, the touch too painful, she jerked suddenly away. A second and a third attempt, each more delicate than before, but still she resisted.

"Kaiva…" Blood or not, I kissed her lightly on the forehead, held a hand softly to her uninjured cheek. Lightly, so lightly, I began to stroke the cotton shirt against her gums. The truck lurched, my hand pushed against a loosened tooth. She screamed out, her arm shoving me violently away.

"Stop it, Wiktor…Please." Her voice was so anguished, angry.

"Darling, we need to stop the bleeding. Hold still."

She sobbed, face away from mine. "Why didn't you fight?"

"I fought, darling, they placed a gun to my head."

I took my free hand to her knee, held it there comfortingly for a few seconds, waited until the truck found a smoother groove in the street. Passing the moments, looking through the tears in her good eye, all the while wishing I could absorb her pain. Pull it from her body, her memory, into mine. Let it disappear down my soul.

Gingerly, I tried again, the surface felt sharp and rough through the cloth, irregular, uneven. The blood soaked past the cotton, my hand quickly growing warm, the fabric sticking heavy to my fingers. Bits of enamel, chips of tooth came free with every wipe. Several times she cried out, pulled back in agony, when I pressed too hard or the truck's movement unsteadied my hand.

My shirt tail was soaked, warm and wet it clung to my stomach, my trousers. The elderly man handed me a sheet from their bundle. I held it to Kaiva's face, my other hand caressing her across the back, until the blood had finally begun to slow. Carefully, I retracted the knotted sheet.

My face must have reflected the horror I found, because Kaiva recoiled and started to weep again. Three upper front teeth, both incisors and a canine, had been bent back twenty degrees. A lower molar was broken off above the gum line, and another was wobbling precariously loose with every reflexive sob. And through it all, beneath pink streaking blood, were assorted chips and cracks in the enamel, each crown a tortured, unfinished puzzle.

She was crying continuously. My free hand comforted her thigh. "It's not so bad, darling." I mopped a slow trickle running down her chin. "We'll get it fixed." As always, the words not enough, condescending, insulting to her.

She asked again, her voice drowned by the motor engine. "Why didn't you fight?"

"I did darling, I did."

She only nodded, a hand pressed lightly against her swelling jaw. "Where are we going?"

A good question. In all the pain and concern for her, it hadn't yet taken hold of my mind. "I don't know."

The reality began to set in. I muttered more to myself than her: "Twice now the communists have forced me from my home."

"For me," said Kaiva, "it's the second time soldiers have."

The sun was high in the clear seven o'clock sky when our now overcrowded truck finally arrived at Rīga's Torņakalns train station. The grey wooden building and its surrounding fenced-in-yard packed with thousands upon thousands of Latvian men, women and children of every class, dress and description. The multitude separated, infested, herded by an equally vast number of tan-uniformed Russian soldiers. In the thick, rapidly heating air, hurried, exhausted prisoners filled every doorway, every meter of free dirt, wood or concrete, clinging equally to luggage and loved ones, all despondently waiting their turn. Through these stationary crowds, channels of humans suddenly flowed as if a great valve had been quickly opened, sent off sporadically to some unseen destination within the dark tunnels or pressed ever closer to the lines of trains, their red-brown cars ominously visible along the far side of the station, a hazy, distant mountain range above the countless heads of mulling passengers.

"How many?" I asked Kaiva.

Her breath horrid, her lips slow and sticky from dried blood, she could give only the answer she knew. "I have no idea."

The guard told us to swiftly dismount the truck. Clutching all our possessions Kaiva and I were pushed through the gate in the fence, suddenly crushed into these desperate mobs, the heat generated by their bodies, their breath, raising the temperature five full degrees the moment inside. Standing near the tunnels, heavily armed Russian soldiers separated people, dividing families, sending mothers and children down different paths than men and adolescent boys.

The fear of separation erupted from my soul. I could not leave her, not like this? The worst fate I could imagine, making every moment in the packed queue, despite the uncertainty, the heat and Kaiva's injuries, bizarrely precious. A desperate second here together, far better than the coming moments apart.

As we waited, a thick featured guard came down the line pulling our suitcases from us, casting them into a huge conical pile, one of many in front of the great pillared central hall.

He shouted out. "Small bags only. Enough for a day or two."

There was some relief in these words. Could the duration be so short? Some urgent but temporary need for manpower? My mind knew it to be a lie, without a doubt a fabrication to keep the queue moving. I looked at Kaiva's battered face. No, I understood their game. The soul clings to hope, no matter how ridiculous the idea or insidious the teller. They could say anything.

Truth or not, it hadn't occurred to me to bring anything small. I handed my remaining item to Kaiva: A loaf of rye bread given to me by the elderly woman in the truck. My wife broke it in half and returned a section to me. When she winced at even the slightest bite, Kaiva forced me to accept her part as well.

After a desperate hour standing there, I was suddenly caught in one of those shifting currents that could mysteriously appear within a crowd. Without warning a Russian sergeant appeared, pushing Kaiva and me apart. She was sent with other women down a path toward the Eastern tunnel, me on ahead to the immediate cars.

The shock in the actual moment of separation was truly horrifying. As terrible, in its own way, as watching that soldier strike her. There were so many things left unsaid, a last kiss, a final pledge of undying love. I tried to press around him to have a last caress of her hand, to pass a simple touch across her fingertips, but the Soviet kept me at the distance:

"Move along, you'll all be together in the end."

"Kaiva." I yelled, but the new wave of bodies swept me backwards. Her bruised amber-haired face eclipsed by three tall Latvian military officers, they too being forced toward the trains by the Russian guards.

I tried to stand off to one side, let them pass, but she failed to reappear after the latest surge. A horrible fear, a desperate realization, even greater than all those terrors since that first knock at the door: Was this the last I'd seen of her? Was this moment that must come in every life, the final look upon my love's countenance? Now only clinging to a memory, fleeting, evaporating, dulling with every second since parting? Was that all I had to feed my soul? Forever? Better death than this, to perish with her image still perfect within my mind, my heart.

I fought to stand my ground, but was swept back again, and again by the undulating crowd. An arm pulled my attention away from Kaiva's disappearance. A young guard, a boy really, pointed to an open cattle car, insisting that I step up into it.

"Now fascist! Inside." He appended his insult by shouting the three classic Russian swear words until I obeyed.

The car had once been a simple cattle container, fashioned of thick, long, reddish planks. Now it was fitted with large double bunks of barren wood on either end, the middle third left open. In this free space, near the opposite wall, a small hole in the floor obviously serving as the toilet. By the smell and the dusty, dried faeces still in the corners, it had been used to move horses before being modified for people.

There were already two men and a boy of about sixteen inside staking territory on the highest bunk of one end. I moved as near to the open door as the guard would let me. Standing on the edge, often helping others climb up inside, I looked out across the crowd for Kaiva. Despite the elevation, I found no trace. I dared not dream they had let her go. No, no, I limited my emotions to more realistic, less desperate desires. Praying she was being put on the same train as me, so that wherever they might take us, somehow we still might be together.

I recognized faces milling through the crowd: neighbors, colleagues, students and former students. Was that Dean Niselovics having his luggage torn apart by armed guards? Could that have been Seskis wandering dumbfounded down the Eastern tunnel?

There were so many others: Ulmanis's stooges, university professors, kindergarten teachers, religious leaders, business moguls, journalists, policemen, publishers, even a few faces from Kaiva's old newspaper, anyone who was listened to or might venture an opinion. Those who dared to do more than quietly go about their lives, even theoretically.

Even now, the guards would allow no display of authority. When one of these leaders would call a few around himself, the soldiers would rush over and dissipate the assembly, seize the man by the coat collar, sending the instigator all the quicker to the cars.

And judging by their dress, they were collecting far less prominent Latvians as well: vagrants, homeless, prostitutes, the mentally ill. The misfits who didn't fit the Soviet ideal of a Workers' Utopia, those poor souls the State was supposed to be helping, easier to haul them away in boxcars than solve their problems. The great parenthesis of Latvian society, stripped away.

And children, everywhere there were children. Thousands. In their mother's arms, on their father's shoulders, lost, alone and crying in the crowd.

The hypocrisy made me physically ill. From a nation that I'd fought for, the government I'd backed in their moment of truth.

How had it fallen to this?

Enraged, I twisted the front of my shirt in my hands, stiff and cracking from the coating of Kaiva's blood. The only remnant of her I still possessed. A blood stained cloth as a last memento? Absence, violence and ruin the valedictory.

My sympathies for the Letts, my love of Kaiva had blinded me to communism's true nature. How could I ever have been fool enough to support this? These people?

"Abductors! Murderers!" I screamed in German to avoid the guards' censures.

My dark words were interrupted by a Latvian shouting behind me.

"Orests! Go ahead!"

A later arrival, the man was standing at one of the horizontally barred windows along the rear, calling to someone on the other side. I crossed the car to find the source of the commotion. A quick glance through the window revealed a thick crowd of people across another set of tracks, massed behind a wire fence at the back of the station, a distance of not twenty meters. A few guards patrolled it, keeping those still free from pushing too hard on the barricade while they shouted for loved ones imprisoned in the railroad cars. With so many faces at the divide, it was impossible for me to ascertain the target of the man's calls.

"Orests marry her, go ahead."

Though too loud for me to hear, someone must have responded because my fellow prisoner quickly nodded. "Yes, yes, it is best. For me, for them."

The interior grew suddenly crowded as a flood of men and teenage boys were directed into our car. They scrambled over each other, filling the free space in the wide bunks. Those remaining began to back toward the rear, as more prisoners were forced inside. I felt the compartment's temperature dangerously rise, a product of packed bodies, warm exhales and the building summer heat. Pressed against a rear wall, I watched the crumpling man who had been shouting through the window.

He was older than me, in his fifties or sixties, roundish, white-haired, a small beard shading his chin. Better dressed than most, the ends of bifocals stuck out of the leather change purse gripped tightly in his hands. I was moved by his pleas across the tracks, through the fence. A last wish to a friend or son? A message to marry a lost love? Or a final approval given to a long frustrated suitor of his daughter?

I kneeled, caught his attention with a touch of the shoulder. "Did he agree? The man outside…to marry her?"

He nodded affirmatively, his voice emotional. "I need my wife to have someone who'll be a good father to our children." He saddled back as a few men were shoved between us, his voice a whisper. "My brother is a kind man, he won't beat them."

As the final passengers pressed me to the wall, there was the creek of a bolt, and the door slid shut, throwing the interior into semi-darkness. Forty or so lungs took the last of the cool, fresh air, as the sweltering heat inside the car continued its meteoric rise.

We heard the heavy snap of a thick lock outside, the metal casing vibrating against the wood exterior.

I was right. This had been the day.

Freedom was only a memory.

Chapter Twenty-six

As the train began to move panic swept the car. People pawed their bodies, dug deep into pockets for anything, no matter how small, to write upon; fought over pens, chalk, lead pencils, desperate to scribble a note for families, lovers, and friends. More than farewells, they recorded practical information: the train, the hour, the station. But no one could honestly say where we might be going.

Packed near me was a young Latvian officer, the insignia and buttons absent from his uniform. Even stripped of the fasteners on his trousers, he had bunched the top into a knot to keep them up. Falling against me as the car vibrated, he quickly unwrapped a cigarette, tore the paper in half, handing the remnant to a neighbor before writing his own in the tiniest of letters:

> *Please deliver to 69/71-20 Gertrudes Iela. On a train leaving Saturday morning from Torņakalns. Tell Līva Kokina I love her and will hold her again.*
> *Lieutenant Felikss Maluhins*

All over the car, they shoved these notes through gaps in the planks or past the bars in the windows. Between the boards I could see the fluttering papers: hundreds, maybe thousands, trailing along the train as it gained speed. Like a huge swarm of white butterflies, floating, spinning in the air, hovering about every car, finally dropping behind, unable to match the engine's acceleration.

I thought to join them, to add my own message, but by then there was no paper remaining. Every cigarette wrapping, clothing tag, or book leaf had been sacrificed. And truthfully, the only person I really wanted to contact was herself almost certainly on another car or train, like me journeying into the unknown.

Hours passed. The car gained a terrible stillness, a pensive and despondent quiet settling under the thick air of noon. Like the prisoner I was, there was nothing to do but lay on a lower bunk staring up at the patterns in the shaking red-wood grain above. The shock of deportation subsiding, unanswerable questions began to creep into my mind: When would I see Kaiva again? Where were we going? What was life going to be like when we reached our destination? Would we ever return?

But the dominant question for everyone, the one hardest to reconcile was "Why?"

Lieutenant Maluhins was next to me, one of seven or eight crowded onto the same platform bunk. He whispered, a pointless exercise in politeness as sound, vibration and anxiety kept anyone from dozing away. "I was off duty. I had gone for a walk outside the barracks to get some fresh Zemgale air. A truck passed full of officers. I think I knew everyone of them."

His eyes were closed, an arm thrown across his brow. A bulbous black-green fly wandered casually across his forearm, licking moisture from his skin. In this heat Maluhins hadn't the will to swat it. He continued: "I asked the men, 'Where are you going?' 'Maneuvers' they said. Being the good soldier, even though I had the day off, I joined them. A little extra training never hurts.

"They took us to this field in the woods. A Russian colonel, I had seen him only once before, he told us to remove our pistols. Claimed it was part of the exercise. It seemed curious but he was a superior officer, what could we do? We followed orders and then they marched us," he made a forward, rising motion with his hand like an airplane taking off, the fly scattering in the air before resettling at nearly the same spot, "straight to the trains. A few resisted but they never made it out of the forest.

"They filled three cars with us. I wasn't even supposed to be there." He smiled remorsefully, eyes still shaded by his arm. "So, I'm the spare, I guess."

Listening to his story, a shrill voice descended from the platform above. I recognized it as Nils's, the man who had shouted to his brother through the fence this morning: "I did nothing wrong either. I should never have been here." His cry was raspy, weak. He sounded truly despondent, far worse than the lieutenant.

I heard the creek of the wood as he turned over, a single eye peeking between the boards above us. "My bookshop…I got rid of every questionable book. I took them in the back lot, burned them. There was nothing objectionable. I don't know why."

Maluhins seemed to pity him, pressing his palm lightly against the platform above as if to comfort Nils: "Did they take anything? Confiscate any items when you were arrested?"

He must have reflexively nodded, the eye floating up and down behind the groove. "A Russian-English dictionary. It could only be…My wife said to be rid of it. I was keeping it only for toilet paper…it's true. They found it in the water closet."

LENIN'S HAREM

The silence renewed after that. What could be said? I thought of my own crimes. More numerous than theirs and far greater in nature: My aristocratic heritage; my service in the Old Bolsheviks, the ones who seemed to be disappearing of late. Or perhaps, it was my vocation? People listen to professors, did it matter that I was only talking about the stars? Maybe having their ears was enough. I thought of the terrible images from this morning, so many of my colleagues in those cattle lines. Were they such a threat to a country of 100 million? Were their words so poisonous?

Or maybe the NKVD knew that my wife printed pamphlets in the backroom. Little tan booklets with dangerous titles like "Socialism is not Totalitarianism." And of course, there was always my connection to Vereshchagin. Still a secret twenty years on? Everybody that seemed to know about it was dead.

A half-dozen reasons to take me, comparatively. I felt strangely guilty. So much more than a dictionary in the toilet.

The day dragged on, the light growing lower in the car, shrinking to only stretched yellow rectangles along the floor. Every thirty or forty minutes the train would shudder to a stop, loading more victims into other cars. But our doors remained locked, sealed. Frustrations grew, internal tensions breaking into frequent altercations. Lieutenant Maluhins and I stopped one particularly nasty assault. Two misguided passengers had attacked an elderly Jew named Yakov, proclaiming him to be a Bolshevik. An ugly, cancerous stereotype. It turned out he was a rabbi.

Ironically enough, I suspected, the only man in this car that had actually been a member of the Bolsheviks was me.

Eventually sleep did come, if intermittently; a narcotic elixir of late afternoon atmosphere and the mind's need to ward off depression with dreams.

But it did not last long. I awoke again to the feeling of perpetual irritation, as if something close-by was moving and would not cease. An old man wedged against me was wiping perspiration from his face. In the darkness of early evening, again and again, his elbow kept hitting me in the cheek, in the temple. After a few moments, I felt my own skin moisten. It was warm and thick, the drops falling on my face. I opened my eyes more fully, letting them slowly adjust to the car's new gloom. They widened in horror: black liquid seeped from the boards above.

Blood.

Horrified words began to rise throughout this end of the car, moans of discomfort building to screams of terror and disgust.

Nils had hidden a shaving razor in his little change bag. He'd slit his wrists as everyone slept.

Following the suicide, there was much debate about what to do with Nils's smuggled razor. Many, including Lieutenant Maluhins, thought to keep it as a potential weapon against the guards. Still others, fearful of reprisals, said it should be thrown down the toilet hole. It was Yakov who correctly pointed out that our captors would need to be informed of Nils's demise at the next stop and would certainly demand to confiscate whatever knife he'd used.

That next station was Daugavpils, where the communists took both the body and the blade, throwing a bucket of water over the bloodstained bunks, washing away the stain, if not the stench or memory.

Nils's space above was taken before it dried. The property too valuable to wait until it was comfortable.

The train remained at the station for some countless hours. Refueling? Changing crews? Adding more condemned to its cargo? Yet another unanswerable question.

It was during this layover that we each received a ladle of garlicky gruel. A soldier distributed it without bowls. We had to sip it all in one swallow or the guard moved on, the meal lost. It was hot and burned my throat, many of my fellows noticeably winced as they sipped, but it was far better than starvation.

I lay still on the bunk, the smell of Nils's blood nauseatingly mixing with the stench of forty unwashed bodies jammed together in the summer night. I passed in and out of consciousness, trying to find a spot where the uneven board beneath my back did not rub my spine raw. It was easier, I had to admit, now that the train was not moving. A comparative reprieve, this temporary stillness, one I could grow to appreciate. How quickly we had lowered our standard of luxury, of what was tolerable. A meek acceptance of our situation? Or survival instincts? I was undecided.

The car door slid open, the torso of a guard shining a hooded lantern into the interior, the faint silhouettes of two others behind him in the dark. The lantern barer called out a name:

LENIN'S HAREM

"Kļaviņš! Ausmiņš Kļaviņš!"

Two men stirred, one near the center of the top bunk, crawling over the others to reach the open space. The other already close, curled on the floor a meter or so from the toilet hole.

There was a discussion at the door as to whose name had actually been called. A moment later, one was shoved back to the floor, while the other was harshly seized and pulled off the train.

Then the door rolled shut, and once again we heard the metallic snap as the bolt locked. The board grating against my back began to vibrate again. The train was pulling away, finally leaving Daugavpils behind. Journeying away from the last city of Latvia, and with a slight detour into what had once been Poland, then straight east.

Through the night into the heart of Russia herself.

The next morning, there was a general feeling in the car that there had been a missed opportunity. That the exiting individual, no matter where his destination, could have been a courier of information to our families. There was a suggestion by Maluhins that if anyone else were removed a list of the car's occupants and the addresses of their kin should accompany him. The problem, of course, was there was no paper to be found. What little that had been possessed was thrown out as notes in Rīga. It was at this point that Yakov, the Jewish man who had been assaulted the day before, produced a thick, well-bound Hebrew Bible and offered it for the service. Lieutenant Maluhins, standing in the center of the free space, bound the prisoners to an oath: If anyone should ever get off this train, they would contact the families of the rest at the first possible opportunity. He had no trouble getting all to comply, even the men that had assaulted the 'Bolshevik' only yesterday. It was a small hope but all we had.

Yakov's book was passed around, each person writing their own information in the margins. To eliminate confusion Maluhins instituted a system: Name of passenger on the top, address and contact in the outer margin, a second in the inner if needed, and a personal message on the bottom. Eventually the book came to me. It was a heavy tome with a face of worn red leather. To my surprise it was written in German, only the cover page adorned with the musical-note-resembling Hebrew characters.

I considered who to put as the contact. My parents in Germany would never get a letter and I had no idea which university colleagues might have been spared, so I put down Agnese's name and address in one margin, and out of desperation, my brother's in the other. Otomars was almost certainly imprisoned on a train like this very one. Yet, he was cagey, there was always the chance. At the bottom I scribbled a note in both Latvian and Russian:

Please tell my family to relay a message to Kaiva Rooka (taken the same day as me, possibly same train): Kaiva, I am sorry. I love you. Please forgive my selfishness, Wiktor.

I flipped to the next free page, and wrote another message in Latvian:

To Orests of Riga, who has a brother named Nils. I am truly sorry to inform you that your brother has passed away. He died peacefully in his sleep on this train, an hour or so outside of Daugavpils. He told me how much he loved his wife and children, and could think of no greater man to take care of them. Please do him proud,
   Wiktor Rooks of Riga.

Since it was sweltering, it took little convincing to find a man to sacrifice his jacket for the common good. And with the book buttoned securely in the inside pocket, all swore that the first to leave would take the coat along as his own.

Standing in the air of the open woods, another prisoner and I folded the sheet around the bodies, and then lowered them into the grave. A mother had smothered her three children, then found a wire from a hat or corset and twisted it around her neck to asphyxiate herself. An entire Latvian family wrapped in a blanket, buried in a hole off the train tracks in the Russian woods. Gone without a trace on this Earth, never to be visited or mourned. Distant relatives always left wondering their fate.

Despite this woman and Nils, suicides were rare. Those that could would fight on. Mostly, we buried the elderly, their bodies unable to handle the hellish temperature or the overwhelming stress. Infants were another common victim, too fragile for the long journey in cattle cars.

A terrible realization washed over me. I was becoming used to death again, as I had in the last days of the wars. My humanity buried with each child in this endless country.

We filled the dirt in with sections of tree bark, the armed guards never very far from us. We were not five meters from the train tracks, the red-brown cars easily visible through the trees. Their doors open to the air as prisoners took the bodies out of those who had succumbed this latest night.

It was terrible, heartbreaking work, but it took me outside the confinement, allowed me to breathe fresh air for twenty minutes and to hear the rumors from the other cars. Nothing on Kaiva as of yet, but we weren't allowed much access, sent straight off to dig the pit.

I would change that. I aimed to make the most of this excursion.

The guards marched up and down either side of the train, only those burying a prisoner or on some other assigned task were allowed to leave the cars. One sergeant shouted out the primary rules every few minutes without variation. "Keep to the tracks. No lagging, no dawdling. A step to the left or to the right means an escape attempt. The guards will shoot without warning."

Regular as church bells, we could keep time to it.

Returning from burying the Latvian family, I apparently wandered a meter or two too far from the rail cars. A young guard, shouted at me to turn about, marching toward me, brandishing his weapon in my direction. Some small part of me thought to run, either I'd escape into the woods or he'd gun me down, and this conflict, this suffering would be settled. But Kaiva could be on the train and nothing was worth jeopardizing a reunion with her. Nothing.

So I walked back toward the rails, hands behind my head. As I passed, the soldier demanded to know which car I was in.

"Number Eleven."

He pointed with his weapon. "That is fifteen." And he pushed me the other way. "Stay nearer the tracks."

My voice was heavy with sarcasm. "Yes, I know how to guard a train. I've guarded trains." I pointed to my chest. "I watched Lenin's train."

The soldier never blinked. Eighteen years old, what did he care about ancient history?

Back on my way toward my pen, I passed the open door of Car Number Fourteen. A teenage girl sat on the edge, taking in the fresh scented air. Accepting her life for what it had become, peacefully waiting until the doors slammed shut once again.

"Kaiva Rooka?"

The youth only shook her head. Everyone knew the methods by now. Kaiva wasn't in the car nor had the girl heard of her.

Car Number Thirteen:

"Kaiva Rooka?"

The old woman only whispered "No."

Car Number Twelve was full of men. I reached Car Eleven, my personal prison. Car Ten and Car Nine tempted, only a few more steps further. I looked back to see if anyone observed. The boy's eyes were still watching, machine gun at his waist.

A distant voice sounded: "Keep to the tracks. No lagging, no dawdling. A step to the left or to the right means an escape attempt. The guards will shoot without warning."

Fate's echo. I silently climbed in.

Despite their best attempts, there was a rumor the Russians couldn't keep secret. Apparently the German army had invaded the Soviet Union. By our guards' countenances and worried exchanges, it seemed to have taken the Russian forces completely by surprise. Though many among us had served in the Soviet government or military, the car was nearly unanimous in its support of the German invaders. Nazi ideology was never discussed. When you're dangling from a cliff, you don't ask the politics of the man throwing the rope, and the news simply gave everyone hope.

A few cynics pointed out that now both of the 'traditional enemies' would be burning Latvian lands once again, but for the most part the objections were strictly practical. We were simply too far inside Soviet Russia. The Wehrmacht would never be able to penetrate this deeply, certainly, not before the Soviets decided to 'erase' any indication of mass-enslavements. Rescue was unrealistic.

No, if there were any joy brought by the news, it was simply spite, to know that our enemy slept a little less comfortably at night.

As the days passed, my mind kept wandering back to that last view of Kaiva: her lip split and bloody, an exhausted, frightened look upon her face. Far from her fairest moment, but a face I'd give anything to see, no matter the state, as long as she was alive.

My head was filled with such images, when I awoke to the sound of the car door sliding open, the poorly greased rollers begrudgingly giving way, groaning as they were forced to turn. There followed the beam of an electric torch, its roving eye crisscrossing the car's interior, slithering over the hills and valleys of poorly-slumbering bodies in search of some individual.

"Wiktor Rooks," a voice called. "Major Wiktor Rooks?"

My heart raced, it could only be for me. There was no other possibility. Despite the mistake in rank, in status, it had to be my personage they called.

I moved off the bunk, the car stirring at the sudden activity.

"I am Wiktor Rooks."

The guard looked at me, his face cast in blue behind the torch's source.

"Come with me."

Quickly I approached the door, Maluhins handing me the preplanned coat. The impatient guard gave me no time for goodbyes, forcing me quickly outside the car. Two more soldiers awaited standing on the cracked concrete platform of a remote train station. A single light pole affixed near the entrance providing the sole visible light for kilometers in the black Russian woods.

There was something in this darkness, in the station's very solitude that turned the course of my soul. Quickly the thrill of emancipation plummeted to the fear of extinction. The reference to 'Major', the last time a military title had been affixed to my name was Titov's terrifying phone call nearly three years ago.

I slowed my steps trying to buy a moment to reason what was truly happening. Seeing me languishing, one guard took my arm, tugging me along while another insisted. "Hurry along, Major."

I glanced back at the car, still open, ghastly white, familiar faces staring back as the remaining guard rolled the door closed. Suddenly the group felt safer. Why was I being singled out? As Juškevičs had been? Dragged away like Līcis must have found himself in his final hours? After long days wanting nothing but to escape the car, I felt exposed, desperate to return to the safety of numbers, to be one of many.

I pulled at the soldier's arm, but my resistance only attracted the other guard to assist, to push me into the darkened entranceway that much faster.

They opened a scarred, peeling wooden door and shoved me forward. An unprovoked aggression in their force, my foot caught the threshold, sending me falling face down onto a concrete floor.

My eyes found a pair of polished, plain black shoes nearby. I upturned my head, fearful to look upon the face of the man who might be my executioner.

I let out a gasp.

"Otomars."

Chapter Twenty-seven

"Did you mention you'd been a Rifleman?"

"I said…I said I was a professor."

"With an enemy army in their lands?" Otomars rocked forward in his chair. "Why didn't you tell them you had skills of value?"

We only stared at each other in mutual disbelief.

I sat across from Otomars at a little table in the office of the train station, trying to take it all in. Sitting with his back to the 'Red corner,' where over-lit ruby and yellow emblems of State, Party, and the Great Teacher had long replaced the traditional Russian icons of Jesus, Mary and the other Orthodox saints, my brother shoved a canvas bag toward me, in it a Soviet officer's uniform. "Fortunately for us the German military made the point for you."

I fingered the fabric. How could I wear this again? After what men in these colors had done? No…

Otomars eyes probed my countenance. "God you look terrible. Have you been wearing the same clothes the entire time you were on the train? All that blood caked on your shirt?"

Obviously, he sensed my hesitation with the uniform. "It was the only way we could justify your release, Wiktor." He pointed at the collar. "You're a major now, a fully decorated…and reactivated… hero. With a slightly more flamboyant record." He smiled. "They weren't going to just let anyone off of there…"

"How?"

He leaned across the table his voice less than a whisper, yet a boyish pride still plainly evident: "A few well-written orders from a colonel too busy in retreat to notice."

It was all so unbelievable. "And you? Why aren't you…"

"I know people who mistype dictation." His tone said the time for self-congratulations was over. We needed to get moving. "Trust me our subterfuge will only last as long as the Germans are throwing everything into chaos. If it settles down, it's back to the trains for both of us. At best."

My pensive mind awakened to the metallic clanking of railcar buckles, the slow churning of an engine. The train outside was leaving.

So shocked was I with Otomars miraculous appearance, I hadn't yet considered: "Kaiva…Otomars, where is Kaiva?"

"Still in a car I presume. I only wish…"

"We must free her!"

He glanced again at the room's closed doors, the soldiers not far beyond, he kept his voice low: "On what grounds? I have no documentation, no rationale, Wiktor. I called in every favor I was owed to find an out for you." He slammed the edge of the table with his palm. "And then some."

I screamed, other ears be damned: "She's the 'War Hero's' wife, isn't that enough?"

There was condescending venom in his response. "It doesn't work that way."

I threw the chair back, stood to take some action. Any action. "Stop the train."

He grabbed my arm across the table. "It's impossible. Count the cars, Wiktor. There are 10,000, maybe 20,000 people who want off those trains! Tonight alone. The whole Baltic…"

"Stop the damn train!" I pulled away, moving toward the door, to halt the engine somehow.

A third voice startled us both, a guard's head popping out from behind the door I approached. "Your automobile is here, sir."

Otomars answered him: "Thank you, Corporal. One moment, please." He waited until the soldier pulled the door shut. "I'm sorry Wiktor, there is nothing I can do."

I turned back to him, voice raging; terrifyingly vindictive that he would dare think about rescuing me and leaving Kaiva. "Then give me a gun. I don't want to live without her."

He shook his head in disproval. "Be a man Wiktor."

I gazed viciously at him. A man? Yes, a man. Fair enough, a man finds a way.

I hurried around the table, shoved the end quickly aside. The sudden violent motion, the horrid screech of wood on cement, seemed to startle him, his face openly shocked. Crouching to the cold cement, I put a hand on Otomars's knee, my head bent low, neck fully exposed. A complete suppliant before my brother and all his abilities, all his prowess. He knew the symbolism. His utter servant, as with the barons of old my life was his to spare or dispose at a whim. I gave all to him, everything, in return for one more favor. This the price of my soul.

"Please Otomars. There must be a way…"

We stood in the mud, trying to keep our cigarettes lit in the drizzling rain of Western Russia not thirty kilometers from the Latvian border. Next to me the hulking body of a Lett who Otomars had convinced to be our driver into Latgale: an overly-talkative Liepāja dock worker named Juris Ozoliņś. He rambled on about his days on freighters to the Americas and Far East Asia, seemingly unbothered by the world disintegrating about him. Neither I, nor the skeletally-thin Russian station manager, exiled from his own office by a roll of bills and Otomars's need for privacy, really listened. Inside, whoever my brother was calling remained a complete mystery to the three of us.

I didn't care as long as he succeeded. On our journey through Russia, Otomars had worked the phones at every stop. Even in a guarded, invaded land, he'd discovered strange out of the way places to make his calls: in shacks at the end of fishing piers, atop country telephone poles, in the bedrooms of farm houses. Always alone and in total secrecy. So far to no avail.

The giant continued his tales. "And the neon board's lights flashed in the shape of all their faces: Judy Garland, and then the scarecrow, the metal woodsman, a sad looking lion, and her little dog too…"

I looked back at the little wooden building: A tilting, desolate shed resting beside the grid-like steel tower of a rural telephone relay station. I doubted it would be here tomorrow. Either the Germans, who had already sprinted past us on several fronts, would demolish it to interrupt Soviet communications or the Russians themselves would bring down the structure to prevent the enemy from using it. I pitied the thing. Poor, orphaned tower, both sides wanted to see it die. I knew how it felt.

This droning Juris would never cease. So loud was his gushing praise of New York's Times Square and all its gaudy wonders, that I barely heard the slam of the door as Otomars exited. His face was noncommittal, no trace of euphoric success or life-ending failure. An excellent poker player my brother: unrelentingly stoic no matter how high the stakes. And as far as I was concerned they could not be higher.

He approached my location, the sound of his boots splashing in the mud, growing louder as he neared. When he arrived at my shoulder, his face was stern as an undertaker's, rain water slowly running down his wide cheeks.

"Alright Wiktor," he let out a trace of a smile, "we've got her off at Bologoye. With the chaos it may take a little while to get her to Pskov." I hugged my brother, unrestrained tears running down my face, left it there a moment, my head resting on his heavy breast, repeating: "Thank you," again and again.

"We've arranged," he smiled at this word, "for her to hitch-a-ride to Gulbene on a Red Cross relief truck. We'll have the locals bring her through Latgale from there. It's best if she meet us in town." He motioned for Ozoliņś, starting toward our car. "She needs to hurry…we all need to hurry. The Germans are closing the loop as we speak."

I rushed to catch up with him. "But Kaiva… you are sure she's free?"

He nodded. "As long as she does what's she's told, for once, we have a chance," he held up a single finger, "a chance…of getting her home."

Was there no miracle my brother couldn't perform? "How? How did you do it?"

He opened the car door, slid himself inside. "Let's keep you an honest man a day or so longer Wiktor."

Our car slipped into Latgale on a muddy, dirt road, designed for horses and winter sleighs rather than automobiles. The engine gunning with Otomars at the wheel, not once, not twice, but thrice the giant and I had to get out and push it from the mire. With every hour, I watched the fuel meter dip tauntingly lower, my mind obsessing to calculate the distance to our destination and the gasoline needed to reach it.

Not that any more-traveled route would have been easier. On the major roads, logs and telephone poles blocked any passing. Railroad tracks had been demolished at every crossing, ties torn up and strewn about to stop car and train alike. Everything designed to delay the German advance.

Indeed, the Russian "Destroyer" units were very successfully ravaging the land while they retreated. The horizon was filled with columns of thick smoke as they burned crops, granaries, and factories, anything the Germans could use. A choking haze hung over fields, between forest trees, and settled on restful lake waters. The tongue, the throat, both uncomfortably trying to shake off a gritty, sooty aftertaste even at great distance. The atmosphere resurrected long buried memories: sights, smells, even tastes of that night in 1905 when the whole countryside seemed ablaze, and again ten years later when the tsar's army razed the crops as the kaiser's men approached Rīga.

The cycle was renewed once again. All this fighting, all these years passing, with the voluminous talk of social engineering and revolutionary new ways of governing; of Workers' States and a Latvian Nation, with thousands, millions dying to realize them, and yet so little progress. Nothing ever changed.

It was all in vain.

We often saw people on foot or in carts moving east. Whole families uprooted everything they owned piled into some skeletal wagon, Latgalians, Jews, gypsies mainly. All following the Soviet army back if they could. For many the exodus was too much, the ill, the elderly, entire families simply sat by road in the smoggy air, waiting for someone to tell them what to do, where to go.

On these backroads my major's uniform and Otomars's charm and pocketbook were all equally useful in allowing us to keeping advancing west. More than once I was sure our excuse would not be accepted by the mounted Russian soldiers we encountered. To our good fortune, we never met anyone that outranked me, never looked eye to eye with a commander of a Destroyer Unit, fully authorized to eliminate any dubious undertaking. In the end, no one ever kept us long. With an uncaring sneer or mystified shrug, they allowed the fools to continue the wrong way. Several times Juris's thick hand pointed a pistol at peasants who wanted to seize our vehicle for their own benefit, but always, somehow, we maneuvered past the obstacle, allowed by rank, force or guile to continue.

We were truly in a no-man's land. German aircraft often circled in the air, buzzing close but mercifully never strafing; in an open field we passed the burned-out shell of a Panzer tank and more than one peasant told us about Wehrmacht soldiers not far ahead. As we zigzagged around the thousand lakes that cover Latgale, a few times Otomars was sure the soldiers encamped on the opposite side were Germans, forcing me to quickly remove my Soviet uniform, shoving it under the seat cushion before their sentries spotted us. Once he was so positive I actually threw it out of the car and when discovering that the hostile forces were simply a camp of frightened Lithuanian refugees, we had to reverse a third of a kilometer to retrieve it.

Always there was the fear in my heart, greater even than that of capture that the path into Latvia would close. That the obstacles we were facing would be too great for the relief car that carried Kaiva down from Pskov. Otomars assured me that it was the safer route, that the neon cross was all the key she needed, but until I actually saw her, held Kaiva in my arms again, felt the warmth of her touch, I could not be comforted, no matter how eloquent my brother's speech.

In the summer rainfall, Juris over-revved the engine once again, carrying the spinning wheels through the mud. In the back, I laid strewn across the seat, wet and exhausted from the latest excursion to move an impediment off our path, the most recent a donkey someone had put out of its misery right in the road.

Otomars sat next to me, my brother briefing me on our destination.

"There is nothing close to the town, Rēzekne is nearly forty kilometers." He tapped my arm to make sure I was listening. "There was a small Russian garrison, operating out of an old granary five kilometers up the road, but they will have retreated with the rest of their army."

He hushed his words, eyeing the back of Juris's head. "The colonel that ran it was a shady character, but a good businessman for a communist." He dropped his voice even further. "We made quite the tidy profit together."

My brother and his dealings, I'd scoff at them but…but they seemed to be keeping us alive. "I don't understand how we'll be safer in such a little town. In Rīga at least there can be a defense."

"Well first, we'd never be able to get into Rīga, the coast is too congested by now. Secondly," he paused for a moment, watching Juris at the driver's wheel again. "Juris?" The giant did not respond, the over-worked engine too loud for him to hear into the back seat.

Otomars tested it once more, his voice a little louder. "Ozoliņś, stop the car."

No response.

My brother smiled, "Juris your mother is a pregnant sow."

Nothing.

Otomars laughed at his silence. "Secondly, Wiktor, I have quite the nest egg stored in my little village, years of hard work. We'll need money to restart our lives in the new government."

"New government?"

"Yes," his eyes fixed on Juris again. "I fully intend to surrender. I hope you haven't added a Lettish tinge to your German, Wiktor?"

"No…" His plans surprised me though they shouldn't have. Otomars was too savvy the opportunist, and realistically, the Soviets forces were in full retreat. The same army, I reminded myself, that had stolen our country's freedom, murdered my friends, thrown me into a box car, and disfigured the only woman I'd ever truly loved. I had absolutely no pity for them. The faster the Germans killed them, the better.

Yet, there was still something in the back of my mind. Some old comments of Kaiva's about Judas rulers and the fashioning of bargains. Would she still call it betrayal after her own recent experiences?

This world had grown uncomfortable. I tipped my hat low, tried to induce sleep, to find sanctuary in a better reality for a few hours. To recall the delicate beauty of my wife's face.

And forget her words.

Chapter Twenty-eight

It was late in the evening, the burning orange sun resting behind tangled forest branches as we reached our destination. Hours later than Otomars had predicted, and the fuel indicator ten full degrees below empty, I considered it something of a miracle that we had arrived at all.

So, this was the village Otomars had spent the last two years making his own? Nothing unusual in my initial impression: Small wooden houses stretching along muddy roads that nearly always ended in wild forest or tended field. Here and there a brick building, or a second story but that was as much variation as the little town would allow. Or at least as far as I could see in the shadowy alleys the car now navigated.

The streets were strangely deserted for a summer's eve, Juris's palm not once approaching the horn. The passing rain was the obvious suspect, but some part of me wondered if the war had made the locals reclusive. The Latgalians had always been a tribe apart from the rest of the Baltic peoples, their dialect slightly different, their ways more truly Eastern than their countrymen. I thought this ravaging conflict might have turned them hermitic, the unsummoned madness coming from far off urban centers like Berlin, Moscow and even Rīga once again disturbing their rustic, unchanging world. The better for them to stay indoors, mind their families, and let the wars of more aggressive peoples pass by the window like a thundering summer storm.

The car reversed, Juris having taken us down a street too narrow for an automobile. Following Otomars's direction we soon turned onto a wider road. Ahead, some large black structure loomed, beyond it the white face of a town clock showing half past ten. As we neared, the details came in focus, and a strange chill ran over my spine. This was unexpected…

"It looks like a prison, Otomars." A large grey-black stone building stood at the end of the road. In front an open courtyard, on the margins the giant brown boxes of warehouse buildings. The whole compound was surrounded by a three meter high iron fence, the top crowned in the toothy curls of barbed wire. Glaring down from opposite corners the empty platforms of watch towers. There was not a light to be seen.

"It was the city hall." My brother pointed out the window. "I spent my days when in residence in an office in the top right corner."

The city hall so guarded? "Is it still in use?"

"I should think it abandoned. The Russians removed the local government, and since it was the largest stone structure in the district, turned it into a political prison, a staging area for those on their way east."

He made reference to the dreaded NKVD headquarters in Rīga: "A sort of 'Corner House Latgale.' Many, many horrible things went on in there."

I shuddered at the thought, taken to a prison in the middle of the wilderness, locked in a cell, waiting for interrogation. Perhaps, it would be better to have a bullet in the head, a less painful route to the same end.

Otomars continued: "Fortunately, the Soviet administration will have long packed up in retreat, along with the prison guards and my colonel friend's local garrison. Frankly, I'm surprised the "Destroyer" units haven't leveled the thing. At best, we'll find some local refugees using it as a sanctuary."

"Where are the prisoners now?"

My brother somehow managed a vindictive sneer. "Buried in the forest. With the Germans coming, the dogs had no time for mercy."

"My God." I felt like a boy in a ghost tale, fearful of approaching the old castle. "We're not staying there are we Otomars?"

He laughed to break the tension. "No, no. I've a residence a little further on." I was momentarily relieved until Otomars told Juris to stop the car. "Let's have a look around."

With an ignored Juris complaining that we had run out of petrol, the two of us left the car outside the fence. Hands on hips, Otomars marched toward the half-opened iron gate, side stepping inside with the empowered aura of a man perusing the family home after a lengthy vacation.

My approach was slower, more cautious, the hesitance natural in ill-considered steps into the unknown.

We passed inside the dark gates, the face of the two-story building cold and black before us. I could see the iron bars on the windows, the hammer and sickle carved above the front door, ill-fitting with the flowing Latgalian designs on the frame. Was this the sort of destination that train would have taken us to in Russia? Would this have been my fate if not for Otomars?

My eyes sought him in the night. He had stopped walking, standing alone in the gloom, a concerned squint as he peered off into the corner of the courtyard. My general apprehension turned to surprise and then a numbing dread. From a door in one of the surrounding wooden warehouses, came three… no four…no five… Russian soldiers their rifles aimed directly at the two of us.

"Well," said Otomars as he put his hands up. "Apparently, not all Soviet forces have retreated after all." His eyes caught mine, the expression not nearly as euphoric as his Russian words: "What luck, Wiktor. We are saved."

How quickly the imagined can become reality.

My brother and I sat in a cell under interrogation deep inside "city hall." Our interviewer was a big man. Not the v-shape or bulging muscles of the separately imprisoned Juris, but a square wall of humanity, wide hips, wide shoulders, wide neck. Everything about him was so wide that he eclipsed the light from the hanging bulb above him, bathing us in his considerable shadow. His NKVD hat hung on the outside door handle – surely to signal something to someone – the few prickly blond hairs left on a shaved head did little to enliven his skull-like visage.

He sat on the interview table rather than across from it, looking down contemptuously at the two of us in low wooden chairs. Major Roman Bloch fumbled for a cigarette in his breast pocket as he commented on my latest response:

"It looks to me like you are a deserter, Major Rooks. Come with your brother to seek shelter in an old haunt of his. Given your German heritage, there is a real possibility that your sympathies are misguided, yes?"

Otomars had remained uncharacteristically quiet during the discussion, replying in terse monosyllables. The absence of eloquence or guile was truly unusual. Was he buying his time, waiting for opportunity, or for once out of ideas? Either way, it made me feel uncomfortably on my own.

I kept my voice level, businesslike. I'd seen his type before: "I have a long and distinguished service record, Major Bloch. My loyalties proved in the field many, many times."

"Yes, I am sure you have." He withdrew two cigarettes, placing the spare on the table next to him and then lighting the other. Was he so addicted he had to have the next already at hand? I wondered how many he went through in a day and where he got them? "Why don't you tell me a little more about where you were going? Hmm, Comrade Rooks? And which unit exactly you were assigned to?"

Was he baiting me into a mistake? We had been left stewing in the cell for quite awhile before Bloch appeared. I suspected Roman may have already had an interview with Juris. I tried to remember exactly the story Otomars had told our driver, the justifications true or not for our journey. Any variation with his could have very unpleasant consequences, especially if they separated me from Otomars as well.

I was about to speak, when a new voice entered the conversation. "That won't be necessary Roman." A thin man in a Russian officer's uniform stood in the open cell doorway. Sixty-ish, short grey hair, dog-eyed and haggard-looking, he was in no way a physical threat to the bullying NKVD Major, yet his voice had the intimidating authority of one who commands. "Major Rooks has been correctly assigned to my staff."

Bloch growled a response as the older man entered, noticeably leaving the cell door open behind. "And why didn't you mention this to me, Colonel Tchuhlanceff?"

My brother came to life at this man's appearance, as if this were the moment he had been waiting for all along. "Ah, Gavriil! Nice to see you again."

Otomars stood up, sliding past Bloch to shake the colonel's hand. "I had feared the Germans...Well, they'll never get you will they Gavriil?" He laughed, clasping the Russian colonel's arm. "Now that we're all assembled let us get down to business." I wondered who was more shocked at the sudden change in my brother, in the atmosphere of the cell itself: me or Bloch. My expression must have been as amazed as his.

Otomars sat back down in the chair, his whole form relaxed, as if we were on Jurmala's sands rather than a subterranean prison cell. He plucked Bloch's spare cigarette from the table. "Let's see how Wiktor and I can best be of service."

He looked about for agreement, a slow nod from Gavriil, a dumbfounded expression from Bloch.

He pressed the cigarette to his lips. "May I have a light Major?"

"No...the interview is..."

Gavriil nudged the major as he sat down next to him atop the table. "Oh, give him a light Roman."

Begrudgingly the major lit a match along the tabletop, held it menacingly close to my brother's face. Otomars took a moment to inhale, and then continued:

"The Soviet government may no longer recognize my magistrate position – Chief Magistrate, I should remind you – but let's deal in practicalities gentlemen. Moscow's authority is not functioning here at the moment. I have…extended relationships with the town leaders. They know me, they trust me. More than a few owe me a favor or two…"

Otomars's prescriptive tone enraged Bloch: "Why should we trust you, Comrade Rooks?"

Otomars smiled behind his cigarette. "I believe I provided Colonel Tchuhlanceff's garrison with quite a lot of useful information in the past? He's always been happy with the intelligence collected, yes? Very profitable…to the Soviet cause."

Gavriil's response was fast-coming, a tad cold in tone but agreeable. "Most certainly."

My brother kept his eyes fixed on the colonel's: "And he has no doubts to my loyalty…"

"No. None."

Otomars smiled satisfied. He slapped a hand on my shoulder. "And as my brother is fighting for the same Soviet cause, and though I am too old and untrained for combat, I feel I can still pull my own weight." He withdrew his hand, laughed. "Which is considerable, you'll all agree."

Gavriil nodded his arms folded. Bloch now wore a hurt frown like an ignored child.

Otomars continued: "Let's be honest gentlemen. The Soviet army is far from here, and moving farther away as we speak. By your very presence, it is clear you are undertaking some sort of covert activity." He shook his head gently, his tone softening as if to calm their nerves at this observation. "I don't know its nature. Such things are beyond my understanding. That is the realm of you military men." He paused to let his praise register slowly. "But whatever you're doing, I am sure keeping a muzzle on the locals is of highest priority."

Bloch had regained his composure, a new found indifference in his tone: "We have control of the local population. There is nothing we need from you."

"True enough, Roman. May I call you Roman? As I am a civilian, I am a little adverse to military titles, you understand. Yes, you can arrest townsfolk, you can even shoot them." His eyes went from Bloch to Tchuhlanceff. "And no doubt you have."

He rocked forward, elbows firmly on knees. "But can you keep them quiet when a truck full of German troops stops at the inn for a hot meal? Do you know people who will tell you when the local baker is putting notes in the bread for the Gestapo? Can you convince the town leaders to preach that German liberation is utter nonsense, even to their own children in their own homes?"

Gavriil agreed. "Your watchfulness to local activities could certainly be of benefit. It always has been."

"Without a doubt. Let us be frank: I can tell you who to threaten and who to woo." His eyes flicked between them. "Who to buy and, if need be, who to kill."

Otomars crossed his legs, reclined in the chair. "Quite simply, gentlemen I can deliver this town to you."

Early the next morning, Otomars and I stood in a little plaza at the edge of town. An oak tree spread shade across the stones at one end, while at the other the locals were already setting up their tables for the morning market. Not far beyond the city's limits, the crumbling remnants of a castle gave an appropriately medieval feel to the summer landscape.

In the plaza center as far as possible from the ears and eyes of the Latgalians we continued our hushed conversation.

"You wouldn't really recommend they kill a townsperson? A local..."

Otomars's voice was earnest, his eyes wary. "I had to close the deal, Wiktor. We could leave them with no doubt of our commitment."

I emphasized the point the best I could, while still keeping my voice low. "I'm not shooting any civilians."

Otomars shrugged my comment away. "Yes, yes. It won't come to that I'm sure."

He watched an old woman set out pottery she'd made at the wheel: bowls, water jugs, decorative figurines. Her eyes caught Otomars stare, to my surprise the elderly matron gave a friendly wave. Everyone really did know him in this town.

He waved back, talking to me out of the corner of his mouth. "Bloch has to be asking himself, 'Why is Gavriil being so accommodating?' Why do I have his ear? Why is he letting you form a town militia? The major senses something is rotten, he just doesn't know exactly what yet."

The woman returning to her busy work, he turned his face back to mine: "Fortunately, Bloch has higher priorities. From everything I can discern, he's coordinating guerrilla warfare groups, intelligence gathering, snipers, saboteurs, that sort of thing. Airdrops to nested infantry if the Russians can ever get a plane in the sky. Anything to damage German infrastructure from behind. It's Bloch's operation but they're Gavriil's soldiers from his old garrison. A precarious truce if I ever saw one. Gavriil's got rank, but Bloch's 'State Security.' Hopefully they'll both spend most of their time in the forest." He smirked. "Or at each other's throats. Anything to keep their minds off us."

"I thought you were certain they'd all be gone by now."

His agitation showed through even as he smiled at a passing child, her arms full of newly woven garments for the tables. "Obviously, I was mistaken." He waited until the girl was out of hearing range. How old was she? Eleven? Was my brother so paranoid?

"I can tell you Gavriil's not happy about it, Wiktor. I'm sure he'd rather be far away from here. I wonder why he couldn't duck this assignment. Perhaps someone else knows about his side activities."

"Maybe we should just avoid them both."

The center getting too crowded, he directed me toward the shade of the oak at the other end. "Not in a town this size. We've a plate spinning on the end of a pole, Wiktor. We don't dare leave it unattended. We'll need to show our loyalty and our benefit soon enough. Otherwise we're all risk to Gavriil. And why have that?"

"How can we show our benefit?"

"Your town militia is a good start. We can control the town easier with Latvians rather than Russians. And it will give us the autonomy we need to lay a path out of here as soon as possible. Sooner or later Bloch will get word through to Moscow, find out we should be on a prison train right now…"

How had my life come to this? I was a professor, with a house…and a wife. My whole body ached at the thought. Otomars swore she'd be here soon, I had to believe in him and his allies. What choice did I have? "You trust Colonel Tchuhlanceff to shield us from Bloch? For the interim, at least?"

"As long as it benefits him. He's a business man as you know. And a good one." A genuine smile, far different than the painted one he wore for passers-by. "A fact he'd like to keep hidden from the NKVD, I've no doubt."

"Then keeping us safe is in his interest."

"To a point. If Gavriil thinks Roman is getting too close or I'm trying to cut some sort of deal to save my hide…"

I dared to ask. "He'll do what?"

"Well, as quietly as possible..." he paused again as a homeless man approached, one of the increasing numbers of war stricken refugees in the town. Otomars dropped a few rubles in his cup. Enough to buy a day's meal.

As the man limped away, my brother let out a long sigh. "I should think he'd have me killed."

Chapter Twenty-nine

"Wiktor, let's talk over tea."

"One moment, Otomars."

I stood in my brother's front garden watching two men push our automobile up the road. They were part of the little militia Otomars had arranged "to control the town" for the Russians. To any passing Germans they were a neutral police force, self-appointed heroes helping to maintain order while the government was influx, though, of course, they were secretly supposed to be aiding to the Soviet guerrillas. In truth, they were on Otomars's payroll and were going to help us escape as soon as Kaiva arrived.

I watched them as a summer drizzle began. Though I had been appointed head of this militia, I didn't know these men. The younger, a teenager named Brīvkalns, was from a religious family. A "Jesus and Mary" in every sentence it seemed, despite the Soviet disapproval. I knew even less about the other, Sergeant Putniņš. He was handsome, gruff, in his late twenties and terribly familiar though he denied any previous meeting.

The downpour increased, the men soaked and losing all traction in the mud. I thought to aid them, but Otomars insisted on a conversation.

"Wiktor," said he, strangely loud and a bit theatrical. "The tea."

I retreated into my brother's small wooden house. The opposite of his wonderful apartment in Rīga, you would never guess an important man lived in such a home. But then that was the point, wasn't it?

Otomars closed the door, motioned me into the kitchen. I found the room stuffy, too hot for summer with the stove lit and a kettle on the burner.

He took a seat at the table, pulled another chair close. "Sit."

I sat. "Otomars, do you really know this Brīvkalns? He's just a child. And Sergeant…"

Otomars placed a finger to his lips, said nothing until the kettle began to whistle, watching me intensely as its screeching increased. At last, he whispered: "We can trust them, Wiktor. They loathe the Russians. Brīvkalns's family was on the same train as you. Putniņš's brother was shot by the NKVD in the forest. They'll go with us to the Germans."

I tried to adjust to talking beneath the kettle's noise. "And Juris?"

"Juris speaks too much. He'll be left behind." Otomars read the distaste in my expression. "This won't be easy, Wiktor, even when we do crossover." He put a hand on my shoulder. "But I have enough monies to sustain us until things settle down."

"And then?"

Otomars sat there a moment, listening to the kettle, eyes very far away. "Do you remember Erich's friend Lukas?" He returned his gaze to me. "You met him at my party a few years ago, when Anne and Erich visited."

"Lukas from Regensburg?"

"Yes." Otomars nodded. "Well, he may be from Regensburg, but Lukas works in Berlin. He's an assistant to Alfred Rosenberg, the Reich Minister of Occupied Eastern Territories – Ostland, they call it. A region that now includes Latvia."

I crossed my arms. "What's this about, Otomars?"

"Minister Rosenberg is Baltic-German. Born in Reval. Educated in Rīga." His voice gained an edge of urgency. "Rosenberg knows, Wiktor. He knows what happened to Baltic-German lands, the thievery. And, they're going to give them back."

This seemed a desperate hope of my brother. "Have you read the newspapers? The aristocrats have tried to piggyback on the Nazis before, Otomars. Do you really trust them? The Nazis are gangsters, thugs…"

"Old history. Erich has been a party supporter for years, Lukas tells him everything. It's going to happen." He leaned closer to me, face centimeters from my own. "After more than three decades to have our estate returned, Wiktor. A home for Father before he dies. To let him regain his birthplace and not be the one who lost it after so many generations. Can you imagine what it will mean to him?"

It seemed impossible. "That would be wonderful."

The kettle howled and rattled on the burner, but Otomars continued. "I was the heir. It wasn't the same loss to you. Do you know the terrible things I've done? To live? To survive? All because my birthright was stolen from me?"

His countenance darkened. "I must tell you sometime what went on during the Great War, Wiktor. It's not a pleasant story."

I felt the ghost of Vereshchagin in the room, said nothing.

He rose, walked toward the stove to fetch the kettle, his tone deliberately lightening. "We'll be a family then, Wiktor, with our parents in their rightful home, and you with a German wife…"

"I have a wife, Otomars."

"Yes…Yes, you do. I spoke in haste." He plucked the steaming kettle from the stove. "Our heritage returned, Wiktor. All the Germans have to do is win the war."

I wasn't quite asleep when the knocking came on the door. I was lost in one of those semi-conscious moments when the body is waking, but the mind fights to continue slumber. A losing battle I had extended as far as possible during the 'White Nights' of summer. To be truthful I preferred dreams now no matter the hour. Kaiva was with me there, uninjured, with no doubts. Let Otomars call it unhealthy, I am simply happier asleep.

But the knocking would not subside. As Kaiva faded and the grey morning rays seeped into my consciousness, I slowly became convinced the NKVD stood outside the house. That Roman Bloch somehow knew I should be on a prison train or dead in the forest and had come for me, as the soldiers had come to our home in Rīga. I rolled over on the couch in Otomars's front room, reached beneath the cushions for my pistol.

Nothing.

I groped around in the ambient light, pulse quickening. It came to me then. Otomars had asked for the gun a few hours ago, before his morning walk to survey the town. I was alone and unarmed.

The knocks continued. Heavier than before. I moved to the window, peered through the dusty pane. A sigh of relief. It was Putniņš, the militiaman.

With the patience of six in the morning, I buttoned my shirt, tucked the tails into my trousers, and then finally opened the door.

He did not hesitate. "Is your brother here?"

In his haste, Putniņš pressed his face closer, and I finally placed the source of his nagging familiarity. He resembled an old colleague of Kaiva's from her newspaper – too well, I thought – the same sky-blue eyes, same dimpled chin, though Putniņš was a much younger man.

I resented the similarity and the memories it brought.

"Otomars is out."

"I need to speak with him."

I reigned in my aversions. One had to be practical. "You can speak with me." I recalled my brother's precautions. "Over tea, I'll heat a kettle. We can discuss…"

"No. There's no time."

I was surprised at his resistance. Even if we were about to desert, I was still head of this farcical militia. "A kettle is needed." I said with emphasis in my voice.

He paid me no mind. "Tell your brother, we found an old automobile to retrieve the fuel. Me and Brīvkalns, we'll siphon it off on our watch." Putniņš glanced behind him, then returned those familiar eyes to me. "But we've got to go tonight. There's too much risk."

Tonight? "No…my wife. You see, we need to wait for my wife, Kaiva, to arrive." I motioned for him to take a step inside, but he wouldn't. "We can't leave before then."

"Magistrate Rooks didn't say anything about a wife."

"I'm sure he did. We have to wait."

He shook his head, defiance in his voice. "Brīvkalns is already making arrangements."

"It's impossible without Kaiva. We must…"

I spied movement in the forest behind the house. A figure was making its way along the wooded path leading toward the garden. Square-shouldered, stocky, for a moment I thought it Bloch. But no…it was my brother.

"The wagon is arriving, Wiktor." Otomars said without greeting. "The one from Gulbene."

The old wooden wagon was full of goods: barrels and boxes, crates with live hens, sacks of flour, hoes, reapers, rakes and other aged and rusted farming equipment. Nearly lost among this assorted payload, I could see the hunched bodies and ducked heads of Latgalian laborers, men in overalls and caps, and a few women, their weathered countenances framed by sun bleached scarves.

Desperately my eyes scanned those shaded faces for recognition, for the one person who had to be there. Who must sit somewhere among them.

The wagon's passengers unloaded themselves quickly, not one stopping to help the driver remove any of the goods. The illusion had taken them to their destination and no one seemed to want to continue playing the part. Most of the 'workers' huddled near one of Gavriil's sergeants. Indeed, I suspected there wasn't a genuine farmhand among them. Nothing as innocent as it seemed.

LENIN'S HAREM

A woman approached…but no, it was not her. Even at a distance the eyes were the wrong shade, the shape too plump, too tall.

One man, his ill-fitting worker's cap pinned to his head with a free hand, turned slowly in circles beside the wagon, scanning the reception as if looking for a familiar face that had not yet arrived. His motion distracted me momentarily, my mind considering his lonely plight. When I returned to my own searching, she was there: Her face wrapped inside a pink Latgalian scarf, her body covered in the simple dress of the farm maiden. An outfit unrepresentative of her Marxist tastes. Yet, I knew those eyes instantly. 'Kaiva.'

She embraced me wordlessly, her soft form pressed firmly against mine. I could feel her heart racing against my breast, nearly as fast as my own. It had only been a month, such a short time truly but it seemed as if seasons, as if years had passed. I felt her lips lock with mine, the tears pressing moist from her cheeks already.

Kaiva was actually here, in my arms, I could not believe it. All the most horrible fears dissolving, all proven joyfully erroneous. If this was a dream, I did not want to wake to a cruel truth. Better to remain lost in the Elysian reality forever and even if fantasy never part again.

She pulled her face away. "I missed you so Wiktor."

"And I you."

I caught a glimpse of her teeth as she smiled in response: chipped, misaligned, the horrible injury still visible. Somehow, illogically, I had thought it might fade. That time's passing might have restored her smile, turned the events of that night to a forgotten nightmare.

But I did not care, she was here and that was all that mattered.

Otomars stood there silently, for once content to remain offstage, giving the moment entirely to the two of us. As Kaiva embraced me once more, I gave an appreciative nod to him. I would never doubt my brother again. He could conjure anything, ask anything of me…

Turning her head, Kaiva's eyes too fell on my brother. To my surprise, she moved away, hugged Otomars, whispering a tender, "Thank You" before returning to my arms. A small but meaningful gesture, it was the first time I'd seen them embrace since our wedding.

I ran my hand through her hair, pulling away the silly scarf. "Are you all right? Your injuries they are healing?"

She only nodded, her mouth smiling slightly, lips locked shut.

I took her hand, "I won't let us be separated again."

"We'll see." she only said. A strangely pessimistic response. Had the harsh world shaken her faith in the inevitability of our remaining together? Oh, to soothe her doubts. But this was not the time.

Holding hands, I took Kaiva back toward Otomars's residence. As I left city hall behind, I found Sergeant Putniņš and young Brīvkalns approaching.

Putniņš stopped directly in front of us almost blocking our path. "Is this your wife, Major Rooks?"

"Yes. Kaiva, Sergeant Putniņš, Private Brīvkalns. Gentlemen, this is Kaiva."

Putniņš gave her a long stare.

I abbreviated the introduction: "The sergeant was head of the local militia during the Independence."

"A long time ago it seems." He took her other hand, and unbeckoned gave it a gentle kiss. "You are a very lucky man to have such beauty on your arm, Major."

Kaiva returned the slightest of smiles, her lips never parting. Despite his awkward attentions, she did not seem overly embarrassed.

He kept his eyes on hers: "I'm sure he tells you so daily."

I took Kaiva by the arm, the two of us moving past him. "Yes, we thank you, Sergeant."

I sat at my bedroom desk in the sparse morning light; Yakov's book spread open, trying to compose the first letter.

> *To the family of Aleksandrs Dūmiņš,*
> *Your son was taken against his will by train from Rīga's Zasulauks Station on the morning of June 14th, 1941. He ~~told me~~ wrote ~~to me~~ that his cousin, wife, and two daughters were...*

I paused. They were not flowing, these words. Never easy to tell a family dire news. Even news they must surely suspect.

I threw the pen in the inkwell. I couldn't send it full of corrections. Or maybe it was that very doubt: Sending it. Would the letters ever be posted now that the Germans had taken Rīga? Was this all pointless?

I was in a foul mood. And the poor lighting didn't help. The sky was still cloudy and grey and the lamp unlit to allow Kaiva a few additional hours of slumber. She had been so tired after her ordeal, her long trip, understandably.

The reunion was not quite all I'd expected. An overreaction on my part? She'd been through so much…

Lost in thought, I barely heard the shouts from outside. Distressing calls in Latgalian and Russian. I could not ignore them. Out the window I spotted a young boy running along the muddy streets in the direction of the commotion.

Already dressed, I found my cap and jacket, and shutting the door quickly behind, ran outside to assess the situation.

In the open street, under the eternal sun of summer, I had little trouble finding the source of the noise: the little plaza at the end of town. A few moments later I arrived, the little square far too busy for this hour. Ignoring their still folded market tables and un-displayed goods, a crowd huddled about one end gazing at some event near the oak tree. Others walked away from the mob, looks of disgust or horror on their faces. One mother dragged her son away, the boy bent on seeing the spectacle hidden from me.

I broke through the market patrons to a startling, horrific scene:

Brīvkalns and Putniņš were lined up against the tree their arms tied around their backs. Four of Gavriil's soldiers stood at a short distance loading their rifles.

"What is going on?" I shouted, running between my men and their executioners. "What is the reason for this?"

Seeing me, they slowed their preparation, eyes turning to the opposite side of the crowd. There, given a fearful space by the local onlookers, stood Gavriil and Bloch watching me with almost mirthful contempt.

"Major Rooks," said Gavriil. "I believe you are in the way."

"What is going on here?"

"One of Roman's sentries discovered them trying to desert to the Germans. Fortunately, they were able to apprehend them first."

"Why wasn't I told?"

"You would have been. Eventually. We waste no time with traitors, Major."

A hoarse voice behind me. "Major, we did nothing." It was Putniņš. "We saw smoke, went to investigate."

Gavriil scoffed at the sergeant. "Alone? At four o'clock in the morning? Carrying a canister of petrol and a funnel? An obvious fabrication. Now if you'll step aside Major Rooks, we'll let the men do their jobs."

"I won't let you kill them. Where is the proof? The process?" Why were the Russians doing this so publicly?

"You won't let us?" Roman's tone was as chilling as the morning air. Only slightly less menacing than the glance between him and Gavriil.

I tried to lower my voice, less hysterical, more reasonable. "By that I mean I'm the militia officer. I will dole out their sentences."

"Yes, you're right, Wiktor." Gavriil nodded agreeably. "Roman give him your pistol. You punish them Major Rooks."

I took an unconscious step back, boot heel nearly on Brīvkalns's toe. "You want me to shoot my own men?" I felt unsteady, horrified at his words.

"You know the penalty for desertion. We haven't the soldiers or the resources for prisoners, Major."

Bloch stepped forward offering the handle of his revolver.

"No! I won't do it."

"We did nothing Major! They don't know a thing." Putniņš shouted a desperate hope in defense. "An empty canister? They have no proof."

Gavriil's face was terrifyingly stern: "Are you refusing my direct order, Major Rooks?" Nearer than the colonel, Roman smiled menacingly at me. A pleased look in his eyes as he pressed the gun handle closer.

Suddenly, an arm was thrown around my shoulder, lips pressed against my ear, and I found myself hurried a few steps away from the Russians and their prisoners.

Otomars's voice was low, calm, steady: "I want you to listen to me very carefully Wiktor. You need to trust in me. I got you off that railcar; I pulled our family away from the burning house. You need to do exactly as I say to survive this."

Where had he come from? Had he stood in the crowd? Watching all along? "Otomars, I can't just kill them…"

"Those men are already dead, Wiktor. You cannot save them and you are not responsible for their fate. You can only choose to save yourself or to perish." His breath burning hot against my earlobe. "Because if you don't obey orders, Gavriil will line you up beside them. Of this, there is no doubt."

To murder these men for a crime we all conspired? That by twist of circumstance these prisoners might have been Otomars and me?

"Major…." Spoke Gavriil in a tired voice. "Is there a problem?"

"They are watching Wiktor; you need to take the gun now."

A terrible fear crawled inside me on the back of his words. Of my life ending in this little plaza. Of being buried in an unmarked forest grave. Of never seeing Kaiva again. Dark images gathered in my mind. A growing hateful jealousy. Of her moving on; making love to another man, raising a family with another man.

Forgetting me.

My eyes turned to my brother's, pleading for some better answer. Some alternative. "They will shoot them anyway?"

"It is true. You aren't killing anyone. They've already decided their own fates."

I repeated these words to myself, as I walked over to Roman, and a shaking hand took the pistol from him. The handle was solid, well-made. Warm and moist from his grip. It fit in my hand too naturally. At Gavriil's command the soldiers forced Brīvkalns and Putniņš down to their knees.

I looked back at my brother. I couldn't do this. "They are already dead, Wiktor. Remember that."

I repeated "Already dead." Two bodies or three. I had no choice. Self-preservation.

Brīvkalns's face was to the plaza stones, repeating final prayers to Jesus. Putniņš looked directly at me, his tearful eyes locking with mine. "We did nothing, Major."

My heart was racing, hammering in my ears. I felt my grip loosen on the handle. So hard to think, I could not reason. Otomars supplied it for me: "You are not responsible."

Yes, I was not responsible. They had agreed, knew the risks, brought it upon themselves. They, Otomars, Gavriil and Roman and their warlike ilk. I was not a part of the equation. Just a man trying to survive.

There was a breeze, but it only made me feel cold. I held out the shaking pistol, pointed it at Brīvkalns.

Not responsible. Not responsible. Not responsible.

A lie.

Brīvkalns repeated the Lord's name.

I fired. My hand unsteady, it took two shots to kill him. Only one for Putniņš.

Fully dressed, I crawled into bed next to Kaiva. Trying not to disturb her slumber.

I felt her move. "Wiktor? Where have you been?" she rolled over against me, placing a hand affectionately on my back. For the last time I was certain.

"Your shoulders are all wet. You're shaking…" Her voice concerned, growing fearful. "What is the matter? What has happened, Wiktor?"

How I would disappoint her. I could not look into her eyes and retell…the events.

I found a crack in the wall, my eyes following up beyond the dresser, to the top of the mirror, always wary of the reflection. "Gavriil ordered two of the militia men shot. My men."

I kept my back to her, staring at the blank, flaking wall. Twisting the sheet in my hand, trying not to sob as I spoke. "They hung their bodies from the oak in the plaza with signs around their necks, Kaiva."

"My god…Oh, Wiktor why?"

"It read: 'The Fate of all German collaborators'"

"How horrible." She stroked my upper arm with her palm. Her voice was low, despising. "Russians killing Latvians once again."

My eyes followed the crack to the ceiling's corner, found a gap where all the plaster had fallen. I could see the wood frame behind. Stripped away to what it really was.

"Yes…again."

Chapter Thirty

The hanging rope was thick, the blade dull, the whole thing taking a very long time to saw through. The chords were tied to the trunk and slung over higher limbs, the boots of the murdered men brushing against my head as I worked, swinging in time to my cutting, softly torturing their killer with every motion.

My thoughts unexpressed, it was Otomars's voice that broke the silence: "That is very foolish, Wiktor. Bloch's men will ask who took them down."

"Men deserve a burial." I didn't look at him, kept cutting. "I can only hope my own murderer is as considerate."

His voice was hoarse, rough, nearly lost, as if he'd spent the day in weighty, unpleasant conversation. "Do you wish to join them in the grave so soon?"

"Frankly, yes."

I heard his footsteps on the plaza stones as he drew nearer. "What will you say then, when you meet our Creator, Wiktor? What wisdom will you carry with you from this world as you enter the next?"

I had no more stomach for his lessons, his games. "Leave me be."

"The Germans and Russians are still fighting over this land. The Latvian state has come and gone. All the struggles, the bloodshed lead to the same point, bodies hanging in the trees."

"When we were boys, it was only a stuffed bag."

"The same message. Now simply more direct. All that matters is family, Wiktor. Blood, not bloodshed. It is the only morality."

"Only words, Brother. And see where they have led us? To murder."

"You survived by those words, Wiktor. If you can't manage gratitude, at least stave off resentment."

With a final, angry thrust, I severed the rope, Putniņš's body at last coming down. So different how the dead fall, flat, no extra motion, not even limp, but sandbag heavy to the surface, a stomach-turning wetness in the thump of impact.

I avoided looking at it, moved on to Brīvkalns. Just a boy, really. I felt waves of nausea, how did this happen?

Otomars frowned, disapproving of my grizzly work. "You're going to make it much more difficult to slip off to the Germans."

Brīvkalns's rope was fuller, thicker, would this never end?

"Do you think it is still possible to escape?" I forced the blade through the first strands. "And will they be any better? The Germans? Have you read Mein Kampf?"

"Yes, and they may even be worse. But we can blend in with them far better than here. Sit in our home, out of the crossfire for awhile…"

"Kaiva can't. A Latvian, a communist…"

"It is a problem." There was hesitance, even regret in his voice. "I…I made a mistake at that Russian train station, I should have said 'no.' But I am soft, where my brother is concerned. You think Kaiva will go over to the Germans? She will have to be left behind, Wiktor. It is the only way."

"We'll convince her."

"Did the murder of these men convince her?"

More dark thoughts. "No."

"Then nothing will. They beat her, imprison her, force her husband…into acts of defense. And yet still she believes. She may even betray us."

I glanced over to him. "To whom?"

"Pillow talk takes strange paths, Wiktor. Even accidentally. You'll have to let her go."

"You know what the NKVD will do if we disappear."

"If we alert the Germans swiftly, there can be a rescue."

"I won't gamble with her life."

He sighed. "Then you gamble with all our lives." He pointed to Brīvkalns. "Look up in the tree, Brother. Our future hangs there. One way or another."

Chapter Thirty-one

There are tasks in every life too dreadful to imagine. That in the sunny meadows of youth, one cannot possibly foresee or dream of undertaking. Yet they are necessary.

Standing unseen behind, my hand clamped across Kaiva's mouth the moment she came in the door. Before she could scream, I forced the pillowcase down over her head, kept those eyes hidden from me.

Forgive me…

She fought feverishly, twisting and turning in my trembling arms. But Kaiva was a slight woman, much smaller than me. Boot heels scraping my shins, elbows battering my ribs, all painless compared to the wounds her cries inflicted on my soul.

I fought the urge to comfort her, to calm her panic with a few precious words.

Yes, she could not know. Not yet.

It will be over soon, Darling.

One hand around her waist, the other pulling the pillowcase taut, I pushed her out the door, where the car was waiting. Requisitioned only yesterday from a farmer who wandered a bit too far from town.

But not as far as I will go. With Kaiva. Otomars's advice be damned.

The car's trunk open, I shoved her in the compartment, pressed her kicking legs down, pried gripping fingers from the lip. All the while, she called for help. For someone.

For Wiktor.

With a few painfully hard shoves, I had her at last inside, but the pillowcase was nearly off, face turning…

I slammed the door. Locked it tight. Listened to the pounding thumps against the inside cover. As fast as my heart, it seemed.

A quick glance at my surroundings, a few old women watching beneath the distant town clock, two boys nearer, abandoning their farm work to stop and stare.

Yes, horrifying. Horrifying to all, but not abnormally so… Just another victim, punished for breaking the rules, nothing unusual. No one hung from the trees today.

I hurried round to the front, slid inside the driver's seat, brushed Yakov's Bible over to the passenger-side cushion. Filled with names, the victims of Railcar Eleven, soon their families would know, the sooner the Germans could mount a rescue.

I will be a hero. Victim no longer, a Crusader armed with a bible, like our forefathers long ago.

The pounding from the trunk.

Yes, a hero…

I turned the key, foot on the accelerator, pulled slowly onto the road. Away from the town as fast as possible.

But not too fast.

A little beyond the rickety bridge, where the old paths turned toward the wider highway, stood Otomars. Alone, off the road, a dark scarecrow in the last field of town.

I slowed to a stop, reached over and unlocked the passenger-side door. But he ignored it, coming around to my window.

I rolled down the glass. "What is the problem?"

"Change of plans, Wiktor. We need to wait for another day."

"Why?"

"Bloch's men have blown the bridge over the Aiviekste River. The road to Rēzekne is closed."

How? How could he know these things? "Then we'll find another route. Another destination."

Otomars glanced down at the gauge on the dashboard. "With a fifth of a liter of petrol? We've not the resources for an odyssey in the woods." He laughed, actually laughed, "And not with those darkening skies…"

"Get in."

Otomars shook his head. "Wiktor, don't be foolish. A storm will flood the roads. There will be another chance. If we go back now, separately, there's nothing to alert…"

"I've made arrangements."

LENIN'S HAREM

His voice turned icy, more fear than outrage in it. "What arrangements?"

"I altered the plan."

He looked away. He already knew, I sensed it. "What have you done? Tell me!" In his anger, he rapped on the automobile's roof.

It was answered by thumps from the trunk.

His eyes turned slowly to the rear, lingered there, narrowing. Otomars dragged a heavy hand across his face in frustration. "Oh Wiktor, you haven't? I told you…"

"And I told you. Did you think me a liar?"

He stood there a long moment, face in hands, listening to the growing sounds from the rear. The metallic pounding gaining strength as if it might soon burst through the back seats of the car.

He shook his head, seemed nearly despondent. "Give me the keys to the trunk."

"No. Get in the car, Otomars. We can still make…make somewhere…"

"Give me the damn keys."

He stood there hand out, flesh grey under the light of a cloudy day, new rain landing on his shoulders, water droplets peppering cheeks and chin.

"What are you going to do?"

"There's only one thing to do, Wiktor. Heaven forgive us…"

I pulled the stolen pistol from my coat pocket, pointed it at him. The second unimaginable crime of the day. "Get in."

He showed no alarm, no surprise, only a sort of parental disgust. He slowly folded his arms. "You'll do nothing. The keys…"

Bluff called. Shrewd as always, Brother, it would never happen. But there were other options…

I floored the accelerator. Wheels spinning in the mud of the road, the car seemed to hover, my eyes and his in one last stare. There was welcome surprise at last, in the motion, the rebellion, before the tread finally gripped and I was propelled forward. Beyond him. Beyond his reach forever.

So I left him there, a shrinking figure on the road behind, quickly lost in the falling rain. I felt no guilt. My brother would talk his way free, explain this disappearance as my own rash behavior. Survive to await the German Army with open arms. He'd live to have his birthright restored.

But I could not wait, not bide my time killing men to survive each day. This die was cast with Kaiva long ago. Let them say that the road to Rēzekne was closed. That the fuel would run out long before we found shelter. That the Germans may be as evil as the Russians. That she would never forgive.

I turned on the radio. A piano solo, Mozart, almost certainly. I thought of Anne, my youth, my home, before the times of killing.

A calmness washed over me, all decisions made, a tranquility in tune with the purr of the engine. All was as it should be. After a lifetime my fate in my own hands, masters, rivals, all causes left far behind in that Latgalian town.

My future my own. My time, our time.

No more the second son.

Acknowledgments

The Author wishes to thank the following people for assistance with the research required to complete this work: Dr. hist. Kaspars Klavins, Professor at Rīga Technical University; Historians Valdis Otzulis, Eriks Jekabsons and Aīda Rancāne; Professor Peter Gatrell at the University of Manchester; Corrie Robinson and the University of Nevada, Reno Department of History; Heinrihs Strods, Laura Aksika, and Lelde Neimane at the Museum of the Occupation of Latvia; Baiba Bela-Krumina at Latvia's National Oral History Project within the Institute of Philosophy and Sociology; Aija Priedite at the University of Latvia; Historian Klāvs Zariņš in the First World War History Department at the Latvian War Museum; Inga Proveja at the Latvian Institute; and Irena Ananjana for the truly enthusiastic instruction in the Latvian language.

Sincere gratitude is owed to all the writers who took time to impart their advice and wisdom: Martyn Bedford, Suzannah Dunn, Shirley Bozic, Ray Philpott, Terry Goodkind, Thomas Mallon, Ben Schrank, Jerry Ahern, Michael Legat, Susan Elderkin, Sarah Holman, Ann Swinfin, Courtney Henke, Anne Moschner, Bill Bowen, Karen Charlton and Jon Spelman at Washington Storytellers Theater.

The Author would especially like to thank Dana Celeste Robinson and the wonderful people at Knox Robinson Publishing; Steve and Andreja Gardner; Seth McCullough; Paul Lucas; Chris and Robyn Gavin; Anda Gerdena and her family; Stacia White; Julia Tabatskaya; Robert McCann; Steve Whitcomb; Julija Berkovica; Erin Cesta; George Stojanoff; Waqas Ali Malik; Bobby King; Karina Mocarjova; Natalia Pavlovna Savchenko; Edward Smith and the members of Youwriteon.com; Lyles Carr; Roger Troupe; Bill King; Olu Adebanjo; my family; my friends at TMG; and my classmates at the University of Manchester's Novel Writing Programme.

Praise for Stalin's Witnesses

Stalin's Witnesses is a riveting blend of reality and fiction — truth and "story truth", woven into a gripping narrative. It conveys the horrifying atmosphere of The Great Moscow Show Trials from a fresh perspective by inviting us into the lives of individuals impacted by the policies of a ruthless regime. The spotlight shines on its leading players — the Romm family, with supporting roles played by "witnesses" to crimes against the state — all historical figures — in this travesty of justice. When historical evidence trails off the author deftly fills the gap with believable thespians and "story truth" to provide a seamless narrative.

A final chapter titled "A Little Bit of History" provides invaluable evidence of the role that history played in the evolution of the Soviet "Theater of the absurd", in addition to the fictional characters that fleshed out the narrative. All of this makes for an engrossing read.

Marian Rubchak, *Senior Research Professor at Valparaiso University*

Jay Wachtel's 'Stalin's Witnesses' is historical fiction at its best—a gripping story that sheds light on one of the most shocking and egregious travesties of justice in modern times. With verve and brilliantly constructed dialogue to fill gaps in the historical record and to bring the historical characters to life, Wachtel chronicles the story of five individuals who were forced to testify against their fellow Communists and in so doing condemned not only the defendants but also implicated themselves in farfetched crimes. He shows what happens when ideology enslaves human beings, hollows out their dignity, and changes their dreams into nightmares. Along the way, he showcases the duplicity and hypocrisy of fellow travelers and others who for various reasons stood by, even lent credibility to the sham proceedings. Above all, he conjures up the spirit of Stalinism — a frightening reality that stills impacts the Russian people.

Dennis J. Dunn, Professor of History and Director of the Center for International Studies, Texas State University - Author of *"Caught Between Roosevelt and Stalin: America's Ambassadors to Moscow"*

Wachtel's lively fictional account offers a fresh look at the cruelty of Stalin's repression from the vantage point of one of its victims, an honest communist official and spy cast in the role of witness to sabotage at one of the three show trials of the Great Terror. The fascinating life story of Vladimir Romm encapsulates much of the Soviet experience, and the reader's natural sympathy with this attractive figure gives his cruel fate added poignancy. A powerful indictment of Stalinism and a great read besides!

Peter H. Solomon, Jr., Professor of Political Science and Criminology, University of Toronto, author of *"Soviet Criminal Justice under Stalin (Cambridge Russian, Soviet and Post-Soviet Studies Series)"* **and** *"Courts And Transition In Russia: The Challenge Of Judicial Reform"*

STALIN'S WITNESSES

BY
JULIUS WACHTEL

Lubyanka prison, 27 November 1936

My cell is a narrow, rectangular affair, three meters wide by four meters in length, with a stained concrete floor, rude masonry walls and a sturdy steel door bearing the disquieting imprint of the labor camp where it was manufactured. There is one small window. High and out of reach, it is so encrusted with dirt that little light enters. My sole source of illumination is a single bulb that burns dimly around the clock, something that was at first bothersome but to which I'm growing accustomed. I sleep, or try to, on a rude metal cot with a thin, badly stained mattress. Into the little space that remains they've wedged a battered old desk and a flimsy chair, probably castoffs from some petty bureaucrat's office. What function they might serve eludes me as I've been denied the right to correspond. I leave for last my lodgings' most unpleasant feature, a metal pail euphemistically referred to as the "honey pot," which generates a stench so unpleasant that during my first days in this hellhole it was difficult to breathe.

Over the years I have heard tales of how prisoners adapt. Now that I've joined their ranks I'm not sure whether getting used to such indignities is something to celebrate. But I refuse to despair. I've done nothing wrong, and before long this horrible injustice will be sorted out.

I was notified of my reassignment three months ago, in August, while posted as *Izvestia* correspondent to Washington. There was little to suggest that anything was amiss. All who serve the Soviet Union are well aware of the pretexts that Moscow Center employs to recall officers who have fallen out of favor, like the sudden illness of a spouse or an accident involving one's child, but such events aren't normally celebrated with elaborate champagne receptions, good-bye gifts and congratulatory speeches by colleagues and well-wishers.

Moments after the embassy's communications officer decoded the message that brought to a close my two years of service as Izvestia correspondent to Washington, my superior, Ambassador Troyanovsky, announced that after a brief sojourn in the Soviet capital I would be sent to Great Britain. It would be disingenuous to say that I wasn't apprehensive, as sham transfers aren't exactly unknown, but his words seemed sincere, and after fifteen years in the Soviet secret service, much of it spent under the guise of being a foreign correspondent, it was easy enough to attribute my unease to a bad case of Bolshevik paranoia.

A few weeks earlier we had gathered in the embassy's projection room to watch clips from the trial this past August where sixteen comrades, among them several leading Party officials, took the stand and one after the other tearfully confessed that they had conspired to assassinate Stalin, wreck Soviet industry and abandon the country to its mortal enemies, Germany and Japan. That high-ranking Bolsheviks would participate in such a scheme seemed astounding – to me, it still does – but they spoke earnestly and their detailed accounts left little to the imagination. A few staffers actually fell ill.

As Soviet law prescribes, each of the accused was shot within twenty-four hours of the verdict, with no right to appeal. To execute comrades of high rank is an unprecedented step, and the auditorium remained quiet well after the projector ceased whirring. Troyanovsky tried to lift the mood with a small speech praising Procurator-General Vyshinsky's tireless efforts and brilliant investigation for thoroughly discrediting the plot's kingpin, the exile Trotsky, then in his seventh year of running around Europe, spouting off against the General Secretary and trying to spur a counterrevolution.

It's no secret that many loyal communists, myself included, favored Trotsky at a time when such sentiments were widespread and, I might add, perfectly legal. It's also true that as the ambassador pointed out – I might add, with a glance in my direction – all had ample opportunity to recant their errors, so the few who failed to live up to their end of the bargain have only themselves to blame. Still, his comments were disturbing. Were any of us at risk? No one dared ask. Truly, all notions of "democracy in the party" vanished long ago.

Throughout the talk I spotted more than a few sallow faces, but as we filed out things livened up. Surely, went the whispers, treachery that severe left the authorities no option, especially now that fascists are breathing down our necks. Looking back on that day I suppose we just wanted to put it all behind us.

In the USSR the verdicts were celebrated with speeches and rallies. But world reaction was mixed. Troyanovsky told me to do what I could to counter the onslaught of virulent anti-Soviet propaganda, but nothing could stop the capitalist press from harping about our reliance on confessions, a curious posture as that is the main way of securing convictions in the West. As for calling the results 'preordained,' a smooth trial hardly seems something to criticize. Is it preferable that the accused deny their guilt?

Then the other shoe dropped. There I was, trying to sell my American counterparts on the wonders of Soviet justice when rumors began to float around the embassy about a second trial. Its scope seemed remarkably similar to the first, with Trotsky reprising his role as the enabler of an Axis-inspired plot to destabilize the motherland. What shook me up was that authorities kicked off their campaign by running Izvestia through the wringer, publicly disparaging my colleagues for their lack of patriotism, then added fuel to the fire by arresting the famous journalist Karl Radek and accusing him of being Trotsky's main go-between.

Radek and I – at the time of his arrest he was nominally my editor – go back a long way. Although not all my memories of him are pleasant, to argue that he was a fascist stooge seemed awfully far-fetched. Still, it was true that Radek was for a time Trotsky's most fervent disciple, at least until Stalin had them both exiled. In those days a bullet to the back of the head wasn't yet the preferred solution, and Trotsky was deported to Europe. Amazingly, Radek was allowed to remain and eventually clawed himself back into the General Secretary's good graces. I hadn't seen him since my going-away party in Moscow, and before that had steered clear of the man for years, so I managed to convince myself that his turn to counterrevolutionary activity was somehow plausible.

On a breezy afternoon only a month ago, as Washington enjoyed its last breath of fall, Galina, our son Georgie and I got together with Paul Ward and his wife at their fine home just outside the capital. While our wives took Georgie for a stroll, Paul and I sat in a 'small' kitchen. Nearly the size of our Moscow apartment, it was equipped in typical American fashion with all the conveniences of a fine restaurant.

Affluence has not blinded Paul to his country's failings. The respected political columnist of The Nation was one of the first to point out Germany's threat to world peace and criticize as incredibly wrong-headed the isolationist tendencies of the American Congress. Regrettably, while many writers and intellectuals openly support the Soviet cause, neither Paul nor I had much success persuading legislators to join in, and he and I both fear that by the time the U.S. grasps that its future and ours are entwined it may be too late. Prick the skin of most Americans and out oozes European blood. What will it take for the most powerful nation on Earth to come to its senses?

Galina and I first set foot in America in early 1934. We were instantly overwhelmed by its apparent prosperity, the spacious apartments and fine homes, many occupied by persons of modest means, the abundance of inexpensive, high-quality consumer goods, and most of all the numerous automobiles clogging the roads, their fumes choking passers-by and casting an eerie pall. Yet in time the rough edges began to show. Coming from the USSR, where it is a serious crime to discriminate based on ethnicity, we were disturbed by racism so pervasive that even in the capital the colored ride in the back of public transport, hold menial jobs and live in the least desirable areas. I have written of the deplorable inequality in the distribution of wealth, with affluent areas bordering neighborhoods beset by the deepest imaginable poverty. Crime and violence are rampant, far worse than what one should expect in a civilized society. Yes, America did have its material comforts. Russians are perennially faced with a scarcity of conveniences – say, good soaps, nice toothbrushes – that could make everyday life a little more pleasant. Yet our sojourn in America convinced us that however well it might provide in the way of consumer goods, capitalism, particularly the unforgiving, every-man-for-himself kind practiced there, can have terrible consequences for those left on the outside.

Paul opened a fresh bottle of vodka and poured two shots. Not quite the Slav, he took only a small sip.

"To my good friend Vladimir Georgievich Romm, may you enjoy the pinnacle of success in whatever it is that you really do, now and in the future. LeChaim!"

"Za vashe zdorov'ye!" I downed my drink in a single gulp. Its unusual flavor prompted me to inspect the bottle. As I suspected, it was Smirnoff, from the Smirnov family, those infamous distillers who fled Russia during the Revolution.

I slid the tumbler forward. 'Well, now that you've entrapped me I might as well have another.'

I was expected to do much more than just take America's pulse. How could we assure its support in the battle against fascism? If war breaks out with Germany and Japan, as our generals are convinced it will, the Soviet Union will need the West's material support and, more likely than not, its armed might. I was to seek out persons of influence – journalists, capitalists, politicians – and bring them to our view of things. It was critical to overcome the isolationist sentiment, particularly noticeable in their Congress, which made it impossible for Roosevelt to fully embrace the USSR.

My relationship with Paul was much more than business, and because of it far more productive. I also had some nice chats with the *New York Times'* manicured, resplendently tailored Walter Duranty. Of course, both were already sympathetic to the Soviet cause. It's not that other reporters were hostile: it's that they didn't care. Most assumed that I spent all my time just like them, engaged in trivial concerns, and when I tried to steer discussions to issues such as the threats posed by fascism they usually groaned. Their editors were interested in drawing in readers, not putting them off. Pressures in the U.S. to return a profit imbue everything with a commercial flavor, affecting even newspapers, which as honest reporters will admit pretend to provide a public service while mostly chasing advertising dollars. American writers expend tons of newsprint and innumerable column inches reporting 'juicy' events that lack any enlightening value or social significance, such as lurid crimes and the comings-and-goings of movie stars, topics that would be ridiculed in Moscow. Urging America to become involved in foreign conflicts is strictly taboo.

If newsmen were difficult, bureaucrats proved nearly impossible. Most were fearful that

I might discover some horrible secret and were extremely tight-lipped, at least until a few shots of bourbon (a horrid drink to which Americans seem addicted) lubricated their tongues. Even then what I mostly got was nonsense. However, I did make inroads with one well-connected person. I first met Allen Dulles in 1932 at the disarmament conference in Geneva during that hopeful time when it seemed that world peace and prosperity was finally within reach. Dulles and I (he was legal counsel to the American legation) established a back-channel to smooth the way for establishing diplomatic relations between our countries. We became reacquainted when I was posted to Washington and he was spending time in the capital in connection with his famous brother's New York law firm. Dulles is rumored to be in line for a top intelligence post, and developing him as a source remains a very worthwhile objective.

But my fondest recollections are of Paul. He and I have a common outlook, a belief that under the right conditions America could transition into a just and peaceful society without artificial social and political boundaries; indeed, without a government of any kind. That's not to say that we are exactly of the same mind, as Paul had come to feel that the path chosen by the USSR was excessively centralized and authoritarian.

"When are you leaving?" he asked.

"Wednesday. We take the train to New York then sail for England the following day."

"Are you sure that you want to do that?"

My friend's somber tone took me aback. "What do you mean? Why wouldn't I be sure?"

Paul fiddled with his drink. "Everyone's heard about Radek. Could you be next?"

That was a startling thing for Paul to say, and it took me a moment to regain my composure. Was I being recalled under pretext? My conscience was clear. Indeed, I felt indebted to the USSR. Through its graces three citizens – Galina, Georgie and I – were participating in a great adventure, enjoying perquisites that would have been completely out of reach for Jewish persons under the Czar, and it seemed unthinkable to pay back that debt by turning our backs on communism.

'Why should I worry?' I asked, trying to convince the both of us. 'I've kept my distance from Radek, and whatever the fool's done, or not, I wasn't in on it.'

"I'm sure you had nothing to do with a plot, if there was one," Paul hastily replied. "But from what I heard there's a trial on the way. You know the man. If he's squeezed he's liable to..."

At that moment Paul's wife Dorothy rushed in. Georgie's brace was giving him trouble and I left to help. Paul and I never did finish that discussion.

Galina was overjoyed at the news of our return. Despite putting on a good show she dearly missed the homeland and was in fact quite miserable. My wife's absence from Moscow had forced her to give up a leadership role in a communist women's organization, and other than for an occasional lecture at the Soviet legation there was little in Washington to satisfy her thirst for political enlightenment. Her opinion of American culture wasn't favorable. She was badly put off by the preoccupation with wealth, the banal entertainments and careless form of speech and dress, and neither our spacious apartment, which in Moscow would be out of reach to all but the nomenklatura, nor the skilled therapists who attended to Georgie seemed to her worthy of squandering one more day in the hub of world capitalism.

Those, as best I can remember, were her exact sentiments.

Our travel plans coincided with the Queen Mary's schedule, and we secured a fine berth, a small luxury that, considering our little fellow's special needs, the ambassador was happy to indulge. Everything had been proceeding well until the evening before our departure, when after making my final round of farewells I returned to the apartment to find Galina hysterical.

"Why didn't you tell me that Radek was arrested?"

I took a deep breath. "I suppose I didn't want to worry you," I replied. Galina had called Dorothy to say her good-byes, and one thing led to another.

"Worry me? They shoot a score of traitors, and then two weeks later that repulsive little man who nearly manipulated you into collaborating gets picked up by the secret police!"

Galina was rarely frightened, and the depth of her concern got me thinking. What if, indeed? "Since those times all we've worked on together are a few newspaper articles,' I insisted. 'If there's anything even vaguely counterrevolutionary about them, give me a pistol, I'll save the bastards the trouble and do it myself!"

We had forgotten all about Georgie, and when our son heard these horrible words he began to sob. I took him into my arms and the three of us hugged for a very long time.

Cookies and a coloring book settled the little man down. But Galina was badly upset. My wife had always been the stauncher communist: deep down, did she think that I had somehow stepped over the line?

"Will you call the ambassador?" she asked.

Her plaintive tone threw me off balance. "What could I say without making him suspicious?" I protested. "Should I ask, 'Comrade Ambassador, exactly what kind of recall is this – the 'good' kind or the bad? Look, everyone knows that we're friends – he's the one who lobbied to bring me here – so if I was really in trouble he'd be the last person whom Moscow Center would tell. Only yesterday you and Elena were making plans to meet in London. Do you really think that Alexander Antonovich would knowingly lead us into a trap?"

My wife's tears returned, and when I tried to comfort her she ignored me and curled up on the sofa. I fell into bed, physically and emotionally drained. Galina had always been the more resilient. When doctors diagnosed Georgie's condition and warned there was already considerable damage she quickly took charge of things, learning everything there was to know about his illness and even arranging to have him treated in a French sanatorium, a placement that vastly improved his prognosis and probably saved our marriage as well. Now it was my turn to hold things together and I wondered if I was up to the task.

A few days later, after a nice send-off by the Troyanovskys and a good night's sleep in a fine New York hotel we stood in awe of the most magnificent steamship ever built, a vessel of such enormous dimensions that when Georgie asked how an object like this could float all I could say was, "It's a miracle!" The lengthy boarding process passed in the blink of an eye, and as I helped my son navigate the gangplank Galina squeezed my hand. Neither of us had brought up that unpleasant business again, and we let the excitement of the journey and the anticipation of reunions with family and friends carry us along.

The voyage was uneventful. Galina and Georgie passed the time reading and playing games while I wrote letters to colleagues whom I did not personally bid farewell. I particularly wanted to stay in touch with Allen Dulles, who remains influential even though his cronies are presently out of power. Sooner or later Allen will return to government, most likely in the intelligence service, which has long been his obsession. I had hoped we could work together when that day came, but that possibility now seems remote.

Our welcome-home celebration was hosted by my brother Alexander and his wife, Elena. Both are well-known Moscow art critics, and Alexander's biography of the French impressionist Matisse is due out as I write. Just before we left for Washington he and Elena were awarded a spacious flat in a Tverskaya Street – brownstone, with high ceilings, a separate dining room and a splendid view of the Kremlin. Galina is terribly jealous, as our family, which includes her mother Ludvika, is stuffed into a tiny apartment that suffers from a bad case of Russian plumbing, meaning that we must often resort to buckets.

To my delight my other brother Evsey and his wife Esfir joined us. They live in Leningrad. Evsey is an engineer in the paper industry. He hasn't been in the best of health, and when I scolded him for making the long trip he responded by loudly bussing my cheeks, making the ladies laugh and reminding me of those times in Vilna when my brothers (I'm the baby of the family) would give me a big smooch as they snuck off to attend meetings of their revolutionary cell. Neither Alexander nor Evsey have children so they brought Georgie many gifts, spoiling him rotten, as uncles tend to do.

Every Russian family has a poet. Ours is Evsey. His passion, unfortunately, is for the Western-style romantic kind, which places him at odds with the proletarian ideals that the Soviet Union expects its artists to promote. It's an interest that he picked up from one of mother's artsy friends and which is bound to land him in hot water, even if he always does use a pseudonym.

Alexander, who has little tolerance for non-conformism, skimmed Evsey's most recent book of verse. 'Can you show me which of these so-called 'poems' speaks to the struggles of the workers?' he asked, trying without much success to conceal his irritation. His attempts over the years to reform his liberally-minded sibling have had little apparent effect.

'What struggles do you have in mind, dear brother? Hell, even if you halve the figures the Commissariats are flaunting – no, if you quarter them! – every Soviet worker must be a Stakhanovite!'

Evsey's digs at the exaggerations of the Five-Year Plans and the glorification of Soviet workers riled Alexander. "Is it still your position, Evsey Georgievich, that art has no obligation other than to itself?"

"Please, call me 'Sallo'. Everyone else does."

Alexander grinned weakly. "Very well, Sallo. You may call me 'Sasha'."

Evsey clapped in excitement. "Wonderful! Now that we're addressing each other as intimates let me explain why evaluating art through the prism of socialism does both a disservice. Better yet, why don't you ask your friend Shostakovich?"

That really was going too far. Everyone knows that Shostakovich is still on the mend politically after the inaugural performance of his "Lady Macbeth" led Stalin to publicly storm out of the Bolshoi. A biting editorial in the next day's Pravda pointed out that glorifying the murder of one's spouse to make way for a lover hardly qualifies as socialist art, and within days the Union of Soviet Composers announced a corrective campaign to assure that future productions support rather than disparage communistic values. A tempest in a teapot if you ask me, but don't get Galina going on it!

"Dmitri Dmitrievich's errors were the products of youth and inexperience," Alexander explained. "We recently had him over for dinner. He personally reassured us that he is working day and night to create more socially conscious works. Elena and I are doing all we can to help."

Evsey refilled his glass with a healthy dose of pepper vodka. "That's exactly my point, Sasha. Here the Government – I mean the critic – advises the composer, who writes a piece, which is criticized, then rewritten, then criticized some more, squeezing out whatever creative juices remain, so when the infernal cycle is done all you have left is a prune. No! Not a prune – the pit! But why worry? We've already let the Party decide for us in every other respect!"

The front door slammed. Galina and her mother were gone, taking Georgie with them. I couldn't blame them. After the ups and downs of collectivization, the wildly exaggerated goals of the plans, the struggles with Trotsky, the trials, and the looming war against fascism, there's precious little room left for differences of opinion, and with the risk of being denounced lurking around every corner it's best not to get into the habit of speaking too much from the heart. Tolerance for competing views is not a quality that Socialists have in abundance, and to that extent we could probably learn something from the West.

When I arrived at the apartment all were asleep. Early the next morning I woke to my wife's sweet breath, a steaming cup of tea and an excited eleven-year-old who couldn't wait to rekindle old friendships. All the unpleasantness seemed behind us. Galina was buzzing around the apartment, thrilled to be back and anxious to resume teaching at the primary school. Catching a glimpse of her fine figure and stunning profile, I considered myself a very lucky man.

On her way out she gave me a nice kiss. "You were right. I was silly to worry."

Ludvika was in the kitchen. As usual, she caught everything. "Worry? What's there to worry about?"

An hour later I was sitting in the reception area of Izvestia waiting for Nikolai Bukharin, the editor-in-chief. He never showed up, so the receptionist eventually turned me over to a preoccupied editor who knew nothing of my pending reassignment or really much of anything else ("we just placed someone in London, why would they send you too?"). He led me to a dusty, vacant office and told me to make myself at home. While cleaning out the desk of its prior occupant I found one of Radek's calling cards, an unnerving coincidence that left me a bit shaken. To clear my head I wandered around the news room. No one seemed interested in having a chat, which wasn't surprising considering what I later learned, in the men's room, when a reporter took pity and whispered the chilling news that Comrade Bukharin was confined to his home awaiting the findings of a Party inquiry into his alleged links with Trotsky.

Radek, then Bukharin. The dominoes were falling, all right.

The editor returned and we agreed that I would write a piece about American isolationism, a topic that was very much on everyone's mind. The hours passed quickly and it was soon time to leave. For a change of pace I tried the spectacular new Metro, opened only last year. As I walked down elegantly arched corridors lined with paintings and sculptures depicting robust workers, bountiful harvests and the USSR's military might it was impossible not to be impressed. Comrade Stalin may not be everyone's cup of tea, but his impact on productivity and morale has been nothing short of amazing. Moments later, seated comfortably in a shiny new railcar, I glanced out just in time to catch a fleeting glimpse of the General Secretary's likeness beaming down from the tunnel entrance. Public transportation in Washington was poor and there was no underground, so when I traveled it was mostly by car, one of those "freedoms" that

Americans enjoy along with frequent jam-ups, breakdowns and accidents. One cannot truly appreciate the orderliness of Moscow without visiting the West.

I exited the train eager to get home and share news of my writing assignment and subway ride. My euphoria lasted all of a few seconds. Not more than twenty meters away, standing in a corner but making no attempt to hide, were the same two dour-looking characters who had been hanging around the paper when I left. I walked home quickly, their presence at the station instilling a sense of foreboding that not even Galina's warm greeting could shake.

I feigned a headache and took refuge in the bedroom. My mind was buzzing. What should I do? Under such circumstances what does one do? Pack a bag? Make a run for it? Destroy incriminating documents that don't exist? Time passed and I gradually relaxed. Maybe these were different men. Maybe my mind was playing tricks.

Alas, it wasn't. I'd been napping for an hour when a squad of secret police – yes, including my two shadows – barged in and spirited me away, their disinterest in looking around for proof of my guilt proving nearly as unsettling as my arrest.